WINE

DARK

DEEP

BOOK THREE:
THE ODYSSEY

R. Peter Keith

This is only what happens, when death comes, to all mortals.
The sinews no longer hold the flesh and the bones together,
and once the spirit has let the white bones, all the rest
is made subject to the fire's fury,
but the soul flitters out like a dream and flies away.

Homer, The Odyssey

One

Unbelievably, they were not dead.

They were not dead, and they were, somehow, somewhere *else*.

The spaceship *Ulysses* hung over an alien world. It rotated beneath them, a pale-yellow gas giant somewhat smaller than Jupiter. The planet's storms curdled into a wash of greens and blues where the gas became more dense. It was haloed by a substantial ring system composed of hundreds of gossamer circlets and shepherded into three nearly equivalent bands by a trinary of large moons. The outer ring seemed to have an inclusion within it, creating a streamer of turbulence.

Far off, a star shined with surprising brightness, revealing another moon nearly hidden in shadow. Cal could see a shimmering blue-green rim of light around it, hinting at an atmosphere.

Cal's helmet speaker crackled. "Can we call them engines now?" Paul Arthor asked with exasperated sarcasm, referring to the mysterious alien objects that had *built* themselves into the *Ulysses*'s hull.

"I have a headache," Xu said, sitting up in the back of the command module.

"Are we not dead?" the Doc asked. She was just returning to consciousness, raising her head, staring in wonder out the command module's panoramic viewports.

"We're not dead," Cal reassured her. "At least I don't think so."

"Is everyone okay?"

Cal tabbed open Inez's page on his spacesuit's arm screen. "Inez?"

"I got knocked around, Cal." She looked dazed. "I'm sorry."

"Doc, get down to the docking ring and check her out."

"Roger, Cal." She floated to the CM's back wall, pushed off against the burnished rim of the rear airlock, and vanished down the central spinal corridor of the ship.

"Where are we?" the pilot, Sarah Samuels, asked.

Xu grabbed at his station and pulled himself toward the spray of screens. "The best I can do right now is *not Jupiter*. Beyond that . . ."

The pilot unlatched her harness and floated into the aisle between the two consoles that arched around the panoramic windows. The big screen still showed the view aft—the yellow limb of the strange gas giant. She oriented herself toward the science station. "How do we find out where we are, mister science-man?"

Xu turned to her, rubbing the back of his head. "I'm not exactly sure yet." He turned back toward his console. "I'll start by having Odysseus look for relationships between stars and see if he can detect any transposed constellations. We should be able to figure out where we are, but it may take a while." He folded out the station's auxiliary screens and began typing. "We'll also need to figure out how we can verify the results we get. I'll need to write a program."

"Might it be easier to come at it from the other end," the pilot said.

"What do you mean?"

"Take the known constellations and calculate what they would look like from other stars. Start with the closest stars to Earth and keep moving out. When the stars match our stars, we'll know where we are."

Xu stared at her for a second. "It might be more computation-heavy, but we already know exactly what those computations are." He smiled. "I'll start right away." Xu Zuoren turned back to his science stations. Its right-hand screen was half blacked out. He reached out and squeezed the housing, and the bottom half of its image returned.

Cal released his own safety harness and kicked out of his seat. Floating in front of the rear-view screen, he gazed upon the twin alien booms. He had seen the registers along the sides of them open and pour out crimson light from between the open vanes.

What did it do?

What was it he *knew* it had done?

He *knew* that it had taken over his ship. But he also knew that it didn't always exercise that control, even if it should. They would have been destroyed in Jupiter's vortex if Sarah had not taken over control of the RCS to guide them out of the hurricane wall. Likewise, into the mouth of the jet stream, although it did nudge them in that direction.

He *knew* that it had created its own, presumably electromagnetic, protective shield around the ship that was orders of magnitude more advanced than their own already miraculous field. Otherwise, they'd have been dead. Crisped by radiation.

He *knew* it had defended them against the crushing effects of gravity—although it was possible that whatever had protected against the gravitational effects could have been a result of the same forces that created the jet stream.

He also *knew* that it kept them fed with more fuel than could have been compressed within the volume of *Ulysses*'s tankers and the alien cylinders combined. Which was, of course, impossible—or previously considered impossible, anyway unless it was converting its own mass into propellant.

What was its purpose? Did it indeed need them for some reason or was it just some faulty tool they'd happened upon?

He pushed off from the ceiling and landed next to Samuels's chair, looking out at the yellow-green planet rolling beneath them. They were speeding beneath its equatorial rings. Sparkling arches of ice and dust reached over, swallowed them, and then were gone. It was as if they had passed beneath the most elegant bridge ever constructed. The green moon was getting closer, a dark object clearly visible against its limb.

"Sarah, I want you to come up with a flight plan to shift into equatorial orbit around *that* moon. Given what we've just been through, our shields should be able to handle whatever radiation this place dishes out. At least for a while. There's something orbiting its equator, and I'm willing to bet it has something to do with how we got here."

"You think?" she asked.

"You don't?"

"I suppose. It's at least probable, right? But if that's the case, why haven't they said *hello* or come to investigate?"

Cal let out an exhausted breath. "The same unanswered questions we have about our friends back there." He jerked a thumb at the twin alien cylinders visible on the rear-view.

The Doc reappeared in the CM hatchway. "Inez is fine; she and Paul were strapped in. She hit her head against the inside of her helmet on a few of those jolts. She just whacked herself around real good."

Cal opened his channel to his comms and IT officer. "How are you feeling, Inez?"

Her voice fizzed over the speaker. "I'm fine."

"So the Doc says. How's our guest?" he asked, referring to the alien growth they'd had only limited success communicating with.

"It's been quiet since we got here, just endlessly zooming through fractal visualizations. I'm recording everything, but I'm not seeing anything like the attempts at categorization that we saw before."

"Disappointing."

"Yeah. I'd hoped it would have something to tell us about where we are. I've been thinking of a few things to try. We—"

Cal cut her off. "Not now. I still haven't gotten used to the view out the window, let alone the fact that we're still alive. I'd rather not add to our list of issues now. If our friend, or friends, are content with being quiet, then I'll take the quiet."

"Roger, Cal."

He turned to his science officer, lost in his library of screens. "Xu?"

"What is it? I'm still setting up Odysseus's comparison sweep."

"It's important to know where we are, but we're going to need to figure out what's around us, in this solar system."

Xu typed a few more commands, slid a window into Odysseus's trireme icon, and turned around. "The normal way to find planets around another star assumes you're on Earth."

"Yes, but since we're already *orbiting* another star . . ."

"Interesting problem." The science officer seemed to lose himself in the thought.

"It is unique," Cal said. The irony was lost on the man. "I'm guessing we should use a combination of transit and direct imaging?"

"Yes, I've already had Odysseus begin searching in a fifteen-degree band on either side of the star's ecliptic, assuming that's where most of the mass would have accreted when this system formed—along the star's rotational angle of momentum. If that's not the case, we'll find out quickly when an orbiting body flashes by our scopes on a different plane."

"Can we have Odysseus run that search concurrently with the constellation sweep or will that slow things down too much?"

"That might bog him down a bit, but I think he can do both at the same time. I'll have him prioritize one over the other."

"Prioritize the search for other bodies within this system. Best we determine the lay of the land as soon as we can."

"We could also look at how much the star wobbles and use that to confirm the kinds of masses that should be out there. Make sure we don't miss anything."

"Excellent, Xu. Add that to your list."

Two

Bisecting the blue-green rim, a vast disc-like silhouette hung in darkness over the moon. It showed no signs of life, remaining in what appeared to be a stable spirographic orbit. As if it had only recently, as planetary timescales go, been captured by the sphere's gravity and was slowly beginning to circularize. Xu had set Odysseus to task analyzing the telescope images, looking for direct evidence of planetary bodies or the perturbations of light, gravity, or electromagnetism that might indicate the presence of other worlds out there.

Xu broke away from gazing at the green moon and its mysterious shadowy disc to look through the CM's docking window. It was a small viewport, but it was directly adjacent to his station. Through it he could see the portside object clinging to *Ulysses* hull and an alien world rushing along beneath them.

Cal put his hand on Xu's shoulder. "How are you doing?"

"I'm fine, thanks. I'm sorry for losing my cool earlier. I had too much personally invested in seeing first contact through a lens of positivity."

"Don't count positivity out yet. We're alive."

"True."

"I think your theory of Jupiter's storms and that jet stream being a purposely seeded self-sustaining atmospheric feature is right on the money, my friend."

"Yes, Its possible that the effect of that jetstream somehow accelerated us into a state where non-euclidian rules apply. The black sphere at the core *may* have transitioned us straight through from non-euclidian to hyperbolic space and then back into a euclidian state–leaving us, somehow, some*where* else."

Samuels swung back out of her seat, around to the rear of the CM, and into their conversation. "That really happened? I thought it was a movie."

Cal laughed.

"Joking aside, I was actually thinking the same thing. It reminded me of the ending to 2001," said Xu.

The Doc floated in from the spinal corridor. "Two thousand and what?"

Cal looked at her blankly.

"A Space Odyssey?" Xu grabbed hold of his console and rotated to face the capsule interior, looking from face to face. "No one? I know it's old, but come on. Seriously?"

"That movie is like one hundred and fifty years old. What do you want from us?" Samuels said.

"Then you *have* seen it."

"My grandfather showed it to me," she admitted.

"Aha!" Xu smiled in triumph.

"What does this have to do with anything?" The Doc appeared annoyed as she asked the question.

"It's relevant, I assure you. The movie's protagonist encountered some kind of space transit system beyond his comprehension and was transported somewhere else."

"A Louis XIV era hotel suite," the pilot interjected.

"That's not the point, it . . . Cal, you just have to see it."

"I'll put it on my list. What happened next?"

"He turns into an old man and then a space baby," Samuels said.

"She's making it sound ridiculous!" Xu was actually riled. "It's one of the most profound and beautiful films ever made."

"Sarah, *stop it!*" Cal turned to his scientist. "Xu, please get to the *point.*"

"I made my point. And I think that is why the pilot is also acting out in such a juvenile way. Our minds know what has happened, but our conscious selves haven't quite come to grips with it yet. I feel a little like I'm going mad, myself." Xu turned and pointed out at the Jovian. "That's not Jupiter, this is not our solar system. We don't know where we are, we don't even know *when* we are, and . . . we may never get home."

Silence.

"And we also might." Cal looked at his people. "Remember that and do your jobs." He looked to Xu. "Science officer. What is your assessment of what's occurred?"

Xu's eyes narrowed. His face cleared of consternation. "I think the atmospheric engineering, presumably in both this Jovian and Jupiter, are part of a space transportation system. One that we, at least currently, do not understand but have somehow become a part of."

They all considered this quietly such that the background sounds of the ship came to the fore.

"What now? Expound on your theory, my friend. What happened? Where are we? And what"—Cal pointed out the window at the discus shape silhouetted against the green moon—"is that?"

Three

Cal took control of the main telescope, interrupting Odysseus's direct imaging planet search. He refocused the instrument on the Jovian's nearby green moon. It was shrinking in his view as the interplanetary—no, *interstellar*—spacecraft swept on toward the gas giant's north pole; the spectacular rings providing a stunning backdrop for the moon. It appeared to be a Europa-like world, a radiation denuded surface of ice with a likely subterranean ocean beneath.

The oblong shape rotated in dark silence, obscuring a limb of the green moon and casting a circular shadow across its face.

"It's not Galactic Central Station, that's for sure," Sarah, the pilot, said sarcastically.

"Are you talking to me?" asked the ship's AI. She wasn't, and so, ignored it.

The object was a fattened discus. Through the scope, Cal could easily make out features on its uniform gray-brown exterior. The discus was scored with regular longitudinal segmentations; some sort of cleavages in the structure—channels or joints perhaps. There were recessed oval depressions, equally spaced around the object in multiple equatorial bands. They appeared to be made of the same pockmarked gray-brown material as the rest of the disc. Perhaps, like the alien object that had bonded itself with his ship, this construction had been in space for eons, covered in space dust, waiting.

It's not Galactic Central Station, but maybe it was, once.

Four

The *Ulysses* crossed over the Jovian's north pole. Temperature gradients similar to those they saw on Jupiter swept the more equatorial bands up into turbulent swarms of colossal atmospheric features. Six counter-rotating vortices bound and stabilized into a six-pointed arrangement. A star of storms enclosing six smaller cyclones—a six-pointed maw of darkness.

"I may have been hallucinating," the Doctor said. "But if this planet is like Jupiter, then that pattern might also be mapped in two dimensions on its core. Maybe we can just go back through?"

"Possibly, Doctor," replied Xu.

"I don't know about you," Sarah said, "but I don't want to just dive randomly into a gas giant.

Xu turned to his screens, tapping with his fingertips. "Arrays of vortices like these have been seen in simulated fluid experiments. Just as on Jupiter and as we see here, they don't simply merge, rather the storms reinforce one another, forming equally spaced arrays around a center. Like a flower. Stable natural structures."

"Or maybe we've just *thought* they were natural."

"Possibly . . ." Xu halted for a second, as if the thought hadn't already occurred to him and then continued expounding. "They're called *vortex crystals.*"

"Seriously?" asked the pilot

"Yes."

"Cool name."

"Yes."

"That's really the name? For real?"

"Yes. Vortex crystals. Actual scientific name."

"Wonderful," the Doc responded in agitation. "They already have a cool, apropos name. It's a machine somehow made of crystal wind. Can we go *back*? Back to Jupiter? Back *home*?"

"The word *crystal* doesn't indicate some magical substance, Doctor. It refers to a state of stability with minimum energy. The storms are likely stable as a result of the violent turbulence beneath - a state of maximum energy gelling into long-lasting features. But we don't know how these systems function together, we don't know any more than the fact that they exist and that we are here. We can't really say how we got here in the first place."

"Are you insane? Yes, we can! We came through Jupiter's north polar storm. What if we go back in?"

"And how would we do that?"

"We do what that *thing* did! We fly back into *this* gas giant's north polar whatever."

"And how do we know that will work?"

The Doc gestured to the pilot. "If the red weed flew us through, Sarah can fly us back!"

"I appreciate the vote of confidence, Doc but . . ."

"We don't know how it works," Xu cut in. "If it *works* at all."

"If it's an *it*," the pilot said with considerable sarcasm.

"To wit," said Xu. "We don't know the rules. Do we fly back through the north pole or the south? Did we exit from the core? I assume so but I was not conscious to see. Not even Odysseus was functioning to record it. If we did exit the core, did the red weed control our ascent or were we brought to the upper atmosphere via another jet stream?"

The Doc stared blankly, out of her element. Xu's mind was too quick, even for her.

"Or both," he continued. "And if so, is there another jet stream that will take us back down? If that's true, how do we find it if the weed doesn't want us to?"

Cal looked at her. "We have to face the facts, Susan, we only survived because of the alien, but we don't know that it will help us go back if that's not in its plans."

"How do we know it even has plans, Cal? Xu said it's part of a transportation system. A machine."

"Yes, one we don't understand and that we don't know how to operate," answered Cal.

"And who says machines can't have plans?" Sarah added.

"The point is that we somehow survived a dive into the core of Jupiter and ended up here, wherever that is. Even if it might get us home, I'm not diving us back into another atmosphere without some evidence and a more compelling reason."

"Cal, if it can't take us back . . . We're dead, we can't survive."

"Who says?"

"Without mission control? Without resupply? How can we?"

"Doc, we don't know what our situation really is yet. We have to keep calm and assess." He shot a glance at Xu and added, "Radar and infrared, please."

"On it."

"Make me a map."

Five

From the preliminary results of both direct imaging and doppler wobble observations, it appeared that the system was a near-binary. A super gas giant was in a tight gravitational dance with a yellow main sequence star as they spun around a mutual center of gravity. The Jovian was so massive and spun so rapidly that its poles flattened and its equator bulged. Four small rocky planets circled further out. Beyond a wide belt of planetary debris, three more gas giants orbited on a slightly tilted plane. It was possible there were other planetesimals further out, but Odysseus's sweeps had not uncovered any as of yet.

The Earth ship orbited the innermost of the outer Jovian worlds. Their first target of exploration, however, simply had to be its green moon. The crew was crowded into the command module. The pilot co-opted the large rear-view screen that hung above the center of the cockpit's forward viewports. She mirrored her console window onto it, a luminescent vector diagram: a spray of helices spinning around two spiraling spheres.

"The flight path to the green moon," Sarah said, waving at the diagram.

"Performing a plane change from the polar orbit we currently occupy would be prohibitively expensive, propellant-wise." She glanced

14

at the docking window and the flanks of the ship beyond. "I don't care how much extra juice that thing, or whatever, is feeding us. Given our location, playing it loose with our consumables is unwise."

Cal met her gaze and nodded.

She pointed at the outermost spot on a highly elliptical path around the larger sphere. "I suggest we shift into what is basically an escape orbit, while still staying within the Jovian's pull. At the apoapsis, the furthest point out on the orbit, our velocity will fall to nearly a standstill. We can then make the plane change with a minimum application of force, alter our inclination and reenter at an equatorial angle. That's our best bet."

"Sounds good, make the calculations. Be ready." He turned to his science officer. "Xu, what have you found out?"

Xu turned away from the console, the articulated screens reordered themselves behind him. "I've used a combination of methods to gain intelligence on the disc-like object in orbit of the green moon." His smaller screens blanked, and an enhanced optical telescopic image of the moon and its companion appeared on the main screen above them. "Here's what it looks like through direct imaging. Radar is estimating the orbital distance of the moon, at least at the points at which we measured, to be 680,000 miles. Further than we thought, the moon is therefore larger than we believed. 3,181 miles in diameter. Much larger than Jupiter's moon Europa, larger even than Earth's own moon."

He switched the image to an enlargement of the orbiting object.

"To get a clear picture of this disc-like object's size, we used infrared light." The screen erupted in a wash of reds and yellows and the obscuring shadows of visible light disappeared. "To know its mass, we need to have an idea of what it's made of. I'm using the hyperspectral spectrometer meant to determine the mineral composition of the Jovian moons to get an idea."

"Hyperspectral spectrometer?"

"Yes."

"Is that . . . ?"

"Yes, that's its real scientific name. I'm glad this amuses you, pilot."

Samuels squelched her grin as Cal shot her a sharp glance.

"Visible and infrared combined show spectral patterns that are not out of line with what I would expect from the surface of an asteroid."

"So, what's that mean?"

"It means, I believe, that like our hitchhiker from the Trojan asteroid belt, this thing has been out in the space environment long enough to be coated by a layer of dirty water-ice. Probably inches thick, likely accreted over decades or centuries or more. Perhaps from a transit through the ice rings. The turbulence in the ring system plus the object's elliptical orbit might suggest that it once occupied a different position."

The image vanished and was replaced with a more detailed magnification.

"You can see here." Xu pointed at darker blemishes at various points around the object. "There are myriad impact formations all along the outer surface. Some of the craters are rather large."

"Do these craters descend beyond the ice layer?"

"Some of them may, but I can't say for sure. Even these areas are covered by the icy soot."

"So, is there a way to get a picture of what the thing itself is made of?"

"Not without breaking through the ice layer and getting at the surface underneath. We could use the beam from the laser altimeter device to—"

"Xu, we're not firing a laser at this thing. We're going to rendezvous with the object and make a closer inspection. Maybe something over there will give us a better idea of how we got here and how we might be able to get back."

Six

In the extended and spinning centrifuge arm leading to Red Hab, Xu caught up with Cal.

"I hope you're on your way to get some sleep too," Cal said, grasping the nylon handle of the tender and letting it pull him up/down into the gently dawning gravity of the habitat.

The science officer replied while wrapping the tender's second strap around his own wrist. "I'm going to the lounge. I have some work I still need to get out of my head. I thought it would be restful *and* productive."

"Sleep is productive. We all need it, even you. Our orbit is stable, Odysseus can handle it. Get some rest."

"I will Cal, I promise. I just can't sleep until I get this stuff out of my skull."

"I got it, what's eating you?"

"You're not going to like it."

Cal's tired smile dropped away. "Spill."

Xu's eyes bored into his. "Something went on at Jupiter's core that is entirely beyond understanding. We don't know where we are— but we also don't know *when* we are."

"Come again?"

"We all lost consciousness, even Odysseus shut down. We have no way to know how long that transition took. First thing I remember, we were rising up through the atmosphere."

"That's my first memory as well."

"It could have been a second or it could have been minutes."

"True." Cal's vision began to cloud over as his mind whirled down the path Xu was leading it.

"It could have been months."

Cal hadn't considered that, his mind initially rejecting the thought.

"Or years."

With all that had happened to them, he had to admit it was possible.

"Or decades."

Cal felt the origins of an immense headache suddenly bubbling up behind his right eye.

"Or—"

"Shut up."

Seven

Xu leaned against the frame of one of Red Hab's large triangular viewports, working from his tablet. Constellations rotated across its glossy surface with a richness of dimension that sometimes made it feel like he held a second window in his hands, one that looked out into some other place. Through the great inverted triangle, the yellow gas planet rode on beneath the ship. As they headed for the equator. They would soon again pass under the arch of the planet's glimmering rings.

The pilot drifted up behind him.

"Hi."

He turned his head. "Oh, Sarah, hello. I've asked Odysseus to concentrate on the constellation comparisons again. I thought you'd like to know."

"Thanks."

"Ready for the plane shift maneuver?"

She nodded. "We can make the burn anytime, but Cal wants to wait until we all get some sleep." She peeked over at his tablet. "How are things going with you? Any clue where we are yet?"

He grimaced. "Not yet. Odysseus is working through the various configurations for more and more stars. He'll figure it out eventually, thanks to you."

"How long *could* it take?"

"It could take two minutes or it could take two days. He says he's located a group of very distant stars within our current sky that look the same as they would if viewed from Earth."

"What's that mean?"

"That means that, on a galactic scale, we are roughly in the same area of the universe from where we started. We'll find out more as he finds further patterns that match."

Sarah let that sink in and looked out at the rolling chasms of the stormy surface flashing by beneath them. The view recalled the experience of flying the ship through the jet stream. She turned away from it.

"The universe likes symmetry, right?" she said. "This planet and Jupiter must be sharing a matter stream."

"Necessarily so, I'd think. Given our experience," Xu replied.

"I wonder if there is actually a reverse stream, bringing matter from this Jovian back to Jupiter?"

"It must be symmetric in some way, or else Jupiter's density would be constantly decreasing. Either the matter is being replaced by this Jovian or its being replaced by some other means. Perhaps even another planet somewhere else? We simply do not know much about this phenomenon yet."

"Is this planet's color due to the influx of gas from Jupiter?"

"Again, unknown, but I would surmise that the disparity in color results from a difference in trace gases. The bulk of this world is probably just like Jupiter, mostly hydrogen and helium."

"Do you think all gas giants have some similar . . . track?"

"If what we experienced was a natural phenomenon, then I'd suppose so. If they are artificially induced features, perhaps not. The presence of our alien hitchhiker would indicate that they aren't natural."

"Why? Rivers are natural and people leave boats by them all the time."

"You're absolutely right, pilot. It's just a feeling I have. However, to take advantage of your metaphor, maybe we should pay less attention to the river and look for more boats."

"Que?"

"Well, what have we learned?" Xu didn't wait for her to respond and continued, "Not all objects orbiting giant planets may be natural. There may yet be hidden elements in orbit that are somehow supporting this transit system, perhaps via processes that have forever been taken for natural phenomena."

"Yeah, or maybe they're not hidden at all," she said, pointing to the object orbiting the green moon.

"Indeed."

"We have to investigate. I'm concerned about our fuel usage, but given our new . . . friend's ability to provide us with propellant, I think we should be good. We didn't dip much below fifty percent during the entire trip through Jupiter. And since our gauges are back to *full*, it stands to reason that it refueled us during ascent."

"Yes." Xu nodded "It would have been a simple matter to scoop in gas from the planet's atmosphere as we rose."

There was an awkward pause during which the pilot scanned the scientist's careworn face, which seemed to have aged years in the past few days. "Right, so . . . I'm going to get some sleep."

"Goodnight, Sarah."

"Good night, Xu. You should get some sleep, too." She paused for a moment, floating at the bottom of the ladder. Gazing at the alien vista through the giant inverted triangle, Xu's human form silhouetted against it. "First people to sleep in another solar system."

Xu turned to her. "Yes."

"Kinda beautiful. To be the first people to do something so fundamentally human, so far from home."

"Yes."

"Do you think anyone will ever know?"

"I don't know. I hope so."

Eight

In the spindle, Inez was asleep, bumping against the limits of the restraints built into the portable chair she had attached to the spindle's pipework corridor wall. Over her right shoulder, on the node server monitor, the mathematical storms zoomed in endless procession. Fractal flowers bloomed and swallowed their elders on an endless fall.

Nine

Hours later, a restless Cal and the Doc met in the CM. It was the middle of the ship's "night." Everyone else was asleep, the artificial intelligence handling the ship's operations. The Doc's zero-G bourbon bottle drifted over the capsule's central dash. She held its bulb in her hand. Cal plucked the bottle out of the air and held it against his chest, gazing out at the green moon and its mysterious shadow. He took a break from obsessing about the object they would attempt to explore in the morning to torture himself over the thing attached to their ship and what it might still be capable of.

"Do you know," Cal said, hugging the bottle, "that for a few minutes I'd forgotten there was an alien infesting the ship?"

She smiled gently. "With everything that has happened, I suppose that's understandable. People can get used to the strangest things." As if to underscore this fact, she pushed the booze-bulb, and it floated over to him.

He caught it and placed it securely back onto the neck of the bottle. "What do you think about Xu's idea that it's a kind of automated booster, part of some ancient space transport system?"

"Maybe. I suppose it did everything it could to protect us. Still, it doesn't seem very friendly."

He squeezed the bulb, pulling a few fingers worth of the caramel liquid up into it. "What kind of beings do you think built it?"

"I don't know, Cal, but I get the sense that they were alien. *Very* alien. That we would find their thinking . . . wrong. I get the sense that they were all alone. That there was no one else out here yet."

"Alone among the stars, huh?"

"Yeah, poetic. But I don't get the sense that there was anything poetic about them."

"Why do you say that?"

"The behavior of the thing, our guest."

"How so?"

"Well, it obviously respects us as life forms. I guess that Xu is right in that sense, it's not trying to harm us. It could just be a tool or a complex system of tools, a booster, maybe. Like Xu says. But that's not what I'm getting at."

"What do you mean?"

Her face twisted into an expression of revulsion. "It just *took* us, Cal. There was no attempt to communicate. No attempt to determine whether we were its theoretical docking partner or something else entirely. That's why it *seemed* violent, predatory. It *was* violent, but it *wasn't* predatory. We were quarry but not prey. There was no attempt to measure consent but also there was no real attack and no consumption either. As if there was no thought, by its maker, that we might not be what it thought we would be. A spaceship approaches? That's my ride. Bang!"

"I wasn't thinking about it that way."

"You wouldn't."

"I guess not. Xu was, I'm sure, hoping it was more of a gift, a token of friendship. The lion teaming up with the mouse."

"Xu's an optimist. You're a romantic . . . I'm saying it's more like the lion and the antelope, but the lion wasn't ever going to eat the antelope in the first place."

"The lion lays down with the lamb?"

"If that's the metaphor, then what happens next?"

They sat quiet for a moment, the strange alien world rolling in front of them.

"Inez says it doesn't even show signs of curiosity. Maybe it *is* just a malfunctioning machine," Cal said, breaking the silence. "Some dumb thing whose instructions have become corrupt over all that time?"

"We don't know that it's as old as Xu thinks it is."

"It was coated with dust. He estimates millions of years' worth, or more."

"It could have disguised itself like that on purpose last year, for all we know. With everything we've seen so far, that's not beyond plausibility." She stretched in the seat. "Regardless, its behavior implies either an imperial point of view or one of a species totally alone in the universe. If it truly saw things through an imperial perspective, you'd think it would have had some means to tell what belongs to it from what belongs to another." She set the bottle rotating in the air in front of them. "Even if just to lay claim."

"You're a smart cookie, Susan."

"That's why you married me."

He smiled and tossed her the bulb. "And why you divorced me."

Ten

From high out on their elliptical orbit, the *Ulysses* had fired its main engine to swing into a wide circular path around the green moon. The discus was now just 245 miles ahead of them. *Ulysses* was maintaining that distance, sweeping it with radar and infrared light to measure its size and distance. Cal ordered them in closer. To change a spacecraft's speed is to change its orbit. Samuels rotated the ship and fired the engine into its direction of travel to slow it down. With less forward velocity, the moon's gravity exerted a greater influence on the ship, and it was pulled into a lower orbit. Now, closer to its surface, they covered the distance around the planet in faster, smaller circles.

Ulysses closed on the object. With ten miles between them Samuels flipped the ship back around and throttled up the engine. The greater velocity caused the ship to pull away from the moon, speeding out to a higher and therefore slower orbit, drawing within a quarter mile of the mysterious object.

"No transmissions detected, no activity seen."

"Thanks, Inez. I kinda expected as much." Cal fidgeted in his suit.

Xu slewed the telescope over the surface of the disc, narrating as the imagery mirrored to the module's primary display screen. "The surface is highly space weathered, pitted. Very low albedo. Looks like ages of exposure to cosmic rays, radiation, and micrometeoroid impacts. Surface markings as earlier observed, there are deep recurring longitudinal furrows originating from the poles of the disc, dividing it into sixteen equal sections. The circular depressions occur on both the dorsal and ventral sides."

The large screen between the windows lit up with a still photo, a magnification of the object. What looked like a puncture hole adorned one of the crescent shaped wedges.

"What is *that*?" asked the Doc.

"Seems that the structure suffered a substantial impact at some point."

Cal rubbed his chin. "Does it penetrate to the interior?"

"Unknown, but the impact site is uniformly covered by dust. I don't see any openings inside."

"Me neither."

They all stared at the shape on the screen in silence for a moment.

"Well, we will know more when we get over there," Cal said.

Xu turned to him. "Have you decided who you're taking?"

"You and the Doc."

"What if I don't want to go?" the Doc asked.

"Then don't go."

She frowned.

"It's almost completed a full rotation."

The image zoomed to the wedge just coming into view over the green limb of the moon and into a squared-circle of a groove that ran around the uppermost circular depression. It appeared to be half-filled with space dust.

"There's something there."

"What is it?"

"I'm hoping it's an airlock of some kind," said Xu. He waved at the screen and the image zoomed. "Look, there is another circular depression beneath the larger one. I don't think that's an impact crater."

The scope zoomed further, and the smaller depression resolved into an inverse tapering cone. Inside its well were indistinct half-moon shapes.

"Either that's debris within or it's part of a mechanism of some sort."

"Hold us here, Sarah." Cal unstrapped from the right-hand seat and floated into open space on the command module's aft deck. Above them, the compartment was filled with the computers that made up most of Odysseus, below an array of instrument packages, radars, and cameras. The brains and senses of the ship that sustained their existence in this impossibly far-off place. There was no sense bringing all that any closer to the unknown object.

"We're going to take the lander over the rest of the way."

Eleven

The *Ulysses*'s exploratory lander was an up-rated version of the taxi lander Cal had previously flown down to Ceres. It was made up of the same gem-shaped pressure vessel and twin articulated engines, with a larger golden-brass descent stage enabling it to carry an advanced lighting rig, more gear, fuel, and consumables. The lander looked like a white diamond enclosed in a baroque setting. Inside, Cal and Xu, in their blue and red spacesuits, had their heads bowed to the two control stations running through the pre-launch checklists. The Doc, in her forest green suit, was strapped in behind, leaning forward to peer out the wide sweep of the window.

The lander had originally been dubbed *Telemachus*, but no one liked the name. It was changed to *Argo* at some point, which made little sense except for it stemming from the Greco-Roman pantheon. Everyone just liked it better. Cal switched on the *Argo*'s lighting array, rotated the engines on their stalks, and accelerated away from the *Ulysses*. The dark bulk of the discus drew nearer as they quickly crossed the intervening space. Xu swept the lander's searchlights over the object. Billions of grains of grit and clumps of icy dirt threw stark shadows and made the surface appear pebbled and shot through with holes.

"I'm going to make one orbit of the structure," Cal twisted a set of virtual dials and slid them to the periphery of the console, "and then we'll move in closer. Say, twenty-five feet above that possible airlock."

"Sounds good, Cal," answered the pilot's voice from *Ulysses*.

The RCS coughed to life, and jets of thruster flame illuminated the lander as Cal took it around the disc. Searchlights playing over its surface, the beams zeroed in, revealing the ragged flanges of the impact site they had seen earlier. Cal brought the lander in closer and pitched forward to center the hole in their main window.

"It's a puncture. The skin is broken and folded inward, but the gap seems to have been resealed and is filled with dust." Xu pointed.

"Let me see if I can get us a better angle on this." Cal squeezed the hand controller and nudged the lander through space, flicking at a series of virtual sliders to raise their height relative to the object. A quick twist of a luminous dial pitched the *Argo* over for a better view of the structure's dorsal surface.

"Yes . . . look." Xu tapped against the inside of the viewport, pointing at the feature. "Something seems to have punched a hole through the side of the disc, but it seems to have closed over, there's a great deal of dust inside the rim."

Cal squinted. "What do you think caused the hole?"

"Likely a meteoroid impact, this thing has clearly seen its share of strikes. It looks like it's been out here for a very long time."

"Every other impact is tiny in comparison," Cal said, scanning the Swiss cheese appearance of the icy sheath.

"Yes . . ." Xu's voice trailed off as he searched around, finding no other impacts approaching such a size.

"And no shielding like our hitchhiker."

"Apparently not."

"Maybe it's dead," theorized the Doc.

"A derelict? It looks the part," mused Cal.

Argo pitched back perpendicular to the derelict and dipped around its far side. The searchlight beam stretched across the curving surface and filtered through the details of the ice sheath as it wrapped over the pockmarked sides. The suspected airlock hove into view. Cal matched orbital speed, canceling out the lander's motion twenty-six feet from the ruined expanse.

"Odysseus, hold position here."

"Roger, Captain."

Nothing could be seen through the forward viewport but the cratered plain of the derelict, ice crystals shining in the light of the distant star. Cal stepped back from the controls and turned to face the Doc, who was already connecting her suit to an EVA backpack. She hoisted it off the clamp and spun in midair to slide her arms into the straps. Cal floated over to his own backpack and rechecked the status indicators. Before removing the pack, he reached beyond to a wall locker and removed the silver briefcase that contained the holster and space-jacketed revolver. The Doc glared at him.

"You warned me not to bring it last time, sure I would use it just *'cause I had it*. I didn't then, I won't now." He Velcroed the holster to his left hip and hooked his arms through the EVA pack's straps.

"I hope not."

"I just hope I don't *have* to." Cal buckled and tightened the pack's straps. "All right. We'll go out through the dorsal hatch. Xu, you have the honor."

The science officer stopped hitching up his backpack and flashed him a look that was genuinely surprised, and grateful. "Thank you, Cal."

"Doc, I'll ask you to hang back and be prepared to assist if we run into trouble."

"That makes sense to me."

"What else really"—He reached up and twisted the concentric rings of the locking mechanism—"matters?" He flashed her a smile as the *Argo*'s atmosphere evacuated and the hatch swung down into the cockpit. Cal was first out to the top of the lander, holding onto a safety guide rail and watching as Xu's red helmet rose up from the hatch, warm light spilling out around him. The derelict hung in front of him, overwhelming the bounds of his vision. Once again, he was about to step completely over the line into the unknown. Cal jetted off toward the giant object, Xu following just off to his side, propelled by compressed gasses spurting from their EVA packs.

The green moon provided a spectacular backdrop as the Doc, perched on top of the lander, watched them shrink toward a surface of cracks and fissured ice. She knew that Odysseus was recording everything, and from multiple angles, but she took a second to snap a few of her own photos anyway.

Cal slowed his descent toward the disc's bulging waist. The wash of his thrusters swept over the icy surface, dislodging unknown years' worth of accrued dust. It floated off and around him as he surveyed the skin of the derelict. Up close it appeared even more worn than it had through the telescopes, freckled with a galaxy of tiny craters. Xu maneuvered closer, examining the smaller of the two circular recesses. Its interior was rifled like a gun barrel. Cal drifted in for a better view. At the bottom of the well was what looked like a set of scissoring parts, locked in ice and dust.

"Break it loose?" Cal asked.

"Let's not get too hasty."

He traced the path of the squared groove. It enclosed the space around both depressions and occurred only on this one wedge. Cal thumbed his controls and maneuvered over to the larger depression. He floated above, adjusting his altitude to bring himself parallel so that he could get a closer look. It was a perfect oval sunk about three inches into the scarred surface.

Cal looked over at Xu, engrossed in his progress. He nudged his thrusters and moved in closer, pulled a sample hammer off his belt, and rapped the ice encrustations in the center of the sunken area.

The ice broke and drifted away in sheets much like the first thaw of spring sends frozen slates floating down creeks and streams. As he'd guessed, the large oval depressions were windows.

Xu looked horrified. "What did you do?"

Cal ignored the question. "This is a window. I think there are other structures inside." There was still quite a bit of clinging debris, and the surface beneath was nearly as pitted as the accumulated ice. He shined his wrist light in through the ages-hazed viewport. The beam scattered, making it difficult to see anything inside. "I'm not sure if there are chambers or if its just a big empty space. If this is a ship or a station or *what.*"

Xu maneuvered over to the perimeter of the window, upside down from Cal's perspective; he aimed his own light in through the fogged material, bobbing his head to try and resolve anything within.

Cal turned his attention to the cleavage in the surface. It ran in a suspiciously door-shaped manner around the window and the secondary opening. He spun the sample hammer around to the chisel end and ran the tapering plastic-sheathed metal into the groove. Clots of ice and dust sprayed away from the plowing chisel.

"What do you think?" Cal pointed at the smaller recess that Xu had first been preoccupied with. "Doorknob?"

Xu had taken out his own sampling tools and was picking ice and dust from the groove. An exceptionally large clump of debris broke free, he swatted it away with a red gloved hand. "There's more than just dust and ice in here, it looks like some kind of manufacturing substrate or excess. Like the residue of a 3D print or sintering job."

Cal jetted closer and mirrored Xu's helmet feed on the suit-screen in his suit's left forearm. The grit in the mechanism looked similar to the debris Paul had found in crevices on the registers and vanes of the alien objects attached to *Ulysses*.

The mechanism was emerging fully from the icy dust. It looked like two inward bent flanges. Something clearly meant to be grabbed and turned.

"That's a doorknob."

"I'd agree."

"Pick the rest of that ice and grit out and let's try it."

Xu worked with his tool, flitting it around the circumference of the collar ringing the flanges. He removed a pistol-grip drill from his pack and dialed it to the minimum of five rotations per minute. He set the vice-grip attachment against the alien flanges and tapped the tool's screen. The vice grip tightened down on the flange. Xu pulled the trigger, and he began to slowly rotate rather than the mechanism.

"I figured."

"Jammed tight."

"Hold on." He swiped a couple of lit squares on his forearm screen.

Cal jetted backwards a few feet, anticipating thruster fire from Xu's pack.

Xu pulled the trigger again, but this time his EVA pack's thrusters blasted to provide force to work against the stuck alien handle. Xu tapped his screen again to raise the torque limit and rotations per minute. The thrusters began to fire almost constantly.

The doorknob didn't budge.

"Maybe you're turning it the wrong way?"

"Give me some credit. I tried both ways."

"Sometimes smart people forget the simple things."

"Not me," Xu said with a smile. "It's just been stuck for a long time."

"Maybe we both try?"

Both suits positioned around the recess, reaching in and gripping the pistol-tool. Cal wrapped both his gloves around the aluminum tape covered body as Xu gripped the handle. They fired their thrusters to compound their forces. The handle stayed stuck.

"Cal, stop. One of us is going to go flying." Xu released the tool and let it drift with the tether attached to his belt.

Cal floated backwards to appraise the situation. He glanced at his thruster propellant indicator. Down to 73 percent already. "Do you want to cut or drill?"

"It wouldn't be my first choice."

"Then we need more muscle or some other way to unfreeze these joints."

"Perhaps the thruster exhaust of an EVA pack would blast enough debris off?"

"Maybe, and perhaps the heat would cause the materials to shrink a bit, but it'd have to be sustained pressure to really have an effect, I'd think."

"We can hold hands?"

"How nice."

"You use your thrusters to try and wash the debris free from the door, and I'll counterbalance your force."

"Worth a shot."

The pair took up positions; Xu gripped Cal by the shoulders and braced his boots against his thighs. "Ready?"

"Ready."

"You guys look cute," the Doc said from the *Argo*'s dorsal hatch.

Xu ramped the thrust level of his EVA backpack straight up to maximum as Cal provided the opposing force necessary to keep them right where they were. He watched his propellant levels drop down into the upper sixties.

After a full minute of thrust, the surface of the airlock door was denuded of ice, freed in a great oblong oval in the shape of Xu's RCS exhaust. The doorknob was still frozen in position.

"Drill now?"

They floated, contemplating the situation. They couldn't just give up, that was clear. They had to come up with something else.

"Hey guys," the Doc said, waving from the roof of the lander, pointing over at the *Ulysses* sparkling off the limb of the green moon. The comms line crackled. "What about the ship's manipulator arm?"

Cal turned to Xu and smiled.

Twelve

The 550-foot long bulk of *Ulysses* crawled toward the derelict using RCS thrusters only.

"Take it easy, Sarah." Cal was standing on the pitted surface, waving her in with his suit's wrist-lights like an airport marshaller guiding a jetliner into the terminal.

Samuels jogged the hand controller forward. Too fast. She pulled back again a few times—blasting the RCS thrusters against the direction of motion to slow its progress toward the hulk.

The Doc watched from far above. She had instructed Odysseus to move the lander out of the way of the approaching interplanetary ship, raising its height relative to the derelict and pitching it over by ninety degrees. She now stood upon its dorsal surface next to the top hatch, boots magnetized to its skin, and looked directly ahead into a view that just a few moments previous she'd have called *down*. She was perpendicular to the long axis of *Ulysses* as it slowly inched sideways toward the mysterious discus, its eighty-foot manipulator arm extended to its maximum, drawing ever closer to the suspected airlock door.

Xu jetted backwards a few more feet and watched the manipulator arm slide past him. Cal had a hand against the surface of the derelict and was reaching out for the arm as it came close, as if he might be able to wrangle it into position by virtue of his will alone.

The three four-foot long rubber-shod claws of the manipulator bumped against the surface, just inches outside the "doorknob" recess. Ice crystals wafted up around them. Cal grabbed hold of the rubber fingers and opened his RCS thrusters. "Gentle, Sarah!"

The manipulator moved just an inch and then slid down and into the striated recess.

"Open the claws." Cal hit the side of one of the fingers, as if he could nudge it further despite it being a part of the great mass of the ship.

"That's it. Can you just beep the thrusters?"

There was the tiniest of movements from the massive Earth ship, and the manipulators slid around the alien flanges.

"Close the grip." The black fingers compressed, the arm itself seemed to rise out of the doorknob recess by microns.

"That's got it."

"It's in?" Xu asked, excited.

"Yep. Great job, pilot."

The comms crackled. "Thanks, Cal."

"Ready?" That was Paul's deep voice, he was in control of the arm itself.

"Ready," replied Xu.

Cal jetted back; if the doorknob wouldn't turn and the manipulator arm came skipping out of the recess, he didn't want to be in the way. He settled to stand on the surface of the derelict.

"Here we go," said the engineer. "Torque at five foot-pounds."

The arm itself stiffened up.

"Ramp it up slowly."

"Seven pounds."

"Slowly."

The shaft of the manipulator arm seemed to vibrate; a small bit of debris bounded up from the recess in the derelict's skin.

"Ten pounds. Twelve."

"I said slowly."

It might have been his imagination but Cal felt he could feel a vibration rising through the skin of the derelict and up into his thighs through his boots.

"Fourteen."

"Cal." Samuels's voice crackled over his helmet speakers. "The ship is starting to move."

"Thrusters. Keep it steady." The doorknob wasn't turning, the rotational energy was transmitting back up the arm to *Ulysses* itself. He began to worry about the stress on the ship.

"Paul, how are we looking?"

"We're fine, Cal. Torque at seventeen pounds."

"Take it up to thirty, let's try and give it a kick."

"Cal—"

The shaft of the arm seemed to flex.

"It's coming."

"Thirty-five."

Bits of grit shot out of the recess, bounding up and along the shaft of the arm.

"It's coming!"

"Forty-three."

Xu looked worried.

"Forty-seven."

Cal felt a sharp crack transmit through the derelict, and its surface appeared to leap up around him. A fine cloud of ice crystals and dust floated amidst his legs. His eyes shot to the *Ulysses* and then to the end of the manipulator arm. It remained firmly in the recess; the airlock door had opened along an unseen seam. The panel above the doorknob was slowly sliding upwards, vanishing into the skin. Beyond the doorway was a small, dark, vaguely spherical room.

Xu let out a whistling breath. He moved in close to the border of the door. Its inner surface was a stark bone white, unstained by the eons of cosmic dust and radiation. A few pieces of debris tumbled end over end out of the supposed airlock.

"Sarah, back *Ulysses* off."

"Roger, Cal."

"Doc, bring the lander back down."

"On it." She gathered her tether, wrapping the strap around her left glove as if pulling on the reins, and braced her boot against the safety railing. She prodded Odysseus, and the *Argo* pitched back upright. The Doc rode it down like it was an ox in the field.

As the lander slowed into position, orbiting in sync just fifteen feet from the open airlock, Cal turned to Xu. "You go first," he said and pointed at the darkened chamber beyond the door.

Xu looked shocked. "Cal, are you sure?" It was a moment in history, should they survive, that humanity would never forget. Cal was giving it to him.

"Absolutely, it should be you."

Xu's face transformed with the brightest smile Cal had ever seen from the man, and he turned, gripped the width of the recessed door, and used the power of his arms to propel himself into the roughly spherical chamber. Cal moved in behind with a squirt of his thrusters. Xu had turned on his full complement of lights and settled to the bowl-like floor of the chamber. Cal hung in the center of the space.

Inset in the left-hand wall of the otherwise featureless chamber were two darkened slots. Cal approached them and turned on his lights. They were jet-black cylindrical openings, oriented vertically, set into the wall. Inside each floated a gleaming ivory disc. The left-hand disc floated near the top of cylinder, the right near the bottom.

"What do you make of this, controls?" he asked.

"Presumably an airlock would have controls."

"Presumably."

Cal reached out and touched the disc on the left. It bobbled in place.

Xu moved in closer, recording.

Cal applied greater pressure on the disc, and it sank to the bottom of the cylinder chamber. At the same moment, the outside airlock door slid closed.

"Cal!"

"We're okay, Sarah. The derelict seems to have power . . . or at least certain mechanisms that still function, anyway."

"Power? Are we sure it's a derelict?"

"Maybe there's a power plant on board that is still operating."

Xu opened his comms. "I've been thinking about this issue in regards to our journey here. This Jovian is similar to Jupiter and the Jupiter-Io flux creates a current of five or so mega-amperes. That's more than two trillion watts of energy constantly being produced. My guess is that this station is tapping into a similar energy field."

He reached out a gloved finger and applied similar pressure to the underside of the low-flying disc. It rose smoothly through the cylinder and the outer door followed, drawing up into the hull of the derelict. He turned to look out the reopened airlock and give *Ulysses* a thumbs up.

"Ready?"

"I'm ready, Cal."

"Doc," he spoke into the comms, "care to join us?"

Thirteen

The derelict's inner door opened and three figures in candy-colored spacesuits, blue, red and green, stepped into a vast hall of pure white. The chamber reflected the proportions, if not the size, of the derelict's outer appearance in negative. Sixteen longitudinal striations interrupted curving ivory walls crowned by a border of swirling imagery. The border fully circumscribed a great disc-like interior space. The striations met in the center of the curving hall, converging into the neck of a large white sphere-topped statue rising some fifteen feet into the air. Two great oval doorways yawned across the far side, one on either end of the oblate hall.

"Xu, what do you think we have here? Is this an archaeological site or have we broken into someone's house?"

The scientist shrugged his red-suited shoulders and aimed his lights across the darkened space. At the far side of the hall, a hole had been punched through the curving ceiling. A star-shaped wound of flayed material curled inwards, twists of stained and pitted outer skin disturbing the monochrome purity. New skin had seemingly grown to seal the hole. The look of the repair reminded Cal of the thing they had acquired, or that had acquired them, near Jupiter.

"Wow."

"*Ulysses*, are you getting this?"

"Yes, Cal. We have an excellent feed from all three of you."

Cal squirted his thrusters and moved out into the hall.

Xu jetted upwards, coming level with the border of frescoes, sweeping his searchlight beams across them. Varied shapes surrounded by swirls of circular geometric patterns ran all through the relief sculpture. The shapes ran from simple triangles, circles, and squares to the entirely unrecognizable; alien, multi-limbed and variegated forms.

Cal moved toward the rent in the ceiling by way of the central column and sphere. The statue was the same spotless white as the rest of the room, as if the entire structure had been cast from the same plaster. As he approached, he began to see dark flecks scattered across the surfaces beyond.

"Take a look at this." At some point, debris had showered down behind the central column. Obscured by the monument, on the gently curving bowl of the floor, was an impact crater. The tail of a cobalt blue torpedo-shaped object projected from the crater, its nose buried. Faded-red circuits radiated from the nose and ran in uneven tracks to its aft end.

"Now we know what made that hole."

Xu traced the object with his searchlight and then swept the beam all around the room. "Something fixed the ceiling but didn't touch this—whatever it is."

"It's a torpedo," the pilot said over the comms.

"Yes, thanks. Torpedo. Fine. No one addressed the unexplored torpedo but fixed the roof. I'm guessing this is another self-repairing machine."

"*Another* abandoned self-repairing machine?" Samuels asked over the comms.

"Apparently."

"This one seems like it's been asleep on the job, though," said the Doc.

"It has obviously been damaged."

Xu examined the red channels in the torpedo's skin more closely.

"Let's not touch that thing, Xu. Treat it as unexploded ordinance."

"Yes, sir." He moved back from it.

"Make sure you get good images of these frescoes. There may be something we can learn from them."

Cal moved back to the sphere, keeping an eye on the torpedo. He pulled out his sampling hammer and rotated it around to the chisel end. He tapped the surface gently.

Nothing happened.

The Doc wandered along the curving wall until she rounded the hall at the far side and stood in front of one of the giant oval doorways. It had to be eighteen feet tall at the apex, so large that the hall's central statue could probably be moved upright through it. Beyond that threshold a tubular corridor snaked away into darkness. She shined her searchlight into the curling tube-way; the right half of its walls sparkled.

Cal was about to try and chip a piece off of the sphere and then considered what history would think of that act. He'd find a less conspicuous spot to try his handiwork and so jetted over to where the Doc was peering down one of the large corridors.

"What do you think this is?"

"This place?" she asked.

"Sure, but this gate in particular."

"An entryway of some sort, I suppose."

"Pretty big door, designed to impress, you think?"

"Maybe, maybe they were just a lot bigger than we are."

"If that were the case, the airlock would have been larger. Its ceiling isn't that much taller than we are."

The Doc stared up at the soaring oval doorway and curving ceiling beyond.

"True, but in here, big doors, tall ceilings, huge monument."

Cal shined his light along a near set of friezes crowning the opening. "What are these shapes, you think? Animals? People?"

"I don't know. They really don't look like anything to me. I suppose we have a problem, what do we pay attention to?"

"What do you mean?"

"Well, all the little Mandelbrot set patterns, in ancient Greek friezes, the draping and leafwork were the artistic filler. Part of the sculpture's framing device. To me, the fractals looks like artistic filler, but what if that's not the case? An alien might look at a page of English text and ask "Do I read the black parts or the white parts?""

Cal cocked his head, scanning the frieze, trying to see it in new ways. There were shapes here common to those on the larger ring of sculpture.

"Is that a dragonfly?" he asked, pointing to a commonly repeated shape.

"A four winged one."

"I don't get it."

"Me neither."

Fourteen

"Xu, let's *go*."

Cal and the Doc had one foot into the curving hallway and were impatient to press forward, Xu was finishing a slow pan over the entire network of friezes, Odysseus was controlling his EVA thrusters, keeping his movement smooth and consistent.

"One second." Cal was panning over a section of frieze that, were he to completely give in to his biases, seemed to show a spider-like shape, on its back, spinning a city instead of a web.

"You said that three minutes ago."

"I'm almost done."

Cal looked at his gauges. They were well in the green. He turned back to the Doc; she had started tentatively down the tunnel-corridor.

"Look," she said. "It opens up into another spherical room just around the bend here." She raised her hand and aimed her spotlight in through the newly discovered room's doorway. "No lights. There are some kind of objects all over the walls."

"Susan, do not go any further."

"Xu, now!"

Xu appeared at the mouth of the corridor.

Cal jetted up behind the Doc. Inside the open circular doorway was a small spherical space. Shadows fled from their lights, leaking in every direction from flat-topped mushroom shapes sprouting from the walls. The mushrooms were ordered into rings, spanning the interior circumference. The tops of the mushrooms sparkled, reflecting the light of their search beams, each mushroom facing a seemingly random direction. At the center of the room, low in the bowl-shaped floor was a circular pad, from which no mushroom sprouted.

There was no other exit from the room.

They returned to the entry hall. Cal led them around the far side of the globe-topped monument and to the identical oval opening on the opposite wall. They made sure to give the torpedo a wide berth.

The second hallway curved around in reverse of the previous and opened into a slightly larger room, spherical again, but its walls were mostly unadorned and smooth. Its entryway was undecorated, but there were smaller circular portals at the cardinal points and each of these was surrounded by a collar of frieze-work about as wide as a man's thigh.

Cal flipped open his suit-screen and tabbed to the team's status display. Plenty of oxygen and battery life. Propellant dropping below half for Xu and him. It wouldn't be critically dangerous were they to push it and run out of fuel. They might have to hand-over-hand it back, manually propelling themselves. That would be fine if all they encountered was empty rooms. If there was an emergency . . . Once levels started to drop below half, he began to feel the prickle of anxiety.

As the Doc said, it likely would not be their last trip over. It wouldn't be the worst decision to head back to the ship and study just what they'd found so far.

"Let's keep this focused," he said. "We should either follow one of these corridors all the way to its end or backtrack and investigate the start of each of passage off that other room."

"Should we split up?" Xu asked.

"*Absolutely* not," said the Doc.

"This room is a convenient nexus. I say we explore the area immediately connected to each of these four doorways." To preclude argument from Xu, Cal added, "We'll expand our explorations on subsequent trips. I don't want us to overextend ourselves, and I do not want to get lost in here."

"Pick a direction."

Cal spun his hammer in the air in front of him. "Heads or tails?"

"Tails."

The hammer spun on all three axes. He reached out and grabbed it. It stopped with its handle pointing to the floor.

"We go down."

The three spacesuited figures gathered around the opening. To Cal, it felt uncomfortably like they were about to drop into a sewer.

"The shapes on these borders match some of the shapes in the entranceway friezes," commented Xu. "The dragonfly shape is repeated a number of times."

"The other hallway was decorated with dragonflies, too. But these are different," said the Doc. She ran her finger over the shapes of the frieze. "These dragonflies look like they have elephant trunks."

"Or they're connected to something."

"Or they're not dragonflies at all."

The figures dropped through the opening and into another cylindrical corridor.

"What do you make of these connecting tunnels?"

"I don't know, except that they probably fit the shapes of whoever built this place."

"Or else their building methods."

The corridor went on for about thirty feet, and they dropped into a transparent bubble about fifty feet in diameter that bulged out into a vast space. A number of other similar bubbles could be seen ranging off into the distance.

Their perspective changed as searchlights cut through the vast chamber beyond. They had fallen out of what had been the ceiling but now appeared to be the floor. Dominating the vista in front of them, a massive trunk-like column rose into a hemispherical expanse. From this column sprouted eight uniform branches, tubes strongly resembling the red weed coursed over them. Surrounding the roots of the tree-shape, dotting the floor of the vast chamber, were spherical shapes and tubes of all sizes. Sixteen crescent petals folded over to meet in the center and enclose the domed volume of sky.

"What is this place?"

"You don't expect me to answer, do you?"

"No speculations, Xu? Come on, you dreamed about something like this since you were a kid. Guess."

"Well, the walls of this room are transparent. Everything else we've seen is white. The vista beyond this bubble introduces more colors to the mix. There are reds, blues, metallic hues. Perhaps this is an observation spot of some kind?"

"Observing what?"

The Doc played her light across the heights of the dome. "Dragonflies?"

"And that giant tree-thing would be?"

"A central docking hub of some kind. I'd guess we are looking at the bottom half of this place, this station, and that these segments were meant to open."

Cal took in the panorama, amazed. He was gripped with a desire to see that roof (or floor) open up and the *Ulysses* floating in space beyond. He panned his beam around. The docking tree gleamed in multiple hues, as did the entire vaulted interior.

"I don't think this place was ever used," said Cal.

Xu turned, staring around them as if seeing the space for the first time.

"Never used?" asked the Doc.

"Yeah. It's not so much abandoned as never occupied. I haven't seen a speck of dust anywhere apart from that torpedo strike. Not a scuff mark, not a wear mark. Look at this docking structure. Not a mark anywhere that I've seen."

The three of them spent several long moments sweeping their searchlights around the chamber, using their cameras to magnify location after location.

"Like I said, this place is new. Built but never used."

"You're right," said the scientist. "Not even the wear marks that you would associate with the initial construction of such a facility. It might have been built autonomously, the way the changes occurred to our hitchhiker."

"We really need names for all these things," muttered the Doc.

Fourteen

They floated back up the tunnel into the nexus room and chose to enter the tube-way directly across from them. The primary imagery in its surrounding frieze was geometric. From the perspective of original entry into the room, they would now be going up. They emerged into a pill-shaped chamber with circular doors on three walls. One of them was closed.

In the center of the room was a smaller version of the monument in the entranceway—with one difference. The sphere on top looked as if it had a neat angular wedge cut from it, forming featureless horizontal and vertical surfaces.

"First closed door we've seen," remarked the Doc.

"Did those other monuments in the docking area have cutouts like this?" Cal asked.

"I don't think they did."

"Me neither."

Xu checked his camera rolls. "They didn't. Not that I can see."

They converged on the central plinth. The cut surfaces looked as if they opened into the hollow interior of the sphere. Cal reached out tentatively to dip the handle of his hammer inside and met solid resistance. The cut surfaces were solid but absolutely transparent, although they did, he realized, reflect light. Cal flipped the hammer around and tapped on the surface.

Xu's gloved hand shot out and blocked the hammer's fall.

"Cal!" He pulled it away and rubbed his fingers. "Don't."

"I was just going to tap it."

"Please, don't."

The Doc was panning her searchlights around the border of the room. "No decorative band here."

"I wonder what that means."

Xu continued to stare at the cut sphere. "I suppose we have no choice but to extrapolate from our own human experience."

"Artwork and decoration are usually for living areas and places reserved for visitors. Not work zones."

"If the friezes are indeed artwork, they could be a form of writing."

"So maybe they're directions? Instructions?"

"Advertising?"

"Could be," Cal said. Looking around. "This place feels like a terminal. A way station. We put works of art in train stations, airports, spaceports . . ."

"And directions, instructions, advertising," said Xu.

"A never-occupied bajillion-year-old way station."

"A station that seems to be technologically related to the things that attached themselves to our ship."

"They, or it, brought us here." The Doc paused, then asked, "Why?"

Cal put his hand flat against the horizontal surface and left it there. "I don't know, Susan."

Xu looked down the hallway from whence they'd come. "To dock," he said.

"What?" The Doc looked confused.

"*To dock*," repeated Xu.

Cal whirled on the Doc. "What did you say to me last night? That our hitchhiker had acted as if its makers were alone in the universe?"

"Yes. It just took us. A process that never took into account that a ship it encountered might be anything other than one of its own."

Cal eyed Xu. "Not a predator, not an infection . . ."

"Just clueless."

"It docked with us—and from its perspective, we didn't do any of the right things," said Cal.

"It thought we were broken."

"And tried to fix us."

"It took us home."

"For repairs?"

"It fits, no?"

Xu held up his hand, as if the torrent of thought was too much.

"I'm not sure," he finally said.

"What's bothering you?"

"I'm not sure. I—" Xu grabbed Cal's arm and pulled his hand up from the surface of the cut sphere. Beneath his palm, seemingly growing up from the depths of invisible clouds was a spray of red weed.

Xu pulled out his hammer and tapped gently on the sphere.

"It's inside."

He touched his finger to the glassy face. The weed gingerly reached upwards and touched the inside of the transparent material, concentrating around his fingertip. He pulled away and the weed began to sink back into invisibility. Cal touched his hand to the surface and the weed reappeared, reaching gently across to him, dancing on the underside of the crystalline surface beneath his palm.

"Is it . . ."

"What's it doing?"

"Let me try." The Doc reached her hand out to the crystal face and the weed bifurcated and a fan of tendrils grew to patter along her fingertips.

54

"Do you feel anything? I don't."

"No."

"You think this is a computer interface or something?"

"If it is, we'd better be careful."

"Do you think it's supposed to be here?" she asked. "Or did it infiltrate this place like it did us?"

"I think it's part of the place. It all looks like it was made by our red weed friend," said Cal.

"Built for people who never came for it."

"Maybe that's who our friend was waiting for?"

"Maybe."

"If it was never occupied . . ."

"What?"

"This is going to sound dumb, but—maybe there's a manual. You know, like a user's manual? For the people who were supposed to come?"

"A nice idea, Doctor, but I haven't seen a single artifact that wasn't physically a part of this station. Have you?"

"No, but that doesn't mean there aren't any."

"True."

Cal moved to the closed door and began examining the friezes; again, the imagery was geometric, circles, squares, and triangles. Xu remained with the sphere.

"So, the thing follows your hand. It seems drawn by touch. What do you think it's keying on?"

"Maybe the same as our screens?" The Doc held her finger to the surface and after a few seconds the weed extended upward; again, as if there was a fog of some kind, invisible except for where it obscured the roots of the weed.

"It's tracking your touch via the surface."

"Couldn't be, could it?

"A gestural interface?"

"Why not?"

"Could be, we don't know the language of its gestures, though."

"Maybe we don't need to? There are common gestures, simple things, that anyone would use."

The Doc countered, "Yes, but even if we were successful, we'd still be giving it random commands. What if we activated the self-destruct or something?"

"Who would build a self-destruct into a space station?" asked Xu.

"The kind of people that get deep-blue torpedoes shot into their space stations?"

"Point taken. I still vote we try something."

"Cal?" He was absorbed in the friezes.

"Yes?"

"Cal, do you have an opinion on us screwing around with this thing?"

"Experimenting," said Xu.

He had been focused on the artwork but was listening. "Try, but don't go crazy. You think it's a gestural interface? Draw a circle. They had to have used these basic shapes since we keep seeing them. I'd think anything dangerous would be more complex. No?"

She reached out and drew a circle. The closed doorway in front of Cal eased open. Beyond was a darkened space speckled with pinpoints of light hinting at a vast recurved interior. Cal bumped his faceplate into another invisible surface. He bobbed his head left and right and caught reflections. More of the same material as the cut faces on the room's central sphere.

"It's a window."

He shined his light through. It was a huge space bordered by the inner skin of the derelict station. The area was lit from the heights of the chamber by a glow emanating from a model of some unfamiliar planet. He could see a warren of spherical and oblong rooms connected by tubular corridors. It looked for all the world like the space was filled by a titanic molecular model kit.

He turned and joined the other two by the room's central sphere.

"I'm going to assume this probably doesn't just open the windows?"

"Probably not."

"This is certainly a command console of some type."

"I vote we stop messing around with it and leave it for the next time," implored the Doc. "We are coming back, right? Before we go?"

"Go where?" asked Xu.

"Home," said the Doc. "I'm being optimistic."

"There are two more doors in this room," said Xu. It was plain he meant that they should continue.

Cal asked, "Are you making a map?"

"My Odysseus copy is."

"Send it to all of us."

"Roger."

"We're only one level up from the nexus room."

"From the look of it," said Xu, "the upper half of this station is an ant's hive of room spheres, and the bottom seems like some type of maintenance or docking bay."

"That has never been used."

"Look at all those rooms," Xu said. "We need to explore them. Maybe we should bring in drones to map."

"Or just to go ahead of us," added the Doc.

"Why didn't either of you think of these things before we left the ship?"

"Sorry, Cal. I was expecting to be exploring Jupiter's moons."

"It's my first time inspecting an alien space station, too," the Doc said, smiling.

Cal returned the expression. "Let's keep to the plan and head back to the nexus room."

The scientist looked longingly at the other two passageways.

"Xu, let's not second guess. We'll be back."

They gathered around the circular opening and dropped back into the nexus room.

Cal glanced around and gestured. "Doc, we've been up and down, we came in through the passageway to your right. So, to our left, straight ahead or the door behind us. Your pick."

She selected the doorway immediately to her left, its portal ringed with sculpture as were the others. These fractals encased multi-legged shapes that had no analog in her experience. Down a short downward curving corridor, they ended up in another dead-end space, a very large pill-shaped room. Mounted to the floor were ranks of what could have been electrical turbines.

Xu floated over to the nearest of them, and shined his light through vents and openings in the surface. A gleam of golden-copper could be seen through the plaster-white.

"Generators?"

"What drives them?" Cal asked.

"We haven't seen a power source yet," responded Xu.

"Or wires," said the Doc.

"Maybe they don't use electricity."

"Or wires," said the Doc.

"Maybe they're not finished."

Cal thought about it. "Could they utilize the magnetic field of the planet?"

"Possibly."

"Let's go back."

Cal stopped.

"All right," he replied after a moment. Something didn't feel right; he felt a staggering melancholy wrap around him. "Let's go back."

They headed through the curved tunnel and into the nexus room. The untried passageways were now to the right and straight ahead.

"My turn," Cal said. "Straight ahead.

The trio drifted across the nexus room and through the far oval passageway. This one was bordered without any central figures—only the fractal patterns that had previously been bordering decoration.

The tunnel ran straight for approximately twenty feet and opened into a very large disc-shaped room. Floating crooked in the center of the room was what looked like a great, dead forest. Shattered trunks and fallen branches orbited slowly amidst a cloud of smaller debris and litter. Cal reached out for a withered branch as it drifted close. It turned to ash at the approach of his blue-shod fingers. Wordlessly, they returned to the nexus and the final unexplored doorway.

The Doc jetted to the opening, now to her left. It was ringed with sculpted egg shapes wrapped in fractal geometries. She shined her light deep into a tight corridor that curved up and around into darkness. They floated in, slowing and falling into single file to make the tight twisting turn. The tube ended in a huge kidney-shaped room. The walls were lined with evenly spaced equatorial bands of circular orifices.

"Now, what's this?" the Doc asked.

Cal opened his thrusters and moved out into the chamber and over to the opening of a random orifice. He pointed his light inside. It was a roughly eight-foot-long tubular space that terminated in a bowl at the far end. The bowl was filled with what looked like padding, flowing out and covering the floor and walls. There were multiple depressions in the walls and what looked like a few cabinet doors, curving up to follow the ceiling.

"These look like . . . bunks. Sleeping chambers. He tried to move inside but his pack was too bulky.

"Xu, help me here."

"What is it?"

"I want to take my pack off."

"Are you crazy?" asked the Doc.

"I think there are objects on the shelves in there."

Xu floated up behind him.

"Just remove the EVA expansion. Leave the batteries and air tanks. Obviously."

"Obviously."

"Doc, get a sample bag."

She pulled a thick transparent bag from a port on the side of her backpack.

The latches popped free and Cal slipped from the EVA pack, reoriented, and pulled himself inside the orifice. His lights dipped into every recess, revealing objects on the shelves. Two cylinders with multiple intertwined bands of pattern work wrapped around them. He passed them out to Xu who transferred them into the sample bag.

He opened the first cabinet. A box took up the bottom of three otherwise empty shelves. Cal touched it and the box slid down to him. It was a drawer, within it a set of three balls hung in webwork supports. He plucked one of the spheres from its cradle and examined it: more mosaic pattern work. He passed the small spheres out to Xu. There was nothing else inside but the presumed bedding.

"The cloth or whatever this bedding is made of seems to be breaking down." He pushed his finger into the padding and it went straight through, breaking apart into threads and desiccated foam.

"It's rotting away."

"I wonder how long this has been here."

"Cal. You need to come back here," the comms channel crackled.

He raised his forearm and the screen lit up with a strip of photos.

"There's something funny on the imaging sweeps."

"Planets?"

"Yes, planets. Spectrographs are in the works but—*this*." A single image expanded on his suit-screen. A fuzzy elongated shape.

"Comet?"

"I don't know, Cal, but we're picking it up on visual and radar and it's *super* bright on infrared." Another image appeared on the screen. The shape was all wrong for a comet, unless it had two nuclei.

"It's coming here."

"How long?"

"Not long"

"On our way."

"Cal." Xu raised the index finger of his right hand. "Why not leave me here to explore a few more of these sleeping chambers, or whatever they are. If there were artifacts in one—"

"Next time, Xu. We're leaving."

Fifteen

They began to cross the space of the entrance hall on their way back to the airlock before Cal noticed the torpedo.

It had opened.

He held out his hands to stop both of his companions silently. Framed by the squared circle of the open airlock door was an amorphous shape. It was mostly cobalt blue, like the torpedo itself. Moving as if examining the door. There was a border around the thing, as if the blue material was encased in a thick transparent envelope.

"Is everything a blob? First a red-black blob, now a blue blob."

"Susan, shut *up.*" He waved them back, and they all started jetting sideways to bring the column of the monument between themselves and the strange blob. The thing twisted, turning the upper portion of the mass toward them. It had a pair of garnet chevrons on its head and they turned on them as if they were eyes.

"Jesus, did it see us?" There was suddenly a jittery quality to the Doc's voice.

"I don't know."

"Why are we hiding?" asked Xu.

"Are you kidding? That thing came out of a *torpedo.*"

"We don't know for sure that's a torpedo."

"Xu, I'm going to strangle you."

"We should try and talk to it."

Cal palmed Xu's faceplate with his left hand and held up the gloved index finger of his right in warning.

The Doc, whispering without cause, asked, "What's it doing now?"

Cal peeked around the corner; it had returned to examining the airlock.

"Cal, please. Let me try and talk with it."

"Xu. It came out of a torpedo."

"It came out of a torpedo-like *thing*. It did not explode. I don't think it's a torpedo."

"It's a delivery device."

"Right."

"One that blew a hole through the ceiling of this place at some point who knows how long ago."

Without a further word, Xu unexpectedly fired his thrusters and floated back out the way they had come, landing in the middle of the entranceway's grand bowl-like floor.

The thing twisted around again. The color bled from its eyes as it fixed it's gaze on Xu. The bottom section twisted to follow its head and it began to move along the curve of the floor, slowly pulling itself along toward the scientist. Xu stood with his hands palms out in front of him.

As the creature moved toward the red-suited scientist it began to differentiate. Two appendages cleaved away from the blob-like shape to speed its progress across the floor. Another cleft split down its sides to form arms which rapidly budded off into mitt-like hands. The top of the torso constricted into a neck, defining a head. The two chevrons formed into a single one, a notched transparency across the center of its face.

The alien was only a few meters from Xu, not accelerating but not stopping. Not hesitating.

"Xu!"

Xu held his hands out, palms up. *I am unarmed. I am friendly.*

"Xu, get back here!"

The thing was not stopping. Concern began to play across Xu's face. Cal could see it from there. He jetted out toward him. "Xu! Come back now!"

As it rushed up to him, Xu opened his thrusters and rocketed backwards. The thing was too fast, sweeping out with one of its newly formed limbs and striking him violently. The scientist spun and flew across the entry hall, bounced off the central monument and skidded against the floor.

Cal pushed the Doc around the far side of the monument's pedestal. "Get to the airlock!"

He grabbed Xu by the backpack and hauled him after. As they rounded the other side of the pedestal, the thing moved to cut them off. There would be no way to make it to the airlock before the alien caught them.

Cal reversed direction, pulling Xu with him and propelling him toward the Doctor. "Back toward the nexus!" The Doc followed but so did the cobalt figure. They might be able to reach the oval passageway before it caught them, but it would be on them soon after. The only exit from the room it could not prevent them from reaching was the short tunnel that lead to the mushroom chamber—a dead end. It didn't matter, there was nowhere else to go. He backed them toward the oval.

Xu moaned, the Doctor was wrapping his right thigh with duct tape, patching a leak.

"This is a dead end, Cal."

"I know that, what choice do we have? You want me to fight it?"

They continued backing toward the oval.

Cal watched the figure. It was moving slowly from side to side, glancing up at the monument as if in wonder. After a moment or two, it carefully stepped around the pedestal, leisurely returning its attention to them. The being held its arms bent away at its sides, imitating an elbow joint that was clearly absent. It swayed forward and took a step.

"Susan, take Xu and get down that corridor. I'll try and delay it, you two see if there's maybe something we missed. Another way out."

Without a word, the Doc and Xu's colorful suits vanished quickly around the bend in the short tube-way. The cobalt figure cocked its head to watch them disappear. When they were gone, the strange being turned its attention back to Cal and resumed its slow advance.

Sixteen

The Doc pulled Xu along, down the corridor, and set him to float gently up against the opening of the mushroom chamber. He grunted as his leg brushed against the wall.

"I'm sorry, Xu." She crouched to check his vital sign indicators. "You'll be okay." She bent and unscrewed the medical access port in his shoulder. Beneath the cap was a resealable membrane. She removed a pain killer capsule and pressed it against the port with her thumb, breaking it open. The hypodermic needle penetrated the seal and then skin, delivering the drug as it dissolved and repaired the membrane at the same time. She screwed the cap back onto the port and left him.

She floated into the center of the circular chamber. The mushrooms circled her in their circumferential bands, flat tops all pointed crazily in a thousand different directions.

"What in God's name is this place?"

She swept her searchlight beam around the room, peering between the stalks, looking in the details for anything that she might have missed. She pointed the light directly above. A single mushroom, larger than the others, presented its flat face to her. She turned the beam 180 degrees. Beneath her was a pad which could have been the sunken top of another large mushroom. There were two translucent studs that rose from the center of the disc. She had not noticed them before.

She opened her comms. "Cal?"

Cal was staring down the approach of the cobalt being. His hand was on the holster at his hip. "Can I help you?"

"I found something I'd missed."

"A way out?"

The cobalt head cocked to the left and then right. It watched Cal stare into his forearm screen with interest. It was less than thirty feet away.

"I don't know if it's a way out, but there are two switches on the floor of the mushroom chamber."

"What do they do?"

"I don't know, I haven't tried them."

"Time to jump in the pool, Doc." He cut the connection.

She stared at the two large buttons on the floor. "Xu, how are you doing?"

"I'm hanging in there, Doc. I'll be okay."

"I think this room might be an elevator of some kind. These buttons. I think they may be *up* and *down*."

Her body rotated at bursts from her thrusters. The Doc set her feet flat against the floor pad, she sucked in a breath and stepped forward. The crystalline stud sank into the floor at the touch of her boot.

Seventeen

An inhuman human shape stood in front of Calvin Jensen Scott. He slid the space-jacketed revolver from its holster. Raising the gun in front of him, aiming at the figure, felt like a betrayal of everything he had lived his life for. Though it couldn't be. *Shouldn't* be. This wasn't his fault. He did not want this to be happening.

He turned on his suit's high beams and shined them on the figure. It hesitated but seemed unfazed. Cal realized there was no way to even begin to try and talk with it. Unless it could receive radio. Which, maybe, it could?

His comms crackled and for a moment, he imagined it might be the creature.

There was an incredible blast of static over his radio. The entire oval entranceway lit up behind him and then fell back into darkness.

The cobalt figure even seemed taken aback. It stopped moving.

His comms crackled again. "Cal." It was Xu. "Cal, you better get down here."

"What's going on? What was that flash?"

"The Doc's gone."

Eighteen

Cal backed down the corridor as rapidly as he could, heart pounding, resisting the urge to pivot around and open his thrusters all the way. He rounded the corner as the cobalt figure tentatively approached the corridor's mouth.

He saw Xu floating at an odd angle, his face slack with shock. Cal looked inside the spherical chamber; the mushrooms had all twisted their heads around into perfect alignment.

Xu's eyes looked glazed. "The Doc was in the chamber, we thought it might be an elevator. She said she was pressing the button to her right. She pressed it, and there was a terrible flash."

The man was too bewildered to notice the gun.

"And then what?"

"Then nothing. That's it, she's gone. I can't get her on the comms, either."

Cal tried, nothing. He played his searchlight around the interior of the chamber and then shot his attention back toward the tubular passageway. He flew back to peer around the corner.

"Is it coming?"

"No. It's not coming down the corridor."

"Can you see it?" Xu asked.

"No."

"Then how do you know it's not coming?"

"Because I don't see it."

Cal's heart continued to pound. Susan. His comms chimed—Samuels. He couldn't answer. Not yet. He powered back over to the doorway and examined the room again.

"What's that?"

"What's what?"

"That." Cal pointed behind Xu, at a rectangle of black on the stark white wall beside the doorway. Above it was another dragonfly relief.

"That wasn't there before," said Xu.

Cal approached the rectangle, glancing furtively down the tube.

"Why isn't it coming after us?"

"I don't know," Cal said, reaching out to touch the black shape on the wall. "Maybe it knows it has us trapped. Maybe it's afraid of us . . . or this room?"

As Cal's fingers pressed against the darkness, red sparks erupted and swirled over the rectangle.

"It's a display."

It twirled out an image of embers, a polyhedron with a blank circle inside, adjacent to another similar shape with a crossed circle in the center. Both circles were flashing.

"What do you think this means?" Before Xu could answer, Cal stabbed out with his gloved index finger and pressed the circle with the cross in it. Nothing happened, so he pressed the flashing empty circle. Blue light spat and arcs of electricity leapt across the mushrooms. A triple burst of illumination flooded the chamber. His faceplate darkened in an instant, but the flash was so bright that he was still blinking away the glare seconds later.

When his vision cleared, the Doc was standing on the pad in the center of the chamber.

"She's back," said Xu, dumbfounded.

"Where did you go?" Cal asked.

She stared back at him and pointed over his shoulder. "Cal!"

Cal pivoted. Revealed in the oval pools from her suit-lights, the cobalt figure came around the bend in the tube-way. He raised the gun.

"Where did that come from?" Xu asked, noticing the weapon for the first time.

"I stole it."

For an instant, Cal was struck by the colors. He had witnessed nothing but monochrome white and the black of shadows for all this time. And now, it was danger that brought color back to the world. The gun's shining nickel body and honey-hued temperature jacket glimmered in the light of the search beams. In contrast, the alien—a deep cobalt blue inclusion within a man-sized sleeve of liquid transparency. A red chevron eye staring with baleful intensity.

The figure continued to advance. Cal's mind spun, his heart pounded, frenzied. It was not going to stop. He held his breath and fired three bullets into the alien. His EVA pack spurted thruster fire to absorb the recoil.

As each projectile hit, the cobalt cyclops's body was wracked with disturbances that spun out from the impact point like ripples in a pond. Each bullet came to a dead stop and hung motionless within the cobalt. The figure toppled over backwards.

"Not sorry I have this now, are you?" Cal said, shoving the gun back into the Velcroed holster.

The Doc scowled.

"Go," Cal shouted.

The three suited figures opened their thrusters and skirted around the fallen alien, moving as quickly as they could through the twisting tube-way. Xu first, the Doc next, and Cal last. Before turning the corner, he stopped and stared at the mass splayed against the floor, just outside the chamber of mushrooms. For a moment, it lay for all the world like a man dead, then the cobalt mass flowed and deformed, pushing its transparent skin upwards. It was as if the figure stood up from within itself. The three bullets hung suspended in its body, glints of brass deep inside the blue. It twisted its head around like an owl to follow Cal's retreat, chevron eye watching with detached curiosity.

Nineteen

The trio crossed the open space of the entryway, past the wreckage of the torpedo casing and the globe-topped monument. The blue figure appeared in the maw of the tube-way entrance.

Cal glanced at his status indicators; his propellant levels had dropped below 10 percent. He didn't bother to ask how the others were doing, they had to make a run for it no matter what. His comms bleeped again, but he ignored it. They had to get to the airlock as quickly as possible.

The figure began to propel itself across the space, pulling itself along the wall and floor in pursuit. Cal rotated around to face backwards, momentum carrying him on toward the airlock. He aimed the gun and fired again. This time, the recoil was desired and no thrusters fired to absorb the motion. As a result, he made up the seconds of acceleration lost pivoting to shoot. Cal's aim was true again. The creature's head rocketed back and its body cartwheeled end over end, slowing its forward motion. It twisted around to reorient and tried to push against the floor, but it had drifted out of reach. The cobalt figure began to float off toward the middle heights of the zero-G hall, its limbs flailing like a turtle stranded on its back.

"Cal!" the Doc called. Both she and Xu were in the airlock.

He turned to them and spared a last glance back at the helpless creature and smiled. *Finally got the better of an alien.*

The thing stopped flailing and pointed its legs at the far wall, and a stream of what looked like thick soap bubbles filled with cobalt material squirted from it. The alien righted itself and began to move toward him, faster and faster. It was ejecting parts of itself as reaction mass.

Or not.

Cal pivoted and opened up his throttle, shooting into the airlock. Xu pressed the right-hand disc controller, and the door slid firmly shut.

The being stopped in front of the airlock window and tilted its head to look at them. It examined the borders of the door, craning its head in a clockwise rotation, and then returned to a neutral position. After a few moments, a stream of expended globules returned to the fold after a long journey of deflections, bounces, and ricochets. The creature turned and pushed off from the door, retreating into the dark interior.

Cal touched the leftmost controller, and the disc floated to the top of its cylinder. The outer door opened to space.

Twenty

Cal touched his faceplate to the pitted outer surface of the lock and with closed eyes took a deep breath. He heard the crackle and pop from his comms channel and the Quindar tone that presaged the pilot's alarmed plea.

"What the fuck! Where were you guys?"

"Sarah, you *reeeally* can't believe what we've had to deal wi—"

Cal turned away from the hull of the station and stared out into space. His jaw dropped open. Beneath the station, beneath the floating *Ulysses* and little *Argo*, was a colossal elongated shape. It was mottled gray and shot through with browns, its prow was flecked with green and flared into a large armored bulb of mass stretching out to a much smaller one far at its rear. It had to be more than a mile long and moved slowly, approaching the station from underneath. It gently probed the derelict station with segmented coils that wafted lazily from its nose. Folded around its head like a mantle and stretching down its flanks, four great wings seemed to fan out a bit, flutter, and then pull back against its sides. For a moment, they glimpsed rippling metallic sheens. It reminded Cal of some strange deep-sea leviathan. One that had been cleaved in two, its entrails stretched over an unimaginable distance to maintain the connection with the severed parts of itself.

Twenty-One

"Is that a dragonfly?" the Doc wondered aloud as the trio crossed the space to the lander.

Odysseus was already bringing *Argo* closer, and it pitched forward and presented its open hatch. Beneath them, an immense elongated shape.

The comms crackled. "It looks more like a whale," said the pilot.

"Have you ever *seen* a whale?"

"Well, it doesn't really look like a dragonfly, either."

Cal clambered inside after the Doc helped Xu maneuver his injured leg through the hatch. He pulled the heavy door shut behind him.

"Is it alive?"

"It looks alive."

Cal pulled himself over to the pilot's station and peered through the viewport. The ship-thing was gently exploring the undersides of the derelict, like a koi lazily searching its pond for food.

The comms hissed, "How can it be alive in space? Just the pressure differential alone would kill it."

"Not necessarily," said the Doc. "Biological life has adapted to some of the most extreme environments on Earth. Hypersaline lakes, the deep seas, acidic soils."

"A far cry from the depths of space, Doc." Cal frowned, accelerating toward the *Ulysses*.

"Not really, there is the widely appreciated theory of panspermia that suggest that life was distributed throughout the universe by comets, meteoroids, asteroids."

"You buy that?"

"I do. Endospores of certain bacilli have been shown to survive temperatures up to nearly 800 degrees Fahrenheit. I think it makes sense that microscopic life, or at least its precursors, could have been spread like that."

"That thing isn't exactly a microorganism," her voice crackled over the radio. "You're saying this thing evolved to survive deep space?"

"I don't know, it might not be alive. Or it might be alive but not natural. All I'm saying is that it's possible."

The thing began to pitch away from the station. It was like watching a mountain range move.

"What's it doing?"

"We have to investigate," said Xu.

"Xu, you're hurt, we don't know what happened to the Doc and our O2 and propellant levels are low."

"Forget about scientific curiosity! What if this is someone or some*thing* that could help us get home? We can't miss this opportunity, Cal. We can't."

"We're going back, Paul and Inez can take *Argo* right back out."

At that moment, the entire length of the dragonfly creature seemed to flex and bend and then snap back like a mile-long spring. The energy imparted caused the ship-being to float backwards and away from the station's underside, pivoting on its long axis. It looked as if it was about to move off.

"Dammit."

Cal pushed the throttle forward and *Argo* leapt toward the

dragonfly as the miles-long thing pitched slowly, end over end.

"It's turning around."

"Keep abeam, we don't want to be at its six if it turns on some kind of engine."

"I don't think that's how it moves," the Doc said.

"What do you mean?"

"Well, first of all, *look* at it. Really look at it. That's not like any spacecraft I've ever seen. It looks organic."

"Looks can be deceiving, Doctor. It may just be the product of technological processes we don't understand," Xu said, squeezing a bead of clear plastic sealant over the split in the thigh of his spacesuit. "Caution aside, however, I would tend to agree with you."

"You're agreeing with me or arguing with me?"

The ship-creature's strange bowl-capped tail rose up ahead of them, filling the lander's forward viewport. The searchlight array threw strange curving shadows across the undulating surface.

"I'm agreeing with you. In fact, I think it's a living solar-sailer."

"You've got to be kidding."

"Which part do you find incredulous, that it could be alive or the method of propulsion?"

"Both. Neither, really. I'm just becoming overwhelmed," said Cal.

"It's true," the Doc said. "This is all becoming too much to deal with all at once. I feel as if I'm ten years old and my parents came home, announced they were getting divorced, and *then* introduced me to their new spouses, who they had already married, and told me that we were moving to a new country."

Cal and Xu stared at her quizzically.

"My entire world is upended, and I don't have the emotional or rational experience to deal with it."

Cal smiled and returned his full attention to the *Argo*'s progress along the creature's length. The ship-being seemed to ignore them entirely. He flipped on the searchlights and swept the beam across its flanks. Once in the Midwest states, he had seen a freight train that never seemed to end. It had gone on for miles and miles, stretching away to the horizon. There was no horizon here, but the effect was the same.

"A solar-sailer?"

"Light can propel something that big?"

"Ask our pilot, Doctor. She had to factor in a displacement of thousands of miles over our outbound journey just to account for the photon pressure of sunlight on *Ulysses*."

"So, you think those wings are sails, then?"

"Yes, four wings around the prow like that. I'll bet they fully unfurl into some approximation of a radial sail pattern."

Cal angled the engines and increased the throttle, the *Argo* proceeded toward the prow of the ship-creature.

"We'll get a better look at those wings presently, science officer."

Xu bobbed on his good leg and swung the telescope from point to point.

The long tail of the creature narrowed as they moved away from the near-featureless stern end of the bulb. *Argo* passed over a hundred-foot long string of illuminated spheres embedded under the ship-creature's skin, suffusing the flanks with a dim light.

"What are those, do you think?"

"They look like eggs."

"I hope they're not eggs. I've watched a lot of movies; space eggs are never good."

"Or maybe they're windows?"

The body of the ship continued to narrow. For a brief distance, perhaps twenty or thirty feet, its diameter was less than the height of the lander, and then it began to widen again.

"We're approaching the head. Slowing." Cal rotated the twin engines on either side of the *Argo*'s pressure vessel to point in the direction of travel and opened the throttle to 20 percent. The bulky bug-shape's progress toward the giant creature's bow slowed to a crawl.

80

They were passing over the structures that Xu surmised were furled wings. They were wrapped around the tapering body of the creature, wound around and around like the closed bulb of a vast tulip.

The comms channel fizzed and popped. "Be careful, Cal."

"*We* will," said the Doc from over his shoulder.

"That thing is starting to pump out a lot of electromagnetic interf—"

As if on cue, Inez's voice dissolved into a sea of crackling static.

The *Argo* continued its slow passage toward the strange vehicle-creature's bow.

"Look over there." Xu pointed excitedly.

There was damage to one of the wings. A hole had been torn in the featureless outer surface to reveal reflective sheets of gold and copper folded tight against one another. There was another gouge in the skin about fifteen to twenty feet long that crossed over an embedded spar. It was clearly metallic beneath. Golden. Like the ribs of God's own umbrella.

One of the spars seemed to flex, and the creature began to drift ever so slightly away from the derelict station. Xu watched with interest as the lander's magnetometer spiked.

"I'd say it was designed, or evolved, to conduct electricity very efficiently, as well. It likely employs a variety of somewhat similar propulsion methods."

The wing rippled again, multiple spars flexing. The magnetometer readings leapt and jiggled.

"My guess is that, when traveling close to a star, it would unfurl those wings to harness the photon pressure of light. Further away from the star, those ribs, if they are indeed electrically conductive, could enable the creature to form sails woven of electromagnetic fields and greatly extend its ability to navigate via solar wind pressure."

"Is that what we just saw?"

"I believe so. If it functions like the experiments I've read about, it should be able to maneuver by altering the charge of individual spines. The size of an electric sail is that of the field it generates, not the dimensions of the physical object creating it."

The *Argo* swept along as the creature's bulk widened beneath. If it were a dragonfly, it was one with no head. Its body flared outward while the stowed wings tapered into towers of muscular flesh that joined each wing root to the body. *Argo* passed over a radial pattern of hollows inscribed around its bow—perhaps its skull—that converged into a nightmarish *face*: an assembly of crab-like eyestalks, waving cilia, and mouthparts, some trailing back along the body for hundreds of feet.

"The eyestalks are watching us."

"How can you tell?"

"What else would they be watching?"

Argo rotated around, flying along just ahead of the massive creature.

"I don't think it's paying attention to us at all," said Xu. "It appears to be entirely indifferent, as if we are beneath contemplation."

The lander crested the far side of the bulbous prow. There was an identical radial pattern of grooves on this side, except that across the upper fan of hollows was spread a glittering stain. The search beam honed in, and a swath of the creature's mantle sparkled as if a great volume of glass had shattered across its surface. Impacted into one of the grooves was a mangled silver cigar-shape, its rear nearly shorn away, exposing a familiar looking internal structure.

"That looks like an aircraft fuselage."

"It is, or at least something built using seemingly familiar techniques."

"*Built*, not grown."

This was too interesting even for Cal's exhaustion to hold him back. "Moving in closer." The lander's engines spun around to face away from the ship-creature, and Cal burped the thrusters.

"There's something flashing."

A transparent expanse like a window ran along one side of the crushed cigar-shape; through it a bright orange light winked on and off.

Argo hovered less than twenty-five feet above the ship-creature's surface and began to circle, giving them a view of the crash site from all sides.

"No spikes on the dosimeters."

"Look, there's a line, or a wire, or something!" The Doc pointed at the crushed vehicle.

There was a partially opened hatchway on the far side of the crashed vehicle and from it ran a thin black cable. It stretched along the perimeter of the glittering debris field and disappeared into the shadow of one of the radial hollows ringing the ship-being's prow.

Cal locked eyes with Xu and said, "I hope you used the transit time to recharge your tanks and batteries." He shouldered his EVA pack. "Odysseus, hold position here."

"Yes, Captain. I can hold this position for thirty-three minutes at present levels of consumption and still have fuel remaining to return to *Ulysses*. If the target changes velocity, my estimate will also change."

Cal moved to the rear of the cockpit and reached up to ratchet the hatch handle around and down. "Who's coming with?"

Twenty-Two

Once again, *into the unknown.*

Or, as his grandmother might have said, *enough with the unknown already.*

Cal watched the Doctor and then Xu leap from the roof of the lander and "fall" up toward the ship-being's mountainous bow. Cal pushed off with his legs, and the solar-sailer's head became the entire expanse of his world. They were dropping onto a surrealistic landscape of muscular integument. The radiating fan of bullet-shaped hollows and the iridescent debris field expanded before him as he dropped. His eyes caught on the wreckage of the craft—it could be nothing else—and he followed the crooked black string that stretched from it into the shadow of one of the hollows. He kept his eye on that spot for the rest of the descent, which lasted less than a minute. He fired his thrusters such that his legs easily absorbed his remaining momentum. A final burst kept him from rebounding back into space, and his feet settled against the fleshy surface. Up close, the skin of the creature had the appearance of an interlocking webwork of scales, as if a spider had spun a turtle's shell. The debris field was before them, a roadway of shiny tatters leading to the wreckage.

The three astronauts skimmed over the surface, heading for the crumpled silver cigar.

The Doc eyed the shredded material. "What is all that stuff?"

"I don't know, we can sample it once we reach the crash site."

"Radiation levels remain steady," said Xu. "Seems safe enough."

As they approached the ruined craft it was obvious that it was not at all a terrestrial airframe but was indeed built with similar methods.

"This is basically a geodesic frame," Cal said to his compatriots. "Like all Earth aircraft stretching back well over two hundred years. Basket-like, redundant structure enabling it to survive localized damage." He peeked into the shredded end of the fuselage; a safety door had closed shut just shy of the destruction.

Xu picked up a few bent curls of the iridescent debris with tongs and dropped them into his sample container, noting the location of collection with a few quickly tapped words and a site photo.

Cal moved down the side to peer in through the transparent section. "It's a cockpit or passenger cabin, I think. These are seats. Strangely shaped but seats, complete with safety harnesses."

Xu and the Doc floated up next to him. There looked to be space for four occupants. The supposed seats were arranged in radial fashion and appeared to be formed from the same material as the floor. The seat back rose up from the sides of the chair but was contoured, holed, and sectioned for a body shape that was absolutely not humanoid. The orange flashing light strobed from a tower in the center of the four seats.

"Seats. Yes, but for what kind of bodies? It looks like it's made for, what? Multiple sets of legs?"

Cal's eyes followed the heavy black wire that ran from an open panel beneath the flashing light tower. It disappeared through the open hatch on the curving wall opposite the window and reappeared on the far side of the wreckage. It snaked off across the surface and down into the curving radial hollow in the creature's measureless skull.

"Come on." Cal jetted off toward the gully, following the wire's sinuous track. The debris became scarce as they approached the hollow. Cal hovered over the bullet-shaped recess. It was some twenty feet wide and shrank in size to disappear into shadow as it got closer to the creature's nose. He pointed his search beam into the darkness. The hollow seemed to twist into the interior of the creature, becoming a roughly ten-foot diameter orifice that hung open in an obscene fashion. At certain moments or angles there seemed to be a tenuous fog wisping away from the lip of the trench.

They approached the aperture, the hollow did indeed dive into the creature's head. There was a great fleshy lid that no doubt should have sealed the orifice but had been prevented from doing so by a Y-shaped piece of wreckage wedged into the opening. The wire ran through and dropped into the darkness inside.

The Doc shined her flashlight beam into the maw. Its sides seemed smooth and slick, with a gauzy fog that rolled up the throat of the tunnel. At the far end, it seemed to curve around or open up, perhaps into a larger space.

"Tell me we're not going in there."

"You don't have to go anywhere you don't want to, Doc. We are well beyond the pale here."

"I'm going," said Xu.

Cal rested one hand on the holster Velcroed to his hip. "I'll be right behind you." He felt a flash of dread that he was becoming accustomed to the weapon. No, more than that—he *relied* on the gun's presence as if it were a new vertebra anchoring the base of his spine. He was an explorer, that's all he'd ever wanted to be, yet he had just learned that violence was an aspect of existence that not even the wonders of the universe could excise. There were times when a directed application of force at a distance made all the difference. He mouthed a silent prayer to all that was beyond his understanding that his future applications of force would be solely in the form of propellant and not bullets. Still, he was glad to have the hated thing at his hip.

86

He dropped into the tunnel after Xu.

Twenty-Three

The tunnel bent around on itself before widening into a bell and opening on a chamber blocked entirely by what looked like a dirty but translucent membrane.

Xu floated up close, and tapped it with his collection tool. White-clear chips floated away from the tool's clawed face. "It's ice."

"Ice?" Cal scanned the barrier; the wire ran through the frost, he could see its murky shadow continuing beyond. Cal pressed his glove against the ice and an entire chunk of it gave way. A four-foot-long sheet of ice tumbled out at him, pushed by the pressure of gas rushing to escape through the hole. The ice shattered against his suit, sending him spinning into the curved wall.

"Are you all right?"

Cal righted himself, frozen chunks crumbling from the recesses of his suit. "I'm fine."

There was a large hole in the ice. The chamber continued beyond, curving around a swelling of bony flesh. Around the broken perimeter of ice, leaking gas was already accreting—freezing at the touch of the cold filtering in from beyond the curve of the tunnel.

Cal moved over to the ice barrier and kicked at it, breaking another large chunk away, creating an easy passage for the three of them. They floated inside.

"I wonder how long that will take to refreeze," wondered Xu. "Interesting design safeguard. If the outer orifice fails, the very internal structure of the organism allows for a backup just by virtue of natural forces."

Cal played his beam around the chamber, settling on the bony mass in the center. "Yeah, incredible sinuses."

The Doc ran her lights over the structures, utterly perplexed.

The wire ran around the bone-like obstruction and through another orifice to a large cavity filled almost entirely by an elongated structure, a central cannon-shaped organ connected to mammoth loops of fleshy coils.

"Very strongly positive EM field in here, Cal." Xu looked at his suit-screen, waving the arm that contained it. "If this thing really is some kind of living photon-electric sailing ship, then it would need to maintain the positive charge of the spines that make up its sails." He hopped up to hover over the top of the structure. "This must be the biological equivalent of an electron gun, compensating for the current created by solar wind plasma striking the sails."

Cal stared at the huge fleshy mound, at the wire, which ran up and over, traveling into another orifice beyond. Following it through that opening led them into another cavity ringed with struts of what looked like membranous tendons.

"It's warmer in here."

Slung from the ceiling of the space was what looked like a seat or chair suspended on a bony arm. Numerous venous tubules swarmed down the armature and into the body of the chair. Cupped within the bowl-like seat was what appeared to be a fluid-filled membrane larger than a human being. Strange objects resembling organs floated within, bound together by a tracery of dendritic structures: a transparent cocoon of body parts curling in on itself like a gestating fetus.

"Jesus." The Doc floated up to it, examining the sac more closely.

The membrane pulsed every thirty or so seconds.

They played their search beams over the thing, Cal followed the arterial piping up out of the chair and into bundles and branches that vanished into the ceiling.

"Is that its brain?" he wondered.

"Or the pilot?" asked the Doc.

"Whatever it is, it doesn't seem to know that we're here."

"Or it knows and doesn't care."

Cal looked around the room for the wire and saw it snake behind an outcrop of strung tendon and fleshy wall. Cal stepped around the bio-wall and aimed his light into the dark recess. The wire vanished behind another organic caul—an amniotic membrane of some sort that seemingly encased a figure curled tightly around itself. Cal shined his search beam directly on the sac. The light filtered through, and although the membrane was only partially translucent, it was clear that the figure inside was wearing a spacesuit.

Twenty-Four

The three of them floated around the caul—red, blue, and green suits bobbing against a gentle current of escaping gasses filtering up from somewhere within the great light-sail beast.

The beam from the Doc's spotlight pierced the thick membrane and illuminated an elongated bowl-shaped helmet with a very Earth-like neck ring. The suit it was attached to seemed ribbed, and appeared, through the membrane at least, to be a silvery color. She was not able to make out any head beneath the dome, just shadows. None of them were sure how many limbs it had, intertwined and curled in upon itself as it was. There was no telling what it might look like.

"What do you think?"

"Some kind of emergency life support?"

"Like a rescue ball?"

Cal picked the wire up in his hands and found it was more rope than wire. The frayed end was knotted around a golden bone-like spar that jutted through the wall of the chamber just above where the strange astronaut curled in its cocoon.

"The wire was just meant to lead us, or *someone,* here. Must have been stripped out of the wreckage."

"Maybe it's in suspended animation, waiting for rescue?"

"You agree that it is clearly an astronaut in need of assistance, then?"

"Wait a minute, Xu—"

"It's wearing a suit, Doc." Cal pitched himself forward and brought himself close to the caul, close to what he thought might be the helmet. He shined the light in through the membrane. It sure *looked* like a helmet. There were shadowy shapes inside, but while he could clearly discern the outer form of the suit, he could not see deeper. He could not untangle the jumble of limbs. He didn't know where the joints might fold or unfold, or if there were even joints at all.

The Doc floated impassively. "It is wearing a suit but—"

Cal floated back upright, "Yes, it is, and that means it's clearly some kind of intelligent being from a technological civilization . . . And we are a long way from home."

She stared at the thing. When the *Ulysses* had first spotted the object approaching them near Jupiter, Cal had asked her to review all of the materials surrounding first contact with another species. She had read books on indigenous Earth tribes and philosophies, but she had also watched a lot of science fiction movies. Some were quite good, a lot of them were quite scary. And the ones that were scary always had situations like the one confronting them. And they never ever turned out well.

"We need help, and it needs *our* help. But I'd like this to be a unanimous decision."

Cal was right, she thought. They needed help, and she had been indignant when Ceres had nearly stranded them. Shocked that any astronaut would leave another to die. It would be hypocritical to refuse. She knew that, no matter the danger and the fear and the utter uniqueness of this situation, whatever this thing was, it was a fellow astronaut. And it apparently needed their help.

"Cal, I don't have any way of assessing this thing. I don't have any medical instruments here apart from the ones built into our suits to monitor our conditions. We don't even know what it *breathes*. We can take samples from the thing and bring them back but . . ."

"And by that time this monster we're riding in may have gone beyond our reach."

"Cal, have you never seen a space horror movie? The one thing you never ever do is bring the cocoon back into your spaceship."

"Doc, that's pretend. Movies end, the good guy wins, and the credits roll. This is life. There are no credits . . . What do you think about setting up some kind of quarantine in sickbay?"

"You're thinking of bringing this thing back to the *ship*?"

"Doc, we have to. Think of it, what we do here might define humanity in the eyes of another intelligent species."

"Doctor," Xu implored. "They make machines like we make machines. We couldn't talk to the weed, we couldn't talk to that damn blue thing, and this creature we're inside doesn't even acknowledge our presence. But a tool-using entity that builds like we build? We've got to be able to communicate with a being like that. Just think what we could learn! It would be the greatest discovery in the history of humankind!"

"We've gone through like ten *greatest discoveries in the history of humankind* since last Tuesday," replied the Doc.

"Susan." Cal turned to her. "If we can communicate with it, maybe it can help us get home."

Twenty-Five

They had the caul between them, pushing and pulling it gently through the recurving sinus and out through the jammed orifice. Cal thought to remove the Y-shaped piece of wreckage once their party had gotten clear.

"There you go, big fella," He said. The heavy curtain of flesh fell closed like an eyelid.

As they pushed the caul up and out of the frozen hollow, they spotted the *Argo* hovering steady above the crumpled cigar-ship and the glitter field. Standing on the surface of the living spacecraft, on the far side of the debris field, was the cobalt blue figure in its sheath of emptiness. It stood motionless, shadow stretching across the landscape, chevron eye staring at them.

They ducked back into the groove in the solar-sailer's surface.

"How did it get here?"

"I don't know."

"There must have been another way out of the derelict."

"We circled that thing, and there was only that one airlock. That and the hole that *thing's* torpedo punched into it, and that had been sealed. There weren't any other openings."

"Then how the hell did it get here?"

"Does it matter? It's here."

Cal sized up the terrain. The only features that could possibly provide cover were the wreckage and the various radial furrows in the solar-sailer's surface. The cobalt being was about two hundred feet away, on the other side of the strewn debris. *Argo* hovered above, its lights blazing.

"Did it see us?"

"I don't think so."

"What are we going to do?"

"Stay down." Cal raised his forearm and tapped in a few commands. "Odysseus, we need pick up, right now."

"Yes, Captain." *Argo* sprang into action, and the shadows thrown over the surface shifted and gyrated.

Cal peeked over the rim of the furrow and saw the being had entered the debris field and was walking across the surface. Its feet adhered in such a way that it seemed as if it was trudging through mud or snow. Its shadow lengthened, reaching out for them as the *Argo* and its lights flew toward their hiding spot. The strange being pivoted its head to watch the lander pass overhead.

Hunkered down in the trench, Cal watched their ride slide into view overhead. Its engines pivoted on their stalks and bright blue flame torched for an instant to stop its forward movement. It hovered above. Maneuvering thrusters fired and the *Argo* gingerly began to descend.

Cal poked his helmet up over the rim again, looking for the cobalt creature. It was a quarter of the way across the debris field, moving faster, almost running. He dropped back into the hollow as Odysseus's voice broke over the comms.

"I cannot descend into the surface feature within which you are currently located. I will have to hover above or land beyond the rim."

Cal looked at his compatriots and then the landscape surrounding them. "Bring 'er down as low as you possibly can," he said to the AI and then looked squarely at Xu. "I'm going up first. When I open the hatch, you and the Doc get inside as quickly as you can."

Xu nodded and pointed to the caul. "What about that?"

Cal spared another glance at the approaching threat. It was more than halfway through the debris field.

"Get it inside fast. You and the Doc go in first, pull it after you. I'll push from behind if necessary."

The Doc crinkled her nose at the caul. "I think it's too big. What if it gets stuck?"

"That's why I want you two inside before you pull it in after you. If it gets stuck, I'll go around to the top hatch."

Argo halted its descent just ten feet from the surface. Cal rocketed out of the trench and up through the lander's golden undercarriage. With its twin engines located outboard on their stalks, the undercarriage was largely open, providing easy access to the hatch at the bottom of the pressure vessel. Cal snagged a reflective brassy strut and grabbed at the hatch handle, wrenching it to the side and pushing up. The hatch began to swing inward. He glanced down at Xu and the Doc, caul between them, and then back at the surrounding cage of struts. *It'll fit*, he thought. At least up through the undercarriage which was designed to allow rovers to drive underneath and dock directly. The bulk of the caul would easily fit, but the hatch was another matter. He looked across the plain, the cobalt blue figure had stopped some forty feet from the lip of the furrow and was staring straight at him.

"Let's go, quickly!" he shouted into the comms. "Go, go, go!" Xu and the Doc, in their red and green spacesuits, began to rise up toward him, the gray croissant-shape of the alien astronaut's cocoon between them. As soon as they had cleared the rim of the furrowed trench, the blue figure's cyclopean eye turned on them. Its head cocked, as if puzzled by their sudden appearance, and followed their path to the lander.

Cal braced his feet against the struts and scaffolding of the *Argo*'s undercarriage and grabbed Xu's red-clad shoulder to help slow them down. Even so, Xu crashed into him, the caul thudded up against the hatch boundary, and the Doc sailed past and clattered into the spiderweb supports of one of the landing legs. She nearly bounced back away but gripped the gleaming silver rod of a hydraulic actuator and hung on, breathing heavily.

"Odysseus, get us out of here!"

"Captain, it is not safe to fire the engines until the crew is secure."

"Now!"

The *Argo*'s engines lit, and the lander pulled away from the surface.

Cal swung over to the Doc, traveling from strut to strut, glancing down, searching for the cobalt blue alien. It wasn't on the surface, but Cal spotted it leaving the ground with a great leap, rising up, drawing inexorably closer to them.

"Get inside, Susan!"

She spared them both a look and then gripped the machined perimeter of the hatch and pulled herself inside. Xu gripped the caul and followed her, sailing up through the hatch. The trailing cocoon bumped against the thick hatch perimeter and snagged. Xu pushed it back out and pulled up again. It bulged against the hatchway but would not fit.

Cal glanced down, looking for the alien figure, but could not find it. He gripped the bottom of the cocoon and opened up his suit thrusters, pushing it up against the confines of the hatch, trying to squeeze it through.

"Doc, do you see the blue monster? I've lost it."

The comms crackled. "No, Cal. I can't see anything from here."

The caul moved, sliding in another foot and stopped.

"It's jammed," Cal said into the comms.

Inside the lander, Xu was frantic. He grabbed a surface sampling pack from the wall and ratcheted the lever to open the *Argo*'s top hatch.

"What are you doing?" The Doc wasn't sure if he was more

concerned for the stuck cocoon or for his friend being outside with the blue alien.

Xu didn't respond, the hatch swung down, and with a quick thrust of his arms, the scientist's red suit vanished through the top hatch.

"Xu!"

Twenty-Six

Cal gave up pushing and gripped the lander's undercarriage, turning himself around, searching for the cobalt blue figure. There it was, crawling upside down around the circumference of one of the *Argo*'s spherical cryogenic tanks. The chevron of its eye seemingly fixed upon him. It was no more than twelve feet away, but there were a good number of struts and golden spars between him and the creature. He gripped the lattice and pulled himself around a landing leg to put another obstacle between himself and the thing and slid the revolver back out of the holster. Two bullets left—he hadn't brought more and didn't even know if the gun could be reloaded while still in its thermal jacket; without protection from the environment of space the metals of the gun would surely cold-fuse together. He wrapped his elbow around the landing leg and aimed the revolver at the center of the creature's mass.

It stopped moving.

"So, you remember this, huh?"

It cocked its head again, and then rotated it all the way around in a move that would have been utterly impossible for a creature with a rigid skeleton. Its upside-down eye was now right side up, staring at him. The motion made Cal queasy.

"Go away!" he shouted at the thing, feeling crazed. There was no way it could hear him, but he shouted at it anyway. "Please, I don't want to shoot you again."

He stared at the open hatch and the jammed alien caul; it was stuck, but there was plenty of space that the creature could conceivably squeeze through considering its demonstrated abilities. But for that concern he would have made a run for the lander's top hatch.

Its arm stretched, oozing out to reach the opposite landing leg. It wasn't going to risk losing its grip this far from a surface it could cling to and move against. Once it had a firm hold, it drew the rest of its body across the empty open space beneath the lander's pressure vessel. Crossing over to get closer to Cal, who just as quickly jetted off to another quadrant of the *Argo*'s undercarriage. He grabbed hold of a different golden leg and thanked the stars that the creature had, so far at least, ignored the open hatch. He had to be careful, at the velocity the lander was accelerating, if he fell away, he could be in trouble.

It reached out again, transparent membrane and fluid blue core speeding across empty space to wrap around a nearby spar. Too close for comfort.

"Enough of this." Cal locked his elbow around a strut. He leveled the revolver and squeezed the trigger. The muzzle flash vanished into the blackness of space, and the recoil spun him around the circumference of the landing leg. He didn't see the bullet hit, but by the time his vision tracked to find the creature, ripples of the impact were spreading across its transparent outer surface. Its grip on the lander remained firm, and it drew itself across space and settled, standing, on the footpad of the landing leg that Cal hung from. It was less than ten feet away.

The chevron eye flashed away to the right, and he caught a red glimpse of movement. Xu's spacesuited form rose over the horizon of the *Argo*'s pressure vessel and cast an orange square as if he were throwing a frisbee. For a second, his red spacesuit glove retained a grip on one corner of the square, causing it to unfold from the force of his throw. It was a simple tarpaulin, standard equipment in any lander. It had a thousand uses. Now one thousand and one.

The tarp opened up like a flag in a storm, expanding solely from the grip he had briefly retained and not from any action of wind or air because there was none. It was a zig-zagged square of plastic sheeting flying through empty space toward the cobalt blue figure. The cyclops turned toward the approaching shape, which struck, wrapping around the creature and the lander's footpad like a second skin. The cyclops began to flail.

"Come on!"

Cal looked up at his science officer and opened his thrusters. A warning tone sounded—his EVA pack's propellant level had dropped below 5 percent. They turned and headed for the lander's upper deck as the thing thrashed against the tarp, seemingly unable to adapt to another form that so quickly altered its shape.

He grabbed at the safety railing that bordered the *Argo*'s top deck, flipped himself over, and stood up, astride the top hatch. The Doc floated inside the cockpit, her eyes wide with puzzlement and fear.

"What the hell's going on!"

Cal ignored her, turning to reach out for Xu, helping him maneuver over the lander's face and the crown of railing. In the flash of a second, Cal thought the creature had thrown off the tarpaulin; something loomed up from below, flat and wide as the tarp, spreading to blot out the stars behind the science officer's red-clad form. Cobalt blue within a shining transparent sheath.

"Xu!"

The thing was on the scientist before Cal's mind could process the gyrations of its shape. It wrapped around him, enclosing, encompassing—and then Xu was inside it. The cobalt folded over him, the red of his suit caused the creature's color to change to a verdant purple. His head rocketed back and forth, eyes searching all around.

"Cal," he said.

His captain was just as stunned. The creature took a step forward, and Xu moved with it, enveloped as he was. Cal leapt forward and crashed into the creature, grabbing it's—and Xu's—wrists. Both figures went over the safety railing into space, scrambling, fighting against one another. Cal's blue gloved fingers dug into the translucent skin, but it did not give way. He let go of one wrist and slammed his glove against the head, over Xu's faceplate, trying to grab hold of the material and pull it away, but his gloves skittered, unable to find purchase, and slipped off.

"Xu! Can you hear me?"

"I can hear you."

He tried to pull at it again, nothing.

"I'm trying to fight against it . . . It's strong. I can't hold it."

It was then that Cal noticed that the creature's free arm was wiggling, vibrating. Xu was fighting to keep it from striking him.

"Shoot it," said the scientist.

"What?"

"Shoot it! Maybe it will weaken, and I'll be able to fight against it!"

Cal grimaced and balled his right fist, striking out with a quick rabbit punch against the creature's gut. His friend's face contorted.

"I felt that."

"Good thing I didn't shoot you, then," Cal quipped, breathing hard. He let go with both hands and slammed them into his chest. Xu grunted. Cal gripped two fistfuls of the translucent outer membrane in his gloves and pulled, but the surface hardly welled up, sliding from between his fingers. They were drifting further and further from the lander, spinning off into space. He caught glimpses as they whirled. The lander's engines were pitching up, and it was moving toward them.

He lashed out with his fists.

"I'm sorry, Xu."

He struck about the sides of the creature's head. Inside, the science officer's helmet sloshed back and forth within the blue substance.

"I can't fight it much longer."

Cal hit again.

"It's . . . strong." Xu blinked and the creature's arms flew to Cal's helmet. Red gloved fingers within splayed across his faceplate. It had him by the head. His own blue gloved hands shot up, batting at the scientist's creature-encased arms, punching its chest and face. The thing's head, and the helmet within, rocked back and forth against the blows, but the only result was that they tumbled through space faster. The thing's grip was unrelenting.

The thrusters on Cal's EVA pack fired, propellant level sinking below 3 percent. He smashed his hands against the creature's arms, trying to get it to release him. Opening up the throttle to full, he rammed his elbows into the creature's hands but could not break free.

His EVA thrusters sputtered and died. The tank was empty.

"Cal . . ."

"Hang on." He pulled his feet up and kicked into its chest as hard as he could. Its grip loosed, and they flew apart, rotating as they spun slowly away from one another.

"Xu!"

The science officer's enveloped form spun just a finger's length away, but with nothing to push against in order to draw closer, not even air, they may as well have been a thousand miles apart. Cal's gaze searched for the *Argo*, but it must have been behind them because he couldn't see it.

"Something's wrong," Xu's voice croaked.

Cal looked at his friend's wide, frantic eyes. He had, in all these years, never actually seen the man frightened. He had seen every other emotion, even humiliation, but never that. Never fear.

"Something's happening. I can hear something."

Xu's suit was dissolving, wisps of red material bubbling away from its surface. It started slowly, but the process began to accelerate. Cal desperately tried to reach him, but the scientist spun helplessly, engulfed in the alien mass, just a few feet out of reach. It was as if the suit was peeling away into nothing. First the outer layer, then the layers of micrometeoroid shielding and insulation. The cooling and heating tubes boiled away and the muscle-fiber pressure garment shredded into wisps of smoke within the cobalt.

Cal was unable to make words form in his throat.

Xu was momentarily revealed, naked within the enclosing mass, his hair fizzing away, vanishing like the bubbles that reach the top of a pint of beer, and then his skin began to burn, opening up in a thousand pockmarks to disintegrate in a wave of annihilation. Cal forced himself to lock eyes with his friend as nerves and muscle flayed away, absorbed into his destroyer. His musculature fled. Cal knew that the man's organs were exposed, encased in a filigree of nerves and venous structures within bone, but somehow, they held each other's gaze. Beneath the maze of organs and nerve nets, the science officer's skeleton was dissolving away. Out of the corner of his eye, he could sense the motion of Xu's pumping heart.

Cal kept his eyes locked with Xu's until they disassociated, his gray-flecked irises flensing away into nothingness. It was only in that moment that he heard a scream, and then the creature rushed toward him. The impact slammed Cal's head against the back of his helmet. The murdering thing reared over him as they spun, and he saw the *Argo*. It was impossibly close. There was another tremendous impact, and then darkness rushed in on him.

Twenty-Seven

Cal woke in the lander, head ringing. He smelled metal. He opened his eyes, and saw he was floating against the restraints of the *Argo*'s co-pilot station. Outside the curving window of the gem-shaped pressure vessel, he could see the familiar shape of the *Ulysses* still in orbit around the green moon, its centrifuge arms in the process of retracting. He turned his head to his left. The Doc's forest green space suit was at the controls. Saying nothing, he craned his head backwards. The caul was pulled up most of the way through the bottom hatch but was still stuck, the door yawning open. That was it. There was no one else in the lander.

He squeezed his eyes shut against returning memory.

"You're awake, are you okay?"

He didn't answer but released his harness and floated back into the *Argo*'s cabin. He was about to kick at the caul but remembered then what it was and stopped. He floated in momentary confusion.

"What happened? Where is . . . the *thing*?"

"I hit it with the lander, it's gone, I think."

"It killed Xu," he said.

"I know."

Silence.

Braced against the decking Cal, looked down at the caul and

gripped it in his gloved hands and began to pull. The Doc released her restraints and came over to help him. Odysseus was safely in control of the lander. She pushed against the cocoon with her boot, as close to hatch as possible. He recognized what she was doing and did the same, compressing its girth and pulling at it with all his remaining strength. The caul moved, hiking further into the lander's interior. The Doc grunted, he pushed and pulled, and the caul heaved up and popped inside. The Doc pushed down on the hatch cover, and it slid into place, locking tightly. There was a film of shorn gray material rimming one quarter of its edge. Cal floated back, breathing hard, looking as if he were about to collapse.

The Doc looked at the caul, an incongruent presence, floating like a great gray croissant. There was a tear along its side.

"Shit."

"What?"

"We ripped it."

"Shit."

The Doc moved to the control panel and pressurized the cockpit. Cal felt the material of his suit squeeze in against him.

"Don't take your helmet off," she said. "But if we've compromised whatever safety seal this thing had . . . Well, I don't want to kill it while rescuing it. I don't know if it breathes what we breathe, but I'm pretty sure it wouldn't do well in a vacuum."

"It's wearing a suit."

"Yes, but—"

"Better safe than sorry, I get it."

They used a cargo net and secured the caul to the lander's curved rear wall and then the Doc opened the comms channel to the ship.

"Inez, I need a favor."

The comms officer's somber voice rang over her speaker—she had obviously already been told about Xu. "Whatever you need."

"I need you to deploy the inner quarantine tent." The tent would enclose an area just inside of the lander's airlock and allow them to decontaminate their suits before entering the rest of the ship.

"Way ahead of you, Doc. It's already done."

"You're the best."

Outside the window, *Ulysses* loomed large. Cal sidled past the Doc and slid into the pilot's station.

"Odysseus can dock the *Argo*," she said.

"I'll do it. I need to."

She didn't argue.

Cal flew *Argo* up the *Ulysses's* flanks, over the twin alien booms and the huge engine bell, down the length of the cradle, and brought it in to hover over the docking ring.

"Ready when you are." The comms crackled with Paul Arthor's voice. He felt like he hadn't heard it in years.

Argo pirouetted and Cal spun the little ship in close to the docking port, adjusting its pitch and yaw slightly. He rotated the big engines around and out of the way and squirted the RCS, bringing the lander in close. The two vehicles mated with a soft bump.

They ran through the close-out checks and powered down the lander's systems, unlatching their harnesses before the process was fully complete. The Doc turned to float up toward the mated top hatch, making sure to check on the caul. It was then that she saw that the tear in its surface was bubbling, frothing.

"Cal!"

The caul itself was pulsing, bulging. The thing inside was moving.

He grabbed the handle and jerked the hatch inwards. "Go!"

The Doc shot up through the hatch, and he followed, pulling the door shut behind him. The Doc tumbled into the heavy plastic sheeting of the quarantine tent wall. Cal hit the button on the side of the airlock, and the inner door clanged shut.

Twenty-Eight

They hurriedly scrubbed their suits with disinfectant and collapsed the quarantine tent. The entire crew stood, peering into the *Argo*'s airlock window as the caul stretched and split open, spilling a volume of viscous liquid to float around the lander's interior. Whatever was still inside strained against the cargo netting until one corner of it gave way and the caul itself floated from the wall. It continued to split, opening along a newly formed seam. The being within thrashed and slid from the wet husk, spacesuited limbs unfolding.

The creature's suit was an iridescent silver, a rainbow of colors flickering through it as it moved. It wore a harness of dark brown around its torso, which wrapped around into a bottle shaped pack on its back. It floated in the center of the lander's cabin, waggling two large reverse-articulated legs ending in booted bird-like feet. A third lower limb that could be another leg, or perhaps a tail, thrashed back and forth, striking the curving walls. Thin human-sized arms extended from narrow shoulders down to large sickle-fingered gloves. The figure was capped with an oddly elongated helmet, humped at its rear.

The creature began spasming and clawing at its neck ring.

"It must be out of air, it can't breathe," said Inez.

"Should we help it?"

"No one is going in there," said Cal. "Not for any reason."

The Doc leaned in closer to the window and saw the creature had a hooked claw in the mechanism of its helmet latch. "We're about to find out whether it can breathe our air or not."

The front half of the creature's neck ring released, its latch folding outwards in a very pedestrian fashion, as if it belonged on a spacesuit made on Earth. The helmet popped off and spiraled away, bouncing off the ceiling. For a moment, it appeared that another limb was folding out through the neck ring, and then it became clear that the creature was stretching out a long, muscular neck. One that had been cramped and folded into an S-shape for who knows how long. The head at the end of the neck was triangular, tapering to a blunt snout. It had forward facing eyes and a rust-red skin of variegated and pebbled scales. The creature blinked forward facing eyes that seemed to be on stalks, pulled in close to the skull, and drew in a deep and wheezing breath. It curled itself into a ball, wrapping its tail over its head and just drifted in the center of the room.

"It's . . ."

"A lizard."

The being floated, curled tight around itself, slowly drifting toward the wall.

"A scared lizard."

"Like an ostrich hiding in the sand?"

They stared at the creature for a moment, and Cal retreated into the center of the docking ring.

"Keep an eye on it," he said and headed for the upper hatchway toward the bulk of the ship. "Don't open that airlock."

"Where are you going?"

"I need some fucking sleep."

Twenty-Nine

Cal sat alone, crumpled into a recliner in Red Hab's darkened rec room, having a cup of coffee. He had said he needed sleep, and he did. He just wasn't going to get it. Not yet. The strange glow of the gas giant's green moon spilled in through the great triangular windows. For the third time, he turned the lights back off, the room's dumb system kept detecting his movements and intruding on his mood. He got up out of the overstuffed seat and walked slowly to the center of the room and the ladder that descended from the hub. He took a deep breath and climbed down into the tiny closet-sized corridor space at the tip of the habitat that provided access to his quarters—and Xu's.

Instead of turning right like he always did, he turned left and placed his thumb on the lock to the science officer's quarters. He was the captain, it was his ship. His print could open any lock, except the Doc's. The door accordioned open. The room was much like Cal's, but where his quarters looked like it had hardly been occupied, Xu's was very much the opposite. Posters for various classic science-fiction properties adorned the walls, overlapping one another, creating a riot of colors and images. The bed was unmade, blanket crumpled in a corner across the room. No doubt it had floated around and then landed there after the habitats were spun back up.

He sat down on the bed and patted the pillow.

"I'm sorry Xu. I'm so sorry."

"He'd tell you that it wasn't your fault, Cal."

He turned and saw the Doc standing in the hallway.

"Can't a guy get any peace on this ship?"

"I'm sorry, I was just coming to see if you were all right. I thought you were going to get some sleep?"

"I tried, can't yet. I'm fine though, Doc."

"Is that right?"

He pursed his lips at her, thinking.

"How are *you*?" They had not had a moment to discuss what occurred in the station's mushroom chamber.

Her face fell a bit, he knew the expression. She had been avoiding thinking about it.

"Peachy," she finally replied. After a moment, she added, "What did you see? From your perspective?"

"When I got to the chamber, you were already gone. We noticed a panel on the door that hadn't been there before. A panel with a single frieze element above it—the dragonfly."

"The solar-sailer, you think?"

"If not, it's quite a coincidence that it showed up soon after, no?"

"What then?"

"There were two symbols on the panel. I touched them both, and when I touched the second . . ."

"What?"

"There was a flash. Like lightning, from inside the mushroom chamber, and you were there." He looked at her, really looked at her. She was the same. He shook his head, scattering odd and unbidden thoughts. "What did it seem like to you?"

"Like nothing. Nothing at all. Frankly, it was as if you had suddenly appeared and Xu had jumped across the room. And then that fucker came round the corner."

Cal's expression twisted.

"I shouldn't have gone after the solar-sailer. We were already exhausted. Low on consumables. I made a mistake." He dropped his head.

"If so, it was a mistake Xu wanted to make as well."

"Yeah. That really doesn't make it any better."

"I'd imagine not."

"It was horrific."

She walked into the room and sat next to him on the bed.

"It peeled him apart, layer by layer."

The Doc grimaced, knowing what a shock like that could do to a person. Her concern was amplified by the hollow look in his eyes.

"I'm sorry, Cal."

He looked at her and opened his mouth as if he were going to say something, but no sound came out. He closed his eyes and clenched his jaw shut.

"I'm okay."

"I know this is difficult, and it's going to stay that way for a while. But, Cal . . ." She put her hand on his. "Cal, we need you. This ship needs you right now. It's not fair, but it is the truth. The *Ulysses* needs her captain."

He took a deep breath and straightened his spine. "I know, Susan. I know."

Thirty

Inez and the pilot floated on either side of the lander docking port, staring through the window at the rescued astronaut—the rescued astronaut that was a lizard.

"I can't believe this," Inez said.

"What? That we are in another solar system with two aliens on board?"

Inez didn't appreciate the pilot's sarcasm. "Maybe we can talk to this one?"

Samuels looked at her. "I thought you'd be the one to know?"

"I don't know why everyone thinks I'm a linguist all of a sudden. I'm the comms officer. If you have trouble with your server or instruments or can't get a signal, I've got your back, but I never studied speaking to aliens. The only alien life we thought we'd face was microscopic."

They both stood in silence for a moment, staring at the creature.

"Still nothing from the server connected to the red growth?"

"No. Nothing since we got here."

They watched the creature floating inside the *Argo*. It was turning slowly, as if on a spit, and although it was tucked in on itself, Inez could catch a glimpse of its right eye each rotation. The lid was tightly shut, and the stalk it seemed to perch upon had been pulled into a recessed socket surrounded by larger, flare-tipped scales. The two watched as it came around again. This time the eye was wide open, like a huge cat's-eye marble staring back at them. No white in the sclera, it was glistening and transparent with a webwork of fine red veins and a curving vertical inclusion for an iris. The creature blinked and then began to uncurl itself, stretching its legs and toes, clenching and unclenching four-digit fists. The head drew back, neck folding into an S-curve of muscle. The snout turned to point at them and the eyes tentatively rose up on their stalks. It gripped one of the handrails with a large hand and then, in a complete surprise, reached out with a tail that turned out to be trifurcated at its tip. The tail reached toward the window and the digits at the end waved at them.

"Did it just give us a little twinkly wave?"

"I think it did."

"With its tail?"

"Yeah."

The creature blinked twice and extended its eyestalks another half an inch or so.

"Call the Doc," Samuels said.

Thirty-One

The Doc floated down into the docking ring, Cal following close behind. As he settled next to her in front of the window, she noticed that he was wearing the holster. She gave him a critical sidelong glance, but he either didn't notice or was ignoring it. She peered back into the window, fascinated. The lizardnaut had stabilized itself by grasping about the cabin with the four huge toes on either of its booted feet. It had pulled its arms up, holding them firmly against what appeared to be a heavily keeled torso. The elongated neck was tracking its head from side to side. At the same moment, it's eyestalks bobbed back and forth as if its entire head and neck were involved in the act of focusing its eyes. Again, the creature stretched out its long, muscled tail and waved at them with the three small digits at its tip.

Cal shook his head involuntarily and turned to his crew. "With Xu gone, I am going to need to rely on each and every one of you, more than I already do. Inez, I am sure you've already been thinking about how to talk with our friend here." He waited for her nod before turning to the Doc. "I'm going to need your counsel, both on how a being like this might think, what we might want to say to it, and at the same time I need you to make sure it will be safe for us, and for our guest, to one day open that door."

"Roger," the Doc said with a nod.

"We're going to feed it eventually, right?" Inez asked.

"We'll get to that. First things first." Cal moved in close to the lander airlock door and held his hand up against the window pane. The creature inside pulled its neck back into a tight S and then hopped forward in the zero gravity. It bumped up against the inside of the glass, extended its eyestalks out full, reached up with one great clawed hand, and placed it gingerly against the glass over his palm.

"I'll be damned."

"Finally, we're getting somewhere," Inez said.

"What do you think, Doc?"

The Doc thought for a moment. This would normally have been a topic that the science officer would have taken the lead on; she'd have interjected only to add the flavor of expertise and information. Now it was all on her. She tried to do her best. "Well, I'm guessing if it comes from a civilization that builds tech similar in at least the basic forms to ours, that crashed ship, it's spacesuit; then it must come from a world subject to the same universal laws that guided the development of life on earth: the laws of motion, thermodynamics, gravity, and entropy."

"Makes sense."

"Granted, I'm a biologist, and I have my own biases, but I'd say that natural selection, fierce competition between organisms over time, has made it the being it is. The same process that resulted in us."

Cal thought about that, looking into the creature's unearthly eyes.

"Obviously, it's from a technological society that has made it to space. That takes concerted effort, therefore, it's likely that they live in something like cities or have some other method where the efforts of many individuals can be concentrated. And for the same reason, to enable concerted effort, it must use some form of a language that is in some sense like our own. Whether it's a spoken language or what, we just don't know yet. It could talk with radar."

"What about its intent? Can we tell if it is from, say, a warlike species?"

"You tell me, Cal. Does it look warlike to you?"

"Did that blue monster?"

"It did, actually. It scared the hell out of me the first time we saw it. I don't get the same feeling from this creature. But still, I'd think any creature that was the end result of the process of competitive pressures would likely carry that underlying structure into its societies. There would be politics and war because how else are disputes settled? And if our new friend is indeed the product of a society, then that society probably has a leadership, be that a president or a parliament or a monarch, and a way for them to enforce said leadership, which would mean police and militaries." The creature kept its palm against the glass opposite Cal's and turned its head to look at her as if understanding that she was talking about it.

She held up her palm and gestured toward the lizard. "It's clearly intelligent," she said. "I'm getting a friendly vibe, but please don't hold me to that. We should remember that it's likely capable of violence, although I am not suggesting it's predisposed to it."

The creature turned its attention back to Cal, as if it were following the flow if not the meaning of the conversation.

"Is there a mic and speaker in the *Argo*'s cabin?" He could not remember if he had ever heard cockpit tones or comms chatter without wearing a helmet or headset.

"There is, for the emergency system," said Inez.

"Can we switch its input to the comms without going in there?"

"I think so. Odysseus?"

"Yes, comms officer. I can change the input. It may damage the speaker, however. It's a bit on the tinny side."

"We'll take that risk."

The connection opened and speakers in the docking ring buzzed to life with a hissing pop of static and the sound of breathing punctuated, now and then, with an odd rattle. The creature craned its neck, stretching out its length, and panned its head across the ceiling, clearly searching for the source of the sound. It discovered the speaker, looked it over, and then returned to the glass. The alien looked at Cal and then looked back toward the speaker and pointed at it with its tail.

Cal glanced at the Doc out of the corner of his eye. *Here goes.*

He placed his hand to his chest and said his name. "Calvin."

The lizard pulled its head back, neck bunching into a tight S. Its eyestalks popped in and then rose back out. The neck loosened up and its triangular snout slid out toward the window. Clawed fingers hooked over its own sharply keeled chest and two bulging sacs protruded briefly from orifices set back in its skull. The mouth opened to reveal a ragged set of semi-sharp teeth, each with many multiple ridges and sharp points. The sacs deflated and a rattling sound came over the speakers that sounded half like an exhale and half like speech. "Seisssss"

"What did it say?"

"Size? Did it say size? Jesus, it sounds like a cartoon lizard," said the pilot.

"Not *size*," Inez said. "It's more of an *ess* sound."

"Seiss," the Doc said.

The thing looked at her. "Seiss," it repeated.

"Seiss," parroted Cal. The creature turned to look at him.

"That's its name."

Cal placed his hand on his chest. "Calvin."

Seiss waved its head from side to side, the sacs behind its eyes bulged again. "Cughllwin" the speaker rattled.

Close enough. Cal smiled and nodded his head. "Calvin."

"Callwin." The creature reared up and a cobra-like hood stood out from the sides of its head and neck, pulsed and flushed, turning a dark, rich red. It dropped its head, waving it from side to side, and retracted the cobra hood.

"That was an impressive display."

"What do you think it meant?"

"I don't know, a smile, maybe?"

"Let's not jump to conclusions, but we may have made a friend. Doc, you need to figure out whether it's safe to take contact to the next step. What do you need?"

"I need samples, Cal."

"Of?"

She cocked her head. He was being obtuse. "I need samples of *it*. Air samples, swabs from the consoles and walls in there. I want samples from the remains of the caul . . . and I want a swab from that thing's mouth and, if it will allow it, a blood sample."

Cal looked at the creature inhabiting the *Argo*. "That means someone is going in there with it."

"Me," said the Doc.

"No. I can't risk losing you. Not now."

"Cal." She knew he was about to insist he go himself. "The ship can't risk losing *you* now."

Cal frowned. She wasn't wrong, but she wasn't entirely right either. Her expertise in the processes of life would become more and more critical the longer they spent away from Earth. Especially as food supplies started to dwindle or the first health issue hit the ship. They couldn't afford to lose *anyone* else. The reality was they couldn't afford to lose anyone at *all* and they already had.

Who should go in was a toss-up, and in a toss-up, he would take it upon himself. Not out of bravery, although he hoped it would be mistaken as such. He just could not bear to sit by and watch.

Thirty-Two

Cal locked his helmet to the neck ring of his suit as the crew gathered around him in front of the quarantine sheeting that framed the lander airlock. The big engineer helped him with his backpack, stripped of everything but air tanks and a battery. Once done, Inez handed him a tablet and said, "Stick to the plan, right?"

"Right."

The Doc held up a plastic packet of tools, swabs, and sample vials and handed it to him. He took it in a blue-gloved hand and secured it to the Velcro stripes across his suit's right thigh.

"Try and take it slowly, start with the swabs from its skin surface and inside its mouth if it will let you—try and get deep in there. Take an air sample, just open the vial and then close it after a few moments, don't wave it around. And swab at least three different surfaces within the lander, I'd like to see what has been growing in there all these hours, if anything."

"Got it."

"And then you've got to try and get it to let you take a blood sample."

Cal grimaced.

"I know, not fun but I need it, and if possible, a tissue punch sample because we probably won't get much DNA out of its red blood cells."

"If it has red blood cells."

"Right, yes."

The Doc held up a set of syringes, one with a rather large needle. "Just one vial is sufficient," she said, looking at the creature as it peered with interest out the airlock window. "Obviously, the larger needle is more threatening, so try the smallest first, but I'm not sure that will get through its skin. It looks pretty tough."

She handed him another device with a single sample container. "This is a punch biopsy tool. I don't know if it's going to let you do this, or if it's even wise to try, but if it's cooperative, try and see if you can get it."

"I don't like the look of that one myself, Doc."

"I know, it's not going to be an easy sell."

"How would you feel if I went to jab *you* with that thing?"

"Not happy." She glanced down at his hip.

"You didn't bring your little friend with you this time?" she asked, referring to the gun.

"I didn't . . . but it's in the silver case in my quarters if you need it."

She nodded and zipped up the quarantine sheeting after Cal had stepped inside.

He stood inside the draped vestibule and calmed himself for a second, then peered in through the *Argo*'s top hatch window. The creature was floating toward the lander's starboard wall, rummaging through the storage lockers there. Cal gripped the hatch handle and slowly rotated it. Instantly, the creature stopped moving, and its right eyestalk pivoted to stare at him.

Cal took a deep breath and pushed the hatch open. The alien pulled its head entirely away from the lockers, turning its long, heavily muscled neck as the hatch door intruded on the lander's interior. It held onto the locker handle and turned slowly to face Cal as he gently drifted inside and closed the hatch behind him.

Except for its periscope eyestalks darting about, the creature didn't make a move. It just hung there by the lockers, steadying itself against the wall with its prehensile tail. Cal floated at the lock, rotating the handle closed, eyes riveted to the reptilian creature. It was bigger than he'd expected, bigger simply by virtue of being on his side of the thick hatch door. He released his grip on the handle and pushed away from the ceiling. His boot touched the floor grating, and he settled to a hover just about ten feet away from the alien.

He took a deep breath and held his right hand up, palm out. The saurian creature blinked and then mimicked the movement, holding up its clawed hand, glancing back and forth between them as if to make sure it was repeating the motion correctly.

"Hello," said Cal, momentarily surprised at the echo of his own voice over the speakers. Of course, otherwise the alien wouldn't be able to hear him through his helmet. *Good thinking, Inez.* It looked toward the speakers, then back to Cal and opened its mouth. A wheezing hiss rattled in his headset.

"Was that a hello?" he asked over his comms.

"Not sure, Cal," Inez replied.

The lizard blinked at him again and its air sacs emptied. "Cullghwin," it wheezed. The sound surprised him, although in retrospect, he wasn't sure why. Perhaps some primitive part of him had already reverted back to viewing the alien as an animal more than a person? Nevertheless, he was again startled to hear something approaching speech from so alien a throat. Cal placed his hand on his chest and the *Argo*'s internal speaker reverberated with his words. "Calvin. Yes."

The alien put its clawed hand against its own avian-like chest cavity and hissed its name.

"Seiss, yes. I am glad to meet you." Cal enunciated carefully even though he knew he wouldn't be understood.

The being's eyestalks bobbed out, and it cocked its head.

"All right, sticking to the plan." He pulled the tablet from the Velcro patch on his left thigh and held it in front of him. The creature, Seiss, blinked at him. Cal tapped the screen to begin playback and carefully watched the alien's reaction. It just blinked.

Inez's voice sounded in his ear. "The video isn't playing."

"Oh?" Cal peeked over the edge of the screen and, seeing it blank, tapped again. The video clips that Inez had found in the ship's medical files and quickly edited together began to play across its surface. In the first segment, a Doctor was gently taking blood from a child who squeezed her eyes shut as her mother held her hand. In another, a military Doctor swabbed the cheeks of a rank of soldiers. A third showed historic footage of early astronauts going through medical checkups. The final clip was a repeat of the first: the Doctor calmly taking blood, the little girl wincing, mother looking on and smiling.

Seiss regarded the moving images with interest. Its head remained still, but its eyestalks were constantly on the move. When the clips finished, it looked back up at him, blinked, and inflated its air sacs. After a moment of waiting to see if it would say something, Cal removed the medical pouch and opened it to show the alien the ranks of sample containers and syringes. It looked from Cal's eyes to the pouch and back again, then its left hand flashed to its right and deftly unclasped the connectors that held its glove to the arm of its spacesuit. With a shake and wiggle, the glove came off to reveal a scaly, bird-clawed hand. Three large fingers and an opposable thumb tipped with sharply curved talons that seemed to retract against the ends of its scaly fingers. The alien extended its arm toward him and waited.

Cal was so shocked that he turned involuntarily toward the airlock window, trying to catch another human being's eye, but they all must have been watching the proceedings on their screens because he saw no one.

124

"You guys are seeing this, right?"

"We are," Inez said from out of his headset. "We're all holding our breath!"

He reached out and placed his hand very gently on Seiss's scaly forearm. It turned its eyestalks to him and finally released the pressure in its air sacs, which came out as another reedy rattle.

"Do we take that as a yes?" he asked through the comms. It's eyes blinked again. Cal picked up the medium-sized sampling syringe and showed it to the alien. A blink and then the air sacs reinflated. The same sound clattered out of Seiss's throat.

"It doesn't seem like a no." He laid the metal of the needle against its skin and looked into its marble-like eyes. The lizardoid stared back and then squeezed its eyes shut, pulling them close against its triangular skull.

"It's mimicking the little girl in the video," Inez said.

"That's a yes, then."

The underside of the creature's wrist and palm were covered in tiny scales, so thin that he could see purplish vein structures beneath the bright red skin. Every crew member had emergency medical training. He'd practiced performing this very procedure in a suit during training, but never had the opportunity arisen where he could put that knowledge to use. Until now. Of course, he missed on the first jab. The creature slit its right eye and looked at him as if to say, *What the hell are you doing?* Cal slid the point of the needle into the skin, it dimpled at the nexus of a grouping of scales, and then yielded. The blood that coursed into the sample container was a deep, rich red.

Thirty-Three

Inez and Cal joined the Doc in the research lab adjacent to her office in Blue Hab.

"Thanks to our surprisingly cooperative guest I got everything I wanted," the Doc said.

"I still can't believe that went so well," Inez commented.

"The day's not over yet." He turned to the Doc. "How's it lookin'?"

"I've split the sample volumes." She turned to the swath of medical and scientific devices built into the lab wall. "I'm incubating half of the material at various temperatures in different kinds of culture media and waiting to see what grows." Windows sprouted open on her console, and she clicked them off one by one. "Meanwhile, I've spent some microscope time with the other half of the sample."

"What are you looking for?"

"Whatever catches my eye." She leaned into the scope and tapped the control that sent its imagery to the lab's largest wall screen. "And what catches my eye is that the alien's blood is *blood*. If you told me it came from a terrestrial animal, I'd be hard-pressed to say otherwise."

"So, it's a lizard."

"No, if you'd told me it was a terrestrial *lizard*, I'd have known something was up. Lizards have nucleated mature red blood cells. Mammals like us don't. This guy's mature red blood cells have lost their nuclei, like the cells of a mammal. The platelets look a little weird, maybe. Earth lizard platelets are nucleated as well, but I'm not sure what I'm seeing here. I'm having trouble differentiating leukocytes from thrombocytes. I don't know if that's because it's an alien or because I'm not much of a veterinarian." She shuffled a set of memory sticks and plugged another into the surface of her console. "But I swear, it honestly reminds me of what we saw on its ship."

"Its ship? How so?"

"You said it yourself, the wreck looked like it could have been built on Earth, the same construction techniques employed by unfamiliar hands. It's the same with its biology."

Cal pulled at his chin. "So, if it's not a lizard, what is it?"

"It's what it is. Remember what I said about similar evolutionary pressures possibly resulting in similar solutions?"

"Yes."

"Well that's what we are seeing here. It might look like a lizard or a dinosaur but it isn't. It's new."

He dropped his hand from his chin. "Any red flags?"

"Not so far, but again, we have to wait for the cultures to grow. In general, we have five or six different classifications of pathogens: bacteria, viruses, parasites, fungi, and prions. Toxins too, usually produced by bacteria. This is where we have to be careful. The more biologically similar it is to us, the greater the danger of infection and vice-versa. Greater than if it was something even more alien."

"Makes sense. We'll proceed cautiously."

"We have to. It is definitely the least-alien alien we've seen so far," Inez said.

"At this point, I'm not seeing anything that makes me any more nervous than I already am, we just need to keep our eyes on those Petri dishes." The Doc gestured at the row of shallow covered dishes locked down inside the incubation chamber. "That's where the real revelations should come from. I've prepped the sample, using synthetic digestive enzymes to break down the tissue for DNA/RNA extraction and replicated it in the PCR unit—"

"PCR unit?"

"Polymerase chain reaction. It's a component of the microbiology lab experiments, designed to analyze the samples we were to have brought up from Jupiter's moons. Stuff to search for life. It's basically a DNA xerox machine, and since I assume we'd rather avoid continually stabbing our new guest, I figured this was a good use of it."

"Good thinking."

"Odysseus is running an entire sequencing of its genome; we'll compare it against the tree of life on Earth and see where it falls out."

"And then we can call it a lizard."

"If it resembles reptilian DNA more than anything else, sure. But I'd bet against that."

"What about the tissue samples and swabs?"

"I'm culturing the swab material on agar plates as well. Thus far, they are interesting only in their banality. As with the blood, the results could pass for having come from one of us." She opened an interface window on her console, checking on Odysseus's progress. "I really hope we get to see where it came from. I'd like to see how closely its world's solutions to environmental and evolutionary pressures resemble those that Earth's ecosystem came up with."

"Of course, me too." Cal hitched his thumb toward the culture dishes. "But that's in the future, Doc. We have more immediate problems. How long is *this* going to take?"

"Well, we have pretty good equipment, despite it all being as miniaturized and stripped down as possible. We should see significant culture growth quickly. I'll isolate some of it, prep for nucleic acid, do the sequencing runs, and compare those to what's known. But it's a process."

"How long?"

"It's going to take a week to ten days for the DNA to be sequenced, although I can run multiple samples concurrently—the creature's and anything else that grows on these plates." She glanced over at the ranks of isolated Petri dishes.

Cal avoided twisting his ring in her presence, no need to remind her that she wasn't his only ex, so he again pulled at his chin. "All right . . . In that case, we can spend the time back in polar orbit investigating the gas giant and our initial alien friend." He jabbed his thumb toward the window and the mysterious twin booms that had, in light of everything else, faded like a commonplace object into the back of his mind. "Maybe whatever happened will happen again."

"It also means we're going to have to try to feed it before any results come back," Inez said. "Assuming it eats and drinks."

"I'm sure it eats and drinks, from what I've seen so far I wouldn't imagine its needs are far from those of terrestrial creatures."

"Maybe it can go long periods without food and drink?"

"I think it just did," said the Doc.

"So how do we feed it without poisoning it?" Cal asked.

"Good question. I've been giving that some thought as well."

"I knew you would. Love you, Doc."

"I know.

Thirty-Four

The Doc and Cal reentered the lander through the top hatch, fully suited. They dropped inside where the alien was waiting for them, perched like a hawk, clinging to the suit racks with its foot claws. It waited patiently for the two human astronauts to settle near the floor. When they had stopped moving, it expelled one of its wheezing rattles and held out its arm as before. The little tuft of gauze and tape covering the spot where Cal had inexpertly drawn blood was still attached.

"Eager to cooperate."

"Grateful for our assistance?"

"I hope."

The Doc reached out with a forest green glove and gingerly took the creature's arm in hand. The gravity of the moment hit her; she was touching a thinking alien being.

Cal's voice in her ear intruded on the thought. "If it's as much like us as you seem to think, it's gotta be starving."

She looked into its strange eyes and could see entirely through the orbs to the network of nerves and blood vessels covering their rear walls. The strange cat irises regarded her, closing to slits as she flashed one of her helmet lights. "I'm sure, but we are going to have to take this as slowly as we can, exposing it to foodstuffs gradually."

She pulled a silver pouch from the back of the medical briefcase she carried slung over her shoulder. "We must be just as methodical in this as we have been in trying to guard against infection."

"How about giving it water? I'd like to show it some kindness if we can. If I were in its situation I'd be looking for some, after being confined and prodded by strange beings."

"I get it . . . I think we can risk giving it distilled water."

"All right. Water, then."

The Doc removed a sliver pouch from her bag and unscrewed the nipple at the top and offered it to the alien. It regarded her for a second and reached out to accept what she had proffered. It examined the package, letting it float, and turning it about on each axis. Its eyes opened wide as it squeezed the pouch and a stream of crystalline water bubbles escaped the silver sleeve. It immediately moved its snout to intercept the escaped liquid and then drained the rest of the pouch's contents. The two human astronauts traded quick smiles.

When it had finished, it handed the pouch back to the Doc with an unfolding of its claw-like hand and emptied its air sacs with a frog's bleat.

"Now what?" Cal asked.

"Now," she said and took a deep breath. "Now I'm going to try and do some needle pricks of its skin."

"An allergy test."

"Yes, exactly. The scales complicate matters, but I think introducing a possible allergen at the nexus between them should work. What we are trying to do is see if its skin reacts with redness or welts." She reached out for its arm, and it allowed her to grip it by the elbow and pronate the forearm in front of her. It looked at her, opening and closing its triangular mouth and briefly revealing the rows of multi-crowned teeth.

She continued, "After a few minutes, we can try and put whatever doesn't cause irritation to its lips, or mouth or whatever, and wait to see if there is any reaction."

"Like?"

"Same as the skin pricks—swelling, redness."

"And if it's a severe reaction?"

"If there is to be an anaphylaxis, it should happen pretty rapidly." She pointed at the case he had carried in with him, and he opened it with the tear of Velcro. Seiss's hood stood away from its neck slightly, vibrating at the sound. Inside, three sets of color-coded ampules clinked against one another. The Doc continued, "The syringe capsules at the top are epinephrine, Benadryl, and levocetirizine. Just in case."

"How do we know *that* stuff won't kill him?"

"We don't, but I don't know what else to do, and we need to address this issue sooner rather than later. Everything has to eat, unless it photosynthesizes, and I didn't see any chlorophyll in his cells, did you?"

Cal glared.

"I didn't think so. We are just going to have to take some risks. This isn't a perfect situation." She opened the other briefcase and pressed both against Velcro strips integrated into the lander's inner wall. Inside the second case were the application needles and a wide array of various basic elements, environmental contaminants, and samples of foodstuffs. She pulled one of three cylinders filled with needles from the case and inserted the applicator handle to withdraw a single sterile sliver, which she dipped into the first of the allergen samples.

Cal squinted at the label. "Cow's milk?"

"There's a lot of it in our foods." She sought the nexus of a number of small scales near where Cal had taken blood and let the needle press gently against the skin. She turned to the creature and made eye contact. "Play the video, Cal."

He held out the tablet, just as before. It was another medical video.

"Where the hell did Inez find footage of allergy testing?"

"It was embedded in the instructional manuals for the medical equipment. She pulled it from there."

"Genius."

The video showed various clips of people happily eating. The creature blinked rapidly and opened its mouth wide, pointing in toward its gullet with a clawed finger. Cal shuttled back through the video and stopped at the testing scene, a soldier laying on his stomach, an array of pinpricks along his back. He pointed at it and then flipped to the end, pausing on a still of a child eating a peanut butter and jelly sandwich.

"First the tests, then we know what we can feed you," he said.

"I should have thought of that," the Doc commented. "Assuming we aren't going to learn its language, we are going to need to teach it English. We should be talking to it."

Cal paused for a moment to take in the scene, the Doc floating, holding a lizard the size of a human adult by its arm, and he felt an involuntary shiver streak through him.

"How hard do you have to push?" he asked.

"I'll just have to give it a little—" She flicked the applicator with a gloved finger, and the creature winced. She pulled the applicator away and showed her palms. "I'm sorry," she said. The attitude of the alien, if not the expressions on its face, was humanly relatable as the emotions of annoyance and patience as it tolerated each subsequent miniature strike. The Doc continued, disposing of each needle after use, drawing a new one up into the applicator, dipping it into the next sample, and following with a little jab. Each time, a being born under another star winced in pain and stared back at them.

"Doc, maybe this is enough?" Cal asked. She was only about halfway through the set of samples, but she glanced up at her patient. Its eyes were narrowing.

"Yeah, maybe you're right. If it doesn't have a reaction to

anything here, we will have a number of things we can feed it. Some of the fruit pastes, at least." She released its arm, and it pulled itself away from them, scooting back through the interior of the *Argo*, using its long three-fingered tail.

"Don't be mad," she said to the retreating being. "I'm just trying to keep you safe."

"I think it understands that."

She looked at its clawed hands and nodded. "If it didn't, I think we'd know."

Seiss relaxed and let go of its grip on the wall netting. It rubbed the arm she had assaulted and extended its long neck, swinging it back and forth between the two human astronauts. It barked an air sac's worth of sound at the Doc and then swung its neck over toward Cal and retracted it back into a bulging sausage of an S-shape. Its eyes stood out on their stalks and blinked at him as if to say *what's with her?*

"I think he's just a bit grumpy."

"Sharing a room with a six-foot-tall grumpy velociraptor is not a comfortable feeling."

"Especially since you were the one with the needle."

"I'm sorry," she said again, holding her hands out toward the alien. It pushed off the wall and sailed right at her. She willed herself not to flinch and almost succeeded as its clawed hands closed gently around her shoulders, its snout directly in her face, just inches away. The creature emitted a soft bleat at her that somehow alleviated her fears. She sensed no malice at all. Naive, she thought. She was being naive. Her muscles trembled as her stomach unclenched. It released her and floated gently away.

Cal also released his tensed muscles. Poised just a foot or two away, his legs braced against the lander wall. He was tightly gripping a handrail near the ceiling, ready to launch himself at the alien.

"I'm fine," she said. "That was more of a hug than anything."

Cal's eyes flashed. "Are you kidding?"

Seiss croaked and retracted its head further, arching the curve of its neck, and looked back and forth between them by moving its eyestalks alone.

"It wasn't an aggressive move. I think bygones are bygones."

Cal's pulse began to slow. He had feared he was on the verge of losing another crew member. He had almost reacted with violence. He exhaled. ". . . now what?"

"Now. . ." She shook her shoulders inside her suit. "Now we give it some time and watch for adverse reactions. Then we'll try and place a piece of food on its tongue, see if that causes any inflammation."

"And you've figured out a way to explain this to it."

"Inez worked up another video."

"These videos are effective. That's how we need to teach it our language."

"I agree."

"Maybe there are language courses, or even children's shows, in the entertainment catalog?"

"It's possible, there's a ton of crap in there."

Seiss blinked, its air sacs puffed up and squeezed out his name, drawing the sounds out this time. "Cullghwinnn". It pointed at him. It turned its clawed finger back at itself and rattled, "Ssseis," and then it curled a long curved claw at her.

"You never introduced yourself, Doc," Cal interpreted

She gasped. "I'm so sorry!" She flushed; she truly was sorry. She had thought of him as an alien and a threat and a medical problem but not as a person. "I've been so rude." She pressed her hand to her chest and said, "Susan."

It pivoted its eyestalks over to Cal and back to the Doc. "Zsooosan?"

"Yes," she nodded. "Susan."

Seiss looked over at Cal again and inflated the bubbles behind its eyestalks. A short sound trumpeted out. "Tok."

"Tock?" Cal shook his head. "I don't understand."

"Tok," the red-scaled lizardoid repeated.

"I don't understand," he said, shaking his head again.

"Susan," she repeated. Seiss swung his scarlet skull over toward her and puffed his crest out. "Zoosan, SssTOK."

"Doc?" she asked.

"Tok." It fluttered its cobra hood.

"It knows I call you *Doc*."

"Paying close attention to our speech, huh?"

Cal watched the alien examine the pinpricks on its arm. A few welts had formed here and there but most of the little spots between the scales were fading from an angry purple.

"Let me see that," the Doc addressed the creature, and it let her hold its arm so that she could carefully examine the series of test spots. "It only really seems to be allergic to ginger. I think it's time we screened Inez's latest film," she said and secured the tablet against the wall while tapping play. Cal and the creature stood shoulder to shoulder and watched the allergy tests continue to oral trials. He turned to the alien and joked, "I can't wait to see how this turns out." It regarded him quizzically with a single turned eyestalk.

The video ended, and the Doc opened up the bottom compartment of her briefcase and pulled out a silvery tube with a picture of a banana on it.

Seiss extended its neck, head cocked.

"I still say it's just going to eat it," Cal said, crossing his arms over his chest.

"If it eats it, it eats it, and we wait twenty to thirty minutes and see what happens. If it swells up or seems in distress, I've got Medrol packs and fast-acting bronchodilator canisters and these here." She pointed to the far side of her medical tray. "These are steroid injectables. If it doesn't get sick, we've solved our immediate problem."

"Yeah . . . another mouth to feed."

"If we can't readily find a way back home, this is a problem we are going to face ourselves. This is a good trial run for when *we* run out of food."

He thought about that for a moment. "Thanks for starting to think long term."

"No problem, *Captain*." She smiled at him. "We have food and water to last for a few months. "

"Yes. The amount of time we were scheduled to spend around Jupiter. After that, we would have counted on a resupply."

"And there's no resupply out here." She made a face at Seiss, opening her mouth and sticking out her tongue. It understood and mimicked her, opening its triangular jaw and extending a long bluish tongue out over jagged multi-peaked teeth.

Cal involuntarily reached to spin his ring, despite the fact that it was under his spacesuit glove, thinking aloud, "But if it can eat what we eat..."

"Then we might be able to eat what it eats."

"Right."

She squeezed a thumb's length of banana paste onto the creature's tongue, which it immediately swallowed.

"Told you."

Thirty-Five

Inez stood in Red Hab's geological sciences lab. The artifacts recovered from the derelict space station had been placed in the quarantine unit originally meant to isolate samples from Europa, Callisto, and Ganymede. Visible and invisible beams inspected the surfaces of the alien objects at nanometer resolutions, constructing computer models that could be manipulated and examined within Odysseus's dataspace. Other beams vaporized the tiniest bits of their surfaces, and the ship's machine mind used gas chromatography to try and determine the composition of the objects. The AI was concurrently performing a similar analysis up in the astronomy lab as part of Xu's still-running program, examining spectrographic readings of light passing close by the other planetary bodies, to determine the nature of their atmospheres. The process differed only in the manner in which the sample data was gleaned.

She opened the comm line to Cal and his helmeted face appeared on the lab's main screen. Behind him, she saw the interior of the lander, the forest green of the Doc's spacesuit, and a dinosaur. It carefully held the Doctor's tablet in its huge recurved claws.

"What's up?" Cal asked. Despite her laser focus on the artifacts she had been examining, the creature in the background distracted her as it held the tablet up over its head, pivoting only its eyestalks to peer at it.

Cal noticed her attention split and glanced back to the creature. "It doesn't like the glare from the lights," he said.

"What's it watching?"

"Sesame Street."

"You're kidding?"

"I'm not. There's two hundred terabytes of audio and video entertainment stored in the lounge's video wall. We found the show there. It's learning English."

"That was a good idea."

"It was all mine," he said, smiling.

"Well, I've had an idea, too. I thought you might think it was too unconventional but . . ."

"There is no such thing as too unconventional now. Shoot."

She nodded. "What if we show the server we connected to the red weed images of some of the artifacts you guys brought back? We haven't removed them from quarantine or anything, but I've mapped the surfaces, taken photos, and I was thinking, if the station and the weed are products of the same civilization—"

"Then whatever else these objects are, they may also be keys to unlocking further communication with whatever has infiltrated our ship and brought us here."

"Right, a picture is worth a thousand words. The only success communicating we have had so far has been visual. I figure the artwork you discovered inside the station must have some greater meaning beyond decoration if it is repeated on the artifacts."

"The friezes are repeated on the artifacts?"

"You didn't know that?"

"No, I didn't. Frankly, I'm surprised you found the time to examine anything we'd brought back." *I'm in a fog, dammit.*

"I haven't investigated them extensively, but Paul and I took a look, and I've rewatched the recordings from while you were inside the station . . ." She drifted off, caught up again in the wonder and excitement, the mystery, and then the remembrance of loss brought her back to reality. "Sorry. Yes, the long rods you brought back . . . they replicate the images from the main frieze in the entry chamber, almost exactly."

"Almost?"

She switched her video feed to mirror the desktop of the lab console, showing the cylindrical artifacts. "The caps of the rods add another element to imagery seen in the friezes, look. I think this pattern here." She pointed to a set of geometric shapes set within nested rings encircling the ends of each rod. "I think it represents this solar system. The same concentric set of rings with one elliptical ring girdling them all. They could signify the three rocky inner planets, the three gas giants, which include the one very large one in the first orbit, and two more rocky planets much further out, which I'm betting we just haven't found yet."

"That's great work, Inez. Truly."

"Here's the same pattern on the spheres, look." A computer model of one of the spheres spun on the video screen. A detail-encrusted globe as ringed with symbology as Jupiter had been girdled by storms. The symbols themselves seemed to be composed of very fine wires or pins that extended up from the track upon which they sat. As if they could change or shift, but they didn't. "The geometric symbol component of the friezes is repeated on the spheres—only here they're clearly associated with the planets themselves. This one is the square, this one triangle."

"Then that nearest rocky planet, the third planet, is circle, then?"

"Yes!"

"Fantastic work, my compliments. He looked her deep in the eye. Even through video, through the reflections off his faceplate, she could see both gratitude and exhaustion. "Thank you, thank you for stepping up."

"No problem, Cal."

"Continue in your efforts at decoding, and you're cleared to show the alien server the imagery of the artifacts from the derelict. Keep me informed, I want to know the moment it responds."

"*If* it responds," she replied.

"We need more information, Inez, and time is not our friend. *Make* it respond." He cut the line.

She turned back to the console, removed a data stick from its port, and headed for the spindle.

Thirty-Six

When Inez got to the docking ring, Paul Arthor was waiting for her. The big engineer floated between her and the spindle access hatch.

"What's going on? What are you about to do?" he asked.

"So far, pictures and video are two for two when it comes to talking to aliens. I'm going to show images of the derelict artifacts to the server."

"And you cleared this with Cal?"

"Of course, I did."

He considered this, his forehead wrinkling. "I don't like how things are going. We've lost a man, and Cal has hardly addressed it."

"We haven't had a lot of spare time, if you've noticed."

"*You* haven't. Since Xu's death, it's you, Cal, and the Doc, and I'm stuck down here while Sarah's been parked in the cockpit."

She examined his face, eyelids drooping toward the bags under his eyes. "I'm sorry, Paul. Is there something in particular you want to address?"

"No, but . . ."

"Is there something you think we should be doing that we're not?"

"No."

She waited a breath and then said, "Then come with me, I'd be glad to have your help if you're not busy."

"I'm not any busier than usual."

She slipped around him and pulled the spindle hatch open. "Then come on."

He followed her into the red-tinged corridor that stretched hundreds of feet down to his engineering sections.

"So, you're going to show it imagery of the artifacts?"

"Yes."

"Why?"

"On the assumption that there is some relationship between the thing that's invaded the ship and whoever, whatever, built that station."

They floated to the black box that hung on the wall of the tight circular corridor. The red weed had grown to engulf a corner of the server, cradling it in a nest of darkly glowing bubbles.

"But you're just showing it these items without any context. You've only *looked* at the items. You may have mapped them, but you haven't *examined* them. Those rods aren't a single piece, are they?"

"No."

"I didn't think so. I thought they may have moved when we transferred them to the isolation chamber. The spheres?"

"The equatorial bands move."

"And those bands repeat the frieze artwork, too?"

"Yes, but with a large amount of additional imagery or pictographs. It could be art, it could be writing, it could be both."

"And the rods? How do they move?"

"The caps turn independent of the rod but in sync with one another. We found two identical rods. The artwork wound along their surfaces is identical to the friezes in the station's grand lobby, but there are eight new symbols on the caps."

Paul pursed his lips. "I know we want to get out of here, but I'm afraid we're getting ahead of ourselves here. You're hoping that the red weed will recognize these things and talk to us? What if it does? You don't know what you're saying to it. You don't know how a turn of one of those caps or bands might change the meaning."

"Look, none of us is a linguist, Paul. Odysseus has the equivalent of a Wikipedia entry on the topic in its database. What are we supposed to do? Wait until one of us rediscovers the entire principles of the science and figures out *exactly* what these things are and what they mean?"

"You know that's not what I'm saying."

"Paul, you don't feel it yet, but there's a fuse burning underneath our feet. We have a limited time that we can survive here unless we figure out either how to get back or how to get help before we starve to death. You're giving me a lot of reasons to do nothing. But doing nothing isn't going to get us out of this. Given those circumstances, I'm going to try. That's all I know how to do. So, unless you have any other ideas?"

The big engineer remained silent but only barely so. There was something screaming in his head, his inner engineer's voice, born of years of education in the values of planning, testing, and measured implementation.

"Fine," she said. "I'm going to show it all of the objects at once. Maybe that will avoid inadvertently communicating some accidental specific goal." She inserted the data stick into one of the server's access ports and loaded the image into the dataspace. Storms of pixels swept over the monitor and deposited an exact replica of their image of the recovered items. They waited a few moments for some other reaction. Nothing.

"So, now what?"

"Maybe . . . we show it the artifacts one by one?"

"You said there are different symbols on the caps of the rods, so the appearance can be varied. Which variation do we show? One? All? How about the spheres? You said the equatorial bands rotate? Is there a relationship between the different patterns of symbol matches that occur when they rotate?"

"No clue. I have no idea if any of this means anything at all. We're trying to elicit a response. To get *somewhere*. Cal's orders: working on the possibility that we inadvertently instructed it to bring us here, we need to figure out if we can tell it to bring us back. All you are offering is reasons why we shouldn't do anything, and I'm specifically supposed to try *something*."

"All right, show it. Show it the rods, fewer possible combinations to contend with."

"Roger that." She fed an image of the rod to the server's shared data space. It appeared on the screen hanging from the server casing on the spindle's cylindrical wall. The cap had been rotated around to match the triangle with the beginnings and ends of the helical strips of artwork.

A graphical storm swept over the server screen, and it replicated the image of the rod, transcribing the friezes and end caps, and displaying them in an entirely new presentation: a strip of symbology.

Then the main engine started.

Thirty-Seven

The acceleration was felt inside the confines of the *Argo* as forcefully as throughout the rest of the ship. Seiss and Cal fell toward the side wall, but the Doc quickly curled her boot around a retaining strap and held herself in place.

The lizardoid hit the wall first and absorbed the impact with its huge reverse-articulated legs and used its tail to prevent Cal from smashing his shoulder.

He turned to the creature and nodded his thanks before tapping his forearm screen and connecting with the command module.

"What the hell's going on up there, pilot!"

"Not my doing, Cal. The ship is adding velocity, swinging us wide. We are either making a plane shift or breaking orbit."

"Paul?"

"I'm here, we're in the same situation we were in around Jupiter. I can try and stop it, but any way I know how means I'll be physically crippling the ship, possibly permanently."

"Sarah?"

"Yes, Cal?

"Where are we headed?"

"I'm not sure. I think you'd better come up here."

Thirty-Eight

Cal entered the command module, still in his spacesuit, gloves and helmet magnetically attached to his backpack. The command module was dark, its curving space lit only by myriad phasing lights pouring from the instrumentation and the glow leaking from the diminishing green moon. Pilot Sarah Samuels was alone, strapped into the left-hand command seat, fingers white-knuckled around the hand controller.

He floated up to grip the headrest of her seat. "What's the situation?"

"First off, I just wanted to say I am sorry, Cal. We haven't had a chance to talk before now."

"We've all been busy," he responded, scanning the readouts illuminating the consoles.

"Still, I know you and he were good friends."

He ignored the statement. "What have you got?"

She blinked her eyes to clear her thoughts. "Sorry. You had asked me to prepare to return to polar orbit around the Jovian. A maneuver like that could be executed at almost any point, swinging us out into an extreme orbit and then shifting to the polar plane and circularizing."

"Are you saying that's what's happening? Did the burn just occur earlier than you expected it to?"

147

"Maybe."

"Maybe?"

"I didn't initiate the burn, and Odysseus is in the dark. The commands are obviously coming from our guest . . . Well, our *first* guest. Given the similarities of the maneuvers, one is different from the other only by degrees, I can't be sure whether we are just making the plane shift or if we're breaking orbit. We could be shifting into a heliocentric orbit that could transfer us to another one of these planets, or to somewhere else altogether."

Cal pulled at his chin. "So, how can we know?"

"If the engine throttles down within the next thirty-seven minutes, it's a plane shift. If not . . ."

"Roger. . ." He emptied his lungs, exhaling as much stress as possible. "All right, if it's just our pole shift, we have nothing to worry about. If not, we'd best start thinking further ahead than we have been." Emergencies tended to put one into a shortsighted mindset. He should have considered that before now. "If we're not shifting into a polar orbit, where would we be going?"

"I suppose that all depends on when the engine shuts down. If it shuts down quickly, we're just shifting to the poles. If it goes beyond the thirty-seven-minute mark but shuts down soon after that, I'd say we were headed *downhill*, counting on the gravitation of the star to pull us in-system. If it keeps firing, then it's heading us *uphill*, continuing to expend energy to work against the star's pull and moving us further outward toward this system's outer planets."

"Which is the more likely?"

"I have no idea. I've been trained to think in terms of fuel economy. That's historically been our limitation but now—"

"The alien devices seemingly eliminate the mass of fuel as an issue."

"Yeah, and without any idea of why the devices brought us here, there's no way to guess until the engine cuts off."

Cal began to think aloud. "Downhill is sunward, and sunward we have the three rocky planets and the super gas giant."

"And outwards we have another gas giant."

"And two rocky planets we haven't discovered yet."

"How do you know that?"

"The artwork in the station, it's repeated on the artifacts we brought back. Inez thinks part of it is a solar system map. If that's true, there are two more distant rocky planets that we haven't discovered yet."

"Well . . ." She checked the timer on her display. "We'll know in thirty-five more minutes.

"Or we can just ask it." Cal pivoted and pushed himself toward the CM's hatch. Samuels began to uncouple her safety harness. Cal pivoted as he flew away. "Sorry, Sarah. In a situation like this, you know the ship needs its pilot at the controls."

She frowned. "This is bullshit."

He clutched at his heart. "I know, but what can I do?" And with that, he vanished through the hatch.

Thirty-Nine

By the time Cal reached the docking ring, the engineer and the comms officer were screaming at one another.

"What the hell's going on? I could hear you guys all the way in the hub."

Both of them were red-faced, casting accusations at one another. "I told *her*. We're flailing around blindly!"

"Paul, calm down! If you want to be angry at someone, be angry at me. It was my order." Cal looked at Inez, who was seething. "Maybe it was a mistake, but I stand by it, we need answers and all we have are questions."

"That's all well and good, *Captain*," Paul protested, "but we went and showed the invader that rod when we had no idea what it meant. It may have *killed* us, but we probably won't even know whether that's the case for weeks, *right?*"

"*Enough*," Cal said, hoping he'd settle down.

"Enough? It's not *nearly* enough. Who knows where in the universe we are? I don't understand *anything* about what's happened to us. Do *you?* What do you mean, *enough?*"

"*I mean enough!*" Cal's shout reverberated through the docking ring torus like a gunshot; all three of their expressions softened as it echoed away. He stared at his ship's engineer. "Go to your quarters and get some sleep."

"I'm not tired."

"Yes, you are. Go to your quarters. Get some sleep."

The big engineer's eyes dropped. He glanced at Inez. "Sorry," he said, and he fell into the ceiling hatch that led down the ship's spinal column.

Cal and Inez stared at one another in silence. It was as if a major structural component of the ship had suddenly shifted and cracked. He felt unsure as to what they could accomplish now. How capable was the ship if he could no longer fully count on its engineer? He pushed those thoughts from his head, it would be a problem or it would not. It was a situation to assess at another time. "Now is for the *now*." Who said that? It was a quote from somewhere, he was sure—or was he? No, he wasn't. He wasn't sure of anything. He might have just made it up. The strain was getting to them, to *him*.

He put his hand on the hatchway window. The door needed to remain closed as long as the *Ulysses*'s engine was firing, so they were communicating with the server via tablet. Its screen output was mirrored on the upper quarter of the tablet's display: the images of the rod artifact and its transcribed sequence of pictograms.

"So, it got that string of glyphs from the rod?" he asked Inez.

"Apparently, yes."

"But what if you had held it differently, shown it a different face?"

"It doesn't actually matter. I didn't notice it before, but the frieze artwork wraps around the rod in a tight helix. The ends of the strip of art only meet the caps at a single spot."

"So, no matter how it would be viewed, there are only eight possible selections that will line up with the intervening art helix?"

"Right. The caps move in sync. So, only eight choices."

"And eight planets in this solar system."

"It can't be that simple, can it?"

"I don't know. There are thousands of possible combinations on the spheres. Paul suggested the rods because of the limited possibilities."

"Thank goodness."

"He was concerned that we were doing the wrong thing, not understanding what we were saying to it, so I suppose he thought the rods would limit the damage."

"Listen, you were right to try. It was a risk, but risk is our business. We're getting somewhere now, the rod is set to the triangle. If you think it's part of a map of this solar system, what planet does that correspond to?"

"The first planet, the Hot Jupiter."

"So, then our Jovian here would be . . ."

"The plus symbol."

"Turn it to the planet closest to us."

"Right." She called the computer model up on the loading space screen to the right of the tablet's primary image. She rotated the endcaps around to the diamond-shaped symbol.

"No, to the planet that's closest to us in miles, not in the next orbit. I think that diamond planet is on the other side of the solar system right now."

"Sorry, Cal."

She twisted her fingers across the screen and the end caps rotated around to the circle. "Okay?"

"Yes, load it."

She swiped the loading screen image over to the window representing the alien server's dataspace. The previous image of the rod vanished and was replaced with the one with the caps set to the circle. Instantly, the screen erupted into the Mandelbrot cyclones, replicating the image, throwing transpositions of the pictographic symbology into what looked like a linear sequence or sentence. A microsecond later, he could feel the change in the engine output, likewise tiny motes of dust swirling in his vision subtly changed the direction of their dance. The RCS system was firing, adjusting the ship's attitude.

The comms system crackled, and pilot Samuels's voice shouted, "Cal!"

"Here."

"It's reoriented the ship."

"And it's stopped?"

"Yes, looks like it was only a minor correction. Or a major correction made with plenty of time."

"That'd be my bet, keep a sharp eye out and let me know of any further changes."

"Roger."

Cal stared at Inez's face. She stared back.

"Yup."

"This is crazy."

"Yup. Although . . . something has finally broken our way," he said, managing a wan smile.

Forty

Later that evening, Cal and Inez descended through the spinning centrifuge arm. Cal landed first, and he waited for her, tottering on the ceiling of Red Hab. She smiled at him as she floated down next to him, landing with a slight jolt in the near Mars-normal gravity. "You doing okay?"

"Everyone's asking me that question, how are *you* doing? Xu was your crewmate as well."

She smiled at his deflection. "I'm dealing with it, Cal. But honestly..."

"I know. All of this, it's too much. I do want to thank you, though. Without Xu—I appreciate the help is all."

"I'm doing my best, Cal."

"You're doing great." He turned and hopped down through the hatchway and onto the ladder.

"Sarah's already down there, she's waiting for you."

"I figured as much," he said.

Cal climbed into the rec-room, gravity's embrace becoming more muscular rung by rung. The pilot sat in one of the overly plush chairs, the display wall set to a rustic New England fireplace. He let go of the ladder and fell on a slow-motion arc to land within a bounce of a luxurious sextet of overstuffed chairs: a hallmark of the *Eureka*-class ships. Never before had a spacecraft, an Earth spacecraft, been appointed so luxuriously: artificial gravity (the best part of which being not having to go to the bathroom in zero-G), generous personal space, and a rec-room filled with entertainment devices, and the chairs. Six recreational lounges designed, unlike everything else aboard the ship, with only luxury and comfort in mind.

He slow-motion flopped into the chair directly across from his pilot.

"I can't believe you let me out of the CM, I never imagined my ass could go numb in zero-G."

"Sorry," he said. "I know you've been feeling trapped in there, but you know that's where the ship needed you to be."

She made a face.

Inez dropped down the ladder and took her shoes off to curl her toes in the brown fibers of the long shag rug. "We figured something out," she said.

The Doc climbed down, not missing a rung as if she were descending in full gravity. "What?" she asked. "What did we figure out?" She crossed the rug and selected her preferred chair, dropping heavily into its embrace, the earthy smell of the soft material filling her nose.

"We're not all here yet, Doc." As if on cue, Paul Arthor's bulk sailed down through the ceiling hatch, swung off the ladder, and stumbled into a walk. He stood next to his chair, the least accustomed to the gravity, and swayed a moment. Cal sized up his expression but the man was either calm or more adept at keeping his feelings from his face than Cal had thought. He nodded at his comms officer to begin.

Inez called up an image of the artifacts recovered from the derelict. It floated ghostlike above the shag carpeting. She explained the recent communications with the growth that had insinuated itself into the ship.

"So, you're saying the artifacts *are* a course selection tool?" Paul asked.

"At least the rods, anyway. We show it an alignment of the geometric symbology on the caps compared to the ends of the artwork strips, and it recognizes the sequence and immediately alters the ship's course."

"It's like an easy-to-use interface for a set of known destinations," Sarah commented.

The Doc tilted her head in thought. "Like a child's interface?"

"Maybe. I don't know."

"What were the items doing on the station?"

"I don't know that either, you didn't see any other artifacts, did you?"

The Doc shook her head as Cal responded, "Nothing that wasn't tied down."

"If it is a space station, maybe it's like a terminal. A place to wait and transfer to your destination . . ." Paul said.

"After arriving in this solar system, via the Jovian," finished Cal.

"Are you saying everything we just experienced was a trip through some space subway?"

"Maybe."

"There's still a lot of questions to be asked about that derelict," Cal reminded them. "We've all been going nonstop since we initially left to investigate it, and so much has happened since."

"And immediately preceding," the pilot snarked.

"True, and we need time to mentally unpack everything, to think logically, and try to make connections that we might have missed. It may just be wishful thinking on my part, being so overwhelmed I'm craving to understand *something,* but our having stumbled onto a transport system is an appealing hypothesis." As he spoke, Cal found himself watching the Doc closely, looking for those small movements and little idiosyncrasies that he knew so well. They were there. Nothing seemed amiss.

She caught him looking at her and held his gaze as she asked a follow-up question of Inez. "So, the rods are ways to indicate each different planet in this system," she said. "What would they have been used for on the derelict?"

"Guidance?"

"Guidance for what? The derelict? We didn't find them in its control room, they were in that bunk or quarters, or whatever they were."

Paul didn't look convinced. "If that's what they really are, a navigational device, then it's a pretty convenient development. With no Deep-Space Network to triangulate us, we're going to have to do quite a bit of work before we can accurately navigate." He turned to Sarah. Piloting the *Ulysses* was her primary domain, and he was aware he was impinging on it. "No?"

"You're not wrong, but Odysseus has already identified reliable references. We can navigate if we have to."

"The rods might not be meant for use with the station itself at all, they might be meant for some other device entirely," said Inez.

"Some kind of larger system, perhaps?" mused the Doc, running her hands up and down her chair's overstuffed arms.

"From your camera angles, I got the impression that the entire underside of the station, beneath those massive doors, was a hanger. That equipment was meant for servicing something. Spaceships, maybe," the engineer said.

"And that's where the solar-sailer was nosing around," the Doc said.

They all sat quietly for a moment, thinking.

"If the rods are the child's tool?"

"I don't think they're a child's toy, Cal, but their complexity is limited."

"Unlike the spheres."

"The spheres," Inez said with a nod. "The spheres are much more complex, both graphically and in terms of the possible combinations. After the discovery involving the rod imagery and the server, I went back to the lab and examined the spheres more closely using drone manipulators to maintain the isolation of the samples . . ."

"You mean you went as far as you did, introducing scans of the rods to the server without fully investigating the other artifacts?" the pilot asked.

Paul Arthor glanced between the pilot and Inez.

"Yes. I had initially sent an image of all of the artifacts into the server's loading space, but that produced no response. I already had a complete and articulated model of one of the rods, and so, I figured that was a logical next step."

"Why not, right?" Paul added sarcastically. Inez ignored him.

The pilot took advantage of the stutter to cut into the conversation. "And just showing a picture of the rod to the server caused it to take action?"

"Yes."

"And why?"

Inez wrinkled her nose. "What do you mean?"

"I mean, why? Why would it know to activate based on a visual image of the artifact and not the artifact itself?"

"Great question, I don't know. Perhaps its original interface is supposed to be visual in some way? I really hadn't even thought to ask that question before, so thank you. I'm going to have to think about it. If anyone has any ideas, *please* let me know."

"Yes, let her know before—"

"Continue," said Cal, cutting off and eying the engineer.

"Yes, well. All we know is that a change in the position of the caps results, when loaded into the server's interface environment, in a change of destination within this system, presumably in relation to the orbital designs on the ends of each cap."

"Unbelievable," the engineer whispered earnestly. He was

unhappy, but he wasn't immune to the wonder of it all.

"And the spheres?" Cal asked.

"Yes, well. The spheres are articulated at the equator and the motion is analog, meaning that it spins freely. There are no detents, no halting of the motion. Twisting it realigns the top hemisphere in comparison to the bottom. Each hemisphere has two rotating bands of pictograms set within it, bordered by non-rotating bands decorated with different geometrical shapes. The movement of these bands is precise and measured—one length forward or backward—as if they're geared. There are two polar caps that spin in sync with the equatorial motion and are portioned into sixteen equal wedges. Each wedge has a different pictographic symbol impressed upon it."

"And what does it do?" Sarah drew her legs up, and she nested further into her chair's wide seat.

"No idea, not even the first clue. Some of the pictograms are repeats of elements of the frieze artwork and some of the other panels and elements you saw, while others are entirely new. The geometric shapes repeat, but there are also shapes that are not present on the rods at all. And before you ask, I have no idea what any of this means."

Paul frowned. "And yet, we are still headed to wherever you inadvertently directed the server alien to take us?"

"Not precisely. We experimented to see if the different shapes did indeed represent different planets."

"And?"

"And apparently . . . they do." Cal said, taking over. "We are headed downslope, gravitationally, toward the star. We were initially headed directly for the innermost planet, the Hot Jupiter, but we altered our destination to the planet currently closest to us, a rocky mars-sized planet two hundred and eighty or so million miles from here." He turned to look at the pilot. "Sarah, I'd like you to independently verify that."

She sat up straighter. "No problem. I said we'd be able to navigate if we had to, but it's going to take some work to have real confidence in these measurements. Xu had Odysseus developing an initial navigational reference system, but we've got a lot of different projects we've been tasking him with. I'll assess and let you know exactly where we are."

"Thank you."

The pilot pulled her legs up underneath herself and into the bounty of the chair. "I had guessed we were headed star-ward, what with the engine throttling like it has been, but do we have any idea what this planet is like?"

"Yes," Inez said. "The overall albedo of the body we are now calling Circle is around 0.14. In infrared, the reflected light is highly directional, displaying a strong oppositional effect much like the light scatter off Earth's Moon. Its readings are typical of regolith surfaces, airless bodies."

"So, why are we going there?"

"For a few reasons," Cal said. "There are additional pictograms associated with Circle on the rod-caps. That may or may not mean something, but we are also already on our way sunwards and it's close. We'll get there in a little over a week. Any other planet is a month or more away given their solar orbital positions and the course we're on."

"Which didn't have to be the case."

Inez turned to the big engineer, and said, "And what would we have done otherwise? Sit here? Go back to the station where for all we know the thing that killed—*killed*—Xu might be?"

"All right," Cal said, trying to calm her down.

"No, it's not all right. The red weed responds to imagery through this server, and those artifacts and that station appear to be related to it. I don't know why that is, but that's what *is*. It's what brought us here, and it's my job to try and talk to it."

Paul Arthor seethed but managed to look more exhausted than angry. The pilot spoke up for him and said, "I think what Paul is saying is that if we'd slowed down a little bit, maybe we'd have a larger choice of options open to us now."

"Exactly," the big engineer said.

"And instead," she continued, "we're limited to what's on our gravitational downslope rather than expending too much of an unknown quantity of energy changing our trajectory."

"And if that were the case, we'd still be sitting in orbit, getting closer to the point when we can no longer survive out here," she retorted.

"All right, this is pointless," said Cal, standing up. "I don't disagree with any of you, but the fact of the matter is that we can't be passive. While I may or may not have made the most optimal of choices, I made *a* choice. We've got a week until we flyby, or brake, into orbit around Circle. In the meantime, we need rest, and we all have plenty of work to do. The best thing we can do for ourselves is get back into something approaching a normal schedule and apply ourselves to the problems we are facing."

"Why do I feel like I've heard that speech before," Paul mumbled under his breath, but he joined the other crew members in nodding assent, each wearing a variation of the same tired expression.

"Doc, you have your samples and our new friend as a patient."

"I'm well aware."

"Inez, I want you to keep analyzing those artifacts and come up with a proposed plan of experimentation for exposing the server to further imagery. I want to have a ship-wide meeting tomorrow. I'll consider everyone's opinions on the subject before I make a decision."

"Yes, sir."

"And anything you learn or ideas you have concerning those rods, I want you to sync in with Sarah on this. It's officially a navigational device as far as I'm concerned, and that means it's her territory."

"I understand." Inez nodded in deference to the ship's pilot and navigator, who seemed less drained than most. Inez admired her. Smart, funny, and attractive, Sarah seemed endlessly and effortlessly at the top of her game.

Cal turned to his dissatisfied engineer. "I want you to do a full check on the ship's systems and basic structure. It's been through a lot."

"It has," he grumbled, "but I've been keeping an eye on things, including any changes in the spread of the infiltration."

"I never thought for a second that you weren't," Cal replied, putting a bit more emphasis into it than he'd wished. "I'd like you also to expend some thought as to how we might disable the engines without damaging the ship."

"You got it."

"Sarah, I want you to confirm our course as best as you can. It seems like you've already stepped up to assume responsibility for the astro-location and navigation computer experiments that Xu was running. Thank you for that. There should be a lot of results to sift through by now."

"Yeah."

"The one thing we haven't figured out about the red weed and that rod is how to cancel the orders it gives."

"Wouldn't surprise me if it didn't have a stop function at all," she said. "Once you're on an orbital path, you can alter it, but you can't stop it."

"Of course." Cal was surprised he hadn't instinctively understood that. Perhaps it was that the simplicity of the selection system led to a simplicity of thought? "I need some sleep," he said. The sentence trailed off as if he were completely drained of energy and spirit.

The crew watched the three-dimensional fire flicker and crackle for a few moments and then slowly dispersed.

Forty-One

When Cal woke, he was floating in the center of the centrifuge hub, curled like a fetus, rotating in synchrony with the 288-foot-long arms. The hub and the hallways that ran up the arms spun past his view until a man he could not see grasped him by the shoulders to halt his movement. He turned around. It was a man of clay, a rude simile of a man with only smudges for features, pits for eyes, an empty black hole for a mouth. It steadied him and began to scan the surroundings, turning its crude head from side to side. Cal, recoiling in horror at the man's face, turned to seek out whatever it was that he might be searching for.

His mother was there. Asking him, "*Why?*"

The *Ulysses* began to disintegrate. Huge chunks of the ship fell apart and crumbled around him until he was alone among the ruins of an ancient western city. Classical structures lay wrecked across the landscape. Ahead was a path that led up a tortuously torn and weathered staircase to the flat top of a small mountain where the wreckage of the *Ulysses* somehow perched as if it were a reclining marble nude. Beauty haunted the statue, suggesting itself between missing limbs and detail lost to pockmarks and pitting.

The marble goddess turned to watch him mount the steps and

ascend, smiling sadly as her face, the Doc's face, fell away from her head.

Cal woke in his quarters, sweaty sheets curled around him. Stars wheeled past his ceiling windows.

Forty-Two

Cal slumped through the sickbay's accordion door, startling the Doc. "Jesus. Didn't you sleep?"

"I slept. Not well."

"You want to talk?"

"Yes, but about your results. I wanted to check on your work."

"Well, I just so happen to have a nice little chemistry unit all set up for capillary electrophoresis. It was originally to be used for the Jovian moon samples." She pulled the bottle of lovely caramel liquid from the bottom right-hand drawer of her desk, but he waved it off. She shrugged and replaced it without sampling. "It was designed to detect even the tiniest signs of life. Not exactly analogous to the situation we find ourselves in, but I figured out what the hell to do with it, regardless."

"That's why you're here, instead of some other lucky soul." He dropped into the chair in front of her desk.

"Punished for my aptitude," she said with a smirk. "The device provides a quick and automated way to collect and compare amino acids. We're looking for functional genetic material, not just from the alien but from anything else living, or once living, within it. Normal symbiotic bacteria, parasites, and anything else that might be floating around. Even waste remnants of other microorganisms that cells within the body have destroyed. I was able to scale up the smallest of samples and get a better sense of what we might be facing, now and in the future." She gestured to the Petri dish-lined interior of the isolation hood. There were Rorschach shapes sprouting in a number of the shallow dishes. "I've been growing these cultures for six days now, and so far, I haven't seen anything that scares me terribly . . ."

"I like the sound of that."

". . .Which does make me worry that I might have missed something."

"I don't like the sound of that."

"There's one aspect that I did find very interesting. Take a look." Her desk screen lit up with a number of swirling molecular models. "Do you know what chirality is?"

"No"

"Chiral is Old Greek, I think, for *hand*."

"Okay."

"Bear with me, but this relates to the theory of panspermia that I'd mentioned earlier. At the chemical level, all of earthly biology has a deep bias: the molecules that make up DNA, RNA, and other nucleic acids inherently *bend* in a certain way, either to the right or the left. That is, the molecules *can* exist in two mirror image forms but only the left-handed version of amino acids and the right-handed versions of sugars are found in living organisms."

"And this is important?"

"Oh yeah. Handedness, chirality, serves an essential function in living beings; many of the chemical reactions that power our cells only work with molecules of the correct chirality. All of life's processes boiling down to one microscopic shape fitting into another."

"And this has to do with Seiss how?"

"Synthetic processes generate equal numbers of both left and right chirality, but when nature makes a molecule, the numbers favor one or the other. It's a molecular form of recognition." The molecules danced in mirror-image on the screen beside the Doc. His eyes glazed over as he looked at them.

She continued, saying, "Molecular locks can only be opened by a key that twists in the right direction, and it looks like the biochemistry that produced Seiss twists, generally, in the same direction as ours."

"Panspermia?"

"More evidence to suggest it, at least." She nodded.

"So, that means it should be able to metabolize our food?"

"Yeah, we should be safe giving him anything it hasn't reacted to allergically."

"And the converse?"

"Indeed, if we can find where it came from, we should be able to metabolize the same food, if toxins or disease don't kill us first."

He considered this. "So, you really mean it when you say that this creature comes from a planet like Earth? Similar, even at microscopic levels?"

"More or less. It's possible, anyway."

He stroked the whiskers on his chin and asked, "If it comes from somewhere so much like Earth, why doesn't it have a more humanoid body shape?"

"Cal, the Earth went through five mass extinction events before humanity evolved. If even one of those hadn't happened, or if one more would have, we wouldn't be here. Remember, we evolved from apes to human beings in a matter of a few million years. If things had gone differently, maybe some other species would have evolved to prominence. Luck is a powerful evolutionary advantage."

"Point taken, Doctor. I'm letting my biases get to me. We need to continue its English lessons and find out what we can from it."

"It *is* a quick learner."

"Yes, and I think it would learn quickest if it was immersed. It's friendly enough, when can we let him loose?"

"Not so fast. We need to make damn sure that it isn't carrying anything that can infect us *or* our food stores—or even the vegetable plants in the bio lab which, all things considered, might be some of the most valuable things aboard."

Cal frowned. They had months until it happened, but the food *would* run out.

"Remember, when the Europeans arrived in the Americas over 95 percent of the native populations, millions of people, died due to lack of immunity to diseases like the flu and smallpox. And ours is the bigger problem, we are dealing with the unknown, and *unknown* life forms could act in ways we can't predict."

Cal collapsed back into the chair, taking half a second to enjoy the gravity and the opportunity to be motionless before replying. "But, on the other hand, if your panspermia theory is wrong, then we could have nothing to fear at all. Our biologies would be so different that anything it carries shouldn't be able to infect us. Just like we can't get diseases from trees."

"That's true . . ."

"But you don't think that's the case, do you?"

She slid away from her desk and pulled the bulb-topped bottle from the bottom of her drawer again. She didn't bother to offer him any this time, she just drew off a few fingers' worth of bourbon for herself. "No, I don't. Given similar problems, the same pressures will drive natural selection toward similar solutions. That creature is not a lizard or a dinosaur, but there are clearly similarities."

Cal absentmindedly twisted the scratched silver band around his finger, deep in thought. "How about it stays in its suit? I'll bet Paul can figure out how to refill its life support system. You can disinfect the hell out of it. How about that?"

"Why are you so keen on this?"

"You saw how much our knowledge and situation advanced from that admittedly foolhardy move with the server? Well, Seiss is a space traveling being. He sure as hell knows a lot more about where we are than we do. We need to do everything we can to improve our communication. That creature is the best and least risky chance we have to increase the amount of information we have."

"All right, I'll buy that."

"So, when can we let it out?"

"The chiral setup of its sugars and amino acids are like ours. I think that means its biology is similar to ours, so we should be exceptionally careful about possible contamination. I'm going to continue to incubate those cultures and see what, if anything, grows."

"Then what?"

"Then we analyze what's there, see if there are any relationships to terrestrial organisms and then see if we can kill them with antibiotics, radiation, or medical nanots."

"How long?"

"Another week?"

"And if it's isolated within its spacesuit?"

"Well, we can disinfect its suit, we've been doing that to our own. I don't see how this would really be any different. It should be safe. As long as it stays in the suit."

"Excellent. I'll set Paul to work. And then how long before we know if its biology is dangerous to us or vice-versa?"

"We still have to wait a week, examine the cultures, and if all looks good, we can start loosening up the quarantine. At that point, I'd suggest one of us goes into the *Argo*, in shirtsleeves, and then stays in quarantine with it for at least seventy-two hours. Then, if all goes well, we open up and let it out."

"If all goes well?"

"Yes. If neither of them gets sick or dies."

"Then I guess I need to pick Seiss a roommate."

"Yes, you do. It's good to be captain sometimes. You can make people you don't like live with a lizard."

He smirked. "I should make Paul do it, he's really pissing me off."

"We all have short fuses lately, and he wasn't exactly wrong. We all just need some rest."

"And some progress," Cal said. "Winning changes mindsets."

"So, it's Paul, huh?"

"No, I'm not going to do that to the poor lizard."

She laughed. "Who then?"

"Who else? We're falling toward a planet with nothing to do but housekeeping tasks. You all take care of your little slices of this ship. I'm happy to be cooped up with the space lizard for seventy-two hours."

Forty-Three

Paul Arthor glowered at the alien pressure suit and gear plunked down on the table in front of him. He sat in the mechanical lab at the top level of Red Hab where the middling gravity made physical tasks easier. The alien objects stunk of disinfectant, wrinkling his nostrils. He pulled at the tangle of cables and straps, moving the components apart from one another. The mechanical nature of the hoses, channels, and grooved connectors all seemed fairly ordinary. Not that they matched any design that he had ever seen, but rather they were built in similar ways to solve the same problems—maintaining pressure, temperature, and atmosphere and enabling an astronaut to move as freely as possible. This suit just had an odd-shaped helmet, an extra limb . . . and a strangely shaped torso, legs, hands, and feet.

He focused back on the materials, the connections, the workings. He began to disassemble the life support backpack and realized he had no tool that would fit whatever passed for its screws and fasteners. This was going to be an endeavor all its own and one, truth be known, that he was not really up for. He rummaged through the maintenance lockers and came away with a roll of sealant tape and a spare set of hoses and connectors, which he spread out across the table next to the odd equipment. He compared the hose diameters and throttled the alien hose with a set of industrial shears. He hesitated. Cal might not like it. The creature might not like it. But it would take days just to begin to delve into the technology, whereas he could connect its suit to one of their own spare backpacks in less than an hour. He wasn't willing to wait for approval, he'd rather ask for forgiveness later. Although, what he actually said aloud was "Fuck 'em" as he sliced through the alien suit's life support lines.

Forty-Four

Sarah was back in the conical command module's pilot seat as the *Ulysses* fell sunward. Great curving arcs filled the display as indicators effervesced, framing the cockpit windows with color and shape. They wrapped around her and flowed down into the main interface console directly in front of her. Although she had complained about being cooped up in the CM, this was her element. She was a pilot and a navigator but one who had absolutely no idea where she was and no idea where she was going.

She didn't approve of Paul's attitude, but she didn't blame the engineer for feeling the stress—or for expressing his opinions. There was an underlying logic in them. Certainly, loading the infected server's database with the model of the artifact, simply because they seemed similar was impulsive, but she wasn't sure it was *wrong*. The consequences of that act were yet another dangerous rollercoaster ride, but as a result, there was a larger picture forming, there was an order to things that they were beginning to sense. And as for the danger, it's not like that wasn't always part of the equation.

Every second brought them closer to the star, distant yet bright enough that its glare washed the backdrop of shining pinpoints into blackness. There were planets out there, but this far away, they were visibly indistinguishable from a number of brighter suns fighting through the starshine.

She was concerned. Not so much about getting home, that was never a guarantee even if the mission had gone according to plan, but about her crewmates' performance as components of the ship she was tasked with flying. None of them had expected to encounter anything like this—how could they? They were all professionals, but this voyage had been nothing but shock after shock. People, like machines, had their limits. She had the bad feeling that parts of her vehicle were overdue for service.

The truth was that they were utterly, if not hopelessly, lost. They couldn't be sure yet how many planets were in the system, how big they were, or what they were made of. Because she had no idea how far they really were from the star, tried and true methods like measuring angular diameter only gave them rough approximations of the sizes of the worlds they were hurtling toward. As for gaining some advance knowledge of the atmospheres of these onrushing worlds, forget it. They hadn't been in the system long enough to be sure they'd gathered enough data. Differential analysis wasn't possible for similar reasons.

They could, however, still rely on spectral analysis of the star's light passing close to a planet to tell them what kind of place it might be. The elements that compose an atmosphere absorb specific portions of light. Analyzing its spectrum and looking for the missing bits would tell you the elements that made up a world's atmosphere.

There was nothing missing from the light passing on from Circle.

She was a lost navigator under a sky full of unrecognizable stars, headed for a dead planet. She trusted Cal, but she felt a creeping sense of doubt. A feeling that there might be no good end to this road. What would they do if they couldn't find a way home? Look for a place where they could find food? They could find an entire planet full of food, but how were they going to get down there? If the imagined supermarket planet had gravity much greater than one of Jupiter's moons, they'd never make it.

And what else was there to search for? Assistance? Refuge?

She reminded herself, what had happened once could happen again. The first sea voyagers must have felt this way. *How many of them died?* She shook the negative thoughts from her head and focused forward. Further exploration of their point of origin, the outer Jovian, would have been the obvious place to look for a way back. *But we've already made multiple orbits around that world's poles and nothing has happened. The alien devices didn't activate, and Cal isn't mad enough to dive the ship into atmosphere on his own.* Not yet, anyway.

They were on a trajectory sunward, and it would take vast amounts of fuel, perhaps more than they could spare, to just turn around. *Who could be sure?* No matter what, they would have to loop around the star in order to return. So, it would be a waste of an opportunity not to explore, at least in flyby mode, as many of the other planets in the system as they could. The Hot Jupiter? It wasn't *too* close to the star. No one had ever seen a world like that up close. Did it have a system of polar vortices like Jupiter? Could it harbor a similar transportation effect? *If so, would that bring them closer or further from home?*

Who knew how it all worked?

Maybe they'd find out from the lizard. *What a thought! Maybe they'd find out from the lizard.* Absurd, but it was reality. *Doubly absurd.*

A graphical representation of their heliocentric orbit shined across the surface of her console. A miniature *Ulysses* composed only of pixels fell through a corridor of ever-expanding green boxes toward whatever awaited it.

Forty-Five

At the far end of the extended centrifuge arm, at the tip of Red Hab, the Doc descended into the tiny corridor between the captain and the first officer's quarters and found both doors open. She peeked into Xu's former room and broke the silence to let the captain know she had once more snuck up on him. "Here we are again."

"Jesus, Doc," Cal said with a start.

"What's wrong?"

"Don't you have an alien lizard to look after?"

"It's deep into watching Bert and Ernie right now, it's fine. What are you doing here?"

"Looking at the posters."

She took in the room fresh—an overlapping panorama of classic science fiction film advertisements covered the walls. "Which is your favorite?"

"My favorite? Let's see . . ." He scanned the beautifully colorful images. "Am I picking based solely on the artwork or does the movie itself factor in?"

"It's up to you."

"Well, this one here." He pointed at a classically illustrated space scene. "It's so beautiful, with the unfinished space station there. Painted at the beginning of the space age. It could be taken for a modern scene. And the film itself, Xu and I watched it together for the fifth time, at least, right before we set sail for Mars."

"What do you like about it?"

"Are you kidding?"

"No, what do you like about it? I've never really been a fan."

"Oh, you're lying, Susan. I know for a fact that you love that movie as much as I do. You're trying to psychoanalyze me."

"No, I'm just coming clean."

"Well, apart from it having turned out to be a training film for this flight, I had always just loved the majesty of the storyline. The full scope of humanity's destiny and all. The questions as to what makes us human and our relationship with our tools—technology."

"A training film is right, at least Odysseus hasn't tried to take over the ship."

"Yet."

"I like this one." The Doc pointed to a garish clash of beasts amidst crumbling buildings.

"I think that's a Polish movie poster for one of those fun old rubber monster movies."

"I just like the look of it," she said.

"This one is great." He spread his palms against the poster and swept across it, just to touch it. *The human adventure is just beginning.*"

"That's the name of the movie?"

"No, the title is overlapped by another poster, it's just the tagline, but it's a wonderful sentiment."

"Yeah, what's that one about?"

"It's about a lot of things, but I guess it's really about how we bring meaning to our lives."

"You came here for that poster, huh?"

"I suppose I did."

"That's okay, Cal. We all need to lean up against something sometime."

"I'm just crushed, Susan," he admitted. "I don't know what to do."

"You just keep going. You keep doing what it looks like you're supposed to be doing, no matter how crazy this gets."

"I don't know if I can. I'm tired."

"Success is not final, failure is not always fatal, it is the courage to continue that matters."

"Who said that?"

"Winston Churchill."

"A war leader?"

"He wasn't famous because of a war, Cal. He's famous for leadership in the face of adversity. He's still famous after all this time because he was there when his people needed him."

"Is that how we bring meaning to life? Being remembered? If any of us ever get back, we'll certainly have achieved that."

"Is that what it's about?"

"Getting back? Or being remembered?"

"Being remembered. I've been assuming we want to get back."

"Remembered? Fame? Not for me. I never wanted that, I just wanted to *do* things. To be a part of something out of the ordinary and maybe push humanity upwards. I suppose in a sense we're doing that, but why does it feel like an animal struggle to stay alive?"

"I don't know, maybe there are no reasons. But pushing humanity's horizons is what we're living right now, Cal. Of all the people who have ever existed, it's you. It's us. We all did the math on the opportunity to be explorers, to see what no one else had ever seen, that was what we balanced against the risk. Even if this isn't what we bargained for. Even if we all don't survive. That math made sense to all of us. Especially to Xu."

They stared at the posters, moving from one to another, *Forbidden Planet* to *Colossus: The Forbin Project* to *Moon*. As isolated as people's inner thoughts are, there was a hard-won depth of understanding between the two of them. She knew, as well as anyone, how much he was hurting. She knew how tired he must feel from looking at the hollows around his eyes, and she knew how easily he might undermine himself, pushed so close to exhaustion. She knew he felt as though he was running out of gas, but she knew that he wasn't. She knew he was up to the challenge. They all were. They had to be; they might fail but they'd make a fine run at it. What else was there to do?

As close as they were, there was no way for her to communicate this to him. As mentally battered as he was, there was nothing he'd listen to but some tough love.

"That math still makes sense," she said. "And if we do manage to survive, it will be because you did your damn job. Shape up, Cal. Your ship needs you."

He stared at her as if he'd just been slapped.

Forty-Six

"So, you're seriously going to let that thing out?" the pilot asked.

"I am." Without thought, Cal rested his right hand on the holster Velcroed to his hip. "Open the hatch, please."

Paul frowned and turned the dial on his station's touchscreen. The shadow of the circular doorway moved behind the plastic sheeting of the reassembled quarantine tent. It opened, revealing a wide circle of brilliance: illumination pouring out from the *Argo*'s interior. A large shadow appeared within the light and hopped up, birdlike, to perch on the circular rim.

Inside the curtains of the quarantine tent, a tablet had been affixed to a rigid support pole and on that tablet a video began to play: instructional films of the post-EVA disinfectant procedure, from the ship's manuals. The strange shadow inside deftly repeated the actions of removing the handle, dipping it into the solution, and swabbing every nook and cranny of its suit, backpack, and newly fabric-welded hoses. After a few long minutes to allow the solution to fizz and dissolve, the air inside the tent was exchanged and the Doc unzipped the partition.

The alien stepped from the tent and floated into the docking ring, out and among the shirt-sleeved human astronauts. It was very much at home in the null-gravity, moving its legs to balance its movement and rotation so expertly that it no longer looked like a lizard but some kind of cephalopod whose limbs were the equal of the next. The being's strange humped helmet, formed to accommodate the bulging S-curve of its retracted neck, made it appear even more alien than it would have otherwise. Cal floated over, realizing that this was the first time the being would be seeing humans without their space suits. He held his hand up, palm outstretched, and pronounced his name.

The creature pivoted to look at him. "Cullghwin", it said, recognizing him as the same creature it had previously associated with the bright blue space suit. It looked around at the other crew members who each pronounced their names in turn. It attempted to repeat them with varying success. Paul's came out a close "Pohl," whereas "Sarah" was almost entirely unrecognizable, reduced to a streaming hissing sound. It shifted its eyestalks back and forth between each of their faces as if trying to figure out which features to focus on in order to best tell them apart.

Seiss pointed at each, repeated their names, and then made a circular hand gesture as if encompassing them all, hissing, "What isss?"

"It's learning."

"Sesame Street works," Cal said.

"What's it asking?"

"Maybe we should just ask it." The Doc gestured to the alien.

Samuels grinned uneasily. "What do you mean?"

"What isss?" It made another sweeping circular hand gesture.

Cal turned toward Inez and the Doc. "I'm not sure what it's asking. Crew? People?"

It turned, slowly pushing itself along toward the panoramic ring of viewports. It gripped one of the chromed handrails and pivoted its neck and eyestalks around to look back at them and began pointing out the window, down the length of the ship, jabbing excitedly with both a wickedly clawed finger and its dexterous tail. It was pointing at the twin alien booms riding alongside the *Ulysses*'s flanks.

"Isss find?" it asked, eyestalks zipping about beneath its distended helmet dome.

"It's talking about the alien bits?"

"I think so."

Cal addressed it. "It found us."

The lizard-alien stared at him and blinked rapidly, something he had learned to interpret as a lack of comprehension.

He held up his left hand and then drew his right closer and closer until it suddenly grabbed its counterpart. Then he pointed out the window at the giant alien booms. "It found us."

The alien angled its saurian head within its helmet and looked back and forth from the window to Cal until it finally wheezed, "Bhiggg hhhappy," and cocked its head again, pulling closer to the window pane and staring down the ship at the remora-like devices. "Bhiiggg."

Cal and the Doc floated up to bracket the creature, looking out along his view. "They're big, yes."

"Hhhappy."

"It makes you happy?" Cal pointed at the creature. It blinked in rapid succession and drew its eyestalks in. "Hhhappy. You. Cullwighn. You ttok. You." It repeated the circular gesture at them and emptied its air sacs. "Bhhhhiggg hhhappy."

"Apparently, we should be happy about those things?" he asked, referring to the alien booms.

"If that's what it is really trying to say."

"Maybe it has a fundamentally different idea of the meaning of the word *happy*."

"Blame Bert," said Inez.

Cal smiled.

The creature slid its weird humped helmet into his field of view and croaked, "Ssseeeemore?"

"More? More of what? The ship?" He waved his arms around,

gesturing at their local environment. "Or the booms?" He pointed out the window.

Seiss's eyes ping-ponged back and forth between its two choices. "Yesssss."

Forty-Seven

The saurian clearly enjoyed the sensation of gravity as much as the human crew did. As they transited the centrifuge arm and descended into the gravity of Blue Hab, its facial features were able to somehow convey both surprise and pleasure from beneath the distorted helmet. This was not to say it smiled or came anywhere close, but damned if it didn't seem that way from the set of its jaw and the motion of its eyes on their corrugated stalks. Nearing the top level of Blue Hab, the creature released the automatic tender and leapt down in the light gravity, easily absorbing the impact with its great reverse-articulated legs. In gravity, it held its long muscular tail out behind, somewhat rigid, balancing its forward-leaning posture. It would rock over on its hips, adjusting its balance the further it extended that heavy head on its long neck.

Cal landed on the roof next to the alien and gestured at the open hatch. The creature bowed, raised its tail into the air, and craned its neck into the opening before hopping once to the hatch's edge and then quickly down the ladder into the habitat's first floor—the sickbay. The Doc landed on the roof and elbowed her way in front of Cal in order to be the second down and show the alien *her* domain—and to make sure it kept well clear of her lab stations. The saurian bobbed its head around the diagnostic tables and recovery stalls, peering between the beds, pointing at various things, asking "nnname?"

Everyone followed the creature, taking turns answering its questions, whether trite or pointed. Pillow, bed, floor, wall, x-ray machine, gas chromatograph. It stopped at the wall inset with Petri dish-lined incubators but the Doc made sure the creature didn't touch. It moved off, circling around the hatch, down to the next floor and stronger gravity.

As soon as the creature dropped off the ladder, it was struck by the huge inverted triangular windows. It hopped over, great arcing leaps in the one-third gravitation and stared through the windows, watching the motion of the stars reveal the habitat's rotational arc. Cal walked slowly up behind it.

"What's it looking at?" Paul wondered.

"I'm not sure."

Inez crossed her arms over her chest. "It feels wrong to keep calling . . . it, *it*."

"Do we know if it has a gender?" Sarah asked.

The Doc broke off from her observations of the creature as it peered around the limits of the great inverted triangles and out into space. "It removed its suit for Paul to modify, I didn't see any external sexual characteristics that I could identify. Everything is covered over with various sized scales. That doesn't mean it doesn't have a gender. I just can't figure out what it is."

"You didn't investigate?"

She cocked her head and frowned. "You want to poke around in its crotch, go ahead."

Inez followed the alien with her eyes. "Maybe we should ask it?"

"We are communicating with an alien being solely on the strength of it having watched four episodes of Sesame Street. You want to try and discuss gender with it, go ahead. I'll stick with *it* or *Seiss*, for now.

Inez crinkled her nose and frowned, temporarily deterred.

The saurian traced the perimeter of the window with one recurved claw, and asked, "What isss? Nnname."

"Window," Cal replied.

"Wwwwindow." It started to make circles in the air with its claw and then pointed out the window. "What . . . isss nnname?"

Cal looked confused and shrugged his shoulders, momentarily looking back at the rest of the crew and their chorus of shaking heads. No one else was sure what it meant, either. It repeated the circular movement in the air, wind-milling its long, slender arm and clawed hand perpendicular to the surface of the window. "What . . . isss? Sssiiircle?"

"Circle?"

"Well, if it's watching Sesame Street, it certainly knows its shapes."

"What *isss?*"

Cal squinted, confusion feeling like concussion. What did it mean? The creature shook its head. This time, the sentiment was comfortably unmistakable even if it was tinged, clearly, with a sense of disappointment. *Never mind*, it seemed to say. Effective communication would take a long time.

The creature's movements and body language were fascinating; sometimes birdlike, sometimes like a lizard, and sometimes unlike either. Sometimes, it moved like something from the depths of the seas, alien and unfamiliar. It pointed to a table. Cal articulated the word *table* in response.

"This seems to work well enough," said the Doc. "Pointing at things and identifying them. I guess this is how communication between peoples has always begun."

"When you have the luxury of face to face contact, at least."

The creature blinked at all of them, erratically splitting its fascination between the ship and its occupants. It hopped over to Sarah and bobbed up and down with its hips, like a drinking bird novelty toy, to look her over from head to toe. She smiled uncomfortably, grateful that its ridges of teeth were locked inside its helmet.

"Okay, so then, what's the best way to proceed?" Cal asked, looking at Inez.

"Me?"

"Who else? You're the communications officer."

"IT and communications officer. My expertise is technical, I can fix the ship's streaming rate and repair a server. I don't know anything about talking to aliens, I'm not a linguist."

"I know that, but you're our communications officer. Who else am I going to rely on? It's your job, whether you've prepared for it or not. I'm sorry, but you're going to have to figure something out."

She stared at him like a deer in the headlights of an oncoming truck. "All right . . . All right, Cal." Her features twisted into a worried frown as she looked at the alien. "This means I'm going all in on Big Bird."

"Whatever works."

Seiss turned back to the inverted triangles looking out onto space. The walls were angled at a slight concavity, and every fifteen seconds, the flanks of the ship and one alien boom could be seen passing by. The lizard's interest was obvious.

"Isss . . . you?"

"I'm not sure what it's asking, are you?" Cal glanced around the room.

"No idea," said Inez.

"Is it our ship? Is it asking about the alien parts?"

Paul slit his eyes. "Ownership, maybe?"

"I don't know."

The creature and the humans looked at one another, confused.

"Let's keep on with the tour," decided Cal. "Show it how we live, sleep."

"Are we going to show it how we go to the bathroom?"

"I think so," said the Doc. "There's no point in being self-conscious about this, I think it's a good idea. We need to know it's requirements, this is as good a way to start that conversation as any."

"Fine by me, but I'm not looking up the reference video," said Inez.

The Doc walked over to the opposite corner of the room and slid open an accordion door to reveal the extruded fixtures of the variable-G toilet. Inez giggled involuntarily. "This is just crazy."

Cal watched the giant alien lizard tilt its head into the small room, its long tail projecting out in counterbalance. "Yeah, it sure is." He watched the Doc pantomime using the toilet. The creature blinked and extended its eyestalks further than he'd seen before. "Ssseisss has," it said.

"Uh oh."

"Why didn't I think it might need to use the bathroom?" the Doc asked.

Inez looked puzzled. "Does that matter?"

"We can't let it," blurted out the engineer. "We don't even know what that means. Maybe it pees acid? *We* don't know! Is it a solid? *How* solid?"

"I agree, it sounds silly, but we can't put the plumbing at risk."

"Yeah, but when you gotta go, you gotta go."

"To do that, it'll have to break quarantine." The Doc stepped in front of the creature to command its attention. "You'll have to wait. Can you wait?"

It blinked at her, pulling its eyes back. "Bathhhroom. Wait."

She turned to the engineer. "Paul, I'm sorry to ask this but—"

"I'll find a bucket or plastic bin. With a lid."

She smiled and turned back to the alien, which was regarding her quizzically with its transparent cat's eyes. "You wait, okay?"

It cocked its head.

"Let's show it the CM, explain the instruments," Cal suggested.

"That'll distract it for a while. Maybe it will be able to tell us something about where we are."

Forty-Eight

Cal preceded the alien into the CM, gesturing at the consoles, the long vertical science and comms stations to aft, and the sweeps of colored instrumentation that lead toward the nose of the conical section, wrapping around and framing the huge panoramic viewports with light. Cal began a cursory explanation of instrumentation and controls, extending and unfolding the rear-view and display screen and then sending it collapsing back into the heights of the module. Cal watched the star growing larger through the wide windows for a moment. When he looked down, Seiss was examining the panels and displays as if expecting to see something that it did not. It looked up at him. "Whhhere isss?"

"Where is what?"

"Isss control for . . . booms?"

"Control for the booms? We don't have a control for the booms." Cal mimed the capture again. "We don't control it."

Seiss's eyestalks turned in to look at one another. It gave him an impression that the creature was looking for anyone, even itself, to share an incredulous glance with.

After a moment, the creature asked, "Word for sssomeone everything has?"

190

"Someone everything has?" Cal asked.

"Rich," the Doc answered, looking at the alien. "Someone who has everything is rich."

"Isss you yours? Things to *Ulysses* grab. Isss yours, rich."

"Are you saying that if that thing is ours . . ."

"Rich, have lots! Rich! Seisss want rich! Seisss reason look creature-ship. Rich." It looked around at them. "Family live happy."

Sarah looked around at her fellow humans, "Well, that's an unexpected development."

Satisfied at having apparently gotten through to them, the alien picked its head up from the displays and stared out the windows at the approaching world, Circle, and the star blazing away in the far distance. It turned to them, asking, "Where isss?"

"We don't know, we are on our way to the third," Cal held up three fingers. "Third planet of this star system but we don't know where we are."

Seiss looked at him, uncomprehending.

"Exactly, we don't know. We don't know where we are." He shrugged his shoulders and held his hands out, palms up. *We've got nothin'.*

Seiss peered through the CM windows. "ship-creature. Where isss?"

"It's also headed inwards, toward the star."

Seiss spread its arms and then its clawed fingers wide.

"Yes, we think it will unfurl its wings when it gets close to the star."

"Where star two?"

"Star two?"

The alien's eyes shot from face to face. "How many ssstars isss?"

"Just one." Cal held up the requisite number of fingers.

Seiss blinked and pulled its eyestalks in close to its head, an unintelligible set of syllables wheezed out of the being, collapsing its already deflated air sacs. It wheezed more deeply, choking to reinflate. "Not sssame. Two starsss. Sssleep long. Now find place one ssstar. Too long ssssleep."

They didn't know what to say, not immediately contemplating the consequences of its simple statement.

"Too long."

Then it hit them, this was not the solar system the alien had gone to sleep in. Seiss had been in hibernation while the solar-sailer spanned the gulf between at least two star systems—at significantly less than light speed. A long time indeed.

"Fffamily."

The words came from the throat of a being born under sunlight that had touched no earthly flower or entered any human eye. They floated around the creature, unsure of what to do or how it would react. It felt understandable, relatable in human ways, but it was possible they were anthropomorphizing. There was no way to tell what it would do next. Cal lay his hand at his hip, resting it on the antique holster, but the alien just continued to look sad, deflated. After a while, it asked if it could sit by one of the big triangular windows and be alone for a while and although it made them all nervous, Cal allowed it.

Forty-Nine

Cal, Inez, and the Doc accompanied the alien, returning to the *Argo*. The Doc put her hand on its narrow shoulder in a gesture she hoped conveyed empathy. It turned its strange eyes to look at her. As they entered the docking ring, Seiss moved listlessly as it headed for the quarantine tent surrounding the lander's hatch. It hesitated at the entrance to the sheeting, pointing at the spindle hatchway as if to ask permission, and when none of them responded in the negative, it floated over to look in the red, pipe-lined shaft.

"That leads down to our engines and power plant," Cal explained, not knowing what else to say. The creature seemed to notice the infected server, mounted to the inner wall and now surrounded with and cradled by distended nodules that glowed deep within their dark red surfaces.

"Isss?"

They looked at one another, none of them understood.

"Isss? Isss why here?" It craned its bubble-encased head back to look at them. "SeisssSeee? Isss you? Found?" It gestured around in the air, as if to indicate what was beyond their current environments. Cal took this to refer to the remora-like constructions attached to the hull. "Go ssstraight home," it continued. Amusingly, Cal could hear the influence of the children's programming in its developing word choices.

"Use. None can sssee. Everyone want. Not good perssssons take. Sssometimes good persssons take. Go straight home. Yes, no?"

Cal looked around, hoping someone wanted to interject with an interpretation. No one did. "We don't understand. Are you saying we are in danger? Are you asking if we just found the booms," he repeated the creature's wide gestures and then pointed, he hoped, to indicate beyond. "Those?"

Seiss followed his gestures with its eyes.

"Yes, we did. We found it, them. They found us, really. We don't know anything about them. They brought us here." He pointed at the ground.

The creature looked confused. "Never know? Before?"

"About the booms, the alien things?" Cal asked. He took out his ship-phone and swiped through the image library to a photo of the *Ulysses* taken just after the alien objects had attached.

Seiss blinked rapidly and retracted a claw and swiped back to the images of Jupiter with the fleshy fingerpad that resided between one sharp claw. "Giant planetsss? Not know? No one tell how to get—how to get to home sssstreet again?"

"No, we don't know how to get back home." He picked up the tablet, getting excited, and called up video of their descent over Jupiter. This was, after all, just the conversation he had hoped for. "We didn't know about the gas planets. Is it a transport system? Is that what brought us here?"

It made a swirling motion with one claw. "Through circlesss of air—transsssport sssystem. Yesss."

"Storms?"

"Ssstorms. Yesss."

"Then we can just go back in?" Inez wondered.

"No. No, don't know, way home?"

"No," she replied.

194

"We entered the north polar storm complex of a gas planet in our home star system," Cal said, he tapped the face of the tablet where photos of Jupiter sprang into existence.

It cocked its head at them.

"We were unconscious," he explained, closing and reopening his eyes. "Asleep when we got here. We aren't sure what pole we came through." Cal flipped from Jupiter to the yellow gas giant, tapped at either pole, and shrugged his shoulders.

"No. Not sssame," the alien replied.

"What's not the same?"

"Not sssame, not planet."

"We know it's not the same planet, we came through the storm tunnel from the other Jovian, the one in our own home star system that we call Jupiter . . ." The creature shook its helmeted head, as frustrated as Cal with their inability to communicate. "Inez, let's get some more video aid here. If—"

The alien shook its head within its helmet and rattled, cutting him off. "Undersssstand! Come here ssstorm planet. Go back, sssame planet, not back to sssame home!" It waggled its head back and forth. "One in, pole, one out. In to, out not sssame."

Cal thought for a moment, extracting the meaning from the rudiments of its English phrasing. Remonstrating himself for his frustration at the same time: the only word of its language he had managed to learn was the creature's name. "You're saying that one pole is an exit and the other the entrance? And that reentering a storm on the planet that brought us here will take us someplace entirely different?"

It just blinked at him, so he turned to Inez. "Is that what it's saying?

"I think so," said Inez.

Cal glanced to the Doc, who shrugged. "One pole is an exit, and the other an entrance, but the entrance doesn't take you back to the place the exit brought you from?" the Doc said, trying to work it out. "Is that it?

The creature's air-sacs filled as waggled its head as a duck waggles its bill. "Ssstorm planet tunnelsss linked, sssstorm planet to planet ssssstorm," it continued. "Links always sssame but links never sssame planet." It was trying hard to make them understand. Overeager, it said, "In from one, out other. North pole go in, to new planet. Sssouth pole of new planet, come out from travel from other planet. Go back in north pole of new —*Not* go back to first planet, sssouth pole. Go to new, new planet sssouth pole."

The Doc shook her head, trying to sort the creature's words in her head.

"Why?" Cal asked.

"Not know."

"You, Seiss, you don't know?"

"No one know."

"No one knows?"

"No one know, everyone use, no one know. Sssome say know, Seiss not believe. Sssay no one know."

"There are many beings," Cal touched his own chest, and then the creature's and then made what he hoped was another all-encompassing gesture to get across his meaning. "Many beings who use the transport system?"

"Yesss. Many. Many beingsss."

Cal felt like his eyes simultaneously met and held those of every member of his crew at once. He let his thoughts simmer until Samuels interrupted with a question. "So, there's a gas planet out there, somewhere, that links back home, but it's not this one?"

"I think that's what it means."

"Is that gas planet here in this system?" She addressed the alien, asking, "Around this star?"

"Not know. Mosssstly not. Maybe?" it replied.

"Good try, Sarah." Cal turned back to the saurian. "How do you find out where a link goes?" He tapped his finger against the tablet, expanding an image of Jupiter's polar storm. "How do we tell where this goes?"

The alien blinked at him, its eyestalks waved. Cal was certain he hadn't communicated his meaning but then it spoke. "Othersss know, tell. Sssome everyone know, sssome not. Sssometimes explore."

"We don't know how to get home. Home. Do you understand that?"

Seiss cocked its head, lifting its eyestalks high. "Home," it said with a sniff. "Not know how to get to home planet ssstreet, how to get to home planet ssstreet." It seemed satisfied with itself. "Understand."

Cal thought about how to phrase his next question. "Do you know how *we* can know how to get home?"

The creature regarded him. "Sssome can know. Sssome know ways to know."

"Do you know?"

"No. Seiss not know. Seiss not know way to know. Seiss know othersss know way to know."

"Can you help us find these people? These people who know?"

"Can. Danger. Seiss tell before, anyone sssee, want. Good, bad. No—all. Try get. Careful."

"Careful?"

"Ssstranger danger," it hissed.

They all shared eye contact again. Cal stepped over and unzipped the quarantine sheeting. "Get me some toiletries and start the seventy-two-hour clock, I'm not stopping this conversation now." He closed himself and the lizard astronaut inside and sealed the quarantine tent.

Fifty

Seventy-two hours in the *Argo*. Eighty-one hours to Circle orbit. He had timed that pretty well. They took their suits off, slowly. Watching one another. Cal remembered he had brought the revolver in only when he felt its weight as he stripped himself of the pressure garment. He folded it inside the multi-layered material and stored it in one of the lockers hugging the *Argo*'s slanting wall. Time to build trust—and to see if either was infectious.

They regarded one another, for the first time, as being to being. Flesh to flesh. "Seiss," Cal said and nodded to the alien. It moved its eyestalks about and extended its head, vibrating the cobra hood that ran along either side of its muscular neck.

Cal picked up the tablet and loaded up a primer on commonly used English words and phrases. The word *about* appeared on the screen.

"Let's talk."

Fifty-One

Everyone else had left the docking ring, except for the pilot and the engineer. Sarah floated in front of the lander's airlock and watched the two figures drifting inside the sterile interior lights. Paul floated up next to her.

"He's in there talking to the lizard."

She turned to him. "And you think that's a waste of time? You don't think it might know something about this place that we don't?"

"It's not that, but you heard the thing, it's not even *from* this system. It didn't start out here, whatever accident put him on that solar-sailer monster happened in some other solar system, light years away. It has no idea how long it was in suspended animation. And why haven't we found out about its aims yet? What's Cal waiting for? Why is he acting like Xu all of a sudden?"

"You think he's putting too much faith in this alien?"

"I don't know, Sarah. You know the guy. He brought you with him to the *Ulysses*."

"Yeah, I know him. I know him well."

"He doesn't know what he's doing."

"No one would know what they were doing in this situation, Paul. I know it's anathema to you and your idea of spaceflight but, right now, we have to do a little bit of flying by the seats of our pants."

Fifty-Two

Cal woke from a dreamless death-like sleep and pulled the drifting flap of his sleeping bag away from his face. Across the way was his roommate, a giant lizard who was also, seemingly, a pretty nice person. He contemplated whether or not he was anthropomorphizing again. But only for a moment. What did the word mean when faced with an intelligent tool-using non-human? The creature was curled up in a ball, floating but tethered to one of the ship's safety railings by the apparently reflexive grip of its three tail-tips.

Over the previous day, a symphony of odors had developed inside the confines of the lander. The most unpleasant part of the musk, he found, came from his own underarms, but the woodsy leaf-litter smell had to come from the saurian. Or maybe its kitty litter box in the far corner by the pilot's controls. It was probably all of those things combined. Except for his t-shirt, which featured a stink all its own.

The lander reeked, but it was also filled with communication and understanding. The two of them had spent two entire days going through English lessons on video and talking. They'd first watch an educational program, talk about it, and then watch some movie that he selected—mostly from Xu's favorites because he felt it somehow an appropriate tribute, as well as a couple of his own.

The creature found them all fascinating, but Cal wasn't sure it really understood what was happening in any of them. More to the point, after discussion, it became clear that although Seiss understood the plots, it was having trouble understanding or discerning the characters' motivations and choices. The Doc had voiced her opinion, while fully suited and checking their vitals, that its culture was just too different for it to readily understand some of the basic underlying structures that define human life choices. Immediately afterwards, Inez, who had been listening in, mentioned a book by Stanislaw Lem that Xu had recommended. Cal had written down the title in his phone's notepad.

He sat up and dispelled the warm cloud that had formed around him as he slept. The cabin evidently didn't heat evenly; he had never slept in a lander before. It was one more thing that he had first expected to do on the surface of Jupiter's moons.

Seiss was looking out from within his curled limbs. That it was a he, was one of the first personal details that the creature had communicated. At least he thought it had. It was a conclusion Cal had gleaned from the statement, made early on the first day of the quarantine, that Seiss "did not make egg but sometimes sat." In any case, continuing to call Seiss *it* seemed insensitive.

Seiss pulled his head from the ball of limbs and body and withdrew leathery lips to reveal his sharp ranges of teeth. This was what the alien intended as a smile, and was something it had taken to consciously doing in an attempt to put him at ease. Cal himself preferred the being's native shaking of his "cobra's hood."

He pulled a packet of water out of the locker at the head of his sleeping bag, and took a swig to wash the traces of sleep from his mouth. "Breakfast?"

Seiss looked at him with his eyestalks and trumpeted, "Breakfassst!" He always got excited for food. Cal batted a meal ration over to him. The creature was quite adept at pulling open the seal and pressing the button that released the energy stored in the structure of the tray, heating the meal to piping hot in seconds.

"Eggsss," he said happily.

"Eggs," Cal nodded. He was genuinely enjoying the creature's company although there were times he could be frightening. His smallest movements dredged deep-seated reptilian fears up from some sinkhole of genetic memory.

"What to talllk about?"

Cal smiled at the question, it knew what he wanted and was more than happy to provide. It—no, *he*—seemed well aware that they were going to these lengths to keep one another safe, always attempting to be friendly to an extent that occasionally caused his internal warning lights to go off. There was no way, currently, for him to know whether the alien was telling him the truth or just a bunch of lizard bedtime stories. *But why would it lie? What would it have to gain?* He grimaced; his mind wouldn't stop.

"Let's talk about the big picture, okay?"

"Bhiiig pitcher."

"Right." He pulled out the tablet and brought up a crude drawing they had begun working on the night before. Cal was trying to get the lay of the land, as it were, to understand the space that surrounded them. If there were indeed so many species that used the transport system, then assembling some kind of map and gaining some intelligence on these peoples and their areas of influence was of paramount importance.

The image on the screen was of a multitude of spheres of all different shades with little bubbles attached, sub files of notes and information. It was common sense that the first step would be to create a map, but common sense was confounded by the very nature of this new concept of travel between the stars. Almost none of the spherical shapes denoting a claimed territory shared their hues with any other nearby spheres. Because the linking of Jovians seemed to be entirely unrelated to distance, territories were not at all continuous from the perspective of normal space. Additionally, the actual locations in space of many important solar systems were entirely unknown to Seiss, and so Cal just stacked those up in rows around the perimeter of the drawn map.

For someone to claim dominion over a solar system they had to control the routes into the system as well as at least one route out. Meaning that not only did they need to control the system itself but they needed to control the space around the Jovian that contained the *in*, wherever that might be, as well as the space around the one that was the destination of your *out*. After all, it would do no good to control a star system if your ships had no safe way to leave. Given that both of these gates, the *in* and the *out*, were apparently *never* present in the same gas giant . . . it became incredibly complicated to establish dominance over a single star system. Many systems were apparently not controlled by any one faction at all, and as a result, often functioned as great trading ports like a twentieth century Hong Kong. They denoted these systems with a sphere shot through with a rainbow of colors like a soap bubble.

Seiss tapped the screen on one of the soap bubbles. "Here sometimes fights. Wars. Pay toll to enter. Not know, change. Sssleep long. Long." He moved his claw tip to another system and was able to shade it a deep blue without assistance. He tapped it. "This here, know link there."

It was a lot to parse, to take in, to fit into some kind of elusive pattern. He struggled to bend his concepts of space to an entirely new geometry. It began to dawn on him that, in a large sense, where they were in space almost didn't matter. What mattered were the paths to the *in* and *out* links that got you to and from your goal. There was no other way to travel between from one system to another except as a solar-sailer does, taking centuries to cross the gulf between stars. You could walk or take the subway.

He needed a subway map.

Fifty-Three

The gleaming white and chrome shapes that made up the *Ulysses* fell through space, slowing. Turning end over end, the ship aimed its tail at the rapidly approaching planet they were calling Circle.

Inez sat in the command seat next to the *Ulysses*'s pilot as Cal was still in quarantine. The jeweled swath of screens, instruments, and indicator lights arched in front of her and around the forward viewports, which now showed them only the way they had come. The gas giant that contained the portal they had entered through was a blue-green smudge about the size of her thumb in the upper right-hand corner of the view. The main screen was unwrapping itself, lowering into position to show them what was "ahead." Inez patched the feed directly through to Cal in the lander.

It was a planet, appearing about the size of a dinner plate but growing rapidly. As their readings had indicated, it appeared dead. An airless wasteland, possibly harboring resources but what good would that do them? It wasn't possible to land since they weren't even sure what the planet's gravity was as magnetometers couldn't function without the starfinders working. The starfinders could only work if they knew precisely where in space they were, which they didn't. On top of everything, the lander's operational range was limited having only been meant to shuttle back and forth to the low gravity of the Galilean moons.

What they *should* do, what she *wanted* to do and was *sure* Cal probably wanted to do, was twist one of those rods from the derelict and select the next planet inwards toward the star and see if that would provoke a flyby. But they couldn't know what would really happen. It *could* result in something catastrophic. She doubted it, but it was possible. Cal had thought it best, at this point, to wait and see what would happen. Gain more information. Take it slow. Besides, she thought, glancing at the propellant indicators, which had not budged off of full, they could spare the gas.

"Looks like we're slowing down," the pilot said, interrupting her train of thought.

"Cal, did you get that?" Inez asked.

"Slowing down to make orbit?" Cal asked over the comms. "Or slowing down to change the angle at which we slingshot around the planet?"

Inez shot a questioning glance at the pilot, who replied without taking her eyes from the displays. "We'll know when we know. Depends on how long the engine keeps firing."

Quarantined in the lander, Cal went to open the comms channel to engineering and hesitated. This in itself was a bad sign if he was hesitating to ask his engineer anything related to his job. There should be no extraneous thoughts in his mind, in moments like this the crew needed to act as one. All of a sudden that wasn't happening, and he had to fix it before it got worse. They were stuck with one another. Forever, if he couldn't maintain an effective chain of command and possibly even then. They could make all the right moves available to them and still never get home, and they all knew it. Somehow, he had to make them feel otherwise or they would completely fall apart, and that was the reason he was pressing so hard for any shred of progress. He was, arguably, being a little impulsive but without some plausible path forward, he knew they'd come apart at the seams.

He looked at Seiss, who just blinked his weird mostly transparent eyes and then opened the channel to the engineer. "Paul?"

"I'm here, Cal, everything is copacetic." His voice resonated with the echo of the docking ring. This was where he managed the ship's operations whenever the main drive was lit.

"I was thinking, if we can't cut off the weed's access to the engine, how about getting some advance warning of its actions? Can we tell when it is about to start or shut down the drive? Is it accessing certain systems first, is there some activity from or within the weed that always precedes these actions? If so, how much advance warning can we get?"

"I'll do my best to look into it, but I've got a lot on my plate as it is. I could use some help."

Cal hesitated as he pinned down the exact locus of what bothered him about the engineer's response. "We've all got a lot on our plates, Paul. You're just going to have to take on a little more. Whenever anyone has free time, I'll send them down."

Inez listened for the comms line to drop before letting out a deep breath. She turned her attention back to the video screen that was providing their view to stern, otherwise known as *the way they were going*. The screen had fully unfolded, and it impinged upon much of the view through the large windows. The engine kept firing until finally the *Ulysses* dropped into a neat circular orbit around the planet's equator.

"Cal, we're getting radar bounce from something on the surface, highly reflective. Are you guys watching?"

"Bring all scopes to bear, let's see what's down there."

"Roger, Cal." The Doctor was manning Xu's—*the* science station while Inez handled copilot duties. She swiped the tabs that slaved the motion of the various telescopes to the radar results. An image of the planet rolling beneath them lit up on screens all throughout the ship.

"Are you seeing this?"

"Yes."

"An absolutely dead world. Moon-like," the Doc said.

Inez narrated for Cal, as if he wasn't already seeing what she was seeing. "Pitted everywhere by craters. No erosion to wipe them away. But look, look at that!"

There were objects dotting the barren world, sparkling in the stark glare, visible even without the magnification of telescopes. They cast shadows that dripped for miles across the surface.

The Doc gaped. "They're everywhere."

"Those must be what's filling the radar with paint," said the pilot.

"They look like cities," said Inez.

The comms line crackled open, and a window with Paul Arthor's face winked into existence on their secondary screens. "Or factories," he contributed.

"If they're cities or factories, where are the roads?" Cal asked. "These things are all over the place, but there's nothing between them. Nothing connecting them. No highways. No rail lines. No landing strips or pads. Nothing."

"Maybe the occupants could fly?"

"Or maybe, like the derelict, they were built but never occupied?"

"Subterranean transit?"

"What does your friend think, Cal?" asked Paul. Cal searched for any sarcasm and mercifully found none. He tilted the camera and the alien's dinosaurian visage filled the screen like a horror movie jump-scare.

"No," it said.

Cal leaned back into frame. "Get that?"

"Yeah, we got it," Inez said, smiling.

"Lotttsss," the creature hissed.

"Lots? Yes, there are a lot of them."

"What isss?"

"We were hoping you might know."

"Sssorry."

The planet's rotation brought another construction into the path of the *Ulysses*'s primary scope. The "city" appeared to have been struck directly by something. It was cratered to a crescent shape with associated debris spread out in rays from the perimeter.

"Increase mag," Inez said. "Zoom in." They were all quiet as the world swung beneath them, putting the immolated structures on display for them. The skylines of the cities were fairly simple, identical, except here and there where an example had been shattered and the simplicity had collapsed into the complex shapes of ruins.

"It's fallen apart."

As the previous one orbited out of view, the telescope zipped to another installation, showing the same thing. Crumbling towers, disintegrating walls, blasted courtyards similar to the rest. The cities had been built and left to be bombarded by space weather for perhaps millions upon millions of years.

Fifty-Four

Seiss and Cal looked over the feed from the ship's telescopes as they orbited Circle, both of their heads practically moving in unison.

"Do you know anything about this place?"

"Not."

"Have you seen other places that looked like this place?"

"No. Not."

They shifted their attention from the telescope feeds to observe the planet directly. The lander's bottom hatch window was perfectly aligned to give them a glorious view of the terrain scrolling by beneath. The cities, or whatever they were, could be seen only occasionally as pinprick reflections of the sun in the midst of a great plain or huddled up against the rim of some massive crater. Otherwise, Circle really did look just like a larger version of Earth's Moon, so much so that it triggered a pang of recognition and longing.

After a few orbits, incredibly, the novelty of a new world, dead as it was, wore off, and he turned his attention back to his conversations with the saurian.

"You had said you knew what this was?" Cal showed him the tablet with pictures of the twin alien booms attached to *Ulysses*, along with closeups of the red weed's various forms and structures.

"Yesss. Never ssseen in perssson. Pictures. Different but sssame. Very ancient. Very rare. Most dead. Broken."

"What is it? What does it do?"

"Make power. Make protect. Build things. Name thing . . . hard. Not have hoonman words yet. Tell?"

"Sure," Cal replied.

"What isss group alll hoonmans?"

"All of them, everywhere? Our planet is made up of many nations?"

"Nay-chonsss?"

"The set of all humans are made up of smaller sets of humans who live in different areas. We call those groups and territories *nations*."

Seiss closed its eyelids and nearly intertwined its stalks. A sign, Cal had learned, of extreme concentration. It opened its strange eyes. "Yes. Understand. Humans make up nations, we too. Not all same. But all nations are what? Together make, together improve? Together?"

"All nations? Civilization. I think you mean civilization."

"Civilization. Yes. These . . ." It pointed to the alien objects on the tablet screen. "Civilization Engine."

Fifty-Five

In the command module, Inez sailed past the glittering bank of her comms and IT station and into the conical nose, settling into the right-hand command seat next to the pilot.

"How's it going?" she asked, strapping herself in simply to keep from having to counter the inevitable drift caused by tapping screens and throwing switches.

"It's going," the pilot replied. "What's happening with our pet monster?"

"Progress. It's a fast learner and seems very forthcoming. It seems *nice*. We're learning a lot."

"About?"

"A lot of things, it's a little all over the place, but Cal is trying to focus on getting a picture of our situation: where we are, who else might be out here, and what happened to us in the first place."

There was silence for a moment as the both of them watched the desolate beauty of Circle rotate beneath them. Every few seconds, the movement of the planet caused one of the ruined structures populating the surface to throw back a glimmer of the star's unfiltered light. Then the pilot spoke again, asking, "Anything that could lead us to a way home?"

"Maybe."

"What's that mean?"

"Cal didn't want me to say yet, but . . . it seems like we can't go back the way we came. Not exactly."

"That doesn't sound good. Why not?"

"The alien says that the poles of some Jovians have transport systems. One pole is *in* and the other pole is *out*.

"Okay, so what's the issue? I'm guessing that, for some reason, we can't just go back in through the other pole of the Jovian?"

"Right. Not every gas giant has these structures, but each one that does, is linked to *two* others. The opposite pole doesn't take you to the planet you arrived from."

"Why?"

"Seiss says he doesn't know. It's apparently not a scientist. But that's just the way things are. It's how it works. There is apparently an extensive transport network, throughout this part of the galaxy at least, built by an ancient civilization. Seiss's people don't fully understand some of the science associated with it, but they utilize it."

"So, we have to find the gas giant that is linked to Jupiter's other pole?"

"Right. We found the way *out* of our system. Now we have to find the way back *in*."

"How do we do that?"

"That's what Cal's trying to figure out."

There was quiet in the command module again. Inez watched the images and indicators illuminate and flow across the sinuous control panels that swept down in front of her. The planet itself continued to turn through the windows beyond. Cold and dead.

"What if," Inez mused softly, "we don't find a way back?"

"What do you mean?"

"Just . . . The creature said that no one has been to this system in forever, otherwise that derelict station would have been claimed, explored, maybe occupied. Obviously, no one has ever, that we know of, come into *our* solar system. That means that no one has ever found the link in. If no one else found it, how can we?"

"That's not a comforting thought."

"It isn't," said Inez.

"We'll get home. We can't afford to think otherwise."

"We can't?"

"We *can't*," said the pilot. She smiled at Inez, knowing the younger woman was having a moment of doubt. They were all entitled to them. "If it's already hopeless, we might just as well give up, right? We have to focus on the next steps."

"Which are?"

"Well, if this transport system is based around gas giants, my guess is that Cal's going to have us head for the Hot Jupiter in the innermost orbit." She cleared the console in front of her and brought up the schematic they'd been building of the solar system. She watched the planets move on their orbits, the innermost perfectly circular, subsequent orbits becoming more and more elliptical the further the planet was from the star. Inez wasn't up to speed on the latest theories they'd developed about the system, but even she could see that the second planet, dubbed Square, was in near coincidence with Triangle, the Hot Jupiter.

"It looks like we could, maybe should, investigate both worlds?"

"That's what I was thinking. They're so close. Why not?"

"What's it like, Square?"

"That's actually not that hard to figure out," Sarah said. "Although I had a tough time initially. I'm no Xu." She cleared the schematic image of the solar system and brought up images of what looked like a series of multi-hued barcodes.

"These are spectrographs. Figuring out what a planet's atmosphere is like at a distance seems like it would be a difficult thing but, much to my surprise, it turns out to be elegantly simple." She swept the colorful barcodes around the screen. "When light is observed reflecting off an object, that light can be measured to figure out what parts of the spectrum are missing."

"Missing?"

"Yes, missing. When starlight passes through the atmosphere of a planet, the different elements absorb the light rather than allowing it to pass through. Each element only absorbs certain parts of the light spectrum. So, what you get from the light coming out is a specific signature. The missing portions of the spectrum tells us exactly which elements are present in the atmosphere."

"It's that simple?"

"Yeah, that simple. The light spectrum coming from Earth is missing frequencies that correspond to nitrogen, oxygen, and argon because that's what composes our atmosphere. 78 percent nitrogen, 21 percent oxygen and 1 percent or so of argon."

"What about non-visible light?"

"Our spectrographs take that into account as well, reading microwaves and X-rays."

"And you've got spectrographic readings from Square and Triangle?"

"Yes, indeed."

"And what do they say?"

"The spectrographic results of the Hot Jupiter are what you'd expect. Unlike Jupiter, most of the lighter elements have boiled away because of its proximity to the star. As a result, the clouds are made of denser stuff. Silicates mostly, with trace elements of methane, ammonia, hydrogen sulfide. That probably accounts for the deep blue color, reflecting mostly that aspect of the star's light. No rings, no moons. That close to the star, they would have been destroyed long ago. A certain amount of its atmosphere is continually boiling away."

"And the magnetic field?"

"Hard to judge, it's all wrapped up with that of the star, but it's

216

big."

"And the other inner world, Square?"

"Let's take a look," the pilot said. She conjured the telescope and spectrographic controls window and ordered Odysseus to slew them from the Hot Jupiter, across to the smaller rocky planet. Halfway through the process, it stopped and alarm windows flowered open.

"Odysseus is detecting something else . . ."

"Something else?"

"Yes, something is reflecting optical light and radar, something between the orbits of Triangle and Square. Look here, on the time lapse plot." She pointed to a red smear across the image. "Over the last few minutes, the background stars have stayed the same, but this thing moved."

"What is it?"

"It's smaller than a planet, but it's still substantial. It's lighting up like a Christmas tree in infrared."

"What *is* it?"

"I'm trying to center the scopes, hold on." The pilot began to frantically move her fingers across the touchscreen, stabbing out to panels on its periphery, ranging around the instrumentation alongside the large viewport. "What the hell?"

"Do you see something?" Inez asked nervously. What strange new thing was about to tax their collective mental state?

Her fingers flew across the controls.

"Comet?"

"Hold on . . ." The telescopic image exploded onto the main screen between them, ranging and zooming. It was an elongated rod-like shape. Bulging at the front and back. Easily a mile or more in length.

"It's . . ."

"The solar-sailer. It must be headed in close to the star."

Fifty-Six

"Okay," Cal said, hanging upside down from the maneuvering rail encircling the hatch in *Argo*'s ceiling. "So, there are many different species that use the transport system?"

"Many."

"Why aren't there any here? In this system?"

"Not know. Not know this sssystem. Sssailer bring. Thisssystem *in* link isss maybe dangerous? Maybe far away lossst? Seiss know is othersss not have come becaussse derelict not taken."

"Makes sense."

"Much rich."

"This system's *in* link was located at the pole of the largest planet in our home system." Cal followed the trail of thought aloud. "Yet as far as our people know, no one has come *into* our system from a gas giant or anywhere else."

Seiss bobbed its long neck and pulled it back into a great humped curve. "In-road to your sssystem dangerous too, maybe? Undiscovered isss maybe far, far away."

"I hope not," Cal said, thinking of how far from home they already were.

"Better," the creature disagreed.

"Better? Why?"

"Far away, go far. No one follows. No one see. Better for now."

"Why is that?"

"If others know, others follow. If wrong personsss follow . . . Better sssecret until Civilization Engine worksss. Build. Make home ssstrong. Galacticsss can't take from humans."

"I think I get the picture."

"Better humans home unknown. Never tell."

"Don't worry, we have no idea how to get back."

"No figure out?"

"No, we've lost our best brain." He tapped his temple. "Our scientist. He was killed while we were rescuing you."

"Killed." Seiss pulled his eyes closed and dropped his snout for a moment. "Sssorry, Cuhhlllgh."

Cal smiled gently at that. "Thanks, not your fault . . . So, no, we don't know how to get back. You tell us that there are others who can figure it out, but you tell us we shouldn't trust anyone. So, how do we solve this problem?"

"Maybe trusst? If right persson. None Seiss know. Think— maybe some teach *how* to find home? Then *Ulysses* figure out home no one elssse know?"

"All right, I'll buy that. Where do we go?" he asked, but before Seiss began to bleat, he knew the answer: the alien didn't know. They had to get out of this system and into a place where Seiss could reorient himself. To get his bearings within his understanding of the transport system. Stumble across a known road, basically.

"All right, forget I asked. We have to find a way out of this system. I know."

Seiss's cobra frill rippled.

Cal sat up, pulling himself back against his seat to keep from floating away, missing the gravity of the centrifuge. "So, these Civilization Engines, who built them?"

The alien adjusted his own position in space with his prehensile tail. "No one know. Sssome sssay know, Seiss not believe." He made a noise like he was blowing his nose. "Most believe sssomething but everyone not believe same ssstory. Everyone different ssstory tell." His air-sacs fluttered and deflated as the syllable extinguished.

"Can you tell me the story?"

"No believe."

"Can you tell me anyway?"

Seiss shivered. "Onsssse upon a time—"

"Oh, knock it off." Cal chuckled.

Seiss rippled its hood again, horrifyingly baring its teeth. "Sssorry. But true how story start. Old, long time gone. Gone before anyone elsssse awake . . . Not know wordsss, Cuhllwign."

"It's okay, keep going."

He bent his snout, wrinkling his triangular muzzle. "What name, parents' parents?"

"Grandparents?"

"Okay. Grandparentsss come into galaxy, firssst civilization."

"Maybe ancestors would be a better word?"

"No one else awake yet. No one else sssee or know to passs along. Only animalsss."

"Yeah, *ancestors* is the word."

"Grandparentsss live long, gather more knowing than anyone even now."

"I guess you're not going to go with ancestors. Less S's, I get it. Did these Grandparents build the storm links?"

"Think ssso, think figured out. Sssent ships. Living ships to help open links from the other ssside. Jovians always link two others not ssssame, no for reason know, maybe Grandparents. Maybe universe."

"The ships they sent out, they were the solar-sailers?"

"Yes but no. No one really know, think yesss. Sssome think sailers know why links work. Sssome try talk about to ridersss of sailers.

220

Sssome die."

"Riders? Kill? In defense, or . . .?"

"Defenssse. Most think sailers seed ssstars for Grandparents but sailers change in long time since Grandparents gone. Sailers sail for themssselves now."

"They seeded the systems with what? Life?"

"Not think ssso, sailers not sssame as Grandparents. Seed syssstem with things Grandparentsss need. Not othersss. No othersss. Birth Civilization Engine."

"They produced them?"

"Yes, sysssstem to syssstem to open links. First thing, spread seed of machinesss. Long orbit in to star. Long time in to find eating rocksss."

"What do the Civilization Engines do, exactly?"

"Not all known, not even in oldessst found." The creature rubbed his arm. The Doctor had been taking multiple daily blood samples from both of them, for their own good he knew, but his arm hurt as well. Without thinking, he rubbed his own shoulder.

"All do sssame but different," the alien continued. "Seiss never sssee before but to picturesss. Not all people who have ssshare knowing. Things to make isss known with all. Ssstrong protection make isss known with all."

"We saw that capability when it took us through the link."

"Yes, link transport all protection. Any rocket over . . . pull from Jovian?"

"Gravity."

"Gravity, yesss. Any rocket over Jovian gravity yesss. Transport about protect. Power. Enginesss make, build."

Cal pinched the bridge of his nose, trying to make sense of what the creature was saying. "Build what?"

"Everything, stories sssay. See nothing but picturesss. Moviesss. Could be true. Could be not."

"A see-it-with-your-own-eyes kinda guy. I get it my lizard

friend." He smiled.

The alien smiled back, hideous and friendly at the same time.

"Civilization *Engine*, can they function like rockets? Propulsion?"

"Not, no. Never. Why think enginesss to work like rocket?"

"In English." Cal thought about how to explain. "In English, anything that makes something go can be called an engine, so sometimes we call our ship's rocket an *engine*."

Seiss cocked his head, retracting his eyestalks in confusion. "Why call rocket *engine*? Why not call rocket *rocket*? Enginesss make, no? Rocket you say make go in ssspace. Why I learn this language? Language should to call things one name, try not confussse. Seiss do big favor learning Earth Englisssh," He finished the sentence with a clatter like the sound of some woodwind instrument with a broken reed. Laughter.

"You're right, but you didn't bring along your version of Sesame Street."

"True," the alien said, chortling. "Enginesss like *Ulysses* has— very rich. Civilization build. Yoursss. Only one know sssame is ours."

"Ours? You mean your people have one?"

"Seiss has never seen. Found old old timesss, first go to ssstars for Vornssthhhp."

"Vorni—?"

"Seiss people. Not all like Seiss, Vornssthhhp, but many and did find the Engine. Many fight but sssoon build ships. Many to ssstars. Civilization Engine built into travel moon. Grand place Vornssthhp leadersss."

"Your people built one of these things into your Capital City?"

Seiss nodded his head and long neck. "Moving Capital City. Protect field invincible. Power biggest. Fuel in moon. Only Vornssthhhp Capital City travel links to stars."

"A moving city," Cal muttered, unable to avoid contemplating the ramifications of the existence of such a thing.

"Moon city. Civilization Engine inside at core. All matter for

222

Engine. Engine make civilization for Vornssthhp."

"How many worlds do the . . . Vornss—your people control?"

"Ssseventy sssseven," the reptilian replied.

Cal thought about that number for a moment. "Is that a lot?"

Seiss mimicked a shrug. "One of most but not the most. Othersss with many more."

Cal thought about *that* for a while as well. "Why were you on that sailer?"

"Harvessst. Need to, not want to. But try. Seiss gone wrong." He hung his head and said, "Family sssuffer. Must try thingsss would not to try else. Sometimesss, must." His eyestalks pivoted to look Cal in the eye, blinked, and continued. "Most in galaxy, sailers eggsss dead but dead eggsss even worth. Life egg worth rich forever! Life egg birth Civilization Engine, maybe. Change all for Seiss. Thisss sssailer, Seiss to find out rider dead. Easssy."

"You mentioned them earlier. What is a rider?"

"Solar sailer mobile unit isss rider. Growsss inside head. Rider to protect, rider placesss to go sailer cannot. Trade with othersss for sailer. If lose rider, take generationsss to grow again but can."

Cal frowned as he processed that, finally asking, "How did the crash happen?"

The saurian shook its head. "Sailers can move fast sssometimes, change attitude gasss release. Not ready for change direction into path. Crash. Others killed."

"I'm sorry."

"Sssad. Not proud. Seiss family need ssso try." His eyes drooped. This behavior had occurred a number of times, the creature's thoughts would turn to his family and he would become morose. "Not now, no need." The creature turned away, snaking his head toward the wall lockers and fished out a tube of banana paste. Cal waited for him to squeeze the entire contents into his mouth before prodding him back into conversation, "So, what happened to the Grandparents?"

"No one know." His frill wavered as he shrugged his shoulders in a synthesis of a natural gesture and a conscious mimicking of human behavior. "Time ssso long, no one know. Time so big, eat almost all traces. Solar sailers ssstill but changed, because alive. Alive change over time. Over long time very much not sssame."

"Yes, Lizard Darwin." Cal smiled warmly. He was growing fond of the alien and was beginning to shrug off the inherent human aversion to reptilian characteristics. He was quite a handsome creature. There was a pleasing symmetry to the patterning of deep red scales and iridescent green tiger stripes that showed up only in certain lights.

Seiss pulled its head back in confusion. "Darrrrwghin?"

"Sorry, we call that *evolution*." The alien's eyestalks turned in as if to look at one another. "The change of living creatures over time," he continued, "generation to generation. A man named Darwin first suggested it."

"Darrghwin?"

"Never mind." Cal waved him off of the topic. "There's nothing left of them but the solar-sailers? What about our . . . Civilization Engine?"

"Also. Many ssstories, Seiss not believe all. Grandparentsss leave Civilization Engines for Parentsss as gift. Seiss not believe true."

"A gift to the Parents? Who are the Parents?"

"Older peoples; sssome still, sssome gone. Not yet . . . evolution, yes? Not evolution yet when Grandparents go, but first to find Grandparents' thingsss. First to find Transport Sssystem. Some Parents say they Children of Grandparents, most sssay that not true. Seiss not think true. Parents old, Grandparents much much older."

"I think I understand."

"Seiss not believe gift. Seiss think destroyed, otherwise where go? No anywhere ever."

"If there were no other species around but the Grandparents, who would have destroyed them?"

"Seiss not know, fun topic all life talk about. Lotsss guessss. Most sssay Grandparents destroy Grandparenss. Or sailers and Civilization Engines or othersss destroy. Some sssay Grandparents leave. Some sssay flee."

"Flee from what?"

"Children."

Fifty-Seven

Alone in the command module, Sarah opened the private comms channel to Cal, still quarantined within the lander. "I've had Odysseus extrapolate the sailer's orbit from the movements that we've already observed," the pilot said. "It's apparently headed for the super-Jovian, but my guess, given what our lizard friend has said about these things, is that it's probably going to use the gas giant to gain even more velocity as it heads for a slingshot around this system's star."

"Interesting."

"It is. If we accelerate at full, we can catch up to it in less than three days."

Cal's fingers grated against the stubble of his chin. "And the gas giant itself?"

"It's like most of the Hot Jupiters that have been detected from Earth—no rings, no moons, just an incredibly engorged spheroid, flattened at the poles by its rapid spin and orbiting incredibly close to the star. We've detected temperatures upwards of three thousand Fahrenheit on the dayside, dropping to a chilly fifteen hundred degrees on the nightside even though the storms transfer heat all around the globe."

"And at the poles?" he asked, thinking about the possibility of a transport system.

"We don't have an angle on the poles, so I don't have a lot of info for you yet, but I can tell you one thing: the solar radiation hitting the planet at point-blank range is supercharging it's auroras. From what we've seen so far, they can spread across the entire hemispheres to the equator."

"Jesus, they're monsters."

"It's biblical, no doubt. Temperatures are significantly cooler than nearer the equator but still over a thousand degrees. Given such gradients, my guess is that the storm activity should be even greater than at Jupiter's poles."

Cal sat and thought about more appropriate biblical similes, thought better of it, and turned his attention back to the solar-sailer. "We'll catch up to the sailer before we reach the gas giant, yes?"

"Oh, yes, however, we are going to expend quite a bit of fuel both accelerating to catch up to it *and* slowing down enough where we can stay coincident with it. We still need to achieve orbit rather than whipping around the planet like the sailer presumably will."

"Given our previous experience, I'd say we have the fuel to spare."

"I agree, but it's still something to consider. We don't yet have a way to accurately gauge how much fuel in the tanks."

"I've got Paul working on that, among a hundred other things. He thinks our fuel system is somehow connected to additional reservoirs within the alien booms."

"It would be nice to know for sure," she said.

"I agree, nevertheless, during the dive into Jupiter, once we had depleted the reserves in the booms, the gauges started working again. So, we are blind only to a point. How long will we be in exploration range of the sailer?"

"A few days? Maybe more, maybe less. I'm only guessing. I have no idea how much our paths will diverge as we near the planet and the sailer, presumably, cleaves off on its slingshot orbit."

If they could manage enough time to salvage elements from the wreckage of Seiss's ship, who knows what options that might open for them? "Excellent," Cal said. "I'll announce it to the crew when I get out of here." Cal closed the channel.

"Announce?" she asked. "Announce what?"

Fifty-Eight

Cal, shadowed by a human-sized lizard, closed down the lander's systems in preparation for ending the quarantine. That the lizard was a seasoned astronaut was clear from the questions it asked about each component as Cal powered them down. Of particular interest to him were the reasons for each step's place in the order of operations. Cal thought about it for a second and decided to answer the creature's questions as openly as it had appeared to answer his.

Replacing the air handling filters and locking the canisters in place was the last item on his checklist. He sealed the old units in airtight bags and pushed them over toward the hatch. Then they each grabbed a duffel filled with personal items and pushed those in the same direction. The entire contents of Seiss's bag consisted of the tablet that the Doc had given him. The creature had nothing of a personal nature on him aside from his spacesuit. Cal's bag was filled with t-shirts, socks, and underwear. He'd worn the same pair of jeans the entire seventy-two hours.

"I'd like to get back to discussing the Galactics," he said as they converged on the hatch.

"Yessss?"

"You said you don't know who or what we might encounter if we find a link out of here?"

"Yesss. Not know where are now. Where system isss. If link, not know who might be other ssside."

"The solar-sailer couldn't have traveled further than your maximum hibernation time, right?"

The creature contemplated a beat before answering, "Yesss."

"Which is how long?"

"Only know Earth clock. Earthers tell all time like clock?"

By *clock* it certainly meant what it had learned from kid's show lessons on telling time—the sweep of the twelve-hour analog clock. "Kinda. Two clocks would be one *day*. Three hundred and sixty-five days is one *year*. A year is the time it takes Earth to orbit once around our home star."

The creature thought about this for a moment, and as he did, Cal wrenched the hatch handle down and they both passed through and into the quarantine tent, where he began to strip off his clothes. Cal pulled the wand from the disinfectant canister and began mopping himself with the fizzing, dissolving substance when the alien croaked, "Longest known sssleep almost two ten tensss yearsss.

The strangeness of that math prevented him from immediately replying. "All right so, that's . . . Xu said a solar-sailer could maybe achieve seven-tenths of lightspeed after a while. So . . . how many stars are within a radius of one hundred and forty light years around the double-star where you met the sailer?"

Seiss cocked his head, his eyestalks extended and curled subtly in toward one another as it was staring itself down. "Have to think. Yesss. Maybe ssseven, eight."

"That many, huh?"

"Yesss. Wasss hoping maybe one? Then know where are usss?"

"Yeah, exactly."

"Good try," he hissed.

Cal smirked, squeezing his eyes shut and pinching his nose

closed while he mopped his face with the foaming substance. It stung his eyes. The lizard made another clattering sound, pulled his eyestalks in close and soaped up his own triangular head.

"I was hoping you might be able to tell me what cultures we might be likely to first come across." Cal placed the mop into the bucket and reached for the fresh jumpsuit that had been left for him on his bench inside the quarantine tent. He sat and began to pull it on. Seiss turned and his long, balancing tail swept around, Cal ducked as the three-fingered appendage grazed the perimeter of the tent.

"Sssorry."

Cal laughed.

"Not able tell other culturesss for sssure what meet. Could be many. Trying to remember names of sssystems. Not have many link routes remembered. Only know for thingsss our names. Not your names." Seiss held up a modified *Ulysses* jumpsuit. From the size of it, it must have been Paul's. The legs had been cut to allow for the passage of the creature's thick thighs. A large hole had been opened into the seat and a long tail cover, made from the material of both pants legs, had been sewn onto it. Seiss regarded it with curious dissatisfaction and tried it on. When it had zipped up, the jumpsuit hung awkwardly off his sloping shoulders, voluminous sleeves cascading down his arms. His claws peeked out of the jumpsuit's cuffs while his massive thighs had literally ripped the seams of what was left of the pants legs.

"How's it fit?" Cal asked, smiling.

"Good in tail."

Cal reached for the zipper to open the tent and break the quarantine.

"If you had to take a wild guess, which people are we most likely to run into?"

"How long, you to keep talking want?" the lizard asked.

Fifty-Nine

The crew, without their new guest, gathered again in the comfort of Red Lounge. The holographic fire crackled. Snow fell in swirls outside of an imaginary window.

"Okay, folks, I'm not sure if you were listening to the entirety of the Hoonman and Lizard show or not, but I think it's time to talk about where we go from here."

"We were listening," Paul said. "Some of us, but I think I speak for everyone when I say that, I'm not sure I understand what you learned while in there. Not everything, anyway. You two seem to have developed some sense of familiarity."

"I hope so. That was the point. We need intelligence, and he is our best source."

"Where is it now?" Paul asked.

"I asked him to stay in Xu's quarters for the moment. He was fine with that; he likes the posters. He asked for more food, so I gave him a few of the breakfast packages we know he tolerates."

"I see. Did you put a lock on the door?"

"No, but I have Odysseus monitoring. He'll let me know if our guest leaves the room."

Cal stared at his engineer as if to say *anything else?* The man didn't respond, and so he continued, "Apparently what we have attached to the ship is a real rarity. An operational relic of an ancient race we are calling The Grandparents.

"The Grandparents? Are you kidding me?" The pilot laughed.

"What do you want from me? It's learned our language primarily through Sesame Street."

"The Grandparents are a near-legendary people. Every spacefaring civilization, and that's another thing, folks—there are a lot of those—has a different story about who these Grandparents were, what they were doing, and what the remaining artifacts of their civilization actually *are*. It is widely believed, however, that the solar-sailer creatures and the few other installations and artifacts that have been discovered are damaged, or *evolved*, elements of an ancient system designed to spread the civilization of the Grandparents across the galaxy. And the thing, or things, attached to our ship are apparently one of them."

"I am sick of saying this," said the Doc, "but we need to agree on some names for all this stuff. We're talking about absolutely earth-shattering events with names picked for us by a being whose only knowledge of English was gleaned from watching three seasons of Sesame Street."

"I think that's a minor point right now," said Cal.

"Maybe," she said. "But I'm looking forward to dealing with minor points like they're major ones. An agreed upon set of names would make discussions like this and those to come easier, it would make notes and reports clearer, etcetera . . ."

"Point taken. Soon."

Pilot Samuels steered the discussion back on course, by saying, "So, the thing that's attached to us?"

"The rarest of the rare. He calls it a *Civilization Engine*. Apparently, his people have had one for hundreds of thousands of years, having found it in their solar system as we found ours. Over generations, they've apparently used it to advance their culture. It forms the core of their capital which is, if this is to be believed, a giant space complex and capital city that they move from system to system. It reportedly has a vast array of capabilities, especially in the realm of construction, and also sports an extraordinarily powerful EM field generator from which Seiss's people have derived their protective ship technologies. In fact, the production of starships based on ancient technology is apparently one of his people's major industries."

"So, what was he doing, trying to get rich looking for solar-sailer eggs?"

"He said his family isn't in the spaceship making business."

"Ah."

"What kind of construction capabilities?"

"I'm not sure yet, but we've seen evidence of this with our version, the way it has been able to grow and reformat itself. Perhaps, given additional resources, it can do more. It's obviously something we are going to want to investigate further."

"Obviously."

"So why is there no one else here? In this system?

"Seiss thinks it's possibly that the only link into this system might be from our Jupiter—otherwise, the derelict would have been claimed by someone, studied, revered, or whatever. If there were any other ways in, the odds are that it would have already been found. Our own system has apparently also remained undiscovered since the time of the Grandparents, I'm still unclear of how long ago that was, but let's say it was an even longer time ago."

"Wait? Our system *was* discovered? How's that?"

"Seiss said that our system would have to have been visited by a solar-sailer, there would be no other way for a Civ Engine to have gotten there. By the same token, something had to have engineered the atmospherics of Jupiter, unless it's a naturally occurring phenomena. Who *knows?* It's so far beyond me. Seiss doesn't know much more about how it all works than I do. We could really use Xu's help right now."

The room fell quiet except for the crackle of fake logs and the soft call of a winter wind that never existed.

"Well, if you ask me, we're finally headed in the right direction," Sarah said.

"The only right direction is the one that leads us home," the engineer said. "We don't know this is that."

"We don't know it isn't. We don't—"

Cal interrupted to prevent the engineer from voicing a contagious litany of fears. "Now here's the thing. There was apparently only one way in here, to this system—the link from Jupiter. There may be other links out, but that would mean there would need to be other ways in. They're always paired. The fact that no one has apparently discovered this system could mean that the only way out is through the opposite pole of the Jovian we entered."

Sarah looked at him with one eye. "And from what Seiss has said about the rules of this transport system—"

"Right. That's the one link in the galaxy that we can be assured will *not* bring us home."

"So, what are we going to do?" asked the Doc.

"Well, it doesn't mean there *aren't* other ways out. There could be other in-roads to this solar system that haven't been discovered for one reason or another."

"Like what?"

"Seiss says in-roads could themselves be isolated by distance or perhaps located in systems bathed in hard radiation or other effects that makes them difficult to navigate for most species."

"So, how does that help us, if they are impossible to navigate?"

"Seiss says that although almost all EM and shielding technology in the known cultures is based on ancient technology, the original devices have never been equaled. They're better. Much better. We can apparently survive where others fear to tread."

236

"So, what now?"

"Now we go looking for another way out. Since we're already headed in-system, our destination should obviously be that Hot Jupiter. The issue is that Seiss himself has no idea where we are and so has no idea where any links might take us."

"Does Seiss know how to activate the transport system?" Sarah asked.

"On his ship, apparently, he knew how to initiate the process. He has never personally seen actual ancient technology before, outside of video or photos or holograms. He has seen the solar-sailer, obviously, although apparently just that one. If the stories are to be believed, the sailers are the most common remnant of what was once a widely spread technosphere. Not really remnants, more like descendants. To hear tell, they have evolved to become an entirely independent and self-sufficient species, so who knows how far they are from their original form. Of other artifacts and entities, he only knows legends. Many of which conflict."

"It's a good story, anyway," said Inez. "This solar-sailer did look like it was interested in the derelict, did it not?"

"Well what this makes it obvious to me," Paul said, frustration bubbling in his voice, "is that our next stop shouldn't be square or triangle—we should try and catch up to the sailer and salvage whatever we can from the alien's ship."

"Agreed."

"Agreed."

"Agreed," said Cal. *Victory*. A plan always went over best when the crew thought they'd come up with it themselves. That Paul was the one to articulate it made the victory even more satisfying. He allowed himself a deep breath.

"The sailer's course and ours should coincide for a while. That's our window for attempting any salvage."

"Does Seiss have any idea why this Civ Engine took us here in the first place?" Paul asked, after a moment.

"Not one damn bit."

Sixty

They dropped through the centrifuge arm, falling out of its gravitation. "I think we're going to need to twist the rod," Cal said.

Sarah choked back a laugh. Inez smiled.

"The Doc's right, we need that meeting on what to call stuff."

Cal and Sarah sailed out of the centrifuge and headed for the command module while Inez split off to head toward the infected server's location in the spindle. Cal stopped her. "You can access that thing from anywhere, maybe it's about time you try it from your station in the CM?"

Inez glanced down the ship's spinal corridor and then followed them. It felt strange, to drop back into her comms seat in the relatively roomier circular rear of the CM. So much had happened since the last time she had performed her job from the intended spot. She folded out her chair, and a multitude of touchscreens opened for her like flowers to the sun.

"So," Cal said, "we're agreed that turning the positioning of the rod to Triangle in order to follow the sailer is the best way to proceed?"

"I think so, Cal," the pilot said, "but predicting the behavior of these devices is a crapshoot at best."

"We know that."

"At *best*."

"All right." Cal went on, "If past behavior is any guide, we should have control of our speed and positioning within the flight corridor it prescribes.

"We'd better."

Subsequent analysis of the sailer's course has it on a slingshot orbit around the Jovian. We should be able to catch up to it in days."

"Which is what I said earlier."

Cal sneered at the pilot, and she gave him a friendly stink-eye as he turned to address the comms officer.

"Inez, load an image of the rod positioned to Triangle."

"Sending the image to the server's loading space now, Cal."

There was a crackle that was more felt than heard, and then indicators across the command module began to go wild in a pattern that was becoming familiar. Paul Arthor's voice crackled over the speakers. "Here it *goes*!"

Icons for the main engine components began to flash across their consoles and displays: propellant injectors, RF generators, helicon coupler, superconducting array, ion cyclotron, and magnetic confinement, all blinking over to green. It was like watching fireworks or the visual spasms of a really good pinball machine.

"Reactor output?"

"358 megawatts at 69 percent efficiency," replied the ship's AI.

The RCS thrusters blared flame as a massive shudder ran up and down the length of the ship. The main engine had ignited. Cal nervously clasped his fingers over the blue dome of his helmet, ready to pull it over his head. "Are we at the point where we can confirm whether we're on course to the Hot Jupiter or not?"

"Getting there, Cal. 81 percent probability according to Odysseus," the pilot replied.

"I'll take that." He nodded back to her. "Let's see if we've got the control over our acceleration that we hope we do."

The pilot loosened up her harness and pulled her command screen closer, gliding her slender digits over the familiar UI discs representing the ship's three axes and the thrust slider—a big yellow tab that turned red under her touch. She pushed it forward and the engine throttled up fluidly.

"Looking good, Cap. Thrust to 70 percent. We're gaining on the sailer."

"How long till we're in range?"

"Four days, nineteen hours," Sarah said.

"And at 80 percent?"

She flicked her fingertips across a side screen. "Three days, six hours."

"Increase thrust to 80 percent."

"Roger." She slid the tab up another ten notches and the engine responded with a suite of satisfying vibrations. "80 percent."

"Calculate turnaround point for braking," he said.

"Roger, Cal."

"Get the scopes focused on the sailer and meet me in Astronomy. I'm going to get the lizard." Cal popped out of the command seat and propelled himself through the CM, out the rear hatch, and into the *Ulysses*'s spinal corridor.

Sixty-One

"Pivoting the high res telescope," the Doc announced from what she still regarded as—and would forever think of—as Xu's chair. She was behind the desk in the ship's main science lab where their most advanced, and bulkiest, scientific equipment lived. She had her own laboratory in Blue Hab, outfitted for the biological sciences—her own area of specialty. That was home. Here, she was in unfamiliar territory, but of course, they were all lost in unfamiliar territory. She needed to get used to it.

She was the second-ranking non-astronomer aboard. Inez, the ship's first-ranked non-astronomer hovered to her right, holding a tablet and reading from the ship's instruction manual.

"That's not it, tab over to HRI. You're on the MRI, and that'll only get you six feet per pixel at a thousand miles."

"But that's the one that's locked onto the sailer," the Doc protested. Inez shrugged.

The pilot watched, leaning against the curved plastic housing of the lab's electron microscope. Bored. "This is what I get for complaining about being stuck in the CM," she said.

"Odysseus?" the Doc asked to invoke the AI. "Is there a way to transfer the positioning data between the telescopes?"

"Yes, Doctor," the ubiquitous machine intelligence replied. "Touch the title bar of the coordinates you wish to copy and hold. The values will flash indicating they have been copied. Touch the tab for the instrument you wish to retarget and repeat the same procedure, holding down two fingers this time. The values should appear in the proper fields. If not, I can do it for you."

"Let's skip to the part where you just do it for me."

Inez smiled.

"Yes, Doctor. You wish to transfer the tracking data from the medium resolution telescope?"

"Yes. To the high res." The Doc rolled her eyes.

"Aiming telescope. Imaging data processing to main screen."

There it was, a shape resolving across the wall behind the desk, becoming more and more refined, more detailed with each processed sweep of data. The form of the sailer, wings still curled tight around its flanks like a flower waiting to blossom.

Cal climbed down the ladder into the science lab followed by the saurian. He slowed, dropping into a seat beside a small work table, eyes locked on the resolving image of the solar-sailer. Seiss seemed struck by the visual as well. It occurred to Cal that the being wouldn't have seen such a view of the ship-creature since his crash.

"Can we get an image of the impact site?" he asked.

"I'm not sure which surface we are looking at, but this is what we've got at the moment."

Cal thought about that, unless it had some other methods of heat regulation and distribution, it would need to turn like a pig on a spit in order to manage the thermal effects of starlight on its surface.

"Is it rotating?"

"Yes, around its long axis, but very slowly," Sarah replied.

"We could launch a camera swarm."

"How long till that would give us significantly better imagery than what we're getting here?"

"They're unpowered, so they aren't that quick. At least a day and a half."

"That's not much of a gain. The sooner we get a look at the crash site, the better our friend here should be able to tell us whether his equipment might have survived in salvageable condition."

"We never expected to have to image a powered object moving away from us."

"Fair point."

"What about a feeler probe?"

"Those are in short supply."

"How quick would it start sending us useful info?"

"If we expended all its fuel to fling it ahead, we'd have significantly better imagery in . . ." Sarah did the calculations in her head. "Eight hours."

"Launch it."

Sixty-Two

Paul Arthor was in the lander, taking a last look around. Replacing anything that had been depleted during its last use and subsequent service in quarantine. They needed *Argo* ready for runs back and forth to the solar-sailer.

The interior of the lander's pressure vessel was generally conical, but there were still corners where fixtures or equipment intruded into the space. In one of those corners, stuffed into a small compartment used to store replacement filters for the air handling system, was a coiled and folded shape. The engineer pulled on a work glove and reached inside, past various packaged air filters, and pulled the folded material out where he could get a good look at it. It looked like a part of the lizard's caul—the skin it had been hibernating within. Paul turned it around, examining it in the bright interior lighting. It had been in there for days and days but had retained quite a bit of moisture, dusty and brittle on the outside but the opposite on the tattered and folded interior. Slime dripped from it like snot from a kid's nose. As the thick mucus slid off onto the deck, Paul could better see a meandering iridescent pattern: a geometric webwork resembling circuitry. Bio-electric lights phased almost imperceptibly within the jellied flesh of the thing.

He laid the quivering mess down and let his work glove slide off with it, abandoning both to the deck, and pulled out his ship phone. He would report this immediately to Cal but found himself connecting with the ship's pilot instead. "Sarah, are you alone?"

Sixty-Three

"I am not," Sarah said quietly into the private comms channel that the engineer had opened. She took a few steps back inside the lab, just to increase the distance between her and her compatriots, although they likely wouldn't have noticed, anyway. They were absorbed by the constantly updating telescope imagery.

"Can you get away? I've found something in the lander, and I'm not sure if it's a problem or not."

"I can't. Talk to Cal."

"I thought maybe I might talk to you about it first. It concerns the lizard."

She hushed her voice even further. "Talk to Cal, Paul."

"I'm not sure Cal will listen."

She dropped her voice to even quieter levels, to a near whisper. "Since when has he not listened to anything any member of his crew has said?"

Silence. She looked around to see if anyone had noticed her conversation. Further details of the solar-sailer had resolved on-screen, so the answer was mercifully negative.

"Talk to the captain, Paul." She clicked the side tab on her ship-phone to end the comms call.

Sixty-Four

The *Ulysses*'s telescopes, as was their function, reached out from the spaceship—no, *star*ship—to render what was far, close. She was reminded that only a few dozen generations ago, human beings once hailed such devices as miracles and feared them as witchcraft. At that moment, the scope might as well have been an instrument of evil, given the visions of shock, horror, and dread it spooled out onto the screen.

"Magnify." Inez reached out and swirled her finger around the tail end of the sailer. It was as if their viewpoint leapt inwards, the magnification rushed in on them. Standing on the vast concave tail of the sailer, as if it were alone in the center of an empty sports stadium, was the cobalt blue figure. It seemed to shine from within, or perhaps it was just the laser-focused attention that the shape demanded of their minds.

"It's . . ."

"What is it doing?"

"It's *looking at us,*" the Doctor said, her words coming out like a shriek.

"I think it's . . . an optical illusion," Sarah said slowly, as if the words just weren't rising from her throat quickly enough. "It can't be looking at us. Can it?"

To Cal, the border of the display screen seemed to lose its cohesiveness, and the images themselves bled out into the room. It was looking at them. Across all that distance, it could see them. Somehow. Another raft of images began to churn onto the screen, sharpening and resolving as the computer folded pass after pass of data into the details. The monster's arms swept from its sides to fan up over its head, meeting and crossing one another.

"Is it . . .?"

"It's waving."

"No."

"It is, it's waving."

"What the fuck?"

Why . . . would it be waving?" Inez turned to Cal. "It's bizarre."

Perverse.

It was waving an arm over the head; a long-distance wave. The same, desperately basic movements he himself had fruitlessly tried in an attempt to communicate with the unidentified object as they approached Jupiter. It was waving. Taunting. No doubt, Xu would caution him about ascribing human emotions, forcing him to examine his human biases. Cal might have taken heed, but Xu was dead, and this thing had killed him. Advice from ghosts? He was not in the mood.

"It's like it's saying, hey, you guys. Hurry up so I can kill the rest of you." He shot the pilot a dirty look and her sarcastic tone melted away. "Sorry, Cal."

That murdering *thing* was literally standing between them and their best shot at finding a way home. Suddenly, the image of Seiss's shattered spacecraft burned through him. He could see it in his mind. He had been right *there*, he had touched it, and then . . . Then the monster had come. No hyperbole, no fantasy stories. A real monster.

Seiss snaked his thick neck around and brought his head into Cal's field of vision. The creature blinked his weird eyes at him. He shifted his attention to the reptilian creature. Hopefully, they'd found more than just monsters out here.

Sixty-Five

The *Ulysses* barnstormed past the planet designated Square, using its gravity to fling them even more rapidly toward the gigantic gas planet and, more importantly, toward the solar-sailer, now less than a day ahead of them. Square, an entire new world, was largely ignored by the exploratory spaceship, rating only the attention of its medium res scope as it flew by. The planet was a glowing ball bathed in bluish-greenish hues. Spectrographs indicated high concentrations of both nitrogen and oxygen. Xu would have demanded the high res be brought to bear. He would have been hard at work poring over mass and density calculations. It could very well be an earth-like world filled with wonders, but Xu was gone and frankly, at that moment, Cal didn't care. He sat strapped into the CM and awaited the braking burn. There would be time for that later. *Hopefully*.

Sarah was, as always, in the seat to his left. The Doc had assumed what was once a fairly common posture for her, floating between the two command chairs, offering her counsel and reveling in the experience. Xu would have been further behind, tempering her persuasiveness. It had been a comfortable and useful dynamic; things had worked well. *Past tense.*

The *Ulysses*'s drive flame had cut out. The ship was nearing the turnaround point where they would position to fire against their direction of travel. The resulting, and fairly rapid deceleration, would bring them close to the sailer and keep them there as long as possible. He wanted maximum time for salvage as anything done in a rush was twice as risky, but now there was the blue thing to contend with. *What did it want? How could they defend themselves against it?* In the log, he recorded, *Are there any prophylactic measures to be taken?* In case anyone ever read it, he wanted to be clear that he was not acting on emotion. This was pure pragmatism. It was a clear danger to the salvage operation. He would kill the blue thing if he could and try not to enjoy it.

They swung by the planet—a little off-blue disc lost in the stardust darkness beyond the CM windows. Magnified views swept across the screen, but the curving console in front of him displayed only the solar-sailer, revealed by the flyby of the feeler probe. The embedded spheres riddling the flanks of the tail glowed more brightly than before, the furled wings rippled in place, not yet unfurling but seemingly ready. A detail of the head of the sailer was front and center, focused on the site where the reptilian's ship had crashed. At the tail, the blue figure had vanished. Cal drummed on his console. Of course, it had.

"I think you're right, Doc."

"Right about what?"

"We need to start naming things." He pulled up a previous strip of imagery. The blue figure, waving. "Let's start with *that*."

"Cyclops?"

"The *Ulysses* thing, huh?"

"It fits."

"I was focusing on its color. What was that cyclops's name?"

"Polyphemus."

"There might be more than just one of those things. We should stick to the Greek tradition. Cyclops as the type, Polyphemus as—"

"*That*," Cal interrupted, mercifully. Polyphemus. As good a name as any, although he'd have been equally fine with *Blue* or *Cobalt*. He just needed a name to focus his hate. *It killed him, right in front of his eyes. Ate him. Ate him to nothing.* Polyphemus.

"Anything seem different about it to you?" he asked them.

The pilot leaned in closer to the image while at the same time expanding its magnification with the skittering of her fingertips. "No, I . . . Maybe. I think it might be emitting light. Yes?"

"That's what I thought," Cal replied.

"It's some kind of glow. What the hell *is* that thing?" the Doc asked.

"I was going to ask the same question," Sarah said, never taking her eyes off her HUD.

Sixty-Six

The *Ulysses* pitched around and vibrated under heavy braking thrust. Sarah gave it far more throttle than during acceleration, slowing rapidly and imparting a temporary gravitation to the entire vessel. All of a sudden, the ship had become a giant tower, a pillar with the command module as its tip. Hatchways were sealed to prevent an accidental fall down the spinal corridor-turned-pit, a well deep as the Washington Monument was tall.

Paul was waiting in Engineering Ring's work lab, where the normally zero-G environment was a benefit to mechanical work and the 3D printers he had been using. In the absence of gravity, structures could be inscribed into thin air. The printers were problematic to use while under thrust, but they could rapidly churn out parts, complete assemblies and even foodstuffs given the right raw materials. Normally when under thrust these chambers would be unoccupied. Nothing was normal anymore.

Cal climbed carefully down the vermillion shaft they called the spindle. He tried not to look down and just hold tight to the ladder. He knew his ship well; he was hundreds of feet above what would feel like the floor if he should fall and hit it.

Paul watched his captain descend through the open hatch,

calling up to him as he got close, "Despite everything, the ship is healthy."

"That's good news."

"But things are starting to get a little wonky," the ship's engineer said.

"How so?"

"RF generator one is slow to start for some reason and reactor output efficiency is down slightly, to 69 percent. I'm not worried, but I'd like the time, sooner rather than later, to be able to dig in and figure it out.

"I'll do my best to keep things quiet," Cal responded, "but —"

"Yeah." The engineer ran a large hand over the dome of his shaved head as Cal eyed a row of three rifle-like shapes. They were laying on a worktable but because of the current direction of gravity's pull it appeared that they hung from some kind of wall display, secured with Velcro straps to keep them from spilling off toward the stern.

"What about the alien device I found hidden in the lander?"

"Device? As far as I know it's just an extra piece of the cocoon that didn't get collected. The rest is in isolation."

"The Doc examined it?" the engineer asked. "She's not concerned?"

"Not that I know of, should she be?"

"It's not organic, not completely. Did the other sections have circuitry embedded within them?"

"There were a few wires that ran throughout, yes."

"But not like this?"

"No, not like this," Cal admitted.

"And this was the only bit hidden."

Paul didn't phrase it as a question, but Cal treated it as such. "Hidden? Maybe. I'll ask Seiss about it."

"It was still holding a charge, possibly still operating."

"I'll investigate it." Cal thought for a moment, then added, "and if you are up for it, I know you're overloaded, but I would love for *you* to take a look at it. See if you can figure out *anything* at all that might help us verify the lizard's story, especially in advance of the salvage."

Paul hesitated.

"And thanks for bringing this to my attention."

Cal loped across the ring, pushing off against the wall that now, thanks to the ship's engine output, would most comfortably be used as a floor, for a little while at least. He stopped in front of the table with the weapons on it. "Where did these come from?"

Paul made some adjustments to his measure of the man before opening his mouth. "You asked me to try and come up with something that might be useful against the blue *thing*."

"Polyphemus."

"Doesn't exactly roll off the tongue, does it?"

"It's what it is, what have you got for us?"

The engineer pulled the first of a series of clumsy carbine-like gun shapes off the table. It was a mix of plastic and metal.

"Where did these come from?"

"I made them."

"No shit?"

"No shit. The stocks and frames, triggers and hammers are 3D printed, the actual functioning mechanisms are gas-powered piton launchers I repurposed from the *Argo*'s landing legs."

Cal regarded the devices with satisfaction. "Paul, that's fantastic."

He held up a long spike-shaped projectile. "Two different kinds of ammo can be loaded; the normal piton spike, which should be quite nasty but against that thing, who knows." He placed the first projectile onto the Velcro and handled a second, its end a cluster of what looked like rubber balls and folded plastic. "And this, a weighted tarpaulin launcher based on Xu's improvised attack, which was pretty effective, to be honest."

"Not effective enough."

"Sorry." He secured the projectile back up against the table. "I didn't mean anything by that."

"Tell me about the tarp launcher."

"Right. I've modified it to add weighted extensions which should wrap the tarp around the target and tangle, trapping it. I've only been able to make one of those so far, but I'm trying to have more ready before we arrive."

Cal pulled one from the vertical tabletop. The metal's gleam was swallowed by the sickly color of the printed plastics. "Careful with them," Paul said. "They're not loaded right now, but you literally can't be too careful with a weapon. The gas cylinder alone can pack a punch." They passed them back and forth, and Cal inspected each with interest, and then replaced them. "Sad to report that these are all single-shot weapons. They can be reloaded, so don't discard them if you don't have to, but I haven't had time to come up with a feasible method to reload in the field."

"These are great, Paul."

"I'll ask you to familiarize everyone with this new equipment before rendezvous."

"No problem, Cal. You going to stick with your wheel gun?"

"Yeah, I am. Sticking with the devil I know."

Sixty-Seven

"Our orbit will be coincident with the sailer for at least a few days," Cal said to the crew, and one giant lizard in a jumpsuit, assembled in Red Hab's lounge. "In light of sighting the cyclops creature, I want this operation to be as fast and as safe as possible, limiting our risk of exposure to attack."

As was expected for this sort of thing, Cal had a sketch of the situation displayed on the lounge's video wall, visualizing the elements of the plan for discussion. The imagery replaced the fireplace but not its crackling audio cues. "We are going to drop down as close as possible in the lander and deploy to the skin of the solar-sailer. We'll bring the *Argo* down next to the crash site but clear of the debris path. With Seiss directing, we will salvage as much as we can as quickly as we can and return to the *Ulysses,* which will stay at a safe distance. 250 miles at least, so that any attempt by the creature to cross will be detected. Afterwards, we'll assess the reclaimed items and make a follow-up landing if necessary."

He scanned the faces of his crew, seeking out the flickering gaze or minute twitch that would indicate a faltering of their confidence or an issue with the plan. Mercifully, he came up empty.

"Which brings us to the cyclops. It's out there, but where? That interior chamber, where the, whatever that was, was gestating?" Cal turned to their alien guest.

The lizard hissed and emptied his air sacs with the noise. "Rrriderrr."

"Right. In the last twelve hours we haven't been able to spot it anywhere on the solar-sailer's exterior. Maybe it's hiding in that rider chamber?

"Posssible. Very good place. Place I went. Also maybe othersss places too. Was to try tail too, if not. Place to grow there." The creature was making remarkable progress learning their language and losing his hissing accent, but many of his sentences still vanished into fogbanks of incomprehension.

"You said the rider was a mobile unit, a sub-entity?"

"En-tity?"

Cal waved his hands in front of his face as if trying to erase the confusion caused by his use of too many words yet unknown to the creature. He tried again. "The riders are capable of traveling and communicating with others?"

"Yes, riders part of sailer but also alone. Can communicate. Simple barter terms. Never more, many try."

"Where do they do this bartering?"

"Wherever others live. Planets, stationsss, ssships, asssteroidsss. Sssailers communicate radio when want. But not unlesss want." When the saurian got excited, the sounds emanating from his air sacs as they inflated and deflated blended into a warbling hiss that still turned his voice into a caricature of an earthly lizard.

It was obvious that the solar-sailers were not designed to enter a planetary atmosphere. "How do the riders get to the surface?"

"They not truly . . . of mind aware? Word?"

"Word for awareness," the Doc said. "Of one's mind? Sentient?"

"Yeah," Cal agreed. "Sentient."

"Yesss. Riders not have true sentient. One dies, exact same

regrown, reborn. So, matter transport okay."

"Matter transport?"

"Yes, matter break apart quantum-level, encoded over EM waves. Transmit? Yes." Seiss bobbed his head on his extended neck. "Transmit. Like shield but not. Grandparents' technology."

"The sailer's have this capability? Matter transportation?"

"Yes."

"All solar-sailers?"

"Yes, internal chamber. Seiss can show when sssalvage go."

"Make sure you do. I'll be very interested to see that," Cal said.

"Me too," said the Doc, her voice tinctured with a deepening anxiety.

Sixty-Eight

The situation was clear in everyone's mind. They and the solar-sailer were each on great elliptical arcs that would coincide for a brief time. The twin trajectories would bring both vehicles close to the Hot Jupiter called Triangle, the massive blunt-poled azure gas giant orbiting closer to its star than Mercury to Earth's. Given their course, the Jovian's gravity would grab hold, capturing the Earth ship and pulling it into its gravitational domain. A few blasts from the *Ulysses*'s main engine would keep them there. The sailer, presumably, would continue along, falling as close to the star as it could in order to whip around and unfurl its giant sails. Riding the pressure of light itself on a decades, or centuries, long journey between stars.

Although they were catching up to it, it seemed as if it was rushing toward them. Outside the forward viewports and on their screens, a deep-sea leviathan slipped out of the inky darkness, growing from a tiny fleck to an unimaginably huge creature—by all accounts a living being—speeding toward them.

After traveling all that distance, they were aligned nearly perfectly for an approach and flyover. Sarah brought the ship in expertly, coming in exactly fifty miles from the solar-sailer for a first reconnaissance pass. Cal nodded a compliment to the pilot. The Doc manned the science station, adjusting its petal-like additional screens. Inez was strapped into her comms position with a new addition to her setup: the tablet she had been using to communicate with the infected server's interface. It had been attached by a flexible stalk to the rear of her IT systems screen.

"Doc, I actually *like* the name Polyphemus. The Greek myth thing is cool. We need a name for the server, too. The one we talk to the weed through. I keep calling it *the server* in my head. It's not very descriptive. How about the *Oracle*?"

"Fine by me," the Doc said with a faraway stare. At the moment, all she was concerned with was determining which of the unfamiliar science instruments to use when, and what indicators to pay the most attention to. She was coming to grips with the idea of letting Odysseus do most of it while she watched and tried to figure it all out.

The Earth ship swept in closer, dropping down below fifty miles. Details became visible to the naked eye: the colossal closed-umbrella shape, the greatly elongated and slightly bowed tail with its concave end, the string of glowing nodules that ran hundreds of feet down the tail's flanks.

The plan was for the *Ulysses* to outpace the sailer and then shed velocity so that they slowly spiraled back around it at a distance of ten miles. The Doc pulled the telescope screen closer and made sure AI control was enabled. Each device would be set to sweep the creature's flanks, and results from one instrument would cause a refocusing of another, and so on until the ideal mechanism(s) were brought to bear on the optimal targets.

Ulysses closed in, dipping beneath the ten-mile limit and powering its way up the solar-sailer's length. The manipulator arm suddenly detached and descended, pointing down at the flanks of the sailer as it passed by miles beneath. Cal's eyebrows rose as powerful searchlights erupted from the clawed end of the robot arm. The beams played over the surface, revealing biologically streamlined details.

"Another surprise," he said, addressing the big engineer via the comms. "Where did you find the time?"

"Right after the derelict station, you were . . . recovering at the time. I couldn't sleep."

"Well done."

"It's just me raiding the lander's spares again."

The turtle-shell-rendered-in-spider-silk appearance of the sailer's outer skin sped by beneath them, stark and clear in the ovals of thrown light. Mottled gray and brown scales shot with an iridescence of blue-green blurred away in streaks and flashes. The giant beast-vehicle spun slowly as it rolled, stretching and contracting shadows, bringing one of the mysterious strings of glowing spheres into view. The spheres appeared to have grown, bulging against the strands and webs of the tail structure, pulsing in various and seemingly random colors, every swollen globe in phase with the next.

They were slowing again. Sarah had throttled up the main engine and was using the RCS to spiral the *Ulysses* around the solar-sailer, allowing it to catch up and start to pass them. As it did, she pitched the ship end-over-end and stabilized their position with a single expertly measured blast from the main engine. She maintained speed enough to keep them even with the location of the crash site. She used the RCS and one more squirt from the main to widen their orbit and move them away to the previously determined *safe* distance. *Whatever safe meant.* From this point on, they'd use the lander to ferry back and forth.

"Here we are folks," the pilot said. "Keep in mind that the sailer is rotating around its very long axis. Its *days* are only about sixteen minutes long, so take that into account when you're headed over there. You might have to chase the landing site a bit."

"We'll manage. Eight hours rest please, people. Bright-eyed and bushy-tailed in the *Argo* at oh-six-hundred."

He got a chorus of nods, *rogers*, and one confused alien lizard staring at his tail.

Sixty-Nine

As the lander boosted toward the strange landscape of the solar-sailer, the enormous Jovian, still days away at their current speed, eclipsed the star. The blue light dimmed and then plunged into an unexpected darkness. Who had ever imagined such an occurrence? With such a large world so close to its sun, of course, such a thing would happen, but who had ever seen such light to know? Cal had a sudden, near overwhelming, sense of place: of where he was, how very far away he was from home. A reminder of the totality of the dark like turning off a car's headlights on a moonless road. The technology-enabled sight vanishes and you remember that you are not safe in the night. It was the primal nature of the fear that struck home; *you can't always know what's coming.*

Cal reached out and clicked the lander's exterior lighting to full. Three additional collimated search beams stabbed out, painting oval patches of illumination onto the mottled surface miles below. They met the larger, fainter circles cast from the *Ulysses*'s new searchlights.

"All right," he said. "Prepare for landing." He scanned the surface for any sign of the cyclops and absentmindedly touched the holster once again Velcroed to the hip of his spacesuit. Seeing the movement, the big engineer hefted the makeshift snare rifle, holding it in front of his broad orange-clad chest.

266

The *Argo*'s cabin was full, overstuffed really, with cargo netting slung between its landing legs for additional cargo capacity. Nearly the entire crew of the *Ulysses* was onboard with only Sarah remaining on the ship itself. Cal wanted as many eyes with them on the surface as possible, including the strange eyes of the lizard alien. They needed to move the salvage along as quickly as possible, not to mention keeping watch for danger and, if necessary, fighting it. He stood at the piloting station, but Odysseus was handling all of the real flight duties, allowing his mind the capacity to wander. This was not something he enjoyed, rarely did it wander into areas he wished to go, but he felt frazzled. It was best for the machine mind to do the driving. He felt as if he were on the verge of making some terrible mistake. Perhaps he already had.

Beyond the sweep of the lander's forward viewport, the sailer's great head grew to blot out the stars. Shadows oozed across the surface as it slowly rotated, and just beyond one of the radial strakes that crowned the head was the glittering fan of Seiss's crash site.

Seiss moved to adjust himself, making a groaning sound as he carefully stretched one limb at a time. He floated just off Cal's right shoulder, folded into a ball in an effort to take up as little space as possible, but his huge spacesuited tail was posing a difficulty. Inez moved to give him room, pressing her yellow-suited shoulder uncomfortably into Paul's thick arm. He grimaced at her, and she smiled back. The lizard hunched, working out muscular kinks no human could imagine and nearly slapped the Doc right in the faceplate.

"Sssorry," he bleated through deflating air sacs.

The Doc shimmied her shoulders, adjusting her backpack. "It's okay," she said to the creature for a moment before asking, "So, how was it again that you crashed?"

Cal paid attention, keeping his hands set against the controls in the illusion that he was doing the flying while the *Argo* powered its way to the surface. Flickering blue flame dwelt within its twin engine bells, eating up the last of its horizontal velocity.

The alien reached out with a gloved talon and rotated himself around to face her, answering much as it had previously. "Learned sssailer was in double star sssystem. Learned to know, no rider. Sailer and no rider, very not common. Friend sssay, come. We get, we *rich*. Seiss need for this, for family. Ssso go."

The Doc contemplated the difference between harvesting and stealing. Did Seiss see the solar-sailer as a nineteenth century person might have seen a whale, or the way a twenty-first century person might look at one? Morals changed with time and understanding. She wondered how deep the lizard's *humanity* went, and she knew what human beings were capable of depending on their definition of that word.

"So, what you were doing was stealing from an obviously sentient being?"

"Yesss." His eyestalks sank within its helmet. "Sssaid not proud. Not happy. Rare chance but sssorry."

She could tell Cal was paying attention and, at that, they exchanged a glance in the periphery of their eyes. The lander dropped closer and closer to the surface. The wide strakes of the radial grooves and hollows were drenched in stark shadow.

"Now think. Now do and for nothing. All gone."

They exchanged glances again.

The *Argo* lowered itself to the ground. It had completely canceled its horizontal motion and was descending slowly, cameras sweeping all around them, searching through the entirety of the spectrum for any change, any sign that the cyclops, or anything else for that matter, might be near. Cal frowned at the wondrous landscape, and the silver vessel smashed against it. They needed whatever they could salvage from that ship, but the thing that murdered his colleague and friend was out there somewhere.

Just get through. Just get to tomorrow. That was all there was now. It simply had to be. That was what this constant state of emergency called for, but it was no way to live. Cal laughed silently; this was the natural state of humanity. *Survival.* But primal thinking meant that there would never be anything *but* tomorrow. The concept, the hope of *tomorrow,* saw today consumed by the act of survival. There had to be something left, for something more. "That's what makes us human," he muttered aloud.

The Doc looked at him quizzically. "What?"

"Nothing, just thinking."

The *Argo* hit the ground with a thump. Normally in microgravity landings, they'd have heard the quick two-two beat of sound and vibration as the anchoring pitons rocketed out and tethered them to the surface. Given that this was the outer skin of a colossal living being, Cal thought it prudent to avoid this step. Odysseus would capitalize on their plentiful fuel reserves and use the RCS thrusters to hold them against the landscape of the sailer.

Cal looked around one more time, scanning the exterior scene through the windows and calling up various camera views on the forearm of his suit. Satisfied, he nodded to each of the others individually. He and Inez had an easy trust. Cal held the Doc's eyes for the briefest instant longer, natural given the complexities of their relationship. There had once been other, larger emotions there that though changed had nevertheless hardened into a similar trust. Paul's gaze held not a twinkle of their earlier disagreements, and Cal was grateful for that. One of the risk factors he'd already mentally factored for was in trusting his engineer as he always had. He decided that did not have the luxury of considering that Paul might fail him. And then there was the lizard. He had been looking for reasons to mistrust the creature, but after spending the equivalent of a long weekend with him in close quarters, teaching, and learning, he felt he had a good sense of him. He reached down and ratcheted the bottom hatch handle and could feel the pressure drop as Odysseus withdrew the atmosphere. Another turn and the hatch opened, rising up into the confines of the interior.

Inez pushed her way toward the ceiling in order to relieve the congestion, and Cal put his hand on the lizard's narrow spacesuited shoulder.

"You first."

Seventy

The five of them spread out, moving to prearranged points around the lander. A pentagon of spacesuited anxiety pointed at the crumpled spacecraft and the debris field fanning out behind it. The cyclops was out—or in—there somewhere. They moved carefully, guardedly, toward the crash site. Seiss's vehicle was exactly as they had left it, a giant crumpled cigar shape wrought in silver and iridescence. The same spars jutted through its skin, the same rents and buckles plagued what was undoubtedly once a smooth and elegant profile. They marshaled around it, the alien peeking through the cracked hatch doorway and shining a flashlight into the darkened interior. The beam played over the ivory mound around which the cockpit was configured. "Is exactly hope." Seiss stroked the housing, clicking his long claws around the periphery of a control panel. "This unit, whole thing, is all. For ship, whole thing. All in." He pointed at the flooring. "Goes through to bottom of craft, measuring parts. That broken, yes. Top parts some no broken, maybe all no broken. This part take."

"All right, Paul. You and Inez see if you can get that thing disconnected without damaging it further." As the two of them moved to join the alien inside the ruins of his craft, Cal and the Doc examined their surroundings.

"Odysseus, anything?"

The AI was constantly probing and sensing with every instrument at its disposal. "There is no change in the background radiation sources apart from the rhythms we have previously attributed to the solar-sailer organism itself."

Cal's helmet turreted in the machined circuit connecting it to the neck of his suit. He continued to scan the horizon, stopping only for a moment to take in the massive shape of the Hot Jupiter encircled by the corona of the eclipse. The cobalt cyclops was nowhere to be seen.

"Doc?"

"I don't see anything." The Doc cradled a second tarpaulin launcher and was keeping her eyes on the deep blackness pooling in each of the large furrows. If something was going to come at them, she felt that's where they'd be coming from. The darkest dark—a shadow in space.

The lizard had separated the damaged hatch door from its frame and let it drift away as he carefully scrambled inside. The alien vanished for a second and then reappeared in the curving transparent cockpit bulge, beckoning them to follow. Inez ducked her head and passed through the bent doorframe into the alien spacecraft, goggling at the exotic appearance of the materials. She had thought she'd missed her chance to experience it in person when the ship-creature had sailed away. The thrill of exploration jarred in strange competition with fear within the loops of her bowels. She gritted her teeth and moved into the ship's bent cabin. There sat the odd chairs she had before seen on video, arrayed around the central hub of instrumentality: the source of the wire that had led Cal to the creature who now perched elegantly on one of the odd fixtures. They weren't seats, they were perches.

Paul stuck his head inside. He wasn't too large to fit, but his bulk was poorly arranged for the cramped interior, so he remained in the doorframe, dipping inside only to provide additional expertise and leverage. Seiss wrapped his claws around the central column and pulled the plastic-looking housing free, splitting it away from where it connected underneath the chairs. He passed the chunk to Paul who sniffed at it and pushed it out through the door. It bounced away into the debris field. With the housing removed, a compact stack of what looked like ordinary electronics rendered in strange colors was revealed. Dense packs of dusky crystal blocks made up a few odd strata. Seiss indicated the locations of screw-like connectors. Getting those out of the way would allow the entire stack to be removed. The heads on the connectors bore a face with four small openings. Seiss rummaged through the shattered interior but could not come up with a corresponding tool.

Paul pulled his pistol-grip tool from his pack and fitted a carbide drill bit. He held it in front of him, toward the lizard. Seiss's eyestalks roamed to inspect it, and then he nodded his head. The engineer passed the tool to Inez who leaned in, acting against the torque of the bit by bracing her feet against the crumbled fuselage's interior wall. The alien screws shredded, shiny pigtails rotating away from the stack. Within minutes, the upper portion of the equipment tower lifted away, tethered only by a few flat wires connecting it to a set of shattered instruments below. Paul wanted to cut them, but Seiss insisted on delicately plucking the connectors loose, which turned out to take less time than either of them would have thought.

Cal watched the cube of stacked instrumentality appear over the side of the crumpled lizard ship. Paul and Seiss held it between them until the alien relinquished it to the maneuvering of the big engineer and his thruster pack. Paul crossed back to the *Argo,* followed by the little comms officer, with a haste that satisfied Cal. The cyclops had still not shown its face.

Seiss drifted over to them, his earth-built EVA backpack moving awkwardly against the straps joining it to his suit. "Finisssh," it hissed.

"There's nothing else we might benefit from?"

"Nothing else is." The alien shook his head. "Only walls, air machine, and engine. Engine gone, air machine gone."

Cal looked over at the wreckage as if he had never seen it before, indeed a decidedly barebones thing. When he turned back, Seiss was staring at him expectantly.

"Yes?"

"Seiss show matter transport?"

Cal looked around. Still no a sign of the cyclops. Perhaps it wasn't interested in them anymore, but if that were so, then why had it been waving at them over the telescopes? He turned back to the lizard. "Where?"

Seiss pointed to another of the radial furrows, one positioned more toward the opposite side and close to the trunk of one of the sailer's long, waving mouth-tendrils. "Through," he said.

Cal looked around them again. This was one of those moments he knew he probably shouldn't split the team, but he was going to anyway. "Inez, I'd like you to stand guard at the lander. Stray no more than two feet from it but keep an eye out."

"Yes, sir," she responded crisply.

"Paul, please do the same with the entrance to this furrow here. Just guard that entrance."

"Will do, where are you going?"

"We are going inside to see what Seiss has to show us."

The Doc appeared lost in thought as she followed Cal and the alien toward the blackness of the furrow.

Seventy-One

They descended an organic tunnel into the head of the sailer, more orifice than edifice. It ended in a tightly sealed set of lip-like doors. Seiss began pressing in against the walls surrounding the fleshy covering.

The Doc shifted her position with a puff from her thrusters. "What are you doing?"

"Looking for . . . word? Make and take signals inside body?"

"Nerves."

"Looking for nervesss." Seiss pressed in a few other spots, and finally, the set of doors opened like a massive eyelid protecting an empty socket. They were completely isolated within their suits, but Cal could tell that some puff of wind had buffeted past them. They went inside, and there, at the end of another short hallway, was a spherical room identical to the one they had found on the derelict—the one they called the mushroom chamber. Lining the walls of the spherical room, just like its twin, were the hundreds of metallic mushrooms, starkly contrasting the organic materials of the passageway. Their caps pointed in random, crazed directions. Like its twin on the station, one larger mushroom in the center of the bowl of the floor contained two large recessed buttons or footpads.

"Matter transport," the alien said.

Cal threw a look at the Doc. Her eyes were wide with dawning terror.

"Sssolar-sailer transport cargo." The lizard pointed to a few additional apertures at various cardinal points around the vestibule. "Tunnels to other ship places. Bring to transport. Transport in what sailer needs, transport out what sailer trades or rider."

The Doc asked, "Does it transport people?"

"No. No. Not ever know, sailer no. Rider, yes but rider not being. Rider grown like new tail. Not thinking thing. Maybe for animals?"

Cal waved his hand in the chamber and a golden inner light suffused the circumferential field of mushrooms. "Why only animals?" The Doc looked like he wished he hadn't asked.

"Most living persons not want matter transport. Matter transport destroy. Rebuilds at other place. When matter transport, person dead. Most think. Rebuilt person new person."

She felt like she had known what the alien was going to say before it said it. She felt it in her bones when she heard the words *matter transport*. Xu said she had disappeared in a strike of lightning. Cal saw her return, or rather that she was not there one second and there the next. A philosophical horror began to whip around her. She felt dizzy.

"What do you mean?" Cal asked.

Seiss looked back and forth between the humans, confused. He could tell there was some subtlety of communication that he had missed. "Maybe not. Believe is only. Some think real death not? Some use transport: body hoppers, machine life . . . Badly injured persons . . . other machines." The lizard was trying to help.

The Doc slumped for a second, and Cal was about to grab her, but her eyes sparked open and glared at his. "I'm all right."

"Let's get the hell out of here," Cal said.

Seventy-Two

They ascended the throat-like corridor more, emerging into the straked furrow on the sailer's surface. They were greeted by the sight of the blood draining from Paul Arthor's expressive face, his increasing pallor obvious even through the glass and shadows of his helmet. He reached out, orange glove firmly gripping Cal's blue, and hoisted him out of the depression, planting him on the rim without ever taking his eyes off something beyond Cal's shoulder. As he landed on the furrow's edge next to the big engineer, he saw Polyphemus.

The cyclops rose from an adjacent furrow, emerging from the shadows. It reached the rim and stopped moving, observing as the five of them took up a chevron of positions in opposition. As a group, they began backing away from the monster, reversing toward the lander. Each of them pointed their weapons at the cobalt-blue humanoid, some more steadily than others. It did not advance. Whether it surmised the purpose of the weapons or not was unclear, but it moved nothing but the eye in its head.

Odysseus extinguished the minimal thrust it had been continually applying to keep the *Argo* in position and opened up the rear-facing RCS nozzles. The *Argo* began to glide over the surface toward the *Ulysses* crew, shrinking the distance they needed to retreat to safety.

Polyphemus remained passive as the astronauts clamored up the lander's undercarriage, past the secured salvage and into the cabin. As soon as they had vanished into the interior, it began to move. Striding forward, heading toward the *Argo,* displaying the same strange implacability. The star's light escaped from the Jovian eclipse and the shadows around them began to seep like spilled ink.

Cal threw open a stream of switches across the console, pressurizing the cabin and instructing Odysseus to rise. The giant outrigger engines blowtorched, and the lander shot from the surface. He expected the monster to charge them, to throw its insidiously beautiful blue shape against them. To stop them. To destroy them. He expected a fight, but as they spiraled away from the surface, the cyclops just stopped. Pivoting its head and casting its baleful, now deep red, eye along their path. It watched them climb away, raising only a single arm, hand outstretched.

Seventy-Three

The magnetosphere of the super-gas giant Triangle was stretched into an incredibly distended ellipse: an ice cream cone shape of intense radiation that constantly swirled within that of its star. The planet rode so close that the solar winds not only boiled off tons of the outer atmosphere per second, but also blasted the planet's electromagnetic field out into a tail that reached well past the orbits of both Square and Circle. This meant that its shape and currents were far different than the EM field of Jupiter, which they had previously navigated. Given the windblown shape and the *Ulysses*'s course, the earth ship crashed into the side of the distended electromagnetic bubble much closer to the atmosphere than they had when approaching Jupiter. The ship's protective field began to sparkle as washes and bands of energetic particles tore around it.

Defying prediction, the sailer had not peeled off toward the system's sun, instead it rode on straight ahead of them. The best Cal could figure was that, because of the size of the Hot Jupiter and its proximity to its star, the sailer was going to use the combination of the gravity of the gas planet and light pressure to propel it even faster toward its next destination. Whatever the reason, the massive ship-creature stayed with them as they fell in toward the super gas giant, so close that the sailer's own naturally generated EM field sometimes shared a wash of deflected particles with that of the Earth ship.

As Cal made the final close out checks before sealing the lander, he sat alone in the vehicle as its lights dimmed. The rest of the crew that had accompanied him on the salvage, Seiss included, had left. Moving the salvaged equipment down into Paul's engineering lab. With any luck, it would contain navigational data on the Jovian-link systems and give them a clear goal and a clear way to get home, although he knew it wasn't a reasonable expectation. As the alien had said, if there was a known way into their system, they would have been contacted already. Perhaps conquered. He got the impression from the lizard's stilted English that they would have been, more or less, exploited if such an inroad was known. It would therefore be hidden, undiscovered. It had to be there, though. There would be some way to ferret out the way home. Most likely, there would not be a complete solution but rather steps toward one. That was fine by him. That was better than nothing. Much better than nothing. It was hope, and hope was what this spaceship ran on now. Hope was a consumable more valuable than oxygen.

He squeezed his eyes shut and gripped the lander's flightstick tightly, summoning some more hope. *If hope is an emotion, then it's something I can control.* He felt something moving, deep within his guts. He didn't think it was hope. When he opened his eyes, the *Argo*'s interior lights had dimmed to nothingness, and the cabin was entirely illuminated by the golden-brown hues of the instrumentation and an ultramarine glow from Triangle that seeped through the viewports. He blinked once, and alarms began to sound. A glance at the console told him that Odysseus had detected a disturbance in the gas giant's atmosphere.

"Odysseus," Cal said wearily. "What's going on?"

"An eruption at the equator."

"An eruption?" Volcanoes were not a hallmark of gas giants, they had no surfaces, no mantles, no magma cores. The eruption obviously was the result of something else.

"Sarah," he called to the pilot over the general comms channel. "What's happening?

"Not sure, Cal. Odysseus classifies it as an eruption of some kind."

"Yes, I know. How does that make any sense?"

"I don't think it knows, but you know what it reminds me of?"

"Tell me."

"It reminds me of our ascent from the yellow gas giant. It's an arc of atmospheric disruption, an exaggeration, a perturbation of gasses out from the planet's equatorial storm band."

"So, you're saying?"

"I'm saying I'm using every instrument on this ship to see if there's another vehicle at the head of that disturbance."

"And is there?"

"I'm not sure yet but—"

"If you had to guess."

"If I had to guess, yes. Something has exited a link within that Jovian. A ship, maybe, spiraling up into orbit at high velocity."

"Escape velocity?"

"Not sure."

Cal was silent.

The pilot waited as long as she could stand it. "What do we do, Cal?"

He waited another beat before answering. "Right now? We hide. Take us around the far side of the solar-sailer. Keep it between us and whatever has just entered this solar system. I want our radar and infrared signatures to be entirely masked by the ship-creature's if possible."

"Roger, Cal." Before he had unstrapped himself from the *Argo*'s control console, he felt the thrumming vibration of the RCS thrusters and watched the starfield outside the windows shift. Sarah was already repositioning the ship.

Seventy-Four

The *Ulysses*'s telescopes slewed about, searching for and sighting the eruption around the equator. The view zoomed via a combination of changes to the shape of the telescope's lenses and the application of powerful algorithmic transformations. They revealed what was clearly a ship spiraling into orbit at high velocity. It trailed great arching cascades as blue as water and yet made up mostly of boiling silicate dust. Something had violently departed a cyclonic transport tunnel.

"What in God's name is it?"

"Get the lizard up here."

"What do we do?"

"Do you think it's seen us?"

"I don't think so, not yet at least. The likelihood is, if anything, that it's only detected the sailer."

"So far."

They were safe, Cal imagined. For the moment at least.

Enhanced telescopic imagery of the equatorial disturbance began to populate the command module's main screen. At the apex of the descending curtains of disturbed gas was an object—regular and yet not. An intertwining of disjointed elements that formed another cohesive shape, like the dome of a dune or the tight sphere of a dead insect curling in upon itself.

Cal's eye caught the lizard's triangular head and elongated neck, slithering into the space between the cockpit's two front seats. The alien took in the projected scenes and emptied his air sacs with a flatulent wheeze. No translation needed: *Oh, shit.*

"You know what that is?"

"Yesss."

There was a prickle of fear deep in him, the urge to run and hide crammed deep by reason, age, and experience was fighting its way back up into the light of everyday thought. *Don't ask. For heaven's sake, don't ask.*

"Tell," he mumbled. A sudden flash of fatigue shot holes through his thought process.

"The People," the lizard answered.

The pilot leaned out from her seat. "Come again?"

"They call themselvesss *the People.*"

"Are they friendly?" Somehow, he thought he already knew the answer, but he was surprised to be somewhat wrong.

"Dependsss."

Not great, but not the absolute worst he'd expected. "Depends on what?"

"The People not . . . flesh? Not all of one mind but can be one or many mind. Understand? Confusing, not have right words." The creature's cobra frill stood out from his neck and vibrated in agitation. "Not sssure if thingsss change since Seiss sssleep. Some the People are belonging to Treaty, they not kill. The People not belonging to Treaty, kill or take us. Me, kill. You, sell biology. Humansss new. Make rich, even for nations. Even more, both Treaty and not Treaty People want take *Ulysses.* Take Civilization Engine."

"Got it, or enough of it, anyway. Sarah, take us in close! Keep us in the solar-sailer's shadow. No matter *what.*"

"Roger, Cal."

Seventy-Five

Pinpoint thrusters flared across the Earth ship as it rotated around the sailer, diving in close to its mile-long flanks. Snuggling up to within 2500 feet of the ship-creature's mountainous head. The reptilian astronaut floated into the *Ulysses*'s command module like a crocodile swam. His arms and legs hung lazily beneath, and he maneuvered and propelled himself with sweeping and grasping motions of his prehensile tail.

"Can hide but what use is hiding where they to be look anyway?"

Cal tossed back a glance from his command chair; over his shoulder, the curving reach of the CM's panoramic windows revealed the crystal-sharp terrain of the ship-creature's head. "What else is there to do? Where else is there to hide? We've got to stay in the solar-sailer's radar shadow as best as we can until our orbit puts the planet between us and *that*."

He pointed at the images of the new arrival. Free of its cloak of dust and gas, it was a startlingly beautiful arrangement of radial accretions twirled around a central pillar. A glasswork castle or a vast sparkling chandelier in space.

"Ssship of the People."

"Right, *that*."

"Maybe move to tail? If sailer opens wings, *Ulysses* too close. Tail safe from wings."

"Good point." He turned and reached past the lizard's snout to clasp his hand onto the pilot's shoulder. "Slide us down along the creature's length, Sarah. Keep it between us and the ship of the People, take us to the tail. But *slowly.*"

"Roger, Cal."

Her hands were already moving, applying thrusters to slow the *Ulysses* and let the ship-creature outstrip it by a few meters per second. The landscape of the sailer scrolled by their shoulders. The lizard snaked its head into Cal's personal space. He placed his index finger on the alien's nostril-less muzzle and gently pushed him back a few inches. "What is it?"

"If they sssee, they not know what you are but will know what you have. They will can sssee."

"You mean they'll know what those are?" Cal asked, pointing out the docking window to the red weed-wrought booms.

"Yes. Civilization Engine. They all out in space do that. Look like that. All do the same, bring bonded ship to some other star. Different each time but space behavior same."

"In space? On a planet it's different?"

"Yes, place change purpose."

"And these People will want it."

"*All* people will want it. The People more than most. Fight wars for Grandparents' artifacts."

"Just to get the artifacts?" Inez asked.

"Before Treaty, the People fight wars over everything. Some still. Just *always* fight war over Grandparents' artifacts."

"What about this Treaty?"

"Not sure, Civ Engines not found since for thousands of years. Think Treaty not hold. Think no Treaty hold. Some will try take, no matter what."

"Who is this Treaty with, anyway? These monsters and *who*?"

"Lots. My people and our sisters, many other civilizations also."

"Sisters?"

"Yes. My people all from home planet but not all people from home planet same nation. My people's nation also many planet empire have. Sister nations, some planet each have."

"Your world, it's not all one people? One nation?"

"No. Your planet is this way?"

"No."

"Then why you think mine?"

"I . . . I don't know." Cal laughed but was cut off by a burst from the thrusters. Sarah was adjusting the position of the ship, keeping the solar-sailer between the *Ulysses* and the sparkling chandelier on its widening gyre around the planet.

"So, the People themselves," Cal asked. "What are they?"

Seiss pulled his neck up into a tense S, puffing up his small cobra hood. It turned a periscope-like eye on each of them independently and then drew them back to focus on one human at a time, remembering they found his ability to split visual attention unnerving. "The People . . . hard glass, bugs."

"Hard glass? Crystal?"

"Maybe?" The alien shrugged his narrow shoulders, employing some learned human body language. "But alive biology."

"Crystal bugs?"

Seiss shrugged again.

"Bugs, insects?" the Doc asked. "A hive mind?"

"No. Look like bugs yes, not think like bugs." Seiss had learned about Earth insects from Sesame Street. "The People, individual minds have but bodies linked, part of whole; serve ship functions. Minds free, command vessel from unreal space."

"I think I understand," said Cal. "They pool the power of their physical selves while their minds communicate in a virtual space. They *are* their ship?"

Seiss seemed to consider this and then swiveled his head to look out the sweep of transparent viewport. "Very very dangerous. Many wars fought. Many together fight. People almost made to be all dead but then other civilizations stop. Say not destroy. Make sign Treaty."

Cal joined the lizard alien, staring unfocused into space, processing his thoughts until the alien re-inflated his air sacs and gave him even more to process.

"Can read and control flesh minds through . . ." The alien groped for a word and then consulted the tablet Inez had given him, scrolling through entries. "Direct chemical-electric stimulation."

"What? What do you mean, direct?" Cal asked.

The saurian ruffled his frill again, which Cal was beginning to associate with agitation. It paged through entries on its tablet again. "Direct. Pith. Punch through skin or bone or carapace into brain."

The CM lapsed into horrified silence, and they all stared quietly at the beauty of the chandelier, twinkling as it moved through space.

Seventy-Six

The *Ulysses* was facing away from the planet, away from the new arrival, awaiting the last possible moment to fire the main engine. Cal could sense the seconds tick away. The window for them to slow down enough to make a capture orbit was closing. The minute they began to slow, their path would diverge from that of the solar-sailer, but for a while, they could keep hidden in its shadows. Sarah was prepping such maneuvers at that moment, sitting quietly next to him and seemingly unmoved by the vista before them. Soon enough, though, the path of the sailer would differ enough to where they would be clearly visible. The puzzle, he figured, wasn't so much how to stay hidden but rather to choose where it would be best for them to be spotted.

He continued to gaze out the command module's window. The scene dazzled: the bright star, the sight of the cerulean super-Jovian and its strangely flattened poles, the glittering speck of the newly arrived alien ship. That a scene of beauty could create such a sense of foreboding seemed perverse.

Where would be best? These new aliens were presumably here to harvest the solar-sailer in some way. Could they wait to run until the People began their harvest? Too risky, they'd surely be spotted before any of that began, and then wouldn't the *Ulysses* be the bigger prize?

The best tactic, then, might be to wait until the chandelier-ship had already launched toward the sailer to make their move. The key unknown was the ability or willingness of the People to use up the fuel it would surely take to change their course. Especially since their original target would be drawing further and further from their grasp. That was assuming, of course, that the chandelier's capabilities couldn't match their own enhanced reserves.

What else was there to do?

He felt movement behind him. He had asked Paul and the Doc to escort Seiss to Xu's quarters and have him wait there. He had watched over the monitors. Once again, the alien was supremely cooperative. He had asked the both of them to return to the CM immediately afterwards but had lost himself in thought once the alien was locked away. He turned to see them slowing to enter the CM one by one.

Cal pondered for a second, wondering how the CM could have ever felt crowded with six people when it now felt cavernous and empty with five. He leaned over and finally spoke to his assembled crew.

"We are going to make a run for the Jovian we're calling Triangle. Therefore, we have to make sure we are spotted where it would be most costly for these new aliens to change their course and intercept us."

There was some surprise in their eyes, except for Sarah's since she already knew his plan, although he wasn't sure what else they might have expected him to say.

"Then what?" the engineer asked curtly.

"Then we hope that they'd rather harvest that sailer than chase after an unknown spaceship."

"You're planning to enter into another one of these link conduits?"

"That has to be a consideration. What can we do now, other than run?"

The big engineer looked to be processing the question. "And you think they're going to be more interested in the ship-creature than us?

Hauling this super-valuable, so-called, Civ Engine?"

"Hopefully. It's just a chance we're going to have to take. Either that or announce ourselves and see what happens."

Sarah perked up. "I vote against seeing what happens. I prefer running."

Paul ignored her. "Now that you bring it up, you *are* just taking the lizard's word as to who these new aliens are and what they might want."

"I'm not going to deny that. But it is the only intelligence we have, and I'm going to use it."

"I'm telling you, if you take this ship in over the poles, this whole thing is going to start all over again. We're going to be sent God knows where, one step further lost. And why?"

This was developing into an unexpected, unwanted verbal ping-pong match. The other crew member's attentions swiveled to follow the volleys.

"What's the alternative, Paul? Stay here and have what brought us here taken away from us? At the very least? Possibly get ourselves killed?"

"Get ourselves *killed?* You're going to get us killed by listening to that *alien.* You're making decisions solely based on what that creature is telling you. Maybe he's our friend, maybe he isn't, but I *know* that when you're lost, you don't just keep wandering around aimlessly. You—"

"What do we do, Paul? Retrace our steps? Sit and wait for help? Those aren't viable options for us."

"You don't even know if what you're suggesting will activate this transport system."

"You're right, I don't. But even if it doesn't, if we are going to have a confrontation with that vessel, I'd rather it be in orbit around the planet than in open space. I think that leaves us with the most strategic options."

Paul hesitated for another moment. It wasn't so much that he felt Cal was being impulsive but rather that so many unforeseen events were progressing so rapidly. He felt a desperate, almost wild desire to slow things down but didn't know how. "This whole thing. It's half-baked."

"We don't have time for your metaphorical bread to rise, Paul. It's time to leave Egypt."

The engineer's face darkened. Cal was so damned quick to twist a phrase. "Every choice you're making is based on the word of an alien," he reiterated.

"And your objections are based on what? The desire to *not* trust an alien? To trust in the good faith of aliens we haven't even met yet?"

"The devil we know, huh?"

"That's my decision, Paul."

"Maybe, just maybe, that's the *wrong* decision?"

"That's always a possibility, but I'm not going to do *nothing*."

"Maybe nothing is the right thing to do?"

Cal and Paul's gazes clashed and grappled, burning at one another. The bigger man became the smaller, and Paul blinked.

"Do your job now, mister. Make sure this ship is ready for the burn. In the future, I suggest you devote your extra time to continuing the investigation of the salvage from Seiss's ship rather than questioning my decision making."

The big engineer turned without a word and launched himself down the spinal corridor, shrinking away toward the docking ring.

Seventy-Seven

The pilot fixed on the chandelier shape glittering in starlight and azure. It was coming. It would swing by them at a distance of over a hundred thousand miles, and then its elliptical orbit would fling it back toward them, or at least toward the solar-sailer, on a perfect intercept course.

She was not the kind of person to let nerves bother her. As a young girl, she had conquered them. Her emotions were under her control, not the other way around. Still, she felt a faint echo of the rush of terror she'd experienced when the ship had failed to stop its braking burn over Jupiter, plummeting them toward what she was certain would be their deaths. *Are we sure they've come for the sailer?*

She also was not the kind of person to let something that bothered her fester, and so she opened the comms line to Xu's old quarters. She would talk to the one person who *could* know, and she didn't really care if the alien was sleeping or not. The comms beeped and no one answered. Either there was no one there, which meant that the alien had left or it just didn't know how to answer the comms. Which was the more likely? She wondered.

The ship had entered its "night" phase. The lighting was subdued, Odysseus was keeping an eye on most things. Cal would be asleep, as would most of the ship, except for her. With the chandelier out there, the captain had made the prudent decision that someone would always be at the helm. She'd sleep when Cal woke and his ass replaced hers in the pilot's chair. She couldn't leave her post. She was about to wake the Doc and ask her to override the comm privacy systems when the picture on her ship-phone changed and the alien's red muzzle appeared on its smooth surface.

"Sssarhaaa?" The alien had trouble discerning human faces in two dimensions.

"Yes."

"I come out now?"

"No, that's not for me to say. I wanted to ask you a question."

"Not for you to say?"

"Never mind. A question?"

"Ssshoot." The creature was picking up some of Cal's go-to expressions. It felt weird.

She shunted the feed of the chandelier ship to her phone, showing the alien. "Are you sure they're here for the solar-sailer?"

"Sure? What is sure?"

"Sure is when—"

"I know word," he interrupted her. "I meaning, not know if word fits. I not know for *sure* why the People here at ssstar sssystem. I know they hunt the sailers. They have always hunted solar-sailersss. They have always hunted mossst creaturesss. Even though Treaty says no, ssstill do. Treaty or non. Not sure everything People do."

Sarah sat with this for a few seconds, mentally rearranging the creature's words and discerning its intent, before speaking. "What do they want with it?" *Do they want what you wanted?* she thought. After all, by his own admission, the lizard alien had crashed while also trying to harvest the solar-sailer in some way.

The creature's eyestalks lowered and its lids slit to near closing. "No. I look for eggsss, artifactsss. The People kill. Strip solar-sailers to bone. Nothing left except sssometimesss skeletons found. No tell why.

No tell what use People have for solar-sailers. People private, don't talk about People."

She had watched much of Cal's interviews and conversations with the alien on video. She noted that the lizard hadn't done much talking about his own people. Cal had been so busy asking about where they were and how they'd gotten there that the background on the culture it came from remained sparse.

"People don't talk about people," she said. "That's true."

The alien cocked its head and its eyestalks rotated to stare into one another.

Seventy-Eight

Cal woke and undid the Velcro bed-belt that kept him, and his blanket, from floating away whenever the centrifuge was spun down and the habitats locked to the hub. They needed to present as small a profile as possible in order to stay hidden within the sensor shadow of the giant beast-vessel. He floated over to his closet and lazily slid himself into a jumpsuit. The gyrations of the act in zero-G left him upside down by the time he'd managed to zip the suit up to his neck. He reoriented himself, slid the accordion door of his quarters open, and headed up the ladder, pushing off every few rungs until he had reached the hub.

The slow burn of his conflict with Paul, coupled with literally everything else, began to brew a fresh pot of anxiety in his gut. He wanted to head down to engineering and try and smooth things out with him, to alleviate an unnecessary strain on himself, not to mention the operations of the ship, but he knew his own instincts for argument were unreliable in such cases. He might easily make things worse. So, he just floated there in the hub for a few seconds of naked indecision and then headed for the command module.

He entered into the dimly lit surroundings of eidetic patterns wrought from indicator lights and endlessly updating displays. The large main screen had been lowered and unfurled. On it the chandelier sparkled in more than just reflected starlight: the ship of the People was expending energy. There was a nova-light glow behind, both silhouetting and illuminating its crystalline structure. The alien ship was increasing its velocity, warping its orbit into a high ellipse angled to intercept the path of the solar-sailer. Not where the sailer *was* but where it *would be* by the time the chandelier had crossed the distance. As the white-hot glare that had turned the chandelier into tiered bars of light faded, Odysseus was able to accurately estimate its path: about the time they would fall into orbit around the Hot Jupiter, the chandelier would have looped back and caught up with the solar-sailer, and *Ulysses,* from behind.

The upside, if there was one, was that the aliens most likely still didn't know they were there. They were probably only aware of the sailer, their natural prey—if Seiss's info could be trusted. *If they diverged significantly from the path of the sailer, would they become the more interesting target? How willingly would these new aliens change the focus of their pursuit?* Those questions, as yet, had no answer.

The solar-sailer was clearly heading to round the planet Triangle at its equator in order to maximize the boost it would receive from its gravitational field. They would *have* to break free into polar orbit if they wanted to keep the transport system as a viable escape option. Not that he really wanted to leap into some other unknown solar system, but it beat being pithed. Cal slid into the seat next to the pilot. She threw him a glance and a nearly imperceptible smile. "Magnetometers are back online. Odysseus hasn't figured out where we are yet, but he's made a good enough map to get the star-finders working again."

"And a good morning to you too, Sarah."

"Is it morning?"

"Not really, but I can't sleep."

"Having trouble making up your mind?" She was talking about the question of *when.* When would it be best to leave the sheltering bulk of the ship-creature? He'd like to drop the *Ulysses* into orbit before the chandelier knew what was happening. Get the planet between them and keep it that way. If it shifted orbit, they could shift orbit to match. Endlessly keeping them at bay. But he knew that was a fantasy. There was just too much space between them and the planet, and they'd surely do something to disrupt that dynamic, like moving out to a higher orbit, launching probes, or other projectiles.

Would they give chase? More? Would the Civilization Engine give us some unforeseen edge? The shielding, the fuel capacity? They were flying by the seats of their pants. Space travel wasn't normally a seat of your pants type endeavor. Normally.

"Are we ready for the burn?"

"Ready whenever you are," she quickly answered.

She had been thinking about the question for as long as he had. Her emotions were under her control, but her logical mind grabbed hold of the argument and obsessed over each side. *When?* Cal was certain she'd already come up with the same answer as he had. *Whenever.* It almost didn't matter, they would be seen, and if they could pursue, they might. There was no way to know. They had no idea of the chandelier ship's top speed or any of its other capabilities, for that matter. To top it off, there was no real place to escape *to*, just further into the relative emptiness of space.

They could try the travel network again, but wouldn't the People just follow? Not if they wanted the sailer as much as their lizard friend suggested they might. Why dive into the Jovian to follow an unknown ship when their expected and valuable target was in their sights?

The counter to that, of course, was the alien constructions clinging like remoras to the sides of *Ulysses*. This Civ Engine, whatever it truly was, was something the new aliens were apparently going to want the moment they laid eyes on it. If Seiss's word could be trusted. *I guess we'll know what the lizard's counsel is worth when that ship spots us.*

The chandelier sparkled on the main screen.

Cal adjusted the straps on his harness. He was second-guessing, taking the lizard's words at face value. What if what the alien was saying was untrue?

Sarah took her eyes off her consoles for a second and surveyed Cal's face, and he took the opportunity to do the same.

What *if*? Everything was a *what if* now.

When would be best? *Now*. Now would be best.

He wasn't sure that he ever even spoke the order, but at that moment, plasma hotter than that burning across the surface of the star vomited from the throat of *Ulysses*'s engine bell. Sarah's elegant fingers moved across the console like a pianist's across the keys.

Seventy-Nine

The Doc was alone in the sickbay. It wasn't quite morning yet, but it was getting there. *Night. Morning.* Words that had no meaning other than what they deigned to assign them. Mere remnants of their diurnal origins, although the words still meant that she was awake when everyone else onboard, as far as she knew, was asleep. She stroked the fleshy leaves of the little succulent plant she had Velcroed to her desk. She smiled at the sensation and then pulled the bottle of bourbon from her bottom drawer. She cradled the bulb in her palms and sat back, listening to the quiet rhythms of the ship. She imagined the pulsing drone of the air-handling system as a throbbing mechanical plea, crying out, *please let us live. Please let us get home. Please let us live. Please let us get home. Please* . . . A plea or a prayer, she wasn't sure which.

Odysseus was handling the ship's operations. She supposed the AI could have explored on its own, but it couldn't really satisfy the mission that way. The mission of the *Ulysses* was always to expand the boundaries of *human* experience. The emphasis was hers, but humanity was entirely the point. Without humanity, the universe was pointless, a symphony with no audience.

At least that was the way she'd thought of it until just recently. Now she knew that there were audiences for the universe beyond humanity.

Let us live. Please let us get home. Please let us live. Please let—

Rhythms, symphonies . . . Her eyes opened to a sound she didn't immediately recognize. Someone was coming. After a heartbeat, she knew just who it was. A hissing, rattling *alien* breathing sound was drawing near. Through the paper-thin walls, she imagined she could see a silhouette: long tail and spine held parallel to the ground, slug-like neck extended and sweeping back and forth. The periscope-like eyes would be searching for her. A cold heat oozed down her back. The alien had agreed not to leave Xu's quarters during the night, but it had. *Why?*

The primal revulsion, the ancient abhorrence of anything scaled and snake-like bubbled up from her intestines. The size of the creature intimidated. Anything human-sized but not human was easily terrifying. *No one saw him on the monitors? No one saw it crossing the hub? Everyone was asleep, so who would have been looking?*

An alien velociraptor entered the sick bay.

"Doctorrr?"

She didn't respond and moved to keep the mass of the desk between herself and the open accordion door. She went to reach for her ship-phone to call for help when it rounded the corner. Its head shot up as soon as he saw her, its neck pulling back into a bunched curve of musculature. Transparent eyes rose on their stalks and exaggeratedly blinked at her.

"Doctorrr? Disssturbing you?" the creature asked.

"No." She swept her hand across the top of her desk, causing it to wake from sleep mode. Windows popped into existence all across its surface. "Just doing some work."

"You willing to with me, talk?" It cocked its head.

"No, yes. Sure."

It cocked its head to the other side, sliding its triangular snout closer to her, inch by inch. "You, I frighten, Doctorrr?" it asked.

She stiffened. "No."

It snaked its head up, adding a foot to its height. "I think *yesss*. I don't mean to frighten."

"You're not supposed to be moving about the ship unescorted."

"I thought, okay. Pilot wake. Too much happening, much important. I not want to bother." It pulled its eyestalks back. "Or frighten." The saurian's jaws slid open, muscles pulling the heavy skin of its muzzle up and away from jagged ranges of teeth. "Wanted to talk withhh you."

Her knees felt weak, but there was another sensation, something worse. Some screaming thing's shrieks echoing down her spine. "About what?" she asked.

"On solar sailer. Matter transssport. You frighten there, worssse than now."

She stared into the alien's eyes, the venous roadmap patterns of his cat's-eye structure were magnified behind the glassy spheres.

"You, that happen to?"

"Yes."

"On sssailer? First time?"

"No, on the derelict."

The alien waited, a pregnant pause, and then hissed quietly. "Sssorry, Doctor. I thinked ssso." It retreated, floating back to the door. "If talk about you need. I to talk to, anytime. Lotsss to thinking about, I know."

What does the alien know? What could it know? What happened to me there? The questions screamed within her, howling through the hollows in her skeleton. Her skin crawled, and her insides felt like jelly. The creature blinked at her again and slunk out of the room, turning awkwardly in the small hallway.

"Seiss?" she called.

The alien turned to look back at her.

"Am I dead?"

It did its rapid blink thing, backing a half-step down the hallway.

"Dependsss on believe?"

"It depends on if I believe in a soul or not, is that right? Something about us that lives on after death?"

It nodded.

"Am I dead?"

"No . . . You alive. Doctor who went to station dead. You new person. Not sssame."

At that moment, the *Ulysses*'s main engine erupted in plasma flame, and the force suddenly brought a new sensation of gravity to the habitat. The alcohol bulb flew from her hand and the lizard was suddenly right in front of her, gently preventing her from toppling over backwards.

Eighty

The chandelier rotated in space, looking more like a castle made of ice the closer one got to it. Its sweeping arches, columns, and projections abided by a larger geometry, acting as solid structures though they were anything but. The columns, arches, and spars were wreathed with crystalline details of entwined ringlets and spidery shapes. Deep within the mass of the vessel, a new space opened, a pocket in what heretofore had been mechanically functional space. All around it, the interleaved structures deformed to accommodate its growth.

A triumvirate of pellucid clumps fell gently in the light rotational gravity, dropping away from the newly created ceiling. They were individual crystalline spider-shapes, translucent with cores of swirling color. They would have been breathtakingly beautiful had any conscious entities been there to witness them. There were only themselves, and being that they differed only in size, the spiders saw no beauty. They just saw what was.

Vermillion and cerulean fluids chased one another through the insectile thing's internal spaces. A current flowed within each creature's triangularly-arranged set of central bodies, propelled by the constant pumping motion of crab-like joints. Even when they stood still, their limbs wavered in place. The activity flushed their various limbs with a glow that purpled over time before shifting back again to red. The faces of these spectacular nightmares were ever-shifting clusters of cabochon eyes and whipping cords.

There was no instrumentation in the room. Each of the creatures knew everything that the others knew since they had become the ship. Yet now they were individuals once again. Each had lived lives of unique experiences before coming together, this had enhanced the effectiveness of the ship, but now they would serve the ship better by being themselves for a while.

With so many enjoined others around them, they could hear thoughts filtering up through the newly manifested floor. A floor that was composed of the interlocked bodies of thousands of their brethren in the same way that they themselves had most recently been a part of what was now the ceiling.

The largest of the three chittered and rotated in place, stretching each of its segmented limbs in turn. *We are no longer of the ship. We will command its fate. There is a new thing to be considered.*

Yes. The new thing. We must know it, said the smallest.

Yes. To know it is a goal. But already there was a goal.

Yet there is a new thing. I believe I know what it is. If correct, it is the more worthy goal, answered the largest.

Yes. The greater goal should be our goal. The most illuminating goal should be the priority, the smallest of the three replied with agitation. Some hidden appendage seemed to momentarily stir from within the vertical cleft between two of its three bodies. *The new thing was hiding behind the ship of the Fleet. It may be of the Fleet. The new thing should be our goal.*

This is why we are ourselves again. If it is a new form of the Fleet, it is a greater goal. The greater goal should be our goal.

Yes. It bears the closest attention. Yes.

Agreed. Agreed. Agreed.

Yes. Agreed. Yes.

What of the ship of the Fleet? It is without its Motile. This may now be a lesser goal but it is a rare opportunity.

Yes. It is a prize. We must not let it escape.

Agreed. It is a prize. But there is now more than one prize.

There are two prizes. Agreed. We must adjust.

We must be in two places at once. Agreed. We must separate.

Yes. Separate. In what manner?

In the manner most relative. I will go with the core. You two will stay with the bulk of us. The largest one proceeded to the center of the chamber. *I will take only the core. The ship of the Fleet must be secured before it opens its sails. You and the bulk will capture the new thing.*

Agreed. Yes. Agreed.

Yes. Agreed. Yes.

The glittering ceiling above the largest spider distended, a rapidly forming stalactite reaching down to wrap a multitude of legs, encircling the largest and drawing it up within itself.

Eighty-One

Shooting through space, on an ellipse over one hundred thousand miles from the solar-sailer and the Earth ship, something began to happen to the chandelier. It seemed to elongate as the central column freed itself and slipped away from its girdle of crystalline curtains. The slender spine continued on course for the solar-sailer while the cored chandelier flipped over to face its tail toward the *Ulysses*. Three engines at its rear exploded into life, flattening the curve of its path, expending huge amounts of energy to stunt its trajectory and whip the bulk of the chandelier back toward the Jovian—the *Ulysses*'s obvious destination.

The star itself expanded into a swollen yellow backdrop highlighting a roiling azure haze that sloughed off the limb of the planet. The outer atmosphere was continuously boiling off due to Triangle's proximity to the star

"Will that cause us any problems?" Cal asked.

"The gas? It seems pretty tenuous," the Doc replied, peering into the science station's multiple screens.

He opened his comms to engineering. "Paul?"

The engineer was organizing blocks of light on the surface of his console. "We're good. The *Ulysses*'s native EM field would be able to handle the star's radiation at this distance, so I doubt it will be a problem with the added protection of the alien one."

"Roger that, thanks."

Cal turned his attention back to his own console and the plots of the multiple objects now streaking toward the planet. The chandelier's engine firing had been elegantly timed. Odysseus calculated that the alien ship would arc over and parallel their own elliptical path into polar orbit to within a distance of no more than three miles.

As they watched the screen, the vertical agglomerations of crystalline towers upended and twisted, forming some new shape for a yet unknown purpose.

The Doctor and the lizard returned, bowing their heads as they sailed through the burnished metal rings of the CM's rear hatch.

"What the hell is going on?" the Doc asked. "Are we making our burn already?"

Cal ignored her question. "Seiss! What the hell is it doing?"

The lizard let out a long hiss before letting a single word escape. "Ssshooot."

A pinpoint of blinding red light appeared, a star of brilliance that coalesced into a tight beam issuing from the empty center of the chandelier. There was no seeing it streak toward them, it happened far too fast for that. Their EM field rippled with fluorescence.

"What's that?"

The Doc frantically unfolded additional science station screens as data spooled in. "It's a . . . Inez, what the hell is this?"

Inez hurriedly flung herself across the diameter of the command module, eyes flaring over the science station results. "It's . . . a *laser*."

"We've been hit by a laser?"

"Did it damage us?" Cal asked.

"I don't think it got through the shield," Inez responded.

The Doc cried out, "They're attacking us."

The lizard interjected, "Not . . ." His eyestalks seemed to want to twist themselves around one another. ". . . yet. Sampling laser."

"Sampling?"

"Yesss. Try to vaporize tiny layer of *Ulyssesss*. Use machinesss to sssee what ssship made of from far away."

"What the hell do you suppose they'll shoot at us next?" Sarah asked darkly.

Seiss looked at her. "More laser? Bulletssss, rocketsss, missssilesss. Drop many mass in path, try overload ssshields. Not work I think, but maybe People try."

In the midst of thoughts of warping orbits and trajectories, a perhaps unfounded suspicion shot into her head, hung for a moment, and then was gone. *Bullets, rockets, and missiles . . . Why does the lizard know those English words?*

Cal watched the chandelier slow, bleeding off velocity to allow the super Jovian's gravity to exert more and more influence, swinging it closer to *Ulysses*. They were speeding up by slowing down. *And within a few hours they'll be speeding right up our ass*, he thought.

"How long until we make orbit?"

The pilot figured she'd best not estimate, so she invoked the AI. "Odysseus?"

"Assume safeguards off," Cal clarified. "Emergency burns. Accelerating as fast as we can, slowing down as fast as we can"

"Ignoring engine and space-frame safeguards, *Ulysses* can make orbit in sixteen hours twenty-three minutes."

"And when will the other spacecraft intercept us?"

"If current conditions remain constant," the machine-mind stated, "thirteen hours, twelve minutes, twenty-two seconds. "

Cal's gaze ranged around the command module and then, as if snapping out of a daydream, he brought the engineer's comms up in a corner of the main screen so that everyone in the CM could see.

"Paul, were you listening to that?"

"Yeah, I was."

"We need time. We need to shave off three hours and twelve

310

minutes somewhere. Between fancy flying and squeezing as much as possible out of the engine, we need to find that time."

"I'll do my best, Cal but—"

"But what?"

"But what the hell are we going to do even if we reach orbit?"

"I don't know, Paul. I've never fought a space battle before. Have you? It seems to me that putting a planet, not to mention a possible escape route, between us is a fair plan."

"Well, if you're going to count on alien after alien, maybe Inez had better start talking to the red weed again?"

"I haven't *stopped*." Inez, taking offense, stuck her nose in. "It just isn't talking back."

"Just find us the time, Paul," Cal said and cut the line.

Sarah cast him a glance but he wasn't sure what it meant.

Eighty-Two

Even though their courses were diverging, the sailer, the Earth ship, and the two pieces of the chandelier remained relatively close. The sailer flew on and away from *Ulysses* as the Earth ship dropped closer and closer to the majestic blue swirls of the titanic gas giant. The bulk of the chandelier continued to slow, arcing inwards, pulling ever closer.

The blue glaze of the planet was a churning dark circle against the furious backdrop of its parent star. Orbiting closer than Mercury orbited Sol, the immense energies pouring into the gas giant's atmosphere resulted in weather systems far larger and more spectacular than even those on Jupiter. The planetary storms had coalesced into four rotating bands ferociously tearing across the planet at upwards of five thousand miles per hour, causing the gravitational effect that gave the planet its flattened appearance. Girdling those blunted poles, Triangle's aurorae twisted like octopi, coruscating tendrils snaking across tens of thousands of miles to reach the equator.

In the CM of the *Ulysses*, the Doc was struggling to keep up with the data pouring onto her screens. Cal had ordered everyone back in their spacesuits, helmets at the ready, and so she was fumbling to sort through the windows that sprang open as her thickly gloved fingers moved over the console.

Scientific wonders flooded in, obscuring previous discoveries, and all she could really do was watch them stream by and hope the ship's AI would alert her of anything that might pose further danger. She was trying to make sense of what she was seeing, trying to provide Cal with insight that he might have missed, but she feared she was doing a miserable job of it.

The nose of the *Ulysses* seemingly pointed directly at the equator of the blue spheroid as its rapid spin brought a single massive storm, hundreds of times the size of Jupiter's Great Red Spot, over the horizon to stare at them. The entire planet took on the appearance of a great purpling eyeball.

"Look at the size of that thing," Inez whispered.

"Triangle is tidally locked," the Doc explained. "Energy hundreds of times more intense than what Jupiter experiences is hitting its permanent dayside. The temperature differential must be responsible for churning the atmosphere into such massive storms. Even on the night side, the temperature is ten times hotter than anything recorded in our solar system."

The ship's EM field lit up as they barreled through a spray of energetic particles. Cal focused the telescope, first on the distant solar-sailer. He could see it haloed in a jacket of sparkling motes confirming for him that it was employing some similar form of electromagnetic protection. He then slewed the scope around, bringing the chandelier into view. A heartbeat later, it too exhibited a protective envelope of cinders as it moved through the same cloud of particles.

They were traveling at incredible speeds, but even this close to the point in the star system where mass warped space to its most extreme and congested, the chase dragged on into tension filled hours. The magnetometers and external dosimeter spiked as a crashing sheet of fluorescence washed over their prow. They had only the most rudimentary maps of the complex flow of radiation zones weaving between the invisible fields produced by the planet and its star. As a result, they were flying by the proverbial seats of their pants, and for a career astronaut, that was not a good feeling. They were accustomed to missions planned out years in advance. Cal had thought that the incident at Ceres was some bump on the road, but he now felt foolish not to have somehow realized that it was the signal of them leaving the road entirely.

He found himself with his eyes squeezed tightly shut and threw them open. Alarmingly, he hadn't really been conscious of ever closing them in the first place. He glanced to his left to see if Sarah had noticed, but her gaze was focused beyond the module's panoramic windows, where the blue super gas giant was eating up the sky ahead.

The massive world swallowed the horizons of their view as they fell further toward the turmoil of its atmosphere. Pulling away, the solar-sailer was cast in silhouette by bands of cyclones; vortices of blue traced in yellow and green as they rose to heights where they wisped away, boiling off into space. Further down in the deeps, the storms churned into purples and black.

Cal shifted his attention to the rear view displayed on the main screen, the chandelier ship magnified by a factor of one hundred. Its crystalline structure turned kaleidoscopic in the combination of the light from the gas giant and the multicolored sparks of its protective field.

The magnetometers spiked again, this time without a commensurate display of fireworks from the ship's EM field. Many miles in front of them, the rear bulb of the solar-sailer appeared to molt away. It exploded from the main body in a shower of gas and brilliant debris. The bulk of the sailer seemed to accelerate away, but perhaps that was an illusion.

"Doc, Inez . . . what the hell is happening? Lightening its mass load?"

"Not sure, Cal . . ." said Inez

"I wish Xu were here," the Doc muttered.

"You and me both," Inez replied, and turning to Cal and the pilot, said, "Odysseus is reporting that the tail piece is slowing."

The Doc pulled the science station's central screen closer. "The expulsions of gas seem to have slowed it down. It's dropping closer to the planet and will not have the necessary momentum for a slingshot out of the system."

"What does that mean?"

Her eyes flit around so rapidly, from window to window and screen to screen, that pain spiked through her skull. "It means the gas giant is going to whip it into orbit around the star."

"Seiss?"

The lizard was suited up as well, floating in the middle of the CM but ready to take refuge in the jump seat harness if necessary. His neck extended snake-like from the iridescent suit's polished ring and poked between Cal and the pilot.

"Not sssure. Never see this. This only sailer I ever see in person. Others sssee on screensss to learn about."

"Maybe it knew it was being pursued?" the Doc suggested. "Sometimes animals will shed a tail to escape a predator."

"Whatever the reason, if the tail is also going to round Triangle, then it's an opportunity for us. Get us behind the tail. We're going to use it as cover for as long as we can."

Blasts from the reaction-control thrusters swung the *Ulysses* into the shadow and shelter of the quarter-mile long tail bulb. They raced as a pair, drawing closer to the gas giant.

"You want to recommend a strategy?"

"If you can see them, they can see us, so keep them invisible. Keep the tail between us and them."

Eighty-Three

The engineer's face appeared on Cal's forearm screen. "I think I've found a way to get us more speed. This isn't going to sound sane, but I think we can push the reactor to 130 percent."

Cal frowned back at him. "That's way beyond the safety limits . . ."

"I know, but hear me out. We keep the reactor chamber in atmosphere rather than a vacuum because the gasses help to transfer heat energy. We get an extra 8 percent in cooling capacity that way. In theory, we could flood the module with something that can transfer heat energy more efficiently than air."

"What do we have that transfers heat more efficiently than air?"

"The cooling water."

"Are you out of your mind?"

"I'm not."

"The entire complex could short out."

"I don't think so. The cooling pipes run all through the chamber and around the reactor. Everything is triple-insulated and water-resistant in case of a leak, and the water is well purified. There isn't much in the way of metallic elements to carry a charge. I'm more concerned about a short boiling the cooling water into steam and rupturing something. I'll remain here, if anything starts arcing, I can shut those circuits down and repair or reroute."

"Paul, you said it yourself. The water is there to cool the reactor. The temperature is going to soar in there, the radiation alone—"

"The suit can take it. I can take it. Besides, what choice do we have?"

Eighty-Four

Paul stood in the engineering module and sealed and locked the hatches. The constancy of their braking thrust enabled him to walk in a semblance of gravity. It felt strange to him. No one was ever supposed to occupy the engineering module while the plasma engine was operating.

But what does that matter? he thought. *What I'm about to do is much crazier.*

He crossed to the cooling water pipes, a squid-like nexus of conduits running up and around the reactor. They connected directly to the reserves and the pumping unit that moved consumables out of the tankers and into the rest of the system. It was not the engine that required all of that cooling water, even though temperatures inside were currently exceeding those of the core of the star. The engine parts were magnetically shielded, the hot plasma never physically touching the mechanisms. The reactor was what powered those protections. It was the reactor that needed the cooling.

He opened a valve never intended to be opened with the system running, and water flooded out into the chamber, splashing around his spacesuited legs, crashing through the grated flooring, and showering down onto the platforms below. Within minutes, the water began rising over the first set of scaffolded balconies at the lowest levels of the engine compartment. Paul began opening emergency bleed vents all up and down the four-story-tall sides of the reactor and engine tower. The water sloshed around due to the braking gravity. Cataracts buffeted the engineer as he waded from station to station, junction to junction, checking for telltale signs of sparks.

By the time he had rushed up the ladders that zigzagged through the various platforms and levels, the water had flooded up to the engineer's helmet. It was racing him up the tower. The waves crested over his faceplate, beginning to burble with heat transfer as he reached the top and opened a final valve, ensuring that the circulation of water through the entire system would continue once it reached that height. The indicators read green, but he put his gloved hand over one of the open intake valves and felt the suction just to be sure.

He tabbed the comms, enjoying the somewhat horrified look on Cal's face at seeing that he was entirely submerged. He gave the captain a thumbs up. The water hadn't quite filled the chamber yet but it should have been enough. "I think we're good."

"Take the reactor to 130 percent," said Cal.

Paul watched the indicators rise beyond the green as bubbles swirled around him.

Eighty-Five

Just ahead of the *Ulysses,* commanding almost the entire view from the starboard window panorama, was the massive tail segment of the solar-sailer. The train of globes embedded in its sides throbbed with color. Sarah didn't need the telescope to see fine details along its quarter mile-long surface. They were nearly nestled up alongside it, relatively speaking. She constantly adjusted their position, shadowing the discarded component from no more than ten miles away, keeping its bulk between them and any further probing from the chandelier ship.

Cal hardly spared a glance at the glowing mountain floating over his right shoulder, his attention instead on the section of console in front of him.

"It's working, Paul! Reactor temps have gone beyond green but are staying within yellow limits!"

The engineer gave Cal a thumbs-up and then cut the line.

"Is that going to be enough?"

He turned to address the pilot's question. "*Ulysses*'s engine can accelerate for as long as it's got fuel, and we've got a lot of fuel. We can't increase the size of the engine, but with more juice from the reactor, we should be able to pump more hydrogen through, strip off more electrons per second and produce more thrust."

"Theoretically."

He ignored her snark. Cal scrolled his console displays off to the left, and a new set of windows exploded open in front of him. The bulk of Triangle was represented by a large blue crescent. Glowing arcs and loops described the multiple objects and creatures chasing one another toward the Jovian. The ejection of the tail and the *Ulysses*'s disappearance in the shadow of its bulk had apparently confounded the People. On infrared and radar, it appeared that the smaller core section of the chandelier had been recalled. It had fired its own engine to presumably intercept the solar-sailer but seemed to have changed its mind. It had shut down its burn and looped around the ship-creature to head back toward it's other component. Cal sent the image over to Sarah's pilot console.

"Why is it coming back?" she asked.

"Who knows? We don't really know why it split off in the first place."

"It wouldn't do that for no reason."

"One would assume not."

Seiss hissed agreement.

"Well, it looks like we've saved the solar-sailer," Sarah teased, fatalistically.

"Whatever the reason, they're slowing down. We can worry about it all we want, so long as we keep accelerating. We're going to make it." *We are.* Cal gritted his teeth.

Eighty-Six

Paul saw a spark, and then another, falling from one of the massive cables that crossed the very heights of engineering. Under the continual thrust, the volume of water was thrown back against the far end of the module and, therefore, the height of the sloshing tide stayed a reliable ten to fifteen feet below the arching curve of the module's forward end. He swam upwards. His helmet broke the surface, and a tide of trickling rivers flowed over the dome.

Another shower of sparks fell, hissing, into the choppy surf. He gazed up at it. It was a bad one to have go. That cable sent power to RF generator one. If it were to fail, much of the hydrogen injected into the engine wouldn't be converted into plasma. The ship would lose much of its thrust, and they'd lose time they desperately needed in order to out-fly their alien pursuer. There wasn't a second to spare, so he hoisted himself onto the emergency service ladder and climbed to the heights of the module. Hand over hand, foot by foot, he moved from span to span in order to access a part of the ship never meant to be touched except in zero gravity. As a result, he teetered fifteen feet above the sea of cooling water. A fall wouldn't kill him, although it could potentially split his suit. As if in punishment for his thoughts, the *Ulysses* hit some thermal updraft or near solid sheet of energetic particles and bucked, swinging him off the railing, turning and slamming him into the side of the conduit-riven module. He gripped a spaceframe girder tightly as the tremendous volume of liquid caromed back and then surged forward, throwing him against the roof. The conduit fizzled and hissed. As the water receded and streamed away, he steadied his grip and threw open the service panel. Grasping the cable, he pulled out his multi-tool and began to fuse the thick insulating layer closed. With all the water splashing about, he didn't bother attempting tape or adhesive.

Electricity raced along his suit sleeves, piercing its layers and scorching his skin, affecting his suit's systems. Half of his HUD went black. He had no idea of his suit's integrity, no idea if it was leaking or bleeding atmosphere. There was fluid sloshing in the bottom of his boots, but it could just be the pooling of sweat. Just as he finished the seal, the ship shuddered again, and he slipped from his perch, smacked his chest against the great bolted curve of the module's inner supports, and fell back into the rough seas.

Eighty-Seven

The large arachnid shivered on its pedestal of crystalline legs, and multicolored fluids pulsed in and out of each of its ten appendages. Eyes that were literally gems dashed about wildly amidst a wriggling field of frenzied mineralized ropes. Something had reached out and struck the core-ship as it approached their original prey—the ship of the Fleet. This had never happened before. Never in all of the history of the People had a ship of the Fleet defended itself in such a manner.

Two new things have happened. I have checked original memories and know nothing. Two new things have happened consecutively.

The creature scuttled across the causeway net and settled back into the core-ship's interface pit.

I am alone and have been fired upon. I contain original memories. I cannot be lost.

It had aborted the core-ship's burn and was looping back to rendezvous with the rest of its bulk.

I must rejoin the ship. I contain original memories. I cannot be lost.

The outer sections of the chandelier lay ahead of the core-ship. Beyond was the massive discarded tail of the ship of the Fleet, which the spider had never cared about at all. It had known the tail would molt for the People had seen this before. It could be easily harvested later if the ship of the Fleet itself was incapacitated. There were only two objects of interest to it. The sailer, which had somehow acted against it without a motile unit, and the unknown spacecraft, which it could no longer detect but must have been there. Somewhere.

Two things have happened that have never happened before. The new thing is most important. Yet original memories must not be lost.

The tetrapod reached out with a spidery leg to touch a jellied projection hanging from the bone-like grid of the ceiling. Minute cilia on the tip of the limb gripped the gelatinous surface and distorted it. In response, the core-ship's thrusters exploded in a pinwheel of flame, increasing its rotation.

A new thing appears. A ship of the Fleet fires a projectile that strikes with little impact? What is happening?

The creature sent a powerful electrical charge coursing through the skin of its craft.

Unknown things act in unknown ways. A projectile is not necessarily a projectile. Original memories must not be lost.

It twisted the jellied stalk again and pushed it flush with the ceiling grid. The core-ship's thrusters fired, opposing the spin, and the ship's rotation slowed to normal.

The new thing must have minds. New things always have minds. Memories must be tasted.

It could not see the new thing. It was playing a game. Hiding behind the tail now instead of the ship-creature itself. But it was there. The spider was certain that it was ancient, certain that it was of the Fleet. Of the Fleet but not a ship of the Fleet, and if it was not that, what? What was it? A New Thing.

Memories must be tasted. Tastes must be shared with the bulk. The bulk will remember.

Eighty-Eight

"Here it comes," Cal said. He was unable to catch a glimpse of the chandelier through the telescope, but the shining splinter of the ship's core was clearly on its way back. Headed wide of the tail, if he had to guess, to rendezvous with the rest of the chandelier. He didn't want to guess, he wanted to know. "What the hell is it up to?"

"It's a little hard for me to tell," the pilot responded. "If you can't see them, they can't see us, remember?"

Cal twisted his mouth into a frown. "Doc, we need to launch a camera swarm. Minimum range, max dispersal. You know how to do that?"

"I've always wanted to shoot that thing." She smiled wanly. "Right away, Cal." She folded the screens up against the science station console and jetted through the circular rear hatch, falling down the spinal corridor. Her green suited form sailed down to the hub and in through the storage ring. She spared a tiny glance toward the food locker holding the treasured sweetness of her favorite gel bars. She spun to land feet first against the hatch to the docking ring and kicked open the lever handle to drop into the torus.

Moving quickly to the wall, she removed a bottle shaped projectile from the rack and transferred it to a gun-like mechanism built into an airlock no bigger than the locker that held her gel bars. She pushed the hatch closed and engaged the mechanism. The swarm launcher projected out through the exterior surface of the docking ring, and with a gout of explosive gas, ejected dozens of baseball-sized camera pods out into space. Unpowered, cameras studding every surface, the disposable pods would give them a myriad of new vantage points. The swarm's momentum and battery life would keep them useful until they reached the outer atmosphere.

She watched them twinkle away, fanning out on their buckshot trajectories.

Eighty-Nine

A procession of pixels marched, seemingly ignored, across Cal's flight console. His gaze remained fixed through the windows as flashing symbols of light representing the sailer, *Ulysses*, the jettisoned tail section and camera swarm, and the ship of the People progressed toward the flattened sphere that signified the planet.

They were dropping close, and the Jovian now commanded the entirety of the horizon. The ship-creature sailed over the twisting blue surface, lofting away toward the blazing star. His eyes flicked downwards to the console, updating the relative positions of the pertinent objects in his mind, and then returned to the towering, churning, mountainous clouds reaching up for them. Although they moved and swirled like the storms of Jupiter, the thunderheads were quite different than anything they had experienced before. The influx of stellar energies made the planet too hot for methane or water clouds. If they had once existed before, they would have boiled away millennia ago. Triangle was so hot that the blue storms sweeping up from the horizon were composed mostly of silicates—silicon and oxygen bound up with extra electrons—essentially charged clouds of molten rock and glass.

"*This* might tax our EM field," worried the pilot, her face losing all color.

Ninety

The two sections of the chandelier met, melding with one another as the *Ulysses* flipped end over end, putting the chandelier, the jettisoned tail, and the solar-sailer into their rear-view. Firing it's engine again, the Earth ship peeled away into an ellipse calculated to bring them down lower over the poles. Their crystalline pursuer fell just behind the great curve of the horizon.

"They're relentless."

The Doc turned to the saurian. "What do they *want*?"

"Already sssay. People want *Ulysses*. Want Civ Engine."

"Isn't there any way to speak with them? We tried so hard to communicate with the weed through the server, and we devoted a lot of time talking with you."

The lizard pulled his eyestalks back and interrupted her. "Not—I spend time. I learn the hoonman language." The creature jiggled his cobra hood in laughter. He was purposefully using the mispronunciation now.

"You're right. These . . . People aren't making much of an effort, are they?"

"That we can *tell*," Inez reminded him.

Seiss shook its snout. "Truth. Hard to communicate with the

People unless allow direct communication."

"Direct communication?" Inez seemed to brighten up at the possibilities, but the saurian cut her off.

"No, remember?" Seiss made a stabbing motion at his helmet with one clawed finger. "That isss sssomething can *never* do."

Cal turned around in his seat, looking back at the creature and trying to catch the Doc's eye. He was about to question the lizard further when the ship contacted the outer reaches of Triangle's atmosphere and lurched. Great thunderous washes of energized particles bulleted across the bow, and long moments passed with them blind inside the field's pulsing fog. Sheets of the planet's aurora blasted sparks and streamers around the circumference of the protective shielding. By the time it fizzled, the tail had visibly pulled away from them, accelerating off on its slingshot orbit to rendezvous with the star.

The colossal chandelier was still behind them, its two components completing their reintegration. The core slid inside the girdling bands and armatures folded out to secure their center. At the tip of the chandelier's core, the highest height of the glass castle's central spire, pools of light converged and began to range outwards as if searching for something.

"Where are those lights coming from?"

"I'm not sure," said Inez.

"Are those ours?"

"No, they're not," she said. "There's nothing else out here that could be . . . wait. The light is being produced by the alien ship itself. The chandelier's surface is being illuminated from within."

"Why?"

"Good question. Are they trying to communicate?"

Light patches swarmed around the alien vessel and unexpectedly converged in a spot on the outermost curtain of crenellated cylindrical structures.

"What the hell was that!" Cal began rewinding through the

camera swarm images, but the kaleidoscope of views, ten for each multifaceted camera pod that made up the swarm, made it nearly impossible for a human to make sense of it. "Odysseus! I need the camera swarm views focusing on the convergence of those lights!" His screen blanked, and then there it was, at the intersection of the ovals of light, like a Venn diagram of dread. Silhouetted against the lights, something strange seemed to be forming, like a pool of wax melting up into a candle. It was Polyphemus, staring straight across space and down the barrel of the Earth ship's scope.

"How is that possible?"

The Doc broke in with a quaver in her voice. "Maybe it can use the sailer's matter transporter?"

"Maybe. Seiss?"

"Not know."

"Maybe it got aboard the smaller part when it rounded the sailer?"

"It doesn't matter how," Cal said quietly without raising his head from the scope. "It's there." He zoomed in, mirroring the scope's imagery onto a segment of the main screen. The cyclops appeared on the glowing surface of the crystalline chandelier, its attention now turned toward the bulk of the strange craft upon which it was standing. Cal magnified the image as much as he could. The same transparent humanoid outline sheathing a glowing fluidic interior now, somehow, appeared to have a human-like nervous system floating within it. The filigree of nerves spiderwebbed throughout the azure gel and cradled a pulsing purplish brain that hovered behind the single blazing red chevron eye. It stood motionless on the surface of the chandelier as the illuminated skin strobed around it.

"Am I seeing things?" Cal asked without taking his eyes off the scope.

Suddenly, chunks of the illuminated chandelier skin began to dislodge, rising like asphalt on a winter's road buckling against the unstoppable force of expanding ice. The pieces broke off, but they didn't fall away. They clung to the surface and began to scuttle forwards, upwards, toward the cyclops.

"What in God's name . . .?"

Cal pulled his hands away from the console as if it had suddenly become hot. "Odysseus, focus the hi-res on those new objects!" The telescope's view shot away, zooming in further and faster than any human could have managed, tracking the scuttling objects.

"Spiders."

"I hate spiders."

The big lizard nodded his serpentine head and shivered his narrow shoulders. "Ssspiderssss."

The crystalline insects swarmed over the cyclops.

Ninety-One

Holy shit, they're enemies!

The Doc had a white-knuckle grip on the sides of the science console's butterfly wing auxiliary screens. "Is it . . . fighting them?"

It was as if no one heard her. They were all ensnared by the sight, dumbstruck.

Inez released the clasps of her harness and floated closer to the image on the cockpit's main display. "Dear lord, look at those things!"

The glittering crustaceans mobbed the cyclops. The blue figure deformed and swung its limbs, sweeping the scuttling things off into space or smashing them against the equally pellucid hull of the ship. The surface beneath Polyphemus's feet erupted into grasping spider legs as more of the creatures unfolded and differentiated from the vessel, rippling out from beneath the conflict. The chandelier's layers split open to disgorge even more scrambling triple-bodied crabs, as if the cells of some deranged organism were gestating into individual defenders.

"What the hell is going on?" Inez asked.

"I sure don't know," replied the Doc.

"Who do we root for?"

"*Us,*" said Cal. "I hope they keep each other busy." He turned to the pilot. "Sorry to do this to you, Sarah." *Sorry to do this to all of us.* "I think you know what I'm going to say, right?"

Of course, she did. She had already begun preparing for the maneuvers. She slid her command screen out from the console and began shifting symbols and patches of various colors across it, creating custom sets of nested commands that she could activate in batches or sequence. As she did, another part of her mind submerged into a very special kind of thought. The possibilities were a million rivers that endlessly branched into more and more complex tributaries. They were all there in front of her, in front of *them*, but only a very few led where they wanted to go: to a future where the *Ulysses* remained intact. She had to find her way there, she had to make sure they stayed in that pocket of time called the present.

She heard Cal speaking. "—can't reach Paul. There's going to be some wildly varying stresses put on the engine shortly. It needs to be ready, and he needs to get the hell out of there." She hoped he was addressing someone else because her ability to pay attention to anything apart from the ship and its motion was quickly dissolving. She knew this would be the greatest test of her ability that she had ever faced.

Considering this new capability of the spider ship—its ability to separate into individual attacking elements—it was even more critical to keep the tail between them than ever. If any of the insectoids threw themselves at the *Ulysses*, she would try to make sure they hit the tail instead. The problem with that plan was, of course, that the tail was going to pull away eventually. There was only one viable way out for them, and she knew it, and she knew Cal knew it. They needed speed, and the key to speed when racing into orbit was in braking. The faster they canceled out their velocity, the quicker gravity would pull them down. Their captain wasn't seeking a suicide plunge though, he would be wanting to bring *Ulysses* down at a very specific point.

She came up for air. "Were you talking to me?"

Cal smiled wanly and shook his head. She slid back into the

deeps of thought. Her cultivated cool was holding, thanks to a certain freedom and comfort she had long ago learned to derive from challenging moments.

Cal flew from his seat, and the lizard's snake-like head turned to watch him go. She hardly noticed. *Do your best and if you, or the ship, are not up to the challenge, so be it.* There was freedom in that.

Someone once said something like *do or don't, there is no such thing as trying . . .* or something. *Whatever it was, it was damned stupid*, she thought. *The only thing that matters is trying.* She recalled a lunch she'd once had with a mentor and colleague. He told her how, if a pilot kept flying, one day they would not be up to the task. He said that he knew that day was right around the corner. So, he was retiring. For her, that same metaphorical day had come and gone weeks ago.

Spirographic patterns of ellipses flowered over her screen; orbits around the Jovian, orbits around the tail. The figures for necessary forces, changes in velocity, attitudes, and positions fell all around the spirals. It was going to be a delicate balance, shedding just the right amount of horizontal and vertical velocities. To top it off, she was going to need to pull off the maneuvers while playing cat and mouse with the chandelier ship around the mountainous, out-gassing, tail section. This was the sort of insane maneuver she'd only imagine attempting in video games, and yet, she was shifting it into the realm of possibility while eliciting hardly a protest from any conscious part of her mind.

She contemplated the space outside the panoramic windows, ignoring the magnified cosmic battle playing out on the video screen. Beyond the solar-sailer's discarded tail section was the curve of the planet. They were already so low that she could see distinct mountain ranges of frothing silicates and bursts of lightning rippling through the convulsing sky.

As things got more and more surreal, she noted, the ridiculous was becoming normal.

Ninety-Two

A voice screamed, *"Danger: personnel are to evacuate the spindle and engineering section whenever the reactor is operating above 60 percent. Danger: personnel are to evacuate the spindle and engineering section whenever the main engine is in operation. Dang—"* The voice finally died as Cal figured out how to cancel his spacesuit's audio alarms. He had a lot of experience canceling various suit warnings, but he'd never heard these before. The spindle hatch rushed up to meet him, and he landed with his hands gripping the handle. He stared through the inches thick plastic window and called out through the comms again, "Paul!"

No answer.

About five or six feet below the hatch was a turbulent mass of bubbling water pressed against the far side by the thrust of the engine, and so it appeared as if he were looking down into a deep silo filled with churning fluid. The ship was firing the main in opposition to their direction of flight, but Cal knew that Sarah might have to cut it off at any minute and throw the ship on some tight orbit around the tail, and then that mass would move. "Paul!"

He wrenched the hatch upwards, and the pressure escaping blew him back onto his ass. He hoisted himself over and poked his helmet out to peer down into the engineering section. There was a garishly painted emergency ladder secured to the module's inner wall, but the place was never meant to be accessed except in zero gravity, and so it was further out of reach than he would have preferred. He slipped inside, maintaining his hold on the handles while ratcheting the hatch closed. The emergency ladder was still too far from the hatch platform. The suit made him ungainly, and he swiped for the top rung more than once before grabbing it and swinging down onto the ladder.

"Odysseus! Where's the engineer?"

"Reactor level two."

The engineering module was four stories tall. Two stories for the reactor, another two for the centrally placed engine complex with the cooling unit running throughout. Cal looked down into the swirling tank of water. Reactor level two wasn't bad. The water churned no more than six feet below, which would put Paul's location at no more than twenty to thirty feet underwater. He swallowed hard and leapt into the rippling liquid. He held his feet together as much as he could, trying to slice into the water rather than smack it hard. He felt the shock against the soles of his boots and the heat encircling him as he fell through a cloud of fizzing bubbles.

Ninety-Three

The *Ulysses* and the chandelier chased one another in a halting manner around the tail, playing a staccato game of ring-around-the-rosy as they all fell toward the atmosphere. Despite the melee still raging on its surface, the alien ship made periodic attempts to swing around the hulk between them. Each time, Sarah cut the main drive and flung *Ulysses* in the opposite direction, only throttling back up once they had rounded the tail and were back in optimal position. Twice smaller objects accelerated away from the chandelier, tracking them. Both times, she moved the ship so that the objects' flight paths intercepted the mass of the tail first, but every evasive maneuver slowed them down, changing the equation as to how to get the ship where Cal wanted it—and in one piece. They spun in lurching bursts around the glowing, throbbing mountain.

The chandelier swung through the cloud of camera probes, revealing it in the utmost of detail. Up close, it more resembled a colossal well-groomed tree. Vast circular curtains of crenellated rods orbited the central spear, joined via a cathedral of crystal arches.

"Crossing over the equator." She watched the plot of the tail's course; their divergence would soon accelerate. "We'll only have cover for another twenty-two minutes."

Ninety-Four

Cal's vision cleared by the time he settled onto the grated floor of the first reactor level. Submerged, the space took on a haunted quality. It was as if he were moving through a dream. The water shimmered with heat, currents rippling around him. The reactor housing and control consoles warped in undulating shafts of light. Cal spotted an open panel with a globe of emergency insulation plastered inside. He hopped quickly to the emergency ladder and followed it down through a gap in the floor and into the equally flooded lower level. His helmet dipped through the grating, and he saw Paul's big orange spacesuit floating up against the ceiling. He swam off the ladder and grabbed a few fingers full of floor grating to steady himself and reached out for the engineer.

Paul bobbed away.

He was either unconscious or dead. Cal reached out and gripped the engineer by his backpack strap when the shafts of light in the chamber suddenly shifted. The main engine cut out, and the volume of water sloshed through the module as the force that had held it in check vanished, smashing Cal and Paul into the grated ceiling, battering them against it.

Cal somehow kept his grip on the engineer's orange suit, struggling to orient himself when what seemed like an explosion blossomed just in front of him, a gout of whitewater, churning and folding around itself. There was a swarming froth of bubbles that obscured his vision, and then he found himself jerked forwards, impelled to and through the surface. He twirled through empty air and smashed into another wave to find himself once again submerged and approaching the spindle hatch. Seiss was behind them, gripping their backpacks and propelling them forward with grand strokes of his muscular tail.

The water suddenly rushed away, and Seiss braced them against the railings, pressing them against the ladder, gripping it with his huge curved and clawed boots to keep them from falling back. The water cascaded over them, but they held firm. Cal yanked down on the hatch release lever, and the buildup of hot gasses nearly shot them through the circular portal. Seiss smashed his helmet against the rim going through and released them, which sent them caroming off against the tubular spindle wall. Cal grabbed at the wildly swinging hatch cover and wrenched it over. Huge orange mitts, the engineer's nearly fused gloves, wrapped over the hatch cover and helped him wrestle it down and lock it into place.

Cal fell back against the "floor" of the spindle, beside the hatch, as the main engine lit up again and the gravitic sensation returned. The lizard hissed and felt his helmet for cracks. Paul smiled at them.

Ninety-Five

The solar-sailer creature continued its dive starward, growing smaller as it fell away. Sarah had kept with the tail section as long as she could, but the giant object had now risen above the *Ulysses*'s orbit. The string of globes arrayed along its flanks pulsed and flashed. Its usefulness as a shield was coming to an end. As it continued on its slingshot path around the super gas giant, the jettisoned tail was venting gas in a coordinated manner. It was adjusting its attitude, positioning itself for something. The tail's course had diverged such that the chandelier was constantly in view, only obscured in the narrowest channel of the flight corridor. It had made a few feints, which she was able to counter by moving the ship out to a distance of fifty miles and positioning the tail between. As long as they quickly detected anything leaving the alien ship, she could maneuver to where the tail would still shield them, but that wouldn't last long.

She found it odd that whatever was being lobbed at them was unable to change course and keep from striking the tail. They just drove into it with little or no variation, producing clouds of dust and debris in rings around the impacts. Whatever they were, they weren't designed as missiles . . . unless they were dumb projectiles like the camera swarm. Disposable.

Ninety-Six

Cal, Seiss, and Paul held themselves against the pipe-lined walls of the spindle, recovering. They each breathed heavily, staring at one another, feeling the waves of directional force as the drive kicked in and out. The sensation was like losing one's stomach repeatedly, going up and over bumps and hills in a ground vehicle.

"Are you okay?" he asked the engineer, finally catching his breath.

The big man wrapped one arm around a flexible conduit, steadying himself. His barrel chest heaved as he said, "I'm okay, Cal."

"Thank God. And good work."

He held his right fist, thumbs up, and glanced over at the lizard. "Good work to you too, thank you."

The alien turned his head toward him, bobbing his eyestalks and letting out a rattling hiss as reply.

Paul nodded and turned back to his captain, tensing his guts against another gravitic wave. He could hear the water sloshing violently beyond the engineering hatch. "I have to go back in there."

"No, you don't," Cal said.

"Yes, I do and you know it. That or we have to throttle back and drain the module."

"We're going to throttle back once the braking maneuvers are finished."

"And they're not finished. Not even close. Listen, the cooling water is pretty pure, but against expectation, it can still carry a charge, one more bad short and . . ."

Cal resigned with a nod. He'd been wrong to doubt the man. Paul would disagree with him, he might even punch him in the face one day, but he'd never fail the ship. Not while he was breathing. A realization of his relationship with the engineer became an encapsulation of the spirit of the entire ship. He had worried that under unprecedented circumstances they might fall apart. Instead, as human groups have done countless times over the centuries, they had all drawn closer together.

"You're right, I know. We need *someone* in there . . ."

"No, Cal. We need *me* in there. I'm the best one for this job. By far. And this job needs to be done as well as it can."

Cal tried to manage a smile, but he couldn't pull it off. He just nodded in assent.

"This is our only way out, isn't it?"

"It's that or take our chances with the spiders," said Cal.

Paul looked back at the hatch, red emergency lights chasing themselves around its circumference. He grabbed the handle and cycled the hatch open. "I'm not a fan of spiders."

"Me neitherrr," hissed the lizard. "Ssspidersss." He shivered in his suit.

The action finally elicited a smile on the captain's careworn and exhausted face. He reached out and clasped his hand on the engineer's massive shoulder. "I hate to say this, Paul. But—"

"I know," Paul said. "It's going to get worse."

Ninety-Seven

Cal and Seiss flew through the spinal corridor on the way to the CM as the drive kept kicking and the ship vibrated and lurched around them. Moving through the burnished steel circlet of the hatch, they were presented with a scene of myriad wonders. The main viewscreen, unraveled to its fullest, displayed a magnification of the alien spacecraft's crystalline surface, while below, the blue cloudscapes of the planet rushed toward the curving windows. Partly silhouetted against the rushing chaos, the Doc, Inez, and far in the nose, enwrapped within consoles and viewport, pilot Samuels wrestled with the controls.

Cal's attention shot to the viewscreen; on it, the cyclops was whirling multiple appendages to strike at its attackers. It had deviated from a humanoid form to adapt to the task. Cobalt tentacles whipped out, smashing at the tripartite arachnids. They broke apart, sometimes with a single strike, creating a cloud of glinting shards—a twirling halo around the battle. The cyclops's chevron eye burned an intense purple.

Odysseus chimed an alert and another window opened at the margins of the viewscreen. On it, the medium resolution scope scrolled across the luminous curve of the chandelier. It stopped suddenly on a limpid blister; a huge upwelling was forming on the surface of the chandelier. On the main window, the cyclops turned to watch the eruption as it simultaneously kept up its fight. The upwelling burst and a stream of glistening shapes squirted away, growing and enlarging. Wriggling multi-limbed crustacean shapes headed straight down the barrel of the telescope.

"Switch the windows, put the sub-window on the main," directed Cal.

"They're spiders!" Inez shouted. "And they're throwing themselves at us!"

Seiss tried adjusting his massive neck within the confines of its helmet. His eyestalks swung back and forth. "People one, People many. People not same as organics. Don't care. Sssingle ssspidersss only whole. Don't care young, only old."

"How can they survive outside their EM field?"

"Some of them aren't, look!" the Doc shouted as the telescope zoomed in on the string of glittering spider shapes coming toward them. A few of the glassy arachnids flexed their legs, but the majority had fallen motionless, their colors fading.

The tail had finally pulled far enough away that Sarah was no longer able to hide the ship behind it. A few minutes later, the first of the dead, or at least immobile, spiders cleared its bulk and sailed on toward *Ulysses*, but they disintegrated against the field in great expanding circles of fizzing light.

There was no longer any point to the grand swings of avoidance, and Sarah rammed the thrust slider far forward. Cal grabbed the back of the empty command chair and slid in against the seat back, grabbing at the restraints.

"What is this? What are they doing?" he asked. "Testing our field?"

"By sacrificing their own?"

"They clearly don't think like we do," said the Doc.

More spiders hit the field, exploding into sparks.

"I don't think they're testing it so much as building up to an overload."

Cal torched a look at her. *Of course.* She was right. A slow drizzle designed to deplete their protective field, trying to prevent them from running. Trying to make a dive into the atmosphere impossible. Without the field at full strength, it was entirely possible that it couldn't carry them safely through the transit link. They'd have to abandon their escape, likely right into the spidery clutches of the People.

Ninety-Eight

The electromagnetic field sparkled around *Ulysses*'s shape as the planet's azure globe enveloped the sky. In the CM, the universe was distinctly divided: the starboard viewports were nothing but cerulean swirls while the portside held the blackness of space and the golden sphere of the star.

Between the two, the dwindling solar-sailer suddenly began to unfurl its vast circumferential wings. It was as if a smaller, rippling sun had exploded into existence between the star and the Jovian planet. The sailer was less than one-third astronomical unit from the blazing sphere, skirting the star's gravitational limits while opening its wings to catch the solar wind. Shimmering and voluminous, the sails reflected the light in a ripple of brassy gold that stretched for miles. Its effective area reached far beyond via invisible electromagnetic extensions. The ship's magnetometers and receivers began to sing and sizzle.

In the CM, at the tip of the stack of modular components that made up the *Ulysses,* the crew shielded their eyes as the ship's systems struggled to adjust to the intensity of the glare.

"Dear *Lord.*"

As the sailer's wings stretched wide, the *Ulysses*'s telescope focused and zoomed in, painting its beauty onto the main viewscreen.

The iridescent wings extended fully, leaving the now slender dragonfly body of the vessel-creature to project outwards from the center like the sexual structures of some stupendous blossom. The sails billowed taut, shining with reflected brilliance.

Ninety-Nine

Paul stood in the flooded engineering module, boots magnetically locked to the floor grate, struggling with a panel that had blown outward. Inside the opened housing, water exposed to high voltage was sublimating into steam, creating a storm of angry bubbles. He threw the cover away to expose the mess, and a gout of steam bubbles rushed out, obscuring his vision entirely. He threw up a hand to shield his faceplate and ducked away. There was nothing to do but cut off power to that trunk. The arcing current converting the cooling water to steam was ramping up the pressure within the module, and that couldn't be allowed to continue. He threw the switch and cut power to almost a third of the ship, sliding the breaker blocks that would shunt power from other areas to only the most necessary systems.

"Paul!" The captain's voice crackled over the comms channel. He ignored it and let himself drift a bit with the current. Water sloshed around his feet, but it wasn't continuing to rise. It was likely just sweat.

"Paul, are you still with us?"

He opened the comms channel. "I'm here, I had to shut down one of the main electrical subsystems. I'll try and keep the essentials running as long as possible, but I'm going to need to drain the module to effect any repairs."

"Roger."

"*If* we can drain it. If we lose power to the pumps . . ."

"I get it. No drain."

"No *cooling*."

Cal grimaced. Without cooling, the reactor would go up. Quickly.

One Hundred

The solar-sailer flared, a weakly burning point hanging between the yellow orange ball of the star and the blue horizon of the super gas giant. Every console in the *Ulysses*'s CM seemed to erupt in shrieks and wails.

"We're detecting massive local change in electromagnetic field intensity!" screamed Inez.

"It's the electromagnetic portion of the ship-creature's sails," Cal figured, aloud.

"It isn't," Inez corrected. "It's coming from the—"

Odysseus wheeled the main telescope around. The mountainous tail was undergoing a transformation. The strings of glowing spheres along its flanks bulged like the eyes of a strangled man. Its alpine bulk was budding open, splitting as if from internal pressure. Sparkling jets of gas erupted from the seams, affecting its attitude on its path toward the star.

The crew stared, eyes wide, mouths agape. A blinding light engulfed the tail. A vast coruscating beam burst into existence between the pulsing palisade and the shimmering wings of the solar-sailer.

"What in God's name!"

"It's . . ."

"A giant fucking laser!"

"It's got to be a hundred meters wide."

The beam pulsed like a beating heart, luminous in a multitude of phasing reds.

"An organically produced beam as big around as a football field?"

"How could anything organic create such a thing?"

"It's impossible."

"Evidently not." Cal's eyes searched the telescope windows, looking for their pursuer. "Inez, I can't find the chandelier."

"What!" She frantically began her own search.

Cal opened his comms to engineering. "Paul, are you seeing this?"

The engineer's face appeared, staring down at his forearm screen. "What the hell is it?"

"Inez thinks it's an organic laser. What could power such a thing?"

"A beam that size, I can't imagine anything aside from the same thing that powers the star."

"Organic nuclear fusion?"

"Why not? The sailer exists, previously I'd have thought that was impossible. We use water to cool the outer jacket of our own reactor, but the inner uses organic fluids. Both as coolant and neutron moderator, they're not as corrosive so . . ."

"So, organic nuclear power. It's possible?"

"Yeah, I'd say it's possible."

"Does it pose any danger to us?"

"Who knows? But I wouldn't think from radiation, the EM field should hold."

"Thanks, Paul." The tail was drawing further away all the time. Whatever danger it did pose was likely shrinking by the second.

"No problem, chief."

Cal closed the channel, already shifting his attention back to the search for the chandelier when the sailer's rippling wings blossomed into an even greater brilliance. The light flared, magnitudes beyond the golden brilliance of the star, and turned red with the energies of the beam. The mile-long body of the ship-creature was a slender spike shadowed in the center of the shining wings.

"It looks like a flower," said Sarah.

"A laser pistil." The Doc smiled, looking around.

"Laser pistol?"

"Pistil. Like, stamen, and pistil. . ."

Cal groaned, Inez and Sarah laughed. The lizard just stared at her, blinking against his lack of comprehension.

"Laser propulsion," Cal said. "Xu mentioned something about it. NASA once drew up plans for an orbital laser. Laser photons add to the light pressure a vehicle would receive from the star and therefore would increase acceleration over the same sail area and mass."

"That's a lot of additional heat and thrust load to absorb," added the pilot.

The sailer seemed to rotate around its slender core as it sped away.

"Of course, it was all theoretical, no one has ever built such a thing."

Seiss looked at Cal, confused.

"No human."

"Yesss."

"You know anything about this?"

"This learned about only. Recordings a long time ago."

"Whatever you can remember would be good."

The alien nodded, missing the sarcasm. "Sailers not always generate laser pistil," Seiss said, missing the joke and adopting the moniker. "Fire laser light at close to star, maximum accelerate for solar-sailer. Best place at close to star. After finish become sailer egg. Very rich solar system. Come back, yesss. Must."

Inez clicked through a number of windows on her touchscreens.

She mirrored a tumbling shape into a sub-window on the main screen. "The chandelier," she said.

They all turned their heads. "Sonofabitch, is it dead?" Sarah replied. "Are we finally catching a break?" Cal just watched it turn, end over end. It was dark, save for a single bright blue spark, lit only with the azure hues of the planetary storms. Sarah pointed through the panoramic viewports. "Did it get hit by the laser?" she asked.

Cal watched its seemingly lifeless gyrations and pulled at his whiskered chin. "I don't think so?"

"The EM burst?" Inez asked.

"Maybe," Cal said, mirroring her console to his and watching her scroll through windows filled with data; rundowns of the values each of the *Ulysses* varied sensing instruments was returning.

"Maybe the cyclops survived," the Doc said, watching the same information pour in. "Maybe it did something to it?"

Cal shrugged.

"It might be tumbling, but it's staying on its orbit, *our* orbit," said the pilot. "It must not have been struck or be leaking anything that could push it off course. Dead or alive, it's still on our tail."

One Hundred and One

Inez's fingers swept across her console, expanding Odysseus's thought pane. "According to simulation, the action distance of a laser is still small, on an interplanetary scale, even for very large sails and beam directors."

"So . . ." Cal processed the implications quickly. "That means the laser should only be providing a boost for a short time."

"Yeah, it's likely consuming itself in the process, although who knows how long that will take. From the intensity of EM emissions, my guess is that it's supercharging the sailer's electromagnetic wings."

"And that beam director is how large?"

"A hundred feet if it's an inch. A beam of that size would have to be . . ."

"Powerful."

"Yes."

"How fast did Xu say a light sail vessel might eventually accelerate?

"Seven-tenths light speed, I think," Inez replied.

Cal watched as the Laser Pistil fell away from the blue horizon and headed toward low solar orbit, its beam firing tangentially to the star. The ship creature fluttered its sails as it sped away, casting off flashes of light and rapidly shifting double-shadows. It oriented its sail attitude toward the sun, reducing the thermal loads while benefiting from the gravity assist. Keeping its appendages taut, it prepared to swivel its wings and catch the flux streaming away from the star.

Cal turned his attention back to his console and the crystalline object spiraling through the telescope display. "They seem to be incapacitated. Whether it's a result of the laser firing or the actions of the cyclops, or both, I don't know but it's another opportunity we need to capitalize on," he said. "Full braking thrust!" He clamped his helmet onto his head and twisted it into the latch with a reassuring click. "Helmets on, people. We're going to let the planet's gravity pull us in as fast as possible." He listened for the click-slide-clack sounds of their helmets sealing. "With any luck, the booms will activate once we're over the pole."

Sarah glanced over at him. "And if they don't?"

"If they don't, we're going to have to flip and fire the main. Add enough velocity to get back up into orbit if we can. At least that way we can keep the horizon between ourselves and that ship, keep out of its line of sight and far enough away to give us time to react to anything that might be launched from it."

Cal turned his attention back to the looming gas giant as they descended into the upper reaches of its atmosphere. Wisps of sapphire cloud sheared away in front of them, propelled upwards by titanic gusts of more energetic gasses. He leaned forward to peer through the CM's viewports. The sailer was shrinking sunward, a spear tip of laser light. He watched it go and turned his haggard gaze to Triangle's north pole, its atmosphere dancing with cyclonic storms.

One Hundred and Two

"And we thought Jupiter was impressive," the Doc said.

The ship swept down over the far reaches of Triangle's northern hemisphere. Incredible thermal eddies and massive convection currents drew the northernmost storm band up toward the pole. The currents swirled into fractal tendrils, sifting the twisting elements of the atmosphere into regular storm structures the diameter of small moons. Blue then white, blue then white, blue then white.

"Approaching the north polar region," the pilot solemnly intoned.

Ulysses descended toward a landscape of Mandelbrot curves and Julia set tempests that dawned, one after another, into view over the horizon. As they rushed down, the pole itself crested the rim to reveal cyclone after cyclone—no, a cyclone of cyclones. Not just a ring of interlocked twisters but rings of *rings* of them, all orbiting the still larger maw of an immense central polar storm. It was as if the great vortex they had seen around Jupiter's north pole had been duplicated here a half-dozen times. Each copied set chased the other, tearing and screaming, about Triangle's flattened pole.

"It's like Grand Central Station!" Inez blurted, trying to make sense of the images Odysseus was flooding into her displays.

Sarah turned to her captain, asking, "Which one do we choose?"

Cal thought for a fraction of a second. "Inez? Any signs of life from the infected server?"

She slid the analyses of the storms off her screen, pulling data rendered into flatline graphs onto her main display. "Nothing, Cal! It's unresponsive."

Cal grimaced. "Let's hope it's still with us, I don't think we're going to survive with just our native field."

The pilot blew out her breath. "Y'think?" *Not even a chance.* The *Ulysses's* native EM field alone might be capable of protecting them at this point, but she knew the ship would never have survived the Jupiter descent without the alien augmentation. And those storms were just made of *gas*. The cloud banks ahead of them were composed of particles of molten glass and stone.

Sarah tilted her purple-helmeted head toward him and whispered through a private comms channel, "I hope you're as right as you think you are."

"Me too."

"You're going to take us right up the middle, aren't you?"

"Yup."

Ulysses balanced on the tip of its drive flame, teetering above the central maw, its horizontal velocity zeroed out. The drive flame vanished, and the Earth ship dropped like a cannonball, the alien-induced electromagnetic field flaring into brightness. Uncounted trillions of atmospheric particles screamed by at thousands of miles per hour. They were dropping through the throat of a gyre whose boundaries were a constantly shifting edifice of unbelievable wind swirling uncounted miles away. The RCS thrusters belched, and the ship pitched over, bringing its nose down. The ship's belly was engulfed in shimmering light as the field there encountered a greater number of gas molecules as the vehicle swung through its arc.

The faraway walls curved around them like the sky curved about the Earth, the scale dwarfing everything that they had yet experienced. If the gullet of Jupiter's central polar storm was the mouth of a whale, this storm was the orifice of a creature set apart from metaphor and beyond the boundaries of the imagination. It could only be the throat of some churning pelagic beast so huge that it was glimpsed but never fully seen. The *Ulysses*'s main drive flame erupted again, and they were rammed back into their seats.

Behind them, the chandelier suddenly lit up and recovered from its tumble with frantic bursts of reaction mass. It followed, dropping into the central maw just a few hundred miles behind *Ulysses*. Given the scale of the chase, that was nothing. It rushed to catch up to them even as they plummeted through the eye of the storm.

Relentless.

The Earth's ship's RCS system suddenly fired of its own accord, throwing them to port.

"Whoa!" Sarah exclaimed as her left shoulder jammed up against the viewport. The *Ulysses* bucked, skittering to starboard, nudging them toward one wall of the eye.

"What's happening?"

The ship rose and then dropped, turning their stomachs.

"I *think* the red weed is awake," said Inez, looking at her displays. The flatline graphs had turned mountainous. In the infected server's loading space, an image of Jupiter's maw appeared again. Perhaps, she thought, that was the only image it had to communicate its intent?

The ship shouldered closer and closer to the careening wall of searing silicates and gas. From inside the CM it appeared as if they were falling sideways toward a rushing solid landscape, and then, it was there. Revolving toward them was a smaller vortex stretching and spinning within the turbining eyewall, opening a channel into the body of the mother cyclone.

Cal reached out and gripped the pilot's shoulder. "Go, Sarah! Go!"

The main engine spurted flame, throttling up. The ship angled over and fell into the roiling pipe of the tributary whirlpool. Flashes of plasma-electricity rode down the twisting passage before them, illuminating random tiny fractions of the way ahead. It was another stable storm, formed by an architecture of wind into an artery branching off the main. Cal recalled similar bending, tipping motions from the voyage that brought them into the system they were now attempting to escape. It followed that the tube they were riding would take them on a spiraling course through the atmosphere, using the planet's gravity, and possibly forces derived from the pressures their EM field was shunting aside, to put them on the wildest slingshot course imaginable: an accelerating fall around and down to the core.

The terrifying dive through Jupiter, where the winds and currents were made up of mere liquids and gas, was being rendered quaint. The gusts and clattering impacts that now rattled the ship were the results of the much heavier elements now striking them. The atmosphere's preponderance of silicates carried a heavy negative charge and elicited a startling reaction from their protective field. It frothed and spiked, bubbling with prismatic eruptions that foamed like a wolf's saliva around a hank of meat. It flared and flickered as the ship was buffeted within the corridor.

Cal clenched his teeth and tightened his gut. *Ulysses handled Jupiter's sea of metallic hydrogen, it can handle this.* He clung to that hope, feeling his innards rise as the ship dropped again.

In the crack of an instant, the field contracted, snugging tighter around the vessel. Cal felt an odd spike behind one eye. *Sinus pressure? The birth of a migraine? Or was the shell of the ship cracking like that of an egg?* A low moan seemed to rumble up through the spinal corridor and echo into the CM. It sounded as if the joints between modules were creaking and straining to hold together. A burst of sparks sprayed from the conduit channel running over their heads, and Inez's panel went completely dark. On Cal's console, the reactor temperature began to climb.

"Paul! You okay down there?"

No answer.

"Paul?"

One Hundred and Three

The spiraling atmospheric current hurled them deeper through the planet. Silicates began to condense into waves of molten glass sleeting over the *Ulysses*'s field. The waves shattered against the protective envelope, sparking and lighting it up. It flickered, failing for a nanosecond, letting sprays of energetic material through to crash against the *Ulysses*'s inner Earth-made field. Once the ship's primary protection, the original EM generator was now the last line of defense. It whined and ramped up its power curve as another stream of leaked particles made it through the alien guardian.

Paul's face resolved into an empty window at the corner of Cal's command console. "I'm alive, the reactor is ramping up to power the native field."

Cal let a relieved breath escape. "Hang on best as you can," he replied and immediately pivoted to a new alert window opened by the ship's AI. It was the alien ship. The chandelier was lighting up as well, its shielding obviously similarly taxed. The two ships descended on their twisting orbits toward a great, dark, flattened shape as if they were descending from space to the surface of some chromic world. It began to resolve through the haze, a vast oblate spheroid. Cal knew instantly that this must be the world's equivalent of the ocean of metallic hydrogen that surrounded Jupiter's core. It was unimaginably large, far larger than the Earth itself, larger than dozens of Earths probably.

Certainly.

Scale was becoming impossible to judge . . . except in their rear-view. The ship of the People was gaining on them, wreathed in lightning and fire.

If the last time they made such a trip was any judge, they would lose consciousness for a period once they reached the core. Hopefully, like last time, they would continue on their trajectory with enough velocity to put them on course to exit the atmosphere of whatever gas planet they arrived within, despite being unconscious during the transition.

He had no idea if the People would suffer the same impairment, but if not, the *Ulysses* would be at their mercy. He had to think of *something*. He had to *do* something. He had to get them off their back *before* they entered the core.

Ulysses barreled through the current. Winds, gusting like sandstorm drapes, fell against the ship in sheets and folds. The shield glowed continuously, flaring into luminous undulations as they crashed through wave after wave of particles both visible and invisible.

"This is much worse than crashing into Jupiter!" cried the Doc.

"Who ever thought I'd live to hear anyone say that?" the pilot snarked as the ship shuddered and leapt, their stomachs following suit. Seiss flew upwards but kept from slamming his helmet into the curved ceiling with a quick motion of his tail. Out the viewports, a centipede of pure electricity writhed over and around the bow. A shower of sparks fell from the ceiling above Cal's console.

"Alien protective field failing. More and more material is getting through to our native shield."

"Inez, *anything* from the server? Any activity at all?"

"Nothing but Mandelbrot sets, Cal!"

He shouted into the comms channel, "Do everything you can to keep our Earth-built field up, Paul! It may be all we have left."

Paul grimaced as an entirely new sound echoed through the ship. It sounded like paper tearing amidst bursting glass. His eyes flew wide. "Pressure loss in Red Hab."

Cal watched warning indicators flower across his console. "Seal off Red Hab!"

Automatic bulkheads slammed closed, sealing the habitat as well as its interface with the hub.

"Sealed! No one in there right now, thank God," Paul said.

Cal's attention shot back to the chandelier. The spiders' protective field flared and stuttered. The *Ulysses* could pull off a miracle and make it through only to fall into the clutches of their pursuer, and who knew what that could mean. The lizard had mentioned *pithing*.

"Seiss! You said that every civilization bases their shielding on Civ Engine technology?"

"Yesss, but not as—"

"Not as good as the originals. The copies are inferior!" Cal finished his sentence for him. "I remember! If *our* Civ Engine shielding is starting to leak, then . . ."

He opened the comms channel to the engineer. "Paul, what's the mass of a camera swarm pod?"

"The mass? Well, they're about a hundred and fifty grams. About five and a quarter ounces. Like a baseball. Why?"

"How many do we have left?"

"About six thousand. We were fully stocked for multiple launches."

He turned to the Doc. "How quickly can you launch them all?"

"*All* of them?"

The ship creaked, conduits bursting.

"All of them!"

One Hundred and Four

Glittering objects sprayed from the *Ulysses*, blasting behind them, into the howling winds of glass and rock that pummeled the powerful EM fields of both ships.

The camera pods flashed across the distance between the two ships in seconds. As they flew, they were crushed, compacted under the intense pressure of the atmosphere, growing smaller and denser by the millisecond. By the time they had reached the chandelier, they had been compressed into something like diamond. The sparkling motes impacted across the chandelier's effervescing electromagnetic envelope like rocks hitting the surface of some iridescent pond. The sparkling ripples washed over the crystalline vessel, pushing its straining shield to the edge. The field flickered, stuttered, and then vanished. A skipped heartbeat later, the entire vessel disintegrated, collapsing into a series of bright flashes—white, then blue, then white again—leaving in their passing a cloud of dazzlingly fluorescent crystalline shards. Another heartbeat later and the shards were squeezed into vapor, vanishing into the storm tunnel.

"Take that," Cal said, smiling.

The ship lurched as if struck, and the Doc screamed. He turned his attention back to the viewports just in time to see the light show. The

Ulysses slammed into an eidetic replica of the interlocking storm shapes they had witnessed swirling around the pole. The shapes geared across the surface of an evil black sphere swathed in sickly gray clouds and the field around them turned blue as an Earthbound sky. Once again, he felt the sickly double-punch of his helmet slamming into his command seat's headrest and his skull hitting the back of the helmet dome.

And then, darkness.

One Hundred and Five

Cal's eyes opened to a view nearly as dark as the blackness of space. Wisps of red and blue faintly defined towering banks of thunderheads dropping away to either side of the ship, giving away the fact that they were rising within a strange new atmosphere. A slow glance to his left found Sarah awake and wrestling the stick, hopping the spacecraft over rising thermal currents.

Ulysses burst from the equator of a Jovian so dark that most of its globe was invisible against the black of space. It was only where great fonts of atmosphere swirled together and rose on thermal currents that the world differentiated from the night, brightening into hot red storms that appeared to burn like the coals of a flame. Arcing over all, a glittering band encircled the equator of the gas giant. It was clearly not natural, machined and riddled with pinpoints of light. Surrounding the ring, enmeshing it with activity, were thousands of colored motes that flit back and forth like gnats over a summer lake. It took just a moment for Cal to realize they were ships.

One Hundred and Six

Ceresian Prime Minister Susan Donovan strolled down the concave corridor and entered the secure mining elevator that descended into the asteroid. The cave had been recently excavated to house the item that had caused more excitement in the colony than anything since the uprising. She was accompanied by Laskey, trundling at her side in his hermetically sealed medical unit. Her chief advisor Argus Crossley strode next to him, helping the unit's too-small wheels make the transition from the clean habitat onto the crude grate of the elevator floor. With a lurch and an electric hum, the gated cage began to drop and darkness closed around them. Underpowered LEDs coughed on, illuminating the cage and throwing a haunted webwork onto the rushing walls of the shaft.

The fall into the depths of the planetoid was swift, assisted by a series of magnetic accelerators similar to those that propelled their exports of fuel, water, and oxygen into space. It only took moments to drop to a fantastic depth. The darkness suddenly retreated as they dropped out of the enclosed rock tunnel and into a latticework elevator shaft that cradled the cage through its final hundred feet of descent.

Through the beaten metal grating she could see the object their makeshift probe had retrieved from Jupiter-space. It, and there had been dozens of them, had been hurled by Jupiter's gravitation outwards into the solar system. And had been detected while searching for any signs of the missing *Ulysses.*

The thing they were descending toward was the only one that anyone had been able to intercept, and as such, the nations of the Earth were waiting impatiently for the release of Ceres's preliminary scientific reports. They would be waiting a very long time, as Donovan had no plans to share. Already red tendrils, weed-like structures, had begun to curl from it, stretching across the roof to weave an awesome scarlet web throughout the cavern.

Continued in Episode Four: *The Galactics*

Author's Note:

For this particular book I want to thank Dr. Bryon Backenson of the New York State Department of Epidemiology for helping me to develop a logical path for characters to approach the biological ramifications of first contact. I was fortunate to gain the benefit of his input before his, and other health professionals, time was consumed with the heroic response to the COVID-19 pandemic. Any errors are solely my own.

In regard to the entire Wine-Dark Deep series, I have had the great honor, and luck, to be able to work with NASA as the chief contact for a Space Act Agreement Partnership for the past four years. It was a gift to work with a number of wonderful people from NASA HQ, the Johnson Space Center, Langley Research Facility, and JPL. They helped us to create an amazing "What If?"—a scientifically plausible future system for the exploration of the solar system (detailed in some cases to the calculation of tank volumes on the landers), complete with environments simulated directly from NASA space probe data. As of this date, over two million visitors have enjoyed this simulation.

Is this system exactly how NASA will approach the future? Of course not, no one can know how the future will unfold, and many of the technologies we will find necessary for colonization of the solar system have yet to be invented—*but* we know many of the obstacles that we will need to surmount in order to do so. We know how we *might* approach solving them. The principles and challenges of spaceflight and science presented here are exactly those that mission designers and astronauts face.

I wanted to create a sci-fi world so grounded that when things got crazy the readers would say "Makes sense to me." A world where the answer to "How do you know?" isn't just "sensors."

I hope you enjoy the books—and remember that every day, there are incredibly smart and dedicated people working to wrestle science fiction into reality. I thank them again for all I learned, and I stress that any errors in the text are mine alone.

Please check into the Uphill Downhill Press Facebook page and website for news, updates, and sneak peeks as well as recommendations on books and programs to further any interests in the real science of spaceflight—and let me know what you think! Please comment on anything you like, and if you find anywhere that I've gone astray, don't hesitate to let me know!

Cheers!

Keith
2020

Made in the USA
Monee, IL
09 April 2021

65209819R00219